DALE BROWN AND JIM DeFELICE

TARGET UTOPIA

A Dreamland Thriller

HARPER

An Imprint of HarperCollinsPublishers

This is a work of fiction. Names, characters, places, and incidents are products of the authors' imagination or are used fictitiously and are not to be construed as real. Any resemblance to actual events, locales, organizations, or persons, living or dead, is entirely coincidental.

HARPER

An Imprint of HarperCollins*Publishers*
195 Broadway
New York, New York 10007

Copyright © 2015 by Air Battle Force, Inc.
ISBN 978-0-06-212287-2

First Harper premium printing: June 2015

Printed in the United States of America

Visit Harper paperbacks on the World Wide Web at www.harpercollins.com

10 9 8 7 6 5 4 3 2 1

Dreamland Whiplash: Target Utopia

Settings

Various locations in Malaysia and the nearby waters; Washington, D.C. and environs.

Key Players

Principals

Breanna Stockard, director, Department of Defense Office of Special Technology; Whiplash Director, DoD

Jonathon Reid, special assistant to CIA deputy director; Whiplash Director representing CIA

Colonel Danny Freah, U.S. Air Force; commander, Whiplash

Chief Master Sergeant Ben "Boston" Rockland, U.S. Air Force; senior NCO Whiplash military detachment

Captain Turk Mako, U.S. Air Force pilot, assigned to Office of Special Technology/Whiplash

Ray Rubeo, President and CEO, Applied Intelligence; key consultant and contractor to the Office of Special Technology

President Christine Mary Todd

Senator Jeff "Zen" Stockard, member of the Senate Intelligence and Armed Services committees (Breanna's husband)

Vice President Jay Mantis

Defense Secretary Charles Lovel

Secretary of State Alistar Newhaven

White House Chief of Staff David Greenwich

Whiplash Action Team Two
Riyad Achmoody, team leader

Chris Bulgaria

Tony "Two Fingers" Dalton

Eddie Guzman

Glenn Fulsom

"Baby Joe" Morgan

Ivan Dillon

Marines

Captain Joe Thomas, head of ground protective forces, Temporary Task Force Tango-Bravo-Mary

Lieutenant Colonel James "Jocko" Greenstreet, commander, Temporary Task Force Tango-Bravo-Mary Air Squadron

Lieutenant Torbin "Cowboy" Van Garetn, pilot, executive officer, TTF Tango-Bravo-Mary Squadron

Kallipolis

Lloyd Braxton, scientist

Thomas Fortine, naval expert, ship captain

Dietz Talbot, recruit

TARGET UTOPIA

MYSTERIES

———

1

Malaysia

COLONEL DANNY FREAH ADJUSTED HIS SUNGLASSES and stared out the passenger window of the Escalade as the SUV wound its way across a jungle ridge, its wheels clinging to a highway so narrow that brush poked against the windows on both sides. The lush jungle of southwestern Borneo in East Malaysia was considered a natural wonderland, one of the few pristine places left on earth. A few years before, this had made it a much-sought-after destination for rich tourists. But the outbreak of virulent guerrilla warfare involving combatants ranging from radical Muslims to sociopathic Maoist throwbacks had dimmed its attractiveness to even the most adventurist arriviste. There were many easier ways to cheat death.

Danny, though, wasn't here as a tourist, and though his eyes scoured the nearby jungle eagerly, he wasn't admiring the sights. Nor were the glasses he was tweaking actually sunglasses. They were high-powered smart glasses, Google glasses on steroids, as the developers called them. Developed from the "smart helmet" technology Dreamland had pioneered a decade earlier, they allowed him to scan in infrared as well as an optically enhanced and magnified mode.

"One time I was in Honduras," said his guide, a portly CIA officer named Melvin Gephardt. "I was in the U.S. Army then, seventeen years old. First or second night there, and we're in the jungle."

"Uh-huh." Danny had learned to throw in a few absentminded remarks every so often to keep Gephardt from bothering him with actual questions, or anything that had to be taken seriously.

"So we're sleeping in these tents, right? Each one of us had one. Canvas, you know the drill. So anyway, one of the guys is sleeping and his arm somehow gets out of the tent, right? All of a sudden, middle of the night, we hear this blood-curdling scream. I mean, someone is dying."

"Mmmm."

"Jump up, run out—this huge Anaconda has his arm like up to the pit in its mouth. Oh my God. The snake had to be like as long as this car."

"Uh-huh."

"So everybody's yelling, and this Special Forces guy, right? He's like there as an advisor for the Honduran army—"

"Stop the car!" yelled Danny, pulling at his seat-belt buckle.

Gephardt hit the brakes. Danny leapt from the SUV before it stopped moving. He trotted down the road about five yards, then made his way into the brush. Pushing his way between the thick vines and trees for about twenty yards, he made his way to a sickly looking Mahang tree, the lone survivor of a clear-cut harvest some ten years before. Older than the other trees, it stood out like a gnarled senior citizen in the middle of a high school prom dance, as thick as its neighbors were slender, stooped where its neighbors were bounding boldly toward the sun.

Eight feet off the ground, a Z-shaped limb rose from the trunk. Fending off the thick vines, Danny clambered up, then pulled himself out onto the limb. Conscious of his weight and the slowly sagging branch, he stretched out toward a black piece of wood wedged in the thin branches at the end.

A piercing screech froze him. Danny glanced to his left and saw an orangutan ten yards away, perched in the swaying top of another tree. The ape bared its teeth in a gesture clearly intended to intimidate.

Danny tried to remember the very brief advice he'd been given on dealing with the animals. The orangutan screeched again, then began shifting its weight so the tree swayed sharply. Ten yards was nothing for an angry orangutan; the animal could easily launch itself and land on Danny's tree, if not his back.

"Go away," Danny snarled, as nastily as possible. He couldn't remember if this was the advice or not; it just seemed like the most sensible thing to do.

The orangutan screeched again.

"Get!" shouted Danny.

The animal gave one last ferocious screech, then retreated.

Danny breathed slowly, then continued out along the limb, moving cautiously but determined to get what he'd come for as quickly as possible.

The branch cracked. Danny felt himself slipping downward, but he didn't fall; the damage was only partial, not enough to sever the limb.

The leaves of several trees nearby rustled violently. A dozen small black figures fled, looking like a swarm of giant bees following their queen to a new hive.

Monkeys. But at least they were going away.

"Sumabitch!" yelled Gephardt below. "Don't fall."

"Yeah, I'm working on that," muttered Danny, stretching a bit more.

"What the hell are you doing, Colonel?"

Danny didn't bother to answer. He inched out closer to the black object, grabbed it and wrestled it from the branch. Just over five feet long, its skin was as smooth as polished stone; the end closest to Danny looked like the nose of a dolphin, with small, round protrusions where the eyes would be. Two oblong stubs marked the middle of each side; the rear looked as if it had been bitten by an animal three or four times larger than the orangutans that were now fleeing.

The object was a little too cumbersome to carry down with him. Danny maneuvered it to an open space in the foliage and let it drop. Then he half shimmied and half climbed back down to the ground. He banged his knee as he went; it complained quite adamantly, reminding him of every other time he had hurt it, which was quite a lot. It strongly implied that he had reached the age when he shouldn't be climbing in trees.

"You gotta watch these monkeys," said Gephardt when he reached the ground. "They're pretty strong when they're mad."

"Yeah," said Danny, trying not to make it too obvious that he was stretching his knee.

"That's it, huh? That's from the airplane? UAV, sorry. That's the part they didn't get?"

"Yeah," said Danny, resisting the temptation to say something sarcastic.

"That's what, from the fuselage? Where's the motor?"

"Got me."

Actually, he knew from the techies who'd been examining the UAV's capabilities from afar that it was likely the motor had broken off, and recovered with the wings and rest of the aircraft by the rebels who were controlling it. But even though he was CIA, Gephardt wasn't cleared to know anything about it. So Danny kept the details to himself.

"We're gonna want to get moving," said Gephardt, looking at the object as Danny picked it up. "Rebels are all over the place."

"Coming." Danny turned the long fuselage around, making sure the glasses were recording every inch. The visuals were being sent back to a situation room in a bunker at Langley, the CIA headquarters in suburban Virginia. When a barely audible beep told him the techies were satisfied that he had examined every conceivable angle, he lifted the slender fuselage onto his shoulder. "Let's go."

"How the hell did you see that thing through all the foliage?" asked Gephardt.

"I eat my carrots. Let's get back."

Gephardt continued his story about the snake as they started back down the hill. It was a story Danny had heard in many different guises over the years: a Green Beret or some other resident expert would come out, measure the victim's other arm, then chop the snake about two inches deeper, releasing the victim. He was then medivacked out, his arm scarred with acid burns.

Anacondas were rare in Honduras and had their pick of much easier prey than sleeping soldiers. Still, the size of the snakes made it exactly the sort of tale suitable to be passed down from generation to generation, a kind of campfire ghost story that many of its tellers—Gephardt undoubtedly among them—told so often that they inevitably became convinced *must* have happened. While Danny had a relatively high opinion of the Agency as a whole—he worked with some of the best officers in the business—the little he knew of Gephardt made it clear that he swam in the shallow end of the pool. It was more indication of how low a priority Malaysia had to not just the Agency, but the U.S. in general. Ironically, upward of forty percent of the world's commerce shipped through the nearby waters, a fact not lost on the pirates operating there.

"So, you flyin' right outta here?" asked Gephardt as they turned off the scratch road onto a slightly wider one.

"Yeah. I gotta get back."

"I'll still stand you that beer when we get into town."

"If there's time," said Danny, hoping there wouldn't be.

"*Shit!*"

Danny looked up. There was a man with an assault rifle in the road ahead.

"I can deal with it," said Gephardt. "Not to worry."

"Two more on the side," said Danny. He touched the right frame of his glasses, switching them into infrared mode.

"Yeah, I see 'em. You know what? We're just gonna blow right by 'em. Screw the bribe. I don't like the idea of stopping."

"Guy with an RPG farther down. Twenty yards. On the right."

"Shit. How are you seein' that?"

The discovery of the man with a rocket-propelled grenade launcher changed the equation; running past would be too risky.

"Back up," said Danny. "We can backtrack."

"Too late. Just be cool," added Gephardt. "It's only going to cost us money. Agency money."

Slowing the SUV's pace to a bare walk, Gephardt rolled down the window and held up a small wad of cash, yelling something at the man in Malay. The man seemed unimpressed—he lifted the rifle in front of his chest with both hands and motioned for Gephardt to stop. Gephardt slowed to a stop by applying the brakes, but kept his right foot on the gas.

"Hello," yelled Gephardt—the greeting sounded roughly the same in Malay as in English. "*Apa yang anda mahu?* What do you want? The tax?"

The man said something in return that Danny didn't catch, then walked over to Gephardt. Meanwhile, the two men Danny had spotted on the side of the road trotted toward them. One went to Danny's window, the other continued around to the back of the vehicle.

"*Tidak, tidak,*" said Gephardt. Danny recognized the word as "no"; the rest of the sentence was indecipherable. He was out of range for the microphone embedded in the frame of his glasses, or the computers at the Whiplash "Cube" could have interpreted for him.

That seemed unnecessary. The man who'd stopped them spoke in tones that suggested they were conducting normal business: he seemed to want more money. Danny glanced at the man standing near the passenger side. He was young, maybe fifteen, or even fourteen. The Chinese QBZ-95 bull-pup assault rifle he was clutching looked several years older than him, and surely had seen more action—the bull pup's dull green surface was scratched and even dented; the box magazine was wrapped with tape in two places, and it looked like a small piece of the top handle grip was missing.

The hand-me-down Chinese weapon suggested

that the man was a member of the 30 May Movement, one of the three rebel groups vying with the East Malaysian government in this part of the island. Not nearly as well funded as the others, 30 May was smaller than the others, though every bit as ruthless.

Gephardt continued to speak with the man on his side of the SUV as Danny scanned ahead. The man with the RPG was pointing it at the front fender. Another man had joined him. Two more figures were heading down a small hill in the distance, just at the very edge of his infrared range.

The man at the back of the SUV grabbed at the handle for the rear hatch.

"That's no good," said Danny loudly. "That's mine."

"I got it," said Gephardt quickly. He turned back to the man at the door, his voice louder than before.

Something he said apparently angered the man, who raised his rifle.

"Easy," said Gephardt. "Relax."

Danny had seen enough. "Whiplash Rotor, command Danny Freah," he said, alerting the system to accept direct commands. "Terminate all targets within one hundred yards of vehicles. All targets are hostile."

In seconds the air began to percolate, as if the very molecules of nitrogen and oxygen were exploding. The men around the truck fell to the ground.

"Gephardt, go!" said Danny. "Go! Get us out of here."

The CIA officer, not quite understanding what was going on, hesitated, though only for a moment. The SUV lurched forward, dirt spinning as it veered first left and then right.

"What the hell?" said Gephardt.

"Just stay on the road."

He did, though barely. They careened through a dozen curves before the road straightened out.

"All right, slow down," said Danny as they hit a wider, well-paved stretch of highway.

"What the hell just happened?" asked Gephardt.

"They were getting dangerous."

"We were just arguing on a price—"

"No. They were too aggressive. I didn't come all this way to lose my fuselage. I can't afford to take chances."

Danny tapped the side of the right temple tip at the back of his glasses, then studied the image that appeared.

"There's a clearing about three-quarters of a mile up ahead," he told Gephardt. "Stop there."

"Why?"

"Just stop there."

"Not without a reason. If those guys had a radio or phones—"

"They're all dead," said Danny. "Just do what I say."

Gephardt tightened his lips. Danny scanned the nearby jungle, making sure there was nothing ahead.

"There," he told Gephardt as they came around the bend. The clearing was small, maybe a dozen yards long and another two dozen deep; the far side was all jungle, and there were some rocks amid the high brush near the road.

Danny got out of the truck and went around to the rear of the SUV. He took out the fuselage he'd retrieved and hoisted it onto his back. It was so light it felt as if it had been made out of Styrofoam, not high-tech carbon and metal fiber.

"You comin'?" he yelled to Gephardt, who was still in the vehicle.

"Coming where?"

"I'll drop you back at the compound."

"I gotta get the Escalade back."

"You sure?"

"Jesus, man. Are you crazy? How are you getting out of here?"

Danny pointed toward the sky.

"Helicopter?" asked Gephardt.

"Osprey," said Danny.

"Why the hell didn't we take it out here in the first place?"

"I didn't want to attract attention if I didn't have to," said Danny. "Unfortunately, that didn't work out."

"Man."

"Are you coming?"

"I got the Caddy. I can't leave it. The drive's easy from here," added Gephardt. "That'll be the only checkpoint. The army's about five miles down the road. Won't even cost me anything."

"OK."

"You didn't have to kill them."

"I couldn't take a chance," said Danny. "You don't have to wait," he added.

Gephardt frowned. "Who are you really working for?"

"I told you. Fact-finding for the NSC."

"The NSC doesn't have magic bullets that appear out of nowhere."

"Neither do I," said Danny, starting into the field.

2

Florida

THE MONSTER LEERED AT THE BASE OF THE STAIRS, ITS mouth open wide enough to display its black teeth. Blood-edged eyes bulged from their sockets, hunting for prey. Suddenly its nostrils pinched together—the scent had been found. It bounded up the stairs with a deathly scream: food was at hand.

Turk Mako steadied his gun and shot the zombie square in the head.

One hundred thirty points floated onto the screen, increasing his score in the video game to 10,400. He was on level 12; things were just starting to heat up.

"Say, babe, are we going swimming or what?"

Turk turned and glanced at his girlfriend, Li Pike, who was standing near the door of the small hotel room suite. The oversized T-shirt she wore over her bikini somehow accented rather than hid her athletic frame. The curve of her breasts and hips teased desire into Turk. His eyes followed the hem of the shirt down her smooth legs, pausing over her sculptured calves and then wandering to her bare toes. She'd painted her nails last night, before they went out; the bright, glossy red seemed to glow.

"So, are we going?" she asked.

"I'm on level 12," Turk answered.

"And?"

"Well, and—" He saw a zombie coming to the right of the screen, dodged the joystick left, spun and fired. As the zombie's head shattered, he hit the key to pause the game.

"And you'd rather play a video game than hang out with me," said Li.

He knew she was joking—Li had a way of exaggerating her smile when she was teasing or being ironic—but still there was the gentlest bit of an edge in what she said.

A small bit.

"No, no," he said.

"What would Dr. Kleenex say?" Li teased.

"Avoidance therapy. I'm killing zombies because I can't kill my boss."

"The Iranians, you mean."

"Them, too."

No doubt Dr. Kleenex—Turk's nickname for the counselor he'd been ordered to see as a mandatory "de-stress" from his last mission—would have read quite a bit into his absorption in the video game. But then, Dr. Kleenex read quite a bit into everything.

The counselor's real name was Washington Galiopis, but he had earned the nickname by prominently stationing boxes of tissues near Turk's chair every time the pilot reported to him. The man seemed to want him to break down and cry.

That wasn't Turk. Nor did Turk feel that he had post-traumatic stress, though he would certainly admit to having been under a great deal of strain on the mission, which involved the secret destruction of two Iranian nuclear weapons bases.

As a test pilot, he was used to dealing with stress. Admittedly, having been on the ground and getting fired at—and firing at others—was a new and not entirely pleasant experience. And immediately upon his return, he had lost his temper, briefly, when confronting his boss, Breanna Stockard, the head of the military side of Whiplash.

The thing was, she deserved to be blasted. In his mind, telling her that she should have had more faith in him was the mildest possible thing he could do.

After all, she'd sent someone to kill him.

As things worked out, Turk had befriended his would-be assassin, Mark Stoner, by saving his life. Together they had escaped, thanks to a plan Turk concocted.

It was only when they were back in the States going through the debrief that Turk realized how close he had come to being assassinated, and why.

He didn't blame Stoner at all. On the contrary, Stoner had saved his life, and he had nothing but gratitude for him.

The same could not be said for Breanna. Until now he'd looked at her as a role model, almost an older sister. Her husband and her father were both war heroes and superb pilots, men Turk greatly admired. But now he knew that her kindness and concern toward him was fake. She didn't care if he lived or died; she didn't care about anything, except for the mission.

Turk, too, was dedicated to doing his duty. He had been prepared to die and even expected to many times, not only on that mission but during his entire service with Special Projects and with the Air Force in general. But the fact that he and Stoner had gotten out alive proved that he shouldn't have been given up for dead. Breanna should have had a better contingency plan for getting him out.

Because she didn't, some of the bravest men he'd ever known, all members of Delta Force, had died in Iran. They'd died protecting him, and helping him do his job. How the hell was he ever going to make up for that?

"So, are you coming or not?" asked Li.

"Just let me—"

She stalked over and kissed him on the lips, leaning her chest into his.

The kiss ended too soon.

"I'll be downstairs." She straightened. "Try to make it by lunch."

Turk watched her walk from the room. Li was

a pilot herself—she flew A-10s—but there was something about the way she filled a bikini that ought not to be allowed.

Kill zombies?

"Damn," muttered Turk as the door closed behind her. He switched off the TV and tossed the controller on the bed.

"Wait up," he called, hustling for the door.

3

White House, Washington, D.C.
Two days later

DANNY FREAH TOOK A DEEP BREATH, THEN ROSE FROM his seat and walked to the front of the secure conference room in the basement of the White House. He'd given a number of presentations in this room, yet he'd never felt quite the flutter in his chest that he felt today. Partly that was because the President herself was here; he'd never directly given her a briefing before.

And partly it was because he was afraid of the implications of what he was about to say.

He cleared his throat and positioned his thumb on the remote control for the laptop, which he'd already hooked into the projection system.

"Thank you," said Danny, clicking through to the first slide in his PowerPoint. "Uh, first of all, I apologize for the, uh, primitiveness of this. I just got back from Malaysia, and uh, I pulled this together . . ."

God, he told himself, *calm down*. He glanced at Breanna Stockard, who was sitting near the end of the table. She gave him a grim nod, as if to say, *Get on with it*.

"For the past twelve months a small rebel group in Malaysia known as 30 May Movement has been active on the island of Borneo, which as you know Malaysia shares with Brunei and Indonesia. Their activities have been primarily in the state of Sarawak, which is the largest part of East Malaysia. You have three countries sharing that island, each encircling the other. Borneo is on the coast, East Malaysia is around it, then Indonesia. That's, um, East Malaysia."

Danny paused for a quick sip of water, then continued. "The 30 May Movement is named after an alleged massacre that occurred on the island, near the border with Indonesia. The group is relatively small, thought to number perhaps five hundred active fighters. That is dwarfed by the size of the other two main groups, which are primarily fighting in the eastern portion of the island, where we've had, uh, where we've sent Marine advisors."

Danny caught a glimpse of Jonathon Reid's bored face. Reid was the head of the CIA half of Whiplash. *Skip over the background*, he'd said earlier. *They know it!*

"So, as you know, the group has not been of much concern to anyone. But a few weeks ago something happened to bring it to our attention. This."

Danny clicked to the first slide. Scratchy video began to play—it was from the camera of a Malaysian fighter-bomber, a Northrup F-5E, which was considered ancient even in Malaysia. The "Freedom fighter" had been pressed into a ground-support role, and at the start of the video was pulling up from a strafing run at a rebel stronghold.

Suddenly, a black shadow appeared on the right side of the screen, flashing toward the plane. It passed quickly overhead.

The object looked like a missile, and apparently the pilot of the F-5E thought that's what it was, since he immediately rolled his plane and fired off chaff and flares—an unnecessary precaution, most pilots would have agreed, since the trajectory of the object made it clear that it had missed his plane. Nothing outside of the U.S. arsenal could change course quickly enough to give him a problem.

But the Malaysian pilot was right to be worried. As his plane rolled away, a warning sounded in the cockpit, announcing that he was being tracked by a weapons radar.

"The sound you're hearing is a warning that the plane is being tracked at close range," said Danny as the video ended. "The plane was subsequently shot down. There are a couple of things to note," he added, "starting with the fact that the object was not detected at close range; there was no threat indicated. And that the shoot-down occurred within moments of the radar being activated."

"What shot it down?" asked the Secretary of State, Alistar Newhaven.

"We believe the object that we saw at the beginning of the video. We think it is a combat UAV."

He flashed a few images on the screen. All were artists' concepts based on the extremely brief and blurry image in the video.

"A combat UAV?" asked the Secretary of State. "Whose? I thought we were the only nation that had them."

"That's why we're here," said the President. She nodded at Danny to continue.

"We don't have enough data to say for certain," admitted Danny. "The aircraft was pretty beat up. The damage is consistent with gunfire, but frankly it could also have been a missile, and whatever hit it, there's no way now of knowing whether it came from the air or the ground. The Malaysians thought it must have been a ground-launched missile, as none of the rebel groups have been known to use aircraft. They dismissed the item in the video you saw as simply another missile that for some reason hadn't been detected."

Danny flipped the slide to a map of an area near the western coast of the island.

"The incident was pretty much dismissed until a group of four Su-29s were attacked in roughly the same area two weeks ago. They were shot down in the space of about ten minutes."

"The Malaysians have Su-29s?" asked the vice president, Jay Mantis.

"Yes, sir, they do." Danny nodded. While the

Russian-made Su-29 was a few decades and at least a generation and a half old, it was still considered a front-line fighter, and Danny wasn't surprised that some members of the government weren't aware that it was in a third-world nation's inventory. "They have a pretty unique mix of aircraft. The fortunate thing that happened here, and it seems by accident—as the UAV was engaging the last aircraft, it appears to have inadvertently been struck by debris from one of the planes it had fired on earlier. The debris sheered one of its wings; it went into a high speed spin and another of the wings came off. Part of the fuselage landed in this area here."

Danny clicked on the slide showing where he had found the main part of the aircraft.

"I picked it up myself two days ago."

"It's been a hectic few days for you, I'm sure," said the President, leaning forward in her chair.

"Yes, ma'am." Danny nodded. "The Malaysians blamed the Indonesians. The two countries have a complicated history. The Indonesians weren't backing the rebels, at least not these rebels—"

"The Indonesians have given us assurances," said the Secretary of State.

"Yes, sir. In any event, the technology that would have to be responsible is far beyond anything the Indonesians are capable of. It's on par with the early Flighthawks. Maybe beyond."

"A group of guerrillas are flying UAVs that are more advanced than ours?" said the vice president incredulously.

"It looks like that," said Danny.

Mary Christine Todd glanced at her watch. The meeting had gone five minutes longer than her aides had allotted; it was time for her to bring it to a close if she had any hope of staying on schedule for the rest of the morning.

"The bottom line is, we need more information about what's going on here," said the President. "Colonel, do you have a recommendation?"

"Yes, ma'am, I do. I'd suggest we send a full team from Whiplash, try and capture these UAVs and find out what's going on. We can have a team out there in three days."

"What would that entail?"

Todd listened as the colonel outlined a plan to move a piloted and unpiloted aircraft as well as Ospreys and a ground team into the jungle. She knew what the objections would be well before he finished. And she knew that the colonel must know that as well.

"If we send that sort of firepower into the area, there's bound to be a reaction from the Chinese," said Newhaven. "Indonesia as well."

China was key. Congress was pushing hard for a rapprochement, which even Todd admitted could benefit the U.S. Her administration was secretly negotiating with Beijing on a number of issues, including territorial claims in the South China Sea. The Chinese indicated they would renounce some of those claims if it could be done without losing face. The political dance was difficult: show too much force in the region, and the Chinese would have to reply with their own. Show too little, and the Chinese would have no incentive to back off their aggressive positions.

"The Whiplash team can operate discreetly," said Danny.

"It hasn't in the past," said Newhaven pointedly.

That was out of line, and the President cut the Secretary of State off.

"I think the Office of Special Projects has an admirable record," said the President quickly.

"You put high-tech gear in there and you might just as well tell the Chinese to triple their aid to the rebels," said Newhaven. "Plus, if these things are being flown by the rebels, then they'll be after them, too."

"Assuming they don't already belong to the Chinese," said Reid.

"The CIA ought to know who owns them," snapped Newhaven.

"I understand your point, Mr. Secretary," said the President. "We have to find a way to get the job done without calling much attention to it. Even among our own people."

That was a veiled reference to Congress, which was dead set against giving more aid to the Malaysians. If the oversight committees found out there was a full-blown Whiplash mission to the island, objections would be quickly raised. Todd was willing to deal with the political fallout, but it seemed premature at this point; there was no firm evidence that UAVs were even there—as she understood the data, it could have been missiles.

"We have a small group of Marines set to support the Malaysians in that area," said the National Security Advisor, Michael Blitz. "Can we fold this operation into them?"

"Any Whiplash presence is too much," said the vice president.

Todd held her tongue. Her contempt for her vice president was well known. Nonetheless, it was obvious as the discussion continued that he was expressing a view that seemed to be shared by the rest of the council and the cabinet members present. The evidence didn't seem to warrant the risks that a Whiplash deployment would entail politically.

"All right," said the President after her scheduling aide pointed at his watch. "As I said at the outset, I have a breakfast meeting to attend. I expect a recommendation by the time I return to the White House." She rose. "Colonel, thank you for coming. Ms. Stockard, perhaps you'll walk with me upstairs."

B REANNA, SURPRISED AT THE INVITATION, FELT HER cheeks burn. She pulled her things together and waited in the hallway for the President, who was stopped by some aides just outside the door and given information about an explosion in a coal mine that morning.

Danny nodded as he passed; Breanna gave him a thumbs-up.

"Good job," she said.

"Thanks." He beamed. For some reason the colonel was more nervous about public speaking than facing combat.

"So, Breanna, how is your daughter?" asked the President as she sailed up the hallway. Breanna had to practically leap to stay up with her. Christine Todd was very much like a sleek sailboat when she moved. Whatever other effect the job had had on her, her energy was undiminished.

"She's great."

"If she's half as smart as her mother and father, she's got quite a future." Todd smiled and stepped into the waiting elevator. She was alone with Breanna, except for her two Secret Service escorts. A man and a woman, they were well practiced at pretending not to hear what the President or anyone with her said.

"I have a few too many enemies in Congress at the moment," said Todd. "Whatever you do to investigate this further, it will have to be done within the Marine contingent. No Whiplash troop or aircraft presence."

"Then maybe the CIA or the Air Force themselves should continue the investigation," offered Breanna.

"No, the parallels to our technology are too provocative. I want the experts working on it. I just want it done quietly. If your full team's presence is warranted, then we won't hesitate."

"If you're sure—"

"And the senator?" asked the President, abruptly changing the subject.

"Same old Zen."

"Yes."

"You know, someone mentioned the other day

that Zen would make an excellent President," said Todd.

"Who said that?"

"It was a party person." Todd gave her a grin the Cheshire cat would have been proud of. "I was forced to agree."

"I don't think he wants to be President," said Breanna.

"That would be a pity."

The elevator door opened and the President abruptly exited, leaving Breanna to wonder what the real purpose of the exchange had been.

4

Arizona

AT ROUGHLY THE SAME TIME DANNY FREAH WAS RUNning the video of the Malaysian air force's encounter with the unknown UAV, Ray Rubeo was staring at the same image. It was playing in the screen on the left side of his desk; the screen next to it was showing a simulation he had constructed that revealed what he thought the program governing the aircraft's movements was doing. Though he had adapted the simulation from one of his company's own programs, it had nonetheless taken him considerable time to construct.

Three hours.

He was dismayed. Years ago it would have been

less than half that. His brain, he was convinced, was starting to slow down.

There were still several hours before the sun would come up over his isolated Arizona ranch, but Rubeo wasn't interested in sleep. He never was when there was a problem to be solved. And this problem was more vexing than most, the issue of his getting older aside.

He turned his attention to the monitor on the right. It was showing an analysis of the code in the middle screen, computing the amount of resources needed for it to run under various systems. The screen was broken into four quadrants, displaying the performance of four different possibilities. The bottom left assumed the program was in the system originally designed for the Flighthawks, some fifteen years before; the chart was off the scale. So was the one next to it, which displayed the system that had replaced it a few years later.

Rubeo was not surprised. Both systems were primarily intended as backups to a human pilot, and the decisions that the computer had to make in controlling a complex airframe were very primitive.

The top two screens were what bothered him. The left showed the system used by the Tigershark in "guiding" its UAV escorts. The Tigershark was Dreamland's own aircraft, and the system it used to guide the UAVs was the most advanced currently in existence.

According to the program, the maneuvers and the decisions that the computer had to make to guide the aircraft they had reconstructed at the speed it had flown taxed this system near the breaking point as well. Only the fourth quadrant showed a system that could handle the plane confidently through the complex maneuvers.

It was an experimental system that used custom-made organic processing chips. It had never been built.

He got up from the computers. Rubeo's house was a combination retreat and high-tech lab. Located in a remote area of the desert, it matched his personality—austere and yet at the same time expansive. He walked into the kitchen and poured himself a cup of coffee, then went out on the back deck.

The wind had died. The clear black sky and sparkling stars foretold a brilliant day.

The abilities of the aircraft were one thing. The behavior was something else. Rubeo's people had pieced together the engagement between the mysterious UAV and the Malaysian Sukhois. There were gaps, but the pattern looked very, very similar to an attack that had been mapped out and preprogrammed for the original service Flighthawks a decade before.

Impossible. Or at least highly unlikely.

Rubeo sighed, and took a sip of coffee.

And then there was this: the material from the fuselage Danny Freah had recovered was made of a carbon-titanium alloy similar to that used in the Flighthawks and the more modern Sabre UAVs. It was the product of a rare and very expensive process, one thought to be well beyond the reach of the Chinese or the Russians, let alone a third-world country.

If he didn't know any better, Rubeo would swear the UAVs were Dreamland's own.

But that was impossible. Wasn't it?

Back to work, he told himself, draining the coffee and turning to go back inside.

5

The "Cube," CIA Headquarters Campus (Langley)
McLean, Virginia
The next day

DANNY FREAH RUBBED HIS CHIN AS TURK MAKO continued speaking. He was more than a little surprised by what he was hearing.

". . . I just want to go back to being a regular pilot again," continued Turk. "I never really intended to stay on this duty with Whiplash."

Half a dozen entries in Turk's personnel file made it clear that was a bald-faced lie.

Danny's office at the Special Projects headquarters was rather large by military standards, a full thirty by thirty feet. Besides his desk there was a sitting area with a couch, chairs, and a large-screen TV. Unlike much of the rest of the bunker, the walls were real, constructed of thick concrete, predating the installation of the energy beams that walled off most of the interior of the three-story, deeply buried bunker.

Under ordinary circumstances, the office felt massive. At the moment, however, the room seemed absurdly small.

"You don't want to work for Special Projects anymore at all?" asked Danny, paraphrasing what Turk had told him. "You want to go back to the regular Air Force. Is that right?"

"Yes, sir. That's it."

Danny watched Turk fidget. "You want to go back to Dreamland as a test pilot?"

"That's not possible. There are no other slots."

"You realize Whiplash is short of pilots," said Danny. In fact, Turk was presently the only pilot; they were seeking funding to expand the roster but it wasn't clear they'd get it.

"Yes, sir. I'll stay until the transition. Whatever you need."

"You don't want to fly?"

"No. I do, I do." Turk fumbled. It seemed obvious to Danny that he hadn't thought this out very clearly at all. "I do want to fly. Just not . . . just not here."

"You've been through a lot, Captain," Danny told the pilot. "Iran—"

"Iran has nothing to do with it."

Danny couldn't hide his exasperation. "Nothing?"

"I—I can't work for Ms. Stockard," said Turk. "That's really the bottom line."

"You can't work for Bree?"

Turk shook his head.

"Sometimes, when we go through something that's . . . difficult . . ." Danny struggled to find the right words. He knew Turk had been through a lot, and wanted to show him the respect he deserved. But a good part of him wanted to turn the captain around and give him a good kick in the behind—maybe that would get him thinking straight.

"Sometimes after a big battle or some other combat," said Danny, "we end up with a tough reaction. Difficult. At first. Then, you know, after a little time off—"

"She wanted me killed, Colonel. Damn it."

"Come on, Turk. That's not fair. That's not what happened."

"Yeah, it is."

"You're getting a little emotional—"

"If someone sent someone to kill you, what would you think?"

"Stoner was sent to *rescue* you."

"To kill me. That was the first option. I talked him out of it. And the Delta boys had that same order. Kill me."

"No," insisted Danny. In his opinion, Turk's anger was just misplaced anxiety, a delayed reaction to everything he'd been through. "If things had gone poorly, then it was understood that you might not come back. I explained that explicitly to you. And you were good with it."

"Yeah, but that's not what the real deal was. It was understood that I would be killed." Turk had started out calmly, but now his face was turning red. "I'd be killed by our own people, under orders. You know it. You know it. Did you give that order, too?"

"I think you need time to think," Danny said. "I think—you really should have more time off. You've earned it."

"I don't want time off. I just don't want to work for Breanna Stockard. That's pretty straightforward, sir. And, uh, I know the situation here. But . . . I think I've earned the right to request a transfer, under the circumstances."

"All right," said Danny finally. "I'll get the paperwork moving. In the meantime—"

"In the meantime I'm back and ready to work. I can fly today if you want. I passed the physical yesterday."

Danny got up from his desk. He always thought better on his feet; the blood flowed to his brain.

"Is there a problem, Colonel?" asked Turk.

"It's a little contradictory, don't you think?" Danny walked over to the credenza, where photographs from some of his earlier exploits were displayed. There was a photo of him, Breanna, and Turk after one of their earliest missions. "I mean, you don't want to work for Ms. Stockard, but you want to work."

"I think that makes perfect sense. I just want a different unit, that's all." Turk folded his arms. "That's never happened before?"

Danny's eyes scanned the credenza. There was a photo of him and his old mentor, Tecumseh "Dog" Bastian. Then a colonel, later a general. He'd given Danny a lot of good advice, though Danny hadn't taken all of it; he wished he had.

"I'm ready to go back to work, Colonel," said Turk. "Use me."

"I do have a possibility of something, but it doesn't involve flying," said Danny. "I need someone who knows a lot about combat UAVs."

"I'm your guy."

"It's not in the States."

"Even better."

AN HOUR LATER DANNY SAT DOWN WITH BREANNA over at the Pentagon to discuss just that. It was one of the more difficult conversations they'd had. As usual, Breanna did her best to make it easy.

"I understand his feelings," she told Danny. "He feels betrayed."

"That's not fair," Danny said.

"Feelings rarely are. And it's beside the point." She smiled. Even if they hadn't worked together for so long, he'd have recognized it as forced. "So what's the solution?"

"I think we give him some space and time to think about it. He'll come around."

"Fair enough. We'll give him as much space as we can. He can have leave—"

"He doesn't seem to want it. And frankly, I think working's probably the best therapy going anyway. He was supposed to be on desk duty at the Cube for a while," added Danny, using the slang term for the special operations bunker. "But that would probably drive him nuts."

"There's no test program at Dreamland for him," said Breanna. "Not for at least two months."

"I was wondering about having him come with me back to Malaysia. Assuming the mission is approved. The duty will be pretty light, and I'll be there to watch him."

"There's a war going on there. You were almost killed."

"Gephardt was a fool," said Danny. "I'll steer way clear of him."

"If we have to integrate with the Marines and the Malaysians, what's his cover?" asked Breanna.

"Ground flight controller. They use pilots all the time. He's had training. He can actually do the job."

"It's too close to combat."

"I don't think combat's the problem, Bree."

"No, I am."

Danny didn't have an answer for that.

BREANNA UNDERSTOOD TURK'S ANGER. EVEN THOUGH she had given the only orders she possibly could, she still felt tremendous guilt. She had, explicitly, directed that one of her own people be killed if he was going to be captured. Not even the genuine relief and joy at hearing that he was alive could erase it.

Turk was a tough kid and a great pilot. And, at least according to the doctors, he didn't seem to have post-traumatic stress. He'd recovered fully from the light injuries he'd had, and in fact seemed to be in the best shape of his life. But throwing him back out in the field—was that really the best thing to do?

"You're worried that something will go wrong when we're out there?" asked Danny.

"I'm just worried that he's been under a lot of stress," said Breanna.

"If I didn't think he could handle the job, I wouldn't be recommending him," said Danny. "And I do need an expert with me."

"You'll be in constant communication with our experts."

"It's not the same as having somebody on the scene. Tech is great, but . . ."

"All right," said Breanna. "Take him." She reached into the in basket on her desk. "The President authorized the mission a half hour ago. You can take one other technical person, but you're just observers. Keep the lowest profile possible."

"That's my middle name. Low profile."

6

Malaysia
Three days later

DANNY FREAH AND TURK MAKO STOOD ON THE tarmac of a small jungle airport, waiting for the advance element of Marine Task Force Tango-Bravo-Mary to arrive.

If Turk was feeling any hesitation at getting back close to combat, it wasn't apparent to Danny. Then again, he didn't seem to be overly excited either. He was just . . . Turk.

Arms folded, the young Air Force captain

watched the sky as the drone of the approaching aircraft echoed over the nearby mountain range. A pair of F-35B Lightning IIs appeared from the east, flying in low over the treetops. The jets— Marine Corps versions of the standard military multipurpose fighters—had full loads of air-to-air and air-to-ground weapons under their wings. Thundering past, they banked into a turn and circled overhead.

While Danny had seen considerable action with various Marine units over the years, he had never worked directly with an F-35B group before, and he watched the aircraft with some curiosity.

The Marine version of the Lightning II was configured for short-runway operations; it could land and take off vertically, and often was called on to do just that. Vertical takeoffs limited the combat weight the planes could use, which generally meant carrying less fuel, fewer weapons, or both, and so as a general rule the Marines preferred to operate the aircraft with short runways rather than direct vertical liftoffs. The runway they were using here was precisely the reason the Marines had fought so hard to get the aircraft in the first place. Officially listed at some 1,200 feet, its usable space ran just over eight hundred; the northern end had caved in some years before due to erosion and was never properly repaired. Barely as wide as a C-130's wingspan, the strip of concrete had been patched in numerous places with cement and aggregate, and just walking along it Danny could feel bumps and see waves in the surface.

As the jets passed overhead, four V-22 Marine Corps Ospreys appeared over the jungle, flying in a staggered follow-the-leader formation. The closest aircraft had already begun tilting its propellers upward, transitioning from conventional airplane flight to that used by helicopters. The Osprey reminded Danny of an Olympic runner who was spreading his arms wide as he approached the finish line.

The aircraft pivoted above the dense jungle canopy as it came in, sliding into a hover in what could only be described as a well-practiced aerial ballet. The rest of the squadron followed, touching down together in a display that would have wowed many an air show audience. Once down, the Ospreys trundled toward the three trailers at the southern end of the strip. The trailers had been delivered by C-130s barely two hours before. Parked near an old cement building that looked like it dated to British colonial times, they were the only other structures at the base.

The rear ramps of the aircraft popped open and Marines began double-timing down to the tarmac, where they were greeted by the small advance force that had secured the base ahead of Danny two days ago. In less than five minutes a total of sixty-eight men and twelve women were deposited on the ground; the ramps were shut and the Ospreys began heading back into the air. Their takeoff was a notch less coordinated but just as efficient as the landing. All four Ospreys were over the nearby mountain before the F-35s dropped down to land.

"Want to go meet the neighbors?" suggested Danny.

"Be there in a minute, Colonel," said Turk. "I need to take care of nature first. You go ahead."

"Be on your best behavior."

Turk grinned in a way that made Danny wonder if maybe this was a good idea after all.

Two more planes landed as Danny walked over. The head of the air detachment was a short, stubby Marine named Lt. Colonel James Greenstreet. His thick torso and long arms reminded Danny not a little of the orangutans he knew were out in the trees watching them. He had a sunburnt face and a scar above his right eye; these complemented the sort of no-nonsense, no-bullshit manner that Danny had long admired in the typical Marine officer. While it was clear from the way Greenstreet stalked across the concrete that he would never be called easygoing, his quick smile and eager handshake signaled that he was exactly the sort of man Danny wanted to work with, the kind of officer who found solutions and didn't stop to calculate what the effect was going to be on his career. The only thing that struck Danny as out of place was the cigarette Greenstreet popped into his mouth as they began talking; it was rare, these days, to encounter an officer in any service who smoked.

"So where are the Malaysians?" asked Greenstreet after he'd finished introducing Danny and Turk to the small group of officers and senior enlisted who'd come over to care for the planes.

"They're due at the base tomorrow morning," said Danny.

Greenstreet nodded. "We'll get them sorted. You're going to handle ground coms?"

"Not me personally. I have a captain with me," said Danny. "He'll train the Malaysians. We met them yesterday. They seem competent."

"Good."

"They're going to set up a camp at the south end of the base," said Danny. "Your Captain Thomas has already worked out the details. He said you have security, but if you need more, the Malaysians can augment you near the hangars and such."

"Captain Thomas knows what he's doing," said Greenstreet. "We've trained with him before. And, uh, as far as the locals go: no offense, Colonel, but most of us feel more secure without them."

"Understood."

TURK FOLDED HIS ARMS AS HE WALKED TOWARD THE F-35. Even before he had begun testing new aircraft for Dreamland and Special Projects, he hadn't been a particular fan of the Lightning II. Like a lot of fighter jocks—at least of the American variety—he saw speed and acceleration as the ultimate virtues of an aircraft; the Lightning II was known to be somewhat below average in those categories when compared to the F-22, let alone the hot rods Turk guided. These shortcomings might have been excused, at least in Turk's opinion, if it made up for it with stellar maneuverability. But the plane's weight and configuration made it less than acrobatic.

Turk tried hard not to be a snob. The F-35 had

real assets: dependability, versatility, and a suite of electronic sensors that were at least a generation ahead of anything else in regular service around the globe. But after flying the Tigershark II in combat, it was hard to look at any other aircraft and not think it was a bit of a pig.

His opinion of the Marine aviators who flew the plane was quite a bit higher . . . mostly.

While the fierce service rivalries that once characterized the military were largely a thing of the past, he'd had a bad experience with a squadron of Marines at a Red Flag exercise very early in his career. The Marines—flying F-35Bs, as a matter of fact—had been led by one of the most arrogant SOBs he'd ever met. The fact that the instructors at Red Flag had regularly spanked his squadron's collective butt would have therefore been very satisfying—except for the fact that Turk and his two-ship element of F-22s was regularly charged with flying with them.

His combined unit only managed to beat the instructors on the very last exercise, and that was because the F-22s followed their own game plan, essentially using the Marines to bait the larger group of aggressors.

Different group, Turk told himself as he walked over to introduce himself. *Give these guys a chance. Not every Marine aviator is a jerk.*

And besides, it was their commander who was the A-hole. The rest of them were decent human beings. For Marines.

Two of the pilots, still in full flight gear, were stretching their legs near the wings of the planes.

"Hey!" yelled Turk.

"Hey, back," yelled the Marine Corps aviator closest to him. Tall for a pilot—he looked like he might be six-eight—he started toward Turk.

"How you doin'?" asked the pilot. He had a southern California twang. "You the Air Force dude in charge?"

"No, that's Colonel Freah. Danny Freah," added Turk, pointing. "He's over there."

"I'm Torbin Van Garetn," said the Marine, thrusting out his hand. "A lot of people just call me Cowboy."

"Why Cowboy?"

" 'Cause they think it's funny that a Swede wears cowboy boots," said the other pilot, coming over. "Don't let his sloppy uniform fool you. He's the best executive officer in the whole damn Marine Corps. My name's Rogers."

"Turk Mako."

"So what's your gig, Turk?" asked Cowboy.

"I'm going to be working with you guys as the ground air controller."

"Cool. You're Air Force."

"That's what it says on the uniform."

Cowboy laughed. "My bro's in the Air Force. Tech sergeant. He is stationed in California, the lucky bastard. Gets a lot of surfing in."

"You're into surfing?"

"Isn't everybody?"

"Cowboy!" shouted a voice from back near the planes.

"That's our C.O.," said Cowboy. "Kind of, uh,

well, I'll let you form your own opinion." He smirked.

"Cowboy. What are you doing?" said the commanding officer as he walked toward them. His tone wasn't exactly friendly. "Is your aircraft squared away?"

Cowboy winked at Turk, then spun around to meet his boss. "Not yet, Colonel. Just making the acquaintance of our Air Force liaison."

"Well get your aircraft taken care of, then deal with your social duties."

Turk braced himself. The snarl of a commander a little too full of himself was universal, but the gait seemed not only unique but all too familiar.

No way, he thought.

But it was—the C.O. of "Basher" squadron was none other than Lt. Colonel James "Jocko" Greenstreet, the man who had commanded the F-35s at Red Flag.

Of all the stinking bad luck.

"I'm Lieutenant Colonel Greenstreet," barked the pilot, stopping about ten feet from Turk. "Who are you?"

"Turk Mako." If Greenstreet didn't remember him, he wasn't volunteering the memory.

"What's your rank?"

"I'm a captain."

Greenstreet frowned in a way that suggested an Air Force captain was too low for him to waste breath on.

"We'll brief when we have our aircraft settled," said Greenstreet.

"Can't wait," said Turk as the colonel strode away. He couldn't tell if Greenstreet had recognized him and didn't think it was worth acknowledging, or if he was simply extending the same warm and fuzzy feelings they'd shared at the Air Force exercise.

"You meet the Marine squadron leader?" asked Danny, walking over.

"Jocko Greenstreet," Turk told him. "Lieutenant colonel. Real piece of work. Don't call him Jocko," added Turk.

"You know him?"

"Unfortunately, yes," Turk explained.

"I assume you'll keep your personal feelings to yourself," said Danny. ·

"Absolutely," said Turk. "I'm sure he will, too—not that it will make any difference at all in how he behaves."

TWO HOURS LATER DANNY, TURK, AND TREVOR Walsh—the Whiplash techie who was going to handle the local monitoring gear—joined the Marine Corps pilots and some senior enlisted men in one of the trailers for a presentation on the UAV.

"This is what we're interested in," said Danny, starting the briefing with blurry images of the UAV in action. "While your primary mission is still to assist the Malaysians, we appreciate any help you can give us. We're very, very interested in finding out what exactly this UAV is and who's flying it. We expect that it may fly into your area."

"You 'expect,' or it will?" asked Colonel Green-street sharply.

"I can't make any prediction," said Danny, who didn't mind the question or the tone. "Unfortunately. But when the Malaysian air force had its fighters on the western side of the island, it appeared."

"Would have been nice if they told us before deploying us here," said Greenstreet.

"That wasn't my call," said Danny.

"We've flown on the eastern side for weeks," said Greenstreet.

"Cowboy says he saw a flying monkey," joked one of the Marines from the back.

"I did," laughed Cowboy.

"Enough," said Greenstreet, immediately silencing his men.

Danny clicked his remote, bringing up a few slides of the fuselage that had been recovered, then the artist's renditions. He detailed the two sightings, with map displays, and reiterated what had happened to the Malaysian aircraft that had attempted to engage it.

"We're not exactly sure that it was the UAV that shot anything down," said Danny. "Not to denigrate their flying but—"

"We've seen 'em," said Cowboy. "You're not denigrating anything."

This time Greenstreet didn't bother stopping the snickers.

"Nonetheless, ground fire can't be completely ruled out," said Danny. "And while the flight patterns *suggest* a combat UAV, we have no hard evidence. That's why we're here," he added. "Myself, Captain Mako, and Mr. Walsh, that is."

"The Malaysians aren't exactly the best pilots in the world," said Greenstreet. "But I'd expect them to know what type of aircraft they were dealing with. And how many. One seems ridiculous."

"Exactly," said Danny. "But whether it's one or ten or whatever, that unknown aircraft is pretty fast and highly maneuverable."

"And you're sure it's a UAV?" asked one of the Marines.

"It's too small to be manned, as far as we can tell," said Danny.

"Where does it launch from?"

Danny shook his head. "Don't know that either. We have elint assets coming on line," he added, referring obliquely to a specially built Global Hawk that would pick up electronic signals. The aircraft was due in the area in a few hours. "Like I say, we're here to fill in the blanks, and there are a lot of blanks."

"You sure this isn't a Flighthawk?" asked Cowboy.

"It's not one of ours."

"Chinese clone?"

"It's possible," admitted Danny.

"The nearest Chinese warship is three hundred miles away," said Lt. JG Kevin Sullivan, the intelligence officer for the task group. "And that's a destroyer. Hard to see it launching something as powerful as a Flighthawk."

"Unless it's just a recon drone and the Malaysians screwed up," said Greenstreet. "That I can definitely believe."

"There is a Chinese carrier task force a little farther north than the destroyer," said Danny. "But that's being monitored very closely."

"They don't have UAVs aboard," said Sullivan.

"Not that we know," agreed Danny. "Nor do they have anything nearly this capable. But like I say—"

"You're here to fill in the blanks," said Cowboy and a few of the other Marines.

"That's right."

"So if we see it, we can engage it?" asked Cowboy.

"If you're in Malaysian airspace and it's hostile, and you know it's a UAV and that it isn't one of ours, absolutely." Danny turned to Turk. "Captain Mako has some notes on its probable characteristics."

He flipped the slide to a video simulation that had been prepared to show the drone's likely flight characteristics. It was smaller than the F-35s and more maneuverable, but presumably would not be as fast. The heat signature from its engine was minimal, but still enough for an all-aspect Sidewinder to lock at two miles, farther if the attacker was behind the UAV.

"Basically, you don't want it behind you," said Turk. "This is just a rough outline."

"The more we can find out about it, the better," added Danny. "But don't put yourself in danger."

"What's that supposed to mean?" asked Green-street.

"Shoot the mother down at first opportunity," said Cowboy.

Everybody laughed.

The briefing turned to working with the Malaysian ground force. The unit would undertake search and destroy patrols in areas where the rebels were believed to be active. Turk would use a pair of backpack UAVs—small remote-controlled aircraft with wingspans about as wide as a typical desk—to help provide reconnaissance. Nicknamed "Seagulls," the UAVs could feed video directly to the Marine F-35s through a dedicated satellite communications channel. The channel allowed two-way traffic, which meant Turk could in turn tie into some of the F-35s' sensor net as well.

Details out of the way, the briefing broke up for a round of beers, recently deposited in an ice chest by a fresh round of Osprey visits. Danny watched the pilots interact; they were young, sure of themselves, pretty much typical pilots as far as he could tell. Greenstreet seemed stiff and a bit too tightly wound; on the other hand, Captain Thomas, the ground commander, was genuinely relaxed.

In his heart of hearts, Danny would have greatly preferred to be working with a Whiplash team, concentrating solely on finding the UAV. The group of Marines he'd been given looked more than solid, but you could never know exactly what you had until the lead started to fly.

In all his years in special operations, the Marine

Corps had never let him down. Hopefully, that string would remain unbroken.

7

Suburban Virginia

"**I** HAD AN INTERESTING DISCUSSION WITH THE President the other day," Breanna told Zen, plopping down in the living room chair across from him. It was late; their daughter had been asleep for several hours, and by rights both should be in bed.

"National security?" asked Zen.

"Hardly," said Breanna. "What's that you're drinking?"

"Pumpkin-chocolate stout." He held the pint glass out to her. "Want some?"

"I don't trust that combination."

"Your loss." He took another sip. "So I'm guessing this wasn't a top secret conversation."

"Not this part." Their respective roles in government—Zen a senator, Breanna in the DoD—made for an awkward set of unwritten rules and, occasionally, difficult protocol between them. Breanna generally couldn't talk about work, even if she thought Zen might have valuable advice. "Ms. Todd said you'd make a good President."

Zen nearly spit his beer laughing.

"I don't think it's *that* funny," answered Breanna.

"I hope you agreed."

"I did. I do. Of course, you'd have to start getting better haircuts."

"What's wrong with this?"

"Twenty years out of date. Maybe if you dyed it."

Zen rolled his eyes. They'd had this discussion many times.

"Seriously," said Breanna. "Why did she bring that up? Do you know?"

"Buttering you up, probably."

"I don't think so."

"She'll be starting her reelection campaign soon." Zen shrugged. "Maybe she figures she can get rid of me by having me run in a primary."

"Ha, ha. She likes you."

"Mmmm . . ." He took a long swig of the beer. While they were members of the same party, Zen and Ms. Todd had had a number of disagreements, and he certainly wouldn't be considered among her closest supporters in Congress. On the other hand, Breanna knew that the President did genuinely trust his opinions and probably valued his willingness to disagree—she had that rare ability among Presidents to actually seek out counterarguments to her own positions.

There was also the fact that he had helped save her life.

"It's a mystery," said Zen. "One of many."

"Wanna go to bed?" Breanna asked.

"There's an invitation I'd never turn down," said Zen, a twinkle in his eyes.

8

Malaysia
Four days later

Turk ducked low to escape the branch as it swung back across the trail. In three days of working with the Malaysians, he'd not only learned to duck when he heard the distinctive sound of a branch swinging through the air, but had developed a kind of sixth sense about the team and how it moved through the jungle.

The eight-man patrols were led by a point man and the team sergeant. Turk was usually the third man in line, trying not to get too close but on the other hand keeping them in sight, which in the jungle wasn't always easy. He remembered the training the Delta boys had given him before his Iranian mission: don't bunch up, be always wary, know where the rest of your team is.

These guys weren't Delta, but they had been working in the bush long enough to move as a team, quiet and wary. Except for Turk's M-4, their main weapons were ancient M-16 assault rifles, supplemented by a single Russian AEK-999 Barsuk, a squad-level 7.62 x 54mm machine gun. The six handguns they had between them included two Smith & Wesson revolvers. They carried an odd mix of Chinese and American hand grenades. By far their most impressive weapons were the large machete-style knives they had at their belts, one sharper than the other. All appeared to have been handed down from at least a generation before, and even the most austere was a tribute to the man who had crafted it. While used to hack through thick underbrush, they could cut off a man's arm or even head with a slight flick of the wrist.

Each man carried extra water, ammo, and rudimentary first aid supplies in a small tactical vest or a web belt; they had no radios, let alone GPS gear or even compasses. Armor and helmets were nowhere in sight. Had Turk not been there, the patrol would have been operating completely on their own; the Malaysian air force was already stretched thin and needed to handle operations in "hotter" areas. Artillery support was a luxury unheard of here.

Only two of the men spoke English with any fluency: the commander, Captain Deris, who had studied for two years in Australia; and Private Isnin, whose nickname was Monday. Monday was the point man, and he had the instincts of a cat. Slight, and barely out of his teens, he managed to get through the brush without making much of a sound, and seemed as comfortable in the thick trees as he was on the road. Though he was at least five years younger than the next youngest man, it was clear they all trusted his instincts, and even Deris deferred to his sense of direction.

Monday and Sergeant Intan, about forty and a devout Muslim, seemed to communicate by telepathy. Neither spoke during a patrol, but the NCO constantly flashed hand signals back to Turk and the rest of the patrol as they walked, somehow perceiving what Monday wanted to do.

Turk wore a set of Whiplash glasses, which allowed him to see the feed from the two Seagull UAVs overhead as they patrolled. The drones were strictly reconnaissance aircraft. Relatively simple but capable of automated flight through a designated orbit, they fed back infrared images without interpretation by a computer or other device.

Operating in a remote section of the jungle a few miles from the Indonesian border, the patrols were designated as "presence and contact" missions by the Malaysian command: the unit swept through different areas, showing that they were there and hoping to come in contact with enemy guerrillas. The settlements here were isolated and tiny, generally with less than a hundred people. Most of the time was spent simply walking along trails. In the three days they'd been out, they had yet to see the enemy.

Today they had a target to check out—an abandoned mine about three miles from the highway. The Malaysians had been given intelligence claiming the rebels were using it to store weapons. A flyover by the Marine F-35s the day before had failed to find anything. The Seagull circling the area showed no activity now. But the terrain around the target area was the most complicated they'd worked through yet, and there was always a possibility that something was hidden in the foliage.

Turk followed as Monday continued up the trail, weaving toward a small rise that would let them see the approach to the mine. Suddenly, Sergeant Intan waved him to the ground; Turk dropped, then turned to signal to the others. Moments later he heard the sound of a truck straining up the hill nearby.

Turk crawled toward Monday and the sergeant; Captain Deris followed.

"Bandits," the captain told Turk. That was the English word they used to describe the rebels, whom they regarded as criminals. "They must be driving to the mine. We will move back and parallel the road."

He gestured with his fingers to make sure Turk understood.

"OK," said Turk. He clicked the back of his glasses, opening the window on Seagull 2's feed. The truck was an older pickup. The bed had been pulled off and replaced with a wooden platform surrounded by wide stakes. It was moving through a pass that led to the mine.

Turk dialed the Marines into his radio circuit.

"Basher One, this is Ground," he said. "Do you copy?"

"Loud and strong, little guy," said Cowboy. The Marines worked in two-ship units, with two planes always on alert as the Malaysians patrolled. The length of the patrols and the lack of refueling assets made it impractical for them to stay airborne when there was no contact with the enemy, but the base was close enough to the patrol area that they could be in firing range in under ten minutes.

"We think we have activity out here," said Turk. "Request you get onboard."

"Roger that. We'll be airborne in zero-two. Check in when you have a definitive word."

"We're moving toward the target now. Check the feed on Seagull 2."

"Looking at it, Ground. I see the truck."

"Roger that."

After a few minutes of walking, the patrol left the trail and moved into the jungle, intending to sweep around from the east in case anyone had been posted near the road. As they were about to start back toward the hill overlooking the mine, the Seagull spotted another pair of trucks heading in the same direction as the other one. A total of a dozen men sat in the back of the pickups.

It was a sizable force for the guerrillas. Captain Deris was pleased.

"A good catch. The airplanes will help," he said confidently. "Bomb them at the mine."

"We need to ID them first," said Turk, citing the rules of engagement.

"Why? It's an enemy site."

"We need to confirm that they're enemy, and not Malaysian army," said Turk. "Or civilians."

"No civilians are here. We're the only army."

"I didn't make the rules," said Turk. "You know them as well as I do. Visual IDs, or we're under fire. Otherwise the Marines can't do anything."

The captain frowned but didn't argue. After talking with the NCO for a few moments, he broke the squad into two units. Deris led the first, with Monday, Turk, and another man in a semicircle toward the hill where they could see the mine. The other half of the squad was assigned to hold the ground between them and the road, in case of an attack or reinforcements.

It took roughly ten minutes for them to reach the position, but it felt like hours. With each step, Turk felt his heart beat a little faster. He checked his M-4 several times as he walked, making sure he was locked and loaded; he kept his finger against the side of the trigger guard, tapping occasionally to reassure himself that he was prepared to fire if he had to.

Inevitably, he thought of Iran. The memories were confused, more about the emotion he'd felt than what had actually happened. He remembered the exhaustion and anger rather than the men he'd killed. His adrenaline kicked in; he was excited in the same way he'd be excited if he were in the air.

But it was different. In the air, Turk felt like a king—he knew his aircraft and his own abilities so well that he was never afraid, never less than completely confident. On the ground, his weapons felt cruder and less dependable, even though he'd been shooting rifles since he was a boy.

The mine was an open pit a little over a hundred yards in diameter, pitched on the side of what had been a low hill. Abandoned several years before, its sides were devoid of vegetation, thanks to whatever poisons, manmade and natural, were left from the operation. A misshapen green pool of water sat at the center.

The three trucks were parked in a semicircle at the entrance ramp to the flat land surrounding the pit. Three men were standing near one of the trucks, consulting a map. The rest of the men had gotten out of the trucks and were milling around the area. Turk counted a dozen.

"Attack now," said Captain Deris.

"We still don't know if they're rebels," said Turk. "They could be miners, just checking the site."

Deris frowned. "You see they have guns."

"Your government wrote the rules, not mine," said Turk. "I'm as frustrated as you."

"What's 'frustrated'?"

"It means—just hold on." Turk examined the feed from Seagull 2. There was a list of items that indicated rebels—a flag was the most obvious, but he couldn't see one. Nor could he identify the black armbands the 30 May Movement regularly wore on operations.

Guns were permitted—as long as they were from a list that included American rifles and the ubiquitous AK-47, all popular out in the bush. But if Turk could identify them as modern Chinese assault rifles, it could be assumed the group were rebels.

The normal Dreamland systems would have ID'ed the gun automatically. Turk had to work harder with the Seagull.

"Seagull 2, move to two thousand feet," he commanded. "Maintain present orbit."

The robot plane began moving downward slowly. Turk cranked the magnification to its highest level.

"Hey, Ground, what are we seeing?" asked Cowboy.

"I'm working on it," answered Turk.

"We cleared or what?"

"Relax a minute."

"I'm way relaxed, dude. Do we have a confirmed target or what?"

"Stand by."

The Seagull cruised over the hillside. Its light body color was practically invisible against the clouds, but veering across a patch of blue it stood out. While the wings were shaped like a bird's, anyone who studied it carefully would realize from its movements that it was an aircraft.

Suddenly, three pops echoed against the hills.

"Gunfire!" said Captain Deris.

Turk studied the guns being raised. They were bull pups—Chinese weapons.

"Basher One, confirmed hostiles at target area," said Turk, involuntarily flinching as a muzzle flashed in his viewer.

There was more gunfire, closer—the rebels had spotted the Malaysians on the ridge.

"Roger that, Ground," said Cowboy. His voice dropped an octave, and there was no hint of humor. "I have three vehicles; roughly a dozen armed men."

"Confirmed," said Turk. "All are hostile."

"We have your position noted," added the Marine.

"Cleared hot. Go get 'em."

"Inbound. Advise you take cover."

In the few moments that had passed since the first gunfire, Monday and Captain Deris had begun firing back. The rest of the rebels had opened up, training their weapons on the hill. Bullets began ripping through the nearby trees.

"Basher is inbound," Turk yelled to the Malaysians. "The fighters are on the way."

He no sooner had given the warning when something whistled in the distance. The ground shook as eight GBU-53 small diameter bombs, all steered by radar seeker to the precise location of the trucks, ignited in quick succession. The explosions destroyed the vehicles and killed or wounded two-thirds of the rebels who'd been nearby.

Monday bolted to his feet, ready to charge down the hill toward the depleted enemy.

"Stay down! Stay down!" yelled Turk. "The planes are still attacking!"

His voice was drowned out by a second round of explosions, these closer to the hill, as the second Marine F-35 mopped up the knot of rebels who'd initially opened fire.

Squatting near a tree, Turk looked at the feed from Seagull 2. All of the rebels were on the ground.

"Basher, stand off. We're going down."

"You got it, dude," said Cowboy, his voice jocular once more. The difference was so striking that Turk would have thought he was talking to another pilot.

Turk followed Captain Deris to the mine. The scent of dirt and explosive mixed with the thick, moist smell of the jungle. Nothing was moving. The F-35s had done the job.

ABOARD BASHER ONE, COWBOY UNSNAPPED HIS oxygen mask and popped a stick of gum into his mouth.

Greenstreet's voice boomed in his helmet. "Basher One, give me a sitrep."

"Three vehicles, fifteen tangos down," replied Cowboy. "We're standing by for the ground team."

"What's your fuel state?"

"Oh, yeah, we're good."

"Cut the bull, Lieutenant."

Used to Greenstreet's prickly ways, Cowboy smiled to himself and read off the exact data, confirming that both F-35s had enough fuel for several hours' worth of flying, with plenty left in reserve.

"Basher One, did you ID the target before dropping your weapons?" asked Greenstreet.

"Friendlies were under fire from the targets," said Cowboy. "We were cleared in via Captain Mako."

"You're sure."

"Absolutely, sir."

"Good."

Lord, don't let me grow up to be a squadron commander, Cowboy thought.

He was just about to tell Greenstreet that he had won the squadron pool on who was going to see action first when the aircraft's warning system blared. The F-35's AN/APG-81 radar had picked up a fast-moving object flying in his direction.

"Stand by," he told Greenstreet. "I have a contact."

He wasn't picking up an active radar. To Cowboy, that meant it had to be an aircraft, rather than a missile fired blindly in his direction.

Which in turn meant it must be the UAV they were looking for.

"Kick ass," he muttered, turning the F-35 in its direction.

The bogie was roughly forty miles away and closing fast. Under other circumstances Cowboy could have launched an AMRAAM with a high probability of a kill. But not only was he prevented from doing that by the ROEs—he hadn't been threatened, nor had the bogie apparently turned on its weapons radar—his job was to gather as much information about it as possible. And that meant getting up close and personal.

"Two, you seeing this?" he asked his wingman, Lieutenant John "Jolly" Rogers.

"Roger One."

"Like we talked about," said Cowboy. "You're high."

The two planes increased their separation, Cowboy moving eastward as his wing mate angled to the west. Cowboy wanted the UAV to come after him; Basher Two would cover him from above and take it down if necessary.

"No radar, no profile like anything we've seen out east," said Jolly. "Not Malaysian. Not standard Chinese either."

"Roger." Cowboy dipped his nose, pushing the jet for a little more speed.

The UAV was coming at him almost straight-on. Cowboy plotted a simple roll and turn to line up for a Sidewinder shot as it passed. That would give his sensors the maximum amount of time to pull data before he downed the aircraft—assuming it did something to allow him to do so.

"Basher One, what's your situation?" said Greenstreet from the ground.

"We have the UAV on our screens. At least we think it's him," added Cowboy. "Preparing to engage."

"Observe it first. Visually confirm it's hostile before firing."

"Yup. Acknowledged."

Cowboy calculated the intercept—a minute and thirty seconds. The UAV still wasn't using a radar against him.

"Come on," he whispered to himself. "Light me up so I can take you down."

The bogie was flying about 5,000 feet above him. Cowboy got ready to turn. It would be in visual range in a moment.

A minute twenty.

Suddenly, the UAV disappeared from his radar screen.

"What the hell?" muttered Jolly over the squadron frequency.

As soon as he heard the Marines chattering about the UAV, Turk switched his communications to the Cube, where Tom Frost was coordinating the data gathering.

"You getting all this?" he asked Frost.

"I have the F-35 data," said Frost. "Global Hawk elint aircraft isn't picking up anything."

"Nothing?"

"I'm resetting the frequency scan. The aircraft is a little too far east. We were worried about the Chinese detecting it earlier."

A few seconds later Frost told Turk that the computers were synthesizing a possible profile for the UAV. It didn't appear armed.

"Also looks like it might be different than the earlier ones," said Frost. "Check out the model."

Turk put his glasses into 3-D mode and spun his hand around, examining the enemy aircraft. It had small stubby wings that reminded him of the Cold War era F-104 Starfighter, a high-speed aircraft. At the rear, the UAV was a very different beast, with a much thicker, wedge-shaped body, a Y-tail, and some sort of directional-vector thrust system—it suddenly cut a nearly ninety-degree turn in the sky.

The turn caused the aircraft to disappear temporarily from the F-35s' radars, a variation on the old trick of beaming a Doppler radar. The American system was too smart to stay blind for very long; the F-35s' redundant systems were able to find it again quickly. But the second or two of confusion, along with the course change, gave the little SUV just enough of an advantage to duck into the ground clutter near the coast, camouflaging itself in the irregular radar returns caused by the ground. It was a command performance, and the fact that Turk had dealt with exactly that sort of maneuver from attacking Flighthawks in simulated combat didn't make it any less impressive.

"Basher, your bandit is two sixty off your nose," said Turk, telling the Marine pilot that the UAV had tucked down to his left. "Ten miles. He's going to try popping up behind you."

"Uh—"

"Trust me. Put your plane on your right wing and look for the bogie to cross your nose in twenty seconds. It's going to be low—he's in the weeds and trying to get behind you. Break now!"

WITH HIS F-35 BLEEDING OFF SPEED, COWBOY KNEW he was a sitting duck for any aircraft that came up behind him. But what Turk was suggesting was very counterintuitive. It seemed almost impossible that the drone could spin around quickly enough to get behind him, let alone get underneath him.

Instinctually, it seemed a dumb move, and not least of all because it would leave him vulnerable to a plunging attack from above, the direction he expected the drone to come from.

Did he trust the Air Force pilot?

Cowboy leaned on his stick, driving the F-35B hard and sharp, exactly as Turk had suggested. The g's hit him hard, pushing him back into the fighter's seat.

A black bar appeared at the right side of his windscreen. The targeting radar was going wild.

Mother!

"Can I fire?" asked the Marine, pushing to stay

with the UAV. But before anyone answered, the black aircraft turned its nose abruptly in his direction and sliced downward, moving and turning at a speed Cowboy didn't think possible. He made his own abrupt turn, losing so much altitude that the Bitchin' Betty warning system blared that he was too low. He scanned his radar and then the sky, but the slippery little UAV and its tiny radar cross section had once more disappeared in the weeds.

Damn.

TURK REALIZED WHAT WAS HAPPENING AS SOON AS Cowboy got the altitude warning. There was no way the Marine was going to catch the other plane now.

Still, they needed as much data as they could get. And they were going to get it by going home.

"Your bandit's heading west," he told the Marine.

"Yeah, we're following."

"You have it on radar?"

"Negative."

"Did he turn on weapons radar?" Turk asked.

"No."

"All right."

"We're going to search this area. Once he's over the water he should be easy to find."

"Easier, maybe."

"Yeah. You see where he launched from?"

"I didn't. I'll check back with my people," added Turk, though he could already guess that the answer would be no: they would be giving the F-35s a vector to the site if they had.

Turk signed off with Cowboy and continued down the slope to the mining area. His boots sank into the soft ground. The place smelled like dirt, and death.

While considered "small," two-hundred-pound GBU-53s still made an absolute mess of anything they hit; the three guerrillas who'd been holding this part of the perimeter had been obliterated. Twenty yards away, half of one of the trucks lay on its side, blown over by an explosion.

A severed leg lay on the ground. Turk stared at it for a moment, frowned, then kept walking.

Three months ago, that would have turned my stomach, he thought. Now it's just one more ugly part of the landscape.

9

An island in the Sembuni Reefs, off Malaysia

FINALLY, THEY'D COME.

Lloyd Braxton stared at the console, even though the displays were blank. He had been waiting for this moment for many months. In a sense, he'd been preparing for it for years.

It was intoxicating. Kallipolis was becoming a reality, precisely as he had envisioned. The days of nation states were passing before his eyes; the elite was ready to take over.

He clenched his fists, controlling his excitement.

There was a great deal to be done. This was just one small step in the evolution.

The next step was to defeat the Dreamland people—Special Projects, Whiplash, whatever the hell bs code name they were using. Defeat them and take their technology, the last piece of the puzzle.

Defeating Dreamland would be sweet. Rubeo and his web of sellout scientists, technodrones for the governments of the world, would finally be put in their places.

Braxton scolded himself. If this became a quest for revenge it would fail. He had argued this many times with Michaels, Thresh, and Fortine—especially the ship captain Fortine—who while still being true believers, bore personal grudges against their governments and a host of officials who had wronged them. Braxton didn't blame them, exactly, but he knew that Kallipolis was a movement of history, a phenomenon like the Renaissance or the Reformation, not something to be sullied by personal grudges.

Kallipolis was both a goal and a philosophy. The philosophy was perfect, unfettered freedom: true dependence on the self, and a true unshackling of the governmental binds that kept men and women from reaching their potential, both personally and as a race. Kallipolis would do away with national borders and provide those who were worthy of it complete freedom and the unrestricted ability to achieve.

The people who made up the Kallipolis movement—aside from the very small group of people he employed, there were over a hundred in close communications with Braxton, and a few thousand more beyond—were members of the intelligentsia, scientists and engineers, and those who had done something with their lives, people who were the builders, not the takers; what they had in common was the ability to see things without emotion and act on them. They acted as he must act: entirely on the scientific principles that had gotten him this far.

So . . . it was on to the next move. Provoke the Americans into showing themselves, and get Whiplash to expose the tech he needed.

He needed to talk to the rebel leader on Malaysia immediately. The sooner the Americans were provoked, the better.

10

Suburban Virginia

Breanna ROLLED OVER IN THE BED, AWARE THAT SHE had to wake up but unsure why. She was in the middle of a dream, caught in an incomprehensible tangle of odd thoughts and a snatch of memory. The setting was her childhood, a home near the railroad tracks. She was running to catch the train. Her father, dressed in his Class A uniform, was yelling at her to stop. The train was a steam locomotive, a huge nineteenth century bruiser stolen from a Christmas display and multiplied a hundred times . . .

Up, she told herself, and she slipped off the covers, grabbing the vibrating phone on her bed stand.

Zen snored as she grabbed a robe from the end of the bed and walked to the hallway.

"Breanna," she said into the phone.

"Need to talk," said Danny Freah.

"Give me two minutes. I'll call."

Pulling on the robe, Breanna went down to the kitchen and glanced at the clock. It was two-thirty in the morning. Indonesia was a day and an hour ahead, making it three-thirty there.

She hesitated for a moment, then hit the button on the coffeemaker. As the water started to heat, she went to the kitchen table and pulled her daughter's laptop open. The Web browser came up; she checked the news headlines on her home page quickly, making sure nothing important had happened in the roughly two hours since she'd gone to bed.

Coffee in hand, she went to her office in the basement. Two minutes later she was talking to Danny over the Whiplash com network's secure link.

"No video from your end?" asked Danny when his tired face appeared on the screen.

"I have it off. Commander's prerogative."

"I have an update on the UAV we encountered today."

"OK," she said, yawning.

"Turk was looking at the flight patterns that were reconstructed by the team Frost heads," said Danny. "He says it followed a defensive pattern he recognized from the Flighthawks, to the letter."

"Is he sure?"

"I had him go over it a couple of times. He looked at everything—the approach, the maneuvers, the way it got away. He said he's flown against that attack a lot."

"Is it a Flighthawk?"

"No. Turk compared it to a late model Flighthawk with stubbier wings."

Breanna tapped on her keyboard, tying into the Cube's computer system. Within a few minutes she had a video of the reconstructed encounter.

"I see what he's saying," she told Danny. "But we still don't have any elint data."

"Turk had a theory about that. This is a preprogrammed pattern, something you could tell the Flighthawks to do. They wouldn't need to be in full communication."

"That's right. Have you talked to Ray about this?"

"He'd gone home."

"I'll talk to him," said Breanna.

"If it is following the Flighthawk's program, the source might be—it could be—"

"Us," said Breanna.

"Yeah. Someone who worked on the Flighthawks."

While there had been Flighthawk crashes and shoot-downs over the years, the aircraft were equipped with a series of fail-safe devices for completely scrubbing the memory and destroying the chips. There was no indication that the systems had ever failed. There hadn't been a crash now in several years.

"This thing gets worse and worse," said Danny before hanging up.

Zen OPENED HIS EYES AS SOON AS HE SMELLED THE coffee. He glanced at the clock—it was a few minutes before three.

He lay in bed, listening to the house. He couldn't hear Breanna; that meant she was downstairs in her soundproof office. She wouldn't have left the house without kissing him good-bye, which inevitably woke him up—though he would never tell her that, for fear she might stop doing it.

Their daughter Teri was sleeping down the hall. He could hear her light breath. The child could sleep through a train crash without waking, something that never ceased to amaze Zen.

The coffee smelled good.

Zen made a halfhearted attempt at drifting off; a grand total of thirty seconds passed before he threw the covers off and pushed himself to the edge of the bed for his wheelchair.

Breanna had grabbed his robe when she'd gotten up, so once he was in the chair he wheeled to the bureau and pulled out a sweatshirt. Then he rolled down to the kitchen. He was pouring milk into his coffee when Breanna came up from her office.

"You took my robe," he told her. "Yours was on the chair."

"Sorry, I just grabbed what was there." She leaned into him for a long kiss. "I'm sorry I woke you up."

"Worth getting up for," said Zen. He took his coffee and went over to the table. "Problems?"

"Eh. Just the usual."

He knew from the tone in her voice that whatever had gotten her up was particularly sticky, but he also knew that he couldn't push her for details.

"Kinda strong," said Zen, sipping his coffee.

"No more than usual."

Breanna sat down at the table across from him. "Couldn't sleep?" she asked.

"A lot going on."

"Thinking about what Todd said?"

"Oh . . . no. I don't think I'd want to be President."

"Why not? You could do a hell of a lot."

"Maybe . . ." He took another sip. Bree was right—the coffee wasn't any stronger than normal.

"What are you doing today?"

"Committee stuff. And fund-raising."

"Your favorite."

"Worse than that. I'm meeting with Jake Harris."

Harris was an entrepreneur who'd made three fortunes and lost two before he was thirty years old. He'd held on to the latest, and over the last few years had become one of the most important political fund-raisers in the country.

"Count your fingers and toes before you go in."

"It's after that I'm worried about. I'd have to do this all the time if I ever ran for President," he added.

"The price you pay."

"Yeah."

Lifting his coffee mug to his lips, he realized he'd nearly drained it. He took a last gulp, then wheeled over to the machine for a refill.

Breanna watched her husband wheel across the floor toward the coffee. For just a moment she saw him as he was before the accident at Dreamland that had taken the use of his legs—a brash young pilot, skilled and already wise beyond his years.

He was extremely bitter after the accident. Even so, it didn't change what was vital about him— the need to strive, the urge to compete and be the best at what he did. The tragedy hadn't made him a better person, but his will to keep going, his struggle to keep contributing to Dreamland and the Air Force and above all his country—those things had made him into a man to be admired, a real leader.

He would make an excellent President.

But should she urge him to run? He'd have to give up a lot, from the trivial—his skybox at the Nationals—to things that had no price, like time with their daughter.

Breanna curled her feet under her, then tucked the robe around her. It was thick and warm, and reminded her of him.

She hadn't taken it by mistake.

She felt an urge to tell him about the plane— he'd know right off if the maneuvers were the same as those programmed into the Flighthawks. He also might have a theory on why that was. Just a coincidence? Or much more?

But she couldn't.

If he ever did run for President, how many things would they never be able to share?

"Need a refill?" Zen asked.

"No, it's full."

Zen balanced the cup between his legs and wheeled himself back to the table. All these years, and he still insisted on an unpowered chair. There was more than a little macho masochism in him.

"Whatever you do, whenever you do it," said Breanna, "Teri and I are with you."

Zen smiled. That was one thing that hadn't changed, ever, and the way his eyes shone, it was clear it never would.

"Thanks, babe," he told her. "You think we can go back to bed?"

"You think we can sleep after all this coffee?"

"Who said anything about sleep?"

"Hold that thought," said Breanna, rising. "I have to make a phone call."

DESPITE THE HOUR, RAY RUBEO ANSWERED ON THE first ring.

"Ray, it's Breanna. I—I'm sorry to wake you."

"You didn't. I'm working."

"Oh. OK. Listen I just talked to Danny. He said that Turk Mako has a theory—"

"Let me guess. He sees parallels between the UAVs and some of our aircraft."

"Well, yes," said Breanna, surprised. "Did you talk to him?"

"No. But I've noticed the parallels myself. I understand the implications," he added. "I'm taking it very seriously."

"I'm sure you are," said Breanna. Rubeo took everything seriously.

"Is there anything else? I am in the middle of constructing a model."

"No, that's it. I'll talk to you in the morning at the Cube."

"Very well," he said, hanging up.

11

Malaysia

Turk ROLLED OVER ON THE THIN MATTRESS IN THE trailer room. Though exhausted, he found it impossible to sleep. After he'd returned from the mission—the Malaysians were bivouacked in tents near the trailers—he'd gone over the mission several times, first for Danny, then the Marines, then Danny again. By the time they were done, his brain was practically buzzing with the encounter; he saw it from all angles, even the enemy UAVs, though of course this was impossible. His mind wouldn't let go.

While he could get sleeping pills from the

corpsman assigned to the Marines, Turk didn't like to use them, or even the more conventional aids available in the form of bourbon, scotch, and beer. He stared at the ceiling, but his thoughts just wouldn't stop, and finally he got up, pulled on his boots—he slept in his clothes—and went out to see if a walk might help.

He heard someone throwing up in the bathroom. The door was open and he saw Lieutenant Rogers kneeling in front of the bowl.

"You OK in there?" he asked.

"Damn food killed me," said Rogers between heaves. "I feel like my stomach is being turned inside out."

"I'll get the corpsman," said Turk.

Rogers groaned, then went back to throwing up.

Turk headed toward the administrative trailer to look for the duty officer and find out who and where the medic was.

He was about halfway there when he heard a whistle above him. It was a strange, unearthly sound, a high-pitched sizzle that seemed to snap against the strong night wind.

The explosion that followed was something else again.

Turk fell as the ground seemed to dissolve beneath him. He landed on his side, and for a moment all the adrenaline that had kept him awake disappeared; he was dazed and confused, not sure where he was or even, in that moment, who he was.

"Incoming!" yelled a Marine nearby. "Mortars!"

Turk bolted upright, energy and consciousness

instantly restored. He turned and ran back into the trailer he'd just come out of, screaming at everyone inside.

"Get to the bunker, get to the bunker!" he yelled, directing them to one of the two shelters the Marines had installed immediately after taking the base.

Men plunged from their rooms, charging into the barely lit corridor in various states of dress.

"Mortars," said one of the NCOs. His voice was loud, but there was no excitement in it, let alone fear. "Move out!"

"The planes," said Cowboy, coming out of his room at the far end. "We gotta get them off the field. Get the rest of the pilots! Pilots, *come on!*"

Turk ran to Rogers in the bathroom. He was still hunched over the toilet, his legs curled around him on the floor.

"You gotta get out of here," Turk said and grabbed him by the back of his shirt.

"Man . . ."

"Come on, Marine. Stand up."

Rogers struggled to comply. Turk helped him out into the hall, then down toward the doorway.

Two rounds hit nearby as Turk pushed Rogers out. He lost his balance, falling against the wall and letting go of Rogers. The Marine went down to his knees and threw up.

The stench turned Turk's stomach, but he managed to grab the shorter pilot and drag him over his shoulder. The compound lit with the flash of another explosion, this one up near the airstrip. The light helped Turk orient himself, and he turned in the direction of the nearest bunker.

"Yo, Rogers," he said. "It would sure help if you could push your feet every so often."

Danny Freah had just finished taking his boots off to go to sleep when the first mortar hit the base. It had been a few years since he was on the receiving end of a mortar attack, but it was an experience few people wanted to relive, and Danny certainly wasn't one of them. He pulled his boots back on, grabbed his secure laptops and the satellite phone, and ran from his trailer toward the command bunker, built around the foundation of an old building at the center of the base.

Captain Thomas met him a few yards outside the sandbagged entrance.

"Great way to wake up," snapped the Marine captain. Two men ran across the field, M-16s in hand, hustling to a perimeter post. "We should have eyes on in a minute."

"You gotta get all the planes off," said Danny. "Where's Greenstreet?"

"He ran up on the strip. I'm sure he's got it under control. Let's get inside the bunker."

Calling the structure a bunker was a bit of an overstatement. The interior had been dug out about three feet, and the sides built up with sandbags. The roof consisted of a series of corrugated steel panels covered with sandbags and dirt. Power came from a gas generator a dozen yards away.

The Marines had launched an RQ7Z Shadow, and its controller was flying the aircraft west, attempting to locate the attack. Based on the original

RQ7B, the drone could carry a slightly heavier pay-load and was designed to be launched by one man rather than two; otherwise the performance specs were similar. Looking like a stick glider with a tri-angle at its tail and a ball turret below its wings, the UAV jetted into the sky from a small metal trailer. Once airborne, its infrared camera provided a 360-degree view of the battlefield; its laser designator could be tied into the F-35B attack systems.

Right now it was getting an eyeful.

"We got over fifty savages in the weeds," said the Marine at the controls. "They're massing for an attack on the west side of the base."

Danny spun around and nearly struck Captain Thomas.

"I heard him," said Thomas. "We'll be ready."

A MARINE RAN OUT TO HELP TURK AS HE PULLED Rogers into the shelter near the airstrip. Just as the weight was lifted off his shoulder, the ground rocked with another nearby explosion. Turk lost his balance and fell straight back, smacking his head on the ground. He rolled to his belly and got to his knees, momentarily disoriented. Then he pushed to his feet.

The Malaysian ground troops were about four hundred yards away, near the outer perimeter. Turk decided that he should head over there in case they needed to liaison with the Marines. But before he could take a single step, one of the crew chiefs for the planes ran up to him, shouting about Rogers.

"We're looking for him—they need him in the air!" yelled the Marine.

"He's sick," said Turk.

"Damn. We need to get the plane off. It's a sitting duck."

"I'll fly it," said Turk. "Take me up there."

"But—"

Turk grabbed hold of the man's arm and pushed him in the direction of the runway. "Let's go!"

Danny stood at the side of the small bunker as Captain Thomas took control of the situation. The rebel force was sizable, nearly four times the number of Marines assigned to guard the perimeter. But the Corps had a slogan: every Marine is a rifleman. And Thomas lived by it: he had already drilled the maintenance and support people in the defense of the base. He now rallied them into position, readying for the assault the Shadow had seen coming.

Ironically, all that preparation left Danny feeling useless; he didn't have an assignment.

"Give me a rifle," he told Thomas. "I'll help on the perimeter."

The captain frowned. "No offense, sir, but—"

"I guarantee I've seen more action than you, Captain," answered Danny.

"Yes sir, but, uh . . ."

Danny knew that Thomas considered it his job to provide security, and that he would feel responsible if anything happened to him. He'd been in the same spot himself, many times.

"Look, Captain, I can shoot as well as most of your men, I'm sure," he said bluntly. "You need bodies. And if anything happens, I gave you a direct order, which everyone here will vouch for."

"What I could use is someone liaising with the Malaysians," said Thomas. "I haven't been able to reach them on the radio. Their equipment is primitive—and that's if they remember to use it. I need someone who can get a radio to them and tell them what to do. They can reinforce the southern side of the perimeter."

"Did Turk go down to talk to them?"

"Uh, Captain Mako ran up to the airstrip to fly one of the planes," said a lance corporal who just entered the bunker, wearing his helmet and carrying an M-16A4. "One of our guys is sick, I heard."

"Give me a radio," said Danny.

Thomas hesitated, but then complied. "Mofitt, go over with the colonel," he said, turning to the man who'd just come in.

"Yes, sir, right away."

"Let's do it," said Danny.

ONE OF THE F-35s STARTED DOWN THE RUNWAY AS Turk ran up. It took him by surprise, and he ducked involuntarily as it roared past, both pilot and steed eager to get into the air.

Turk continued toward the other planes. Two crew dogs were attaching bombs to the hard points of the nearest aircraft, despite the continuing whistle of the mortar attacks. A pair of rounds landed every thirty or forty seconds, with an occasional single shell breaking the pattern. They were getting closer to the runway, walking up in fits and starts.

Turk spotted Colonel Greenstreet in front of the wing of the plane being armed. He was shouting at the ordnance men, yelling at them to finish their business so he could get in the air and do some "f-in' good."

A second F-35 taxied out from behind the aircraft. It hesitated a moment, then seemed to explode off the runway so fast that Turk thought it had been hit by a mortar shell.

One of the crewmen spotted Turk and ran to him.

"Captain! Have you seen Lieutenant Rogers?" he shouted.

"He's sick," said Turk. "I'm going to fly. Get me to his plane."

The crewman pointed to the very end of the tarmac and began running toward it. Turk caught up in a few seconds and then passed him, racing to the F-35B as the shriek of incoming rounds pierced the air. The shells exploded a hundred yards away, off to the right; while they landed harmlessly, Turk realized that the enemy had changed its sights and was now aiming at the planes and the runway.

A crew chief met Turk as he reached the airplane. "Captain Mako?"

"Rogers is sick!" shouted Turk. "I'm getting his plane up!"

"Uh—"

"I'm checked out on it," he said. "We leave it on the ground it's dead."

That was apparently enough of an argument for the crew captain, a gunnery sergeant who'd heard Turk during the briefings and knew he was a pilot.

"She's fueled!" shouted the gunny. "We just put some bombs on the rack."

"Good! Let's go."

"You need gear!" yelled the NCO. "Where the hell is your helmet? You need a flight suit!"

"Get them quick or I'm going up like this," said Turk. Technically, he didn't need either, but one of the gunny's men was running up with a helmet, and Turk knew he'd have a much easier time with the plane if he was geared up properly. Fortunately, the suit was a little big and he was able to get into it quickly.

"Careful where you step, Captain," said the gunny as he climbed into the plane.

"Call me Turk!"

"Get your helmet on!"

"In the plane!" Turk pulled himself over the fairing and slipped in.

It had been two years since he'd been in an F-35B, let alone flew one. Though the plane shared a large number of parts with the Air Force's F-35A, in truth it was a much different animal, certainly when taking off and landing.

And it had been quite a while since he'd flown an A model as well, come to think of.

"Damn." Turk momentarily blanked. He stared at the controls. "What the hell do I do first?"

The crew chief appeared on his right with the helmet.

"Here, Captain!" he shouted as two more

rounds landed somewhere behind them. These sounded much closer than the last set. "You sure you're good?"

"Yeah, yeah. Come on. Let's go!"

"What the hell are you doing!" yelled Greenstreet, materializing on his left.

"Rogers is down in the bunker puking his guts out," said Turk. "He's sick."

"What?"

"He's sick. Something he ate. We have to get the plane off the ground."

"Where's the rest of your gear?"

"We don't have time—I'm just going to get it off the ground."

If Greenstreet thought that wasn't a good idea, the *thud-thud* of two more rounds falling, these near the edge of the runway, convinced him otherwise.

"Go! Get him off the ground!" he shouted to the crew. "And don't wreck my plane!"

"I won't. Don't worry about that," snapped Turk, reaching to start the engine.

"You good, Captain?" asked the crew chief, his voice considerably kinder if just as loud as Greenstreet's.

"Yeah, I'm good. Get yourself to shelter."

The Marine gave him a thumbs-up and disappeared off the wing as the ground shook with a fresh explosion.

Turk looked back at the panel.

"What the hell have I gotten myself into?" he said aloud.

BRAVE MEN
AND COWARDS

———

1

Malaysia

MOFITT LED DANNY DOWN TO THE MALAYSIAN CAMP.
The corporal, with the tall, lean build of a natural runner, trotted at a strong pace, glancing over
his shoulder every few paces to make sure Danny
was still with him. By the time they reached the
edge of the Malaysian army bivouac, Danny was
winded and had to pause for a moment to catch
his breath.

"You all right, Colonel?" asked the Marine.

"I'm OK. You can go back now."

"No offense, sir, but the captain wouldn't like
that."

"All right. Come on."

The Malaysians' tents were arranged in a semicircle, with their commander's tent in the middle;
they were all empty.

"They might be in the trenches," said Mofitt,
trotting in the direction of a sandbagged defensive position about thirty yards downhill from the
tents. But the Malaysians were nowhere in sight.

"Hang tight for a minute," said Danny. He took

the radio and called back to the Marine commander, asking if the Malaysians had checked in.

"Negative. Where are you?"

"In their camp," Danny told him.

"They're not there?"

"Roger that."

"Stand by."

Captain Thomas came back on the line a moment later, having checked the video from his overhead UAV. "They've gone down to the spot on the perimeter already," said the Marine. "They're in defensive positions."

"All right, we're going," Danny told him.

"Is Mofitt with you?"

"Yes."

"All right. Roger. Be advised, the rebels look like they're getting ready to attack."

Danny looked over at Mofitt, crouched nearby against the sandbags. The corporal was scanning the area in front of them with his night vision.

"They're holding the line near the road," said Danny. "But they have no coms."

"Let's get there, then."

"Good."

"Uh, one thing, sir. I gotta tell ya . . . I don't speak Malaysian, sir. I'm sorry."

"Neither do I," said Danny, scrambling to his feet.

TURK'S FINGERS TIGHTENED INVOLUNTARILY ON THE F-35B's stick as the mortar shell struck the field to his left, close enough for the air shock to push the plane sideways as it lifted off. For an instant he was sure he would lose control. But the aircraft was extremely stable, even in short-takeoff mode, and while the explosion had spooked him, it wasn't strong enough to actually disturb the plane. The plane's computer adjusted the angle of the rear nozzle, and the plane continued up and off the runway, quickly gathering speed. The massive fan behind the cockpit churned furiously, adding its own impetus to the thrust of the engine at the rear. Airborne, Turk cleaned the landing gear, folding the wheels inside the plane. The large panel above the fan and the two smaller ones behind folded down for level flight, the F-35B becoming "just" another fifth generation fighter.

I'm up, Turk thought. Not too bad. So far.

"Basher Four, Basher Four, are you reading me?" asked Greenstreet over the radio.

Turk clicked the mike button. "Yeah, I'm up. I'm still getting used to the, uh, controls."

"Get south and stay out of the way."

"I'll give it a shot," said Turk sourly.

GUNFIRE ERUPTED ON THE WESTERN SIDE OF THE base as Danny and Mofitt reached the position where the Malaysians were supposed to be. The positions—a few logs and sandbags with good sight distance down the hill—were empty.

"Colonel Freah, are you reading me?" blared the radio.

"This is Freah. You're loud and clear."

"The Malaysians moved all the way down to the road. They're another two hundred and fifty yards from your position," said Captain Thomas. "We need them to pull back—we're going to hit the rebels with bombs when they come up the road. Then they can sweep in behind us."

"All right."

"Can you send Mofitt down to them?"

"We can get down there."

"The rebels are moving—we need it quick."

"We're on our way."

Danny told Mofitt what they had to do, leaving out the fact that Thomas hadn't wanted him to go. There was no way Danny was staying behind.

"I don't know exactly what's down there," said Mofitt. "I can't see through the brush."

"I know. We'll go as fast as we can. But don't get too far ahead of me."

"Colonel, you don't have a weapon."

"I have my sidearm." Danny unsnapped the holster of his personal weapon, a Glock 20 chambered for 10mm. It was a big gun, and the ammo packed an extreme wallop. The recoil was nasty as well, though not quite as extreme as might be expected from such a large round. "Lead the way."

Mofitt took off, sorting through the trees in a zigzag pattern, occasionally stopping to let Danny catch up. He heard two trucks on the road, as well as more gunfire from the western end of the base. He visualized what was going on: the rebels had split their ground force, with a small group making an attack to the west. Meanwhile, the main group was coming up the road, intending to sweep up from the southeast while the defenders were occupied on the other side. The Malaysians had either somehow realized this and gone down to meet them, or simply blundered into the right spot at the right time.

Or wrong spot at the wrong time, depending on your point of view.

The F-35s would make quick work of the trucks, but they couldn't hit them if the Malaysians were too close.

Mofitt stopped about ten yards from the road. Danny went down to his knees as he reached him.

"They must be moving up the road," said Mofitt. "You can hear the gunfire. I'm thinking they realize the flank's vulnerable."

"Yeah," agreed Danny. "But we gotta pull them back. Come on."

"They may be trigger happy, Colonel. Better stay behind me, just in case."

"You move so damn fast, I don't have a choice," said Danny.

ONCE IN THE AIR AND MOVING LIKE A "REGULAR" AIR-plane, the F-35B was relatively easy to fly. She wasn't one of the racehorses Turk was used to, but she wasn't a dog either. She went where she was told to go, responding crisply to his inputs.

Turk climbed through 5,000 feet, moving into a gradual orbit around the airfield as he sorted himself out. His helmet was an extension of the plane's display panels, providing critical information on the systems; it was similar enough to the systems he was used to that he had to keep reminding himself he couldn't handle the controls with gestures or voice commands, but actually had to fly with his hands and feet.

Not that this was a bad thing. It forced his mind and body to work together in a familiar and reassuring way, one that chased away trivial cares and worries. It was both a release and an exhilaration, a combination he had felt the first time he slipped into a pilot's seat, as if his DNA had been programmed exactly for such an environment.

But he was more than a pilot. He was a warrior as well, and as he climbed he started looking for a way to join the battle.

The experience in Iran had cemented that identity. Thrust into an environment that was completely foreign to him—one where control was quite frankly beyond his grasp, where there were no checklists and where logic had almost nothing to do with what happened—Turk had not simply survived, but thrived. Iran's nuclear warheads and their secret stockpile of weapons grade uranium had been destroyed because of Turk Mako. Plenty of other people had helped, but at the very end it had been him, his actions, that completed the mission.

In another man that realization might have caused extreme conceit. But in Turk it had the opposite effect—it tempered him, made him realize he should be humble. If he was a great pilot and a great fighter, then he surely didn't have to prove himself, much less boast about it; what he had to do was his job. Destiny had given him tools, like a kid born with special math skills who had to work twice as hard to put them to work in the best way.

And so as he saw the other planes mustering for

attack, Turk brought his plane into the tail end of their formation, forming as wingman on Basher Three, flown by Cowboy. Greenstreet, in Basher One, immediately noticed.

"Four, what's your sitrep?" said the squadron commander.

"Forming up. I have Three's wing."

"Negative. I want you to maintain orbit over the base. Stay out of the way."

"I'm armed and ready to help."

"You're armed and dangerous," snapped Greenstreet. "Just chill, Air Force. You've done a hell of lot already."

Three months before, Turk might have responded angrily, interpreting the remark as a slam against his abilities. Now he just shook his head, shrugged, then acknowledged. He'd find another way to contribute.

Danny could hear the trucks moving on the road as he and Mofitt finally reached the Malaysian captain.

"We have to fall back," he told Captain Deris. "Come on. Pull back."

"The enemy are going to attack," said Deris. His thick accent took Danny a moment to decipher. "We must fight."

"The planes will get them," said Danny. "Come on. It's OK. We're not giving up. Let the planes do their job, and then we'll take over."

The captain nodded, then began shouting to his men, ordering them to fall back. A few moments later a pair of mortar rounds exploded behind them. The Malaysians hit the dirt. Bullets began raining through the brush. The enemy had seen that they were falling back and misinterpreted it as a panicked retreat.

Danny got on the radio. "We're taking fire," he told the Marine captain. "Where are those jets?"

"They'll be there in a few minutes. They're going after the mortars first," said Thomas. "We have the mortars zeroed in for them."

"We're pinned down here," said Danny. "Looks like they have machine guns mounted on the pickups."

"Copy that. The planes will be ASAP."

ASAP wasn't going to do it. A fresh volley of fifty-caliber machine-gun bullets sent Danny prone. The Malaysians began returning fire, but that only intensified the attack. Another set of mortar shells fell behind them, these closer.

Captain Deris came over to Danny. The battle had changed dramatically in the last few moments; the Malaysians not only were no longer on the attack, they were now cut off from any reasonable defensive position.

"I have men down," Deris told him. "We are going to be overrun."

"The planes are coming," said Danny. "The mortars are hitting above the hill. You can't go up there. You'll be cut down."

"We will have to move," said Deris. "At least if we take our chances through the shells, some will make it. Here, all will be killed. We have only these thin trees for cover."

"How many men do you have?"

"Ten now, and two of those are wounded."

Mofitt rose next to him and peered through his sight.

"Bastards are coming fast," he said, then squeezed off a three-round burst, plunking one of the rebels.

It was too late to try running for it, Danny realized. He clicked the radio to talk to the Marine ground commander. But Thomas beat him to it, transmitting before Danny could say a word.

"Colonel, stand by for a transmission from Basher Four." The Marine captain's voice sounded hoarse; the gunfire in the background sounded very close. "Go ahead, Basher."

"Colonel, this is Turk. Say location."

"We're about twenty yards from the road, on the southwest side directly below the Malaysian camp. There are two—"

"Yeah, roger, I got you. Hold your position. I'm taking the trucks out. I'll check in before the next pass."

"Everybody get down!" shouted Danny. "Down!"

THE BOMBS CAME OFF THE WINGS IN QUICK SUCCESsion, like the snap of a drummer's wrist as he rolled on his snare. Turk banked, lining up to take a run with the cannon strapped to the F-5's belly. The lead vehicle was on fire and the other had been broken in half by one of the bombs. He lit the cannon as his targeting pipper came up on a small pack of figures behind the second truck. They disappeared in a tornado of smoke.

Pulling back on the stick, Turk had a fleeting vision of what it would be like on the ground—chaos and death, the stink of burning metal and flesh in your nostrils.

It was truly hell. But you fought for your own, and you protected them, and that meant the other guy had to die.

The *other* guy. Which was why he was so mad at Breanna. She should have protected him, not sent an assassin.

"Basher Four to ground—Colonel, how are you looking?"

"Nice job, Four."

"Do you need more? My gun's full."

"We have it under control. Trucks are on fire. Rebels are retreating. I owe you one," added Danny. "Thanks."

"Roger that. See you back at base."

2

Washington, D.C.

ZEN WHEELED HIMSELF OUT FROM BEHIND HIS DESK IN his Senate office, revving himself into full-blown senator-at-work mode. There was a lot to do in the next few hours, starting with a vote in the chamber.

"OK, people," he said, zipping into the outer office. "I'm off. See you all around three."

"Senator?" His appointments secretary stood up from her desk, waving frantically to get his attention as he passed. "I have the President's office on the line."

"Tell 'em I just left for a vote," he said, not bothering to stop.

"The President wants to set up a lunch. Today."

Zen stopped at the door. President Todd didn't call often, let alone ask to have lunch. When she did, it was usually trouble—for him.

But Breanna's recounting of Todd's comment the other night made him wonder what she was really up to. If he wanted to find out, lunch was the price he'd have to pay.

Maybe.

"I can't do lunch," he said, fudging, since his appointment could be easily put off. "But if she wants to see me at some point after three, that's OK. Schedule it and text me."

Zen saw Fran Knapp, his recently hired political aide, giving him a wary eye—blowing the President off for lunch was not considered a good political move.

Zen smiled at her, and kept smiling all the way to the Senate.

3

Malaysia

"The attack on the base had to have been helped by whoever is handling the UAVs," said Danny, speaking to Breanna and Jonathon Reid a few hours after the attack had ended. "They're trying to get rid of us."

"It could easily be a coincidence," said Reid. "There were no UAVs."

"They had precise locations."

"That airstrip dates to the 1950s," answered Reid. "You have to be mindful of the politics here, Colonel. Both domestically and in geopolitical terms."

"If they're going to be this aggressive, we need to step up our force," said Danny. "Or the Marines are going to take casualties. That's going to be a disaster."

"I think Danny has a point," said Breanna. "We should have a full force there."

"You know the problems with that," said Reid.

"How about more observation assets, for starters?" said Danny.

"Even that will require the President's approval," said Reid. "And I don't know that she's going to give it."

"We might as well ask for everything we want," said Breanna.

"I'm not arguing with that," answered Danny.

Three Malaysians had been killed and four

wounded in the attack; the wounded had been medevacked via a Marine Osprey to the eastern Malaysian capital. Two Marines had been hit by shrapnel; both were taken back to the MEU's flagship, offshore on the eastern side of the island several hundred miles away. The MEU was supporting Malaysian operations there.

"We still don't know where the UAV came from," said Reid.

"But we do know that it flies like one of ours," said Danny. "And to me, that's a bigger problem than whatever politics we're worried about."

"We're well aware of the implications, Colonel."

"All right," said Danny.

"We've moved Team Two to Hawaii," said Breanna. "So if the President does green-light us, they'll be ready quickly. Sergeant Rockland is there with them. We have the Tigershark and four Sabres ready as well."

"Right."

"I'm not arguing with you," put in Reid. "I'm just telling you what the situation is."

They talked a while more about contingencies and different plans, but Danny couldn't wait for the conversation to end. He was tired and beginning to feel frustrated, the inevitable result when politics or admin bs got in the way of action.

GREENSTREET PUT HIS FACE BARELY TWO INCHES from Turk's. "You still haven't explained who said you could bomb those trucks."

"I didn't figure I needed permission to save the

base," answered Turk. He had to struggle to keep his voice level.

"I told you where to fly and what to do," said Greenstreet. "We were coming back as soon as we took care of the mortars. We were back on target inside of five minutes."

"Our guys might have been dead by then," said Turk. "With respect."

The conversation had been going on now for at least ten minutes. *Conversation* was the wrong word—it felt more like an inquisition.

"Hey, Colonel, you oughta lighten up," said Cowboy, coming into the flight room at the end of the trailer. "Or at least lower your voice. We can hear you outside."

"Who the hell asked *your* opinion, Lieutenant?"

"Just sayin'."

"Do your sayin' somewhere else."

"Yes, sir." Cowboy gave Turk a sympathetic look as he left the room.

"I know you're a hotshot," said Greenstreet, lowering his voice a few decibels. "But here you work for me. You got it?"

"I got it."

"Just because I'm easygoing doesn't mean I go for insubordination. I give an order, I expect it followed."

Turk was at a loss for a response, wondering how Greenstreet could consider himself easygoing. Maybe because he hadn't ordered him flogged.

"If you were a Marine, I'd have you busted to ensign," continued the colonel.

"I don't think you would," said Turk. "I think if I were a Marine, you would have expected me to take out those trucks. You would have kicked my ass if I didn't. Because my guys and my commander were in danger, and sure as shit it was my job to protect them. If I didn't do that, and I was your pilot, you'd have me court-martialed. And I would deserve it."

Greenstreet looked as if he'd been slapped across the face.

"Dismissed," he told Turk.

"I don't work for you," said Turk, rising. "Even when I'm on the ground."

"Get the hell out of my sight."

Turk walked from the room at a deliberate pace. He knew he was right, and he knew that Greenstreet knew it, too. The knowledge filled him with an odd if grim satisfaction, as if he were the hero in an old-fashioned western like *Shane*—the misunderstood good guy never given credit for saving the day.

It was a dangerous notion, though. Different service or not, Greenstreet outranked him, and while the colonel would never in a million years sustain a charge of insubordination against him for saving the base, he surely could find a way to make things uncomfortable for him. This wasn't the military of the Cold War, where an unreasonable officer could literally break a man just on a whim. But it was still the military, and Turk knew that by standing up to Greenstreet he was skating very close to the edge.

Still, he was right.

Getting brow-beaten had left him with an appetite. He went over to the tent that was serving as a mess area. Cowboy and Haydem, the Marine's fourth pilot, were sitting at one of the tables when Turk walked in. Both men rose solemnly and applauded—albeit very lightly—when Turk went over with his coffee.

"Hey, Air Force," said Cowboy. "Thanks for saving our plane."

"Screw that. Thanks for saving the base," said Haydem. "I hear our beer supply would have been blown up if the attack went on much longer."

"It was nothing," he told them. "Push button stuff."

"We're also applauding your entry into the brotherhood of abuse," said Cowboy. "Now you're one of us."

"You've been christened," said Haydem. "By Greenstreet's spit."

Turk laughed.

"He didn't mean any of what he said," Cowboy told him. "He knows you did the right thing."

"I don't know about that," said Turk.

"He gets his underwear twisted up," added Haydem. "But he's a good pilot and a decent commander."

"He's a decent pilot," said Turk, aware that he might be judging him on a harsh scale. "But as a commander . . ."

"He is definitely a hardass," conceded Haydem.

"Prick's more like it," said Cowboy. "But it takes all kinds."

"Our squadron's the highest rated in the wing," said Haydem.

"You can get good results without being an asshole," said Turk.

"I'm not going to defend him," said Haydem. "I'm just stating the facts."

"And the facts are, these eggs suck," said Cowboy.

"I heard that," growled a Marine over by the food trays. "You think you can do better, you come up here and try it."

Haydem and Turk laughed. Cowboy jumped up. "Hey, Slugs, I thought you'd never ask."

Slugs—the cook—shook his head. Cowboy was well known in the unit as a wise guy with a good heart, and treated as such.

"I better apologize," he told Turk. "Or I'll end up like Rogers. He's still flat on his back."

"Jolly got that way because he ate some of the Malaysian shit," said Haydem. "He was bragging about it."

"Oh." Turk realized he'd eaten with them, too, several times a day. He wondered if he was also going to get sick.

"You flew pretty well," said Haydem. "You fly F-35s a lot?"

Turk shook his head. "Not too much." He wasn't sure how much to explain. "I fly a lot of different things, so, you know, variety."

They talked about the F-35 for a bit more. Turk avoided mentioning the planes he flew, since the details were all pretty much classified. They were just discussing how much faster the aircraft might be with a bigger engine—no pilot was ever satisfied—when Cowboy came back to the table with a tray of doughnuts.

"How'd you manage that?" asked Haydem.

"Me and Slugs are friends from way back," said Cowboy. "I appreciate his time in the kitchen. Help yourself."

"Thanks."

"Wait a few minutes and you can get some fresh coffee," added Cowboy.

"I don't need any more caffeine. I won't be able to sleep."

"You aren't going to sleep, are you?" asked Cowboy.

"I was thinking about it."

"No time. They'll have us up for another mission ASAP."

"Really?"

"What do you think, this is the Air Force?"

Turk laughed. "The Air Force was flying two and three missions a day in Libya when I was there."

"You were in Libya?" asked Haydem.

"I've been in a few places." Turk took one of the doughnuts.

"Our mysterious stranger," said Cowboy. "Where do you keep your cape, Superman?"

"Hey, I wasn't trying to brag."

"He's just a top secret man," Haydem said. "He flies all sorts of things."

"Flying saucers?" asked Cowboy. "They have those at Dreamland, right? That's where that UFO landed."

"Before my time," said Turk. "Where's that fresh coffee at?"

4

The Cube

"AS YOU CAN SEE, THE FLIGHT PATTERN IS EXACTLY THE same as WX2-BC, an early evasion path for the Flighthawks." Ray Rubeo paused the video, a simulation that showed the actual path taken by the unknown UAV and the preprogrammed Flighthawk path. "Captain Mako identified it correctly."

"Coincidence?" asked Jonathon Reid.

"Doubtful." Rubeo touched his right earlobe, an old habit when faced with a difficult question. The gold stud earring was well worn. "The pattern is precisely the same. Not only do you have the initial maneuver, but you have the acceleration and escape as well. Any of the Flighthawk family would have acted precisely the same way, assuming that they are in autonomous mode."

"It's certainly not a Flighthawk," said Breanna.

"No," said Rubeo. He'd managed to nap a bit before the meeting, but it hardly compensated for the hours and nights he'd missed over the last two weeks. "Smaller, and faster than series Two or Three. Nor have we intercepted control transmissions."

Rubeo flicked his hand in front of the screen

to change the slide. The fuselage that Danny had recovered a week earlier appeared.

"As you know, the electronics of the aircraft that Colonel Freah came back with had been destroyed. First fried—to use the vernacular of some of my assistants—and then blown up by a small explosive, which severed this portion of the aircraft from the rest. However, we were able to recover some small bits of one of the chips, which were embedded in this portion of the remains."

He flipped to a new slide, which showed what looked like a slag of brown dirt laced with silver tints.

"To give you an idea of scale, here is the chip, or what remains of it, with a dime."

The coin loomed over the tiny bit of silicone.

"The chip is a computing unit," continued Rubeo. "It is quite sophisticated. It appears to make use of ten-nanometer chip technology. That is significant for a number of reasons, beginning with the fact—or I should say apparent fact—that it had to have been custom-fabricated. It is at the high end of the scale."

Rubeo continued, talking about how the technology allowed for massive processing power in a relatively small space. To give the others an idea, he mentioned that Intel's Ivy Bridge processors— commonly used in high-end desk and laptop computers—contained in the area of 1.4 billion transistors (or actually the chip equivalent). The processor could change state roughly 100 million times a second. That was beyond the processing power of a supercomputer in the Cold War.

Assuming it was anywhere close to a standard size, the chip they had examined would have been several orders of magnitude more powerful than the Ivy Bridge, both in terms of size and speed. Rubeo's people weren't entirely sure how much faster—there was just too little to go on—but the technology appeared comparable to that in the nano-UAVs so recently used to wipe out Iran's nuclear weapons.

The biggest problem for the chips was the heat they generated; this seemed to have been solved with a rather ingenious and extremely elegant air piping system, where microtunnels were bored into the surface of the aircraft and used to bathe the processors with cooling air. The so-called pipes were thinner than human hair, and webbed in a way so that the structural integrity of the aircraft was not harmed. The discovery of those pipes—Rubeo didn't mention that he had been the one to spot them—were significant in many ways.

"What we're looking at here is enormous man-ufacturing ability," concluded Rubeo. "Even as-suming these aircraft are essentially one-offs, hand-built. The skill necessary to create the airframe—let alone the brain that fits into it—is very, very high."

"So it's definitely not Chinese," concluded Reid.

"I didn't say that." Rubeo touched his ear. "It doesn't fit with the Chinese capabilities that I'm aware of. But that doesn't mean it's not Chinese. I have no evidence. I know several companies that could have manufactured the processors. All are in the United States. Including mine," he added, feeling he ought to make explicit what Reid was probably thinking. "We have a laboratory facility dedicated solely to government work, and it would be capable of producing these chips."

"But it didn't," said Breanna quickly.

"Our ten-nanometer chips are all accounted for," said Rubeo.

"The nano-UAVs?"

"They were destroyed in Iran," said Rubeo. "But those use eight nanometer chips. Which you will recall is why they are so absurdly expensive. And my company didn't create those processors. We believe the CMOS limits no longer justify the technology, and so we're moving in a different direction. Perhaps incorrectly," he added.

"We should check every fab site we can think of," said Breanna.

"Yes." Rubeo had already made his own discreet inquiries without finding the actual manufacturer. "I would guess, though, that it was somewhere in Asia, maybe even Malaysia. An underutilized facility that has been overhauled with new equipment at much expense."

"That could be anywhere," said Reid.

"Yes."

"So what are we dealing with?" Reid asked.

"Impossible to tell until we capture one," said Rubeo. "If they are this sophisticated in chip technology, I can only make guesses about the weapons."

"Twenty-five-millimeter cannon?" asked Breanna.

"I believe something lighter."

"There were no weapons used in this last encounter," said Reid.

"True. Maybe some carry weapons and some don't. Or they weren't correctly positioned for attack. Or many other possibilities," said Rubeo. "But planes were shot down previously, and we have to assume that if they have the base technology, they can weaponize it. The Gen 4 Flighthawks would have carried lasers. And the Gen 4 Flighthawk appears to be an excellent model."

He waved his hand for the next slide, which showed an artist's rendition of the unknown UAV next to a Gen 4 Flighthawk. The Gen 4's wings were a little longer, its tail a bit stubbier, but the airfoils were very similar. The Gen 4 had not gone into production, superseded by the smaller and faster Sabres, which were capable of distributed autonomous control—they made real-time decisions on their own.

"Lasers small enough to be on that class of UAVs are too impractical for combat," said Reid. "The Air Force studied the matter in great depth."

"They're impractical only in a high-threat environment," answered Rubeo. He had strongly disagreed with the Air Force's assessment of small weaponized lasers, though the decision to choose the Sabres instead of the Gen 4s made the point moot. "And the report didn't consider the latest evolutions."

"It was a cost problem as much as anything," said Breanna. "Outfitting a fleet of UAVs with lasers was a budget buster. The Flighthawks and the Sabres have proven that lightweight cannons are enough in aerial combat, and have an advantage in ground attack. For the foreseeable future, at least, they make a lot of sense."

"All right. We need to tell the President that we need more data," agreed Reid. "And we need it quickly. Clearly, it's a critical threat. And it's not coming from China."

"No," said Rubeo. "Ultimately, I'm afraid, we are probably the source of the technology."

"We?"

"Dreamland, Special Projects, or my companies," said Rubeo. "The links may seem vague, but their sum total is unmistakable."

5

Malaysia

THE MALAYSIAN UNIT HAD BEEN HIT HARD, WITH FOUR of their men wounded and four dead. So Turk was surprised when Captain Deris came and told him he wanted to get back into the field immediately.

"There are only two places they could be now," the captain told Turk after asking for his help. "If we can get flyovers we can see where they came from and strike at dark."

"There were a lot of rebels. Most of them got away. Are you going to have reinforcements?"

"If the planes back us, we have more than enough."

Deris sketched out a plan on a map of the area, then asked Turk to take it to the Marine squadron for approval. Turk, unsure what sort of reaction he would get from Greenstreet, decided to discuss it with Danny before doing anything else.

"I was worried you'd be sleeping," he told the colonel when he spotted him in the mess tent.

Freah held up his coffee cup. "Not with the coffee these guys brew. I won't be sleeping for a month. What's up?"

"The Malaysians want to attack. They think they have the rebel bases figured out."

Turk explained the plan to Danny.

"They're brave, but that's no substitute for firepower," said Freah. "They don't have enough people to do all this."

"Yeah. I didn't think so either," said Turk. "But they want to get these guys."

"The Marines are talking about finding the rest of the rebels who attacked them," said Danny. "Maybe we can figure something out."

CAPTAIN THOMAS HAD ASKED FOR A PLATOON OF REinforcements to be sent in from the MEU to go after the rebels who'd attacked. With three rifle sections or squads, the unit totaled forty men, and would be there by nightfall.

"We could send two squads with the Malaysians," suggested Thomas. "That will be more than enough to deal with these guys, as long as we have air support."

Greenstreet was in a better mood, or at least one that allowed him to ignore Turk when he saw him. Reviewing the plan with Cowboy, he gave a grudging nod, then said he was handicapped with Rogers still sick.

"I'm down to three pilots," said Greenstreet. "I can only get three planes up."

"We can do it with two," said Thomas.

"You have to worry about the UAV showing up," said Danny. "Are two planes enough?"

"You'd want two planes to deal with it," suggested Turk. "So really, two planes handle the attack, and two fly cover."

Greenstreet bristled, but didn't contradict him.

"Then one jet on the attack, if we only have three," said Thomas.

"It's tight if they're at both spots," said Greenstreet. "It's just a question of how much ordnance we can bring. Maybe we mix the loads, have one flying CAP and the other two attacking but ready to tangle with the UAV."

CAP was an old acronym for command air patrol, meaning that the single aircraft would fly top cover for the others when they attacked.

"What about Turk flying?" asked Danny. "He did pretty well."

"These are Marine aircraft," snapped Greenstreet. "Marine aviators will fly them. I'll work it out."

Danny and Thomas exchanged a look, but there was nothing more to be said. Greenstreet stomped off, Cowboy in tow.

"He'll come around," predicted Thomas. "He's

just protecting his turf. Some guys are like that. Even Marines."

"WE'RE MARINES, NOT PUSSIES," COMPLAINED COWboy as soon as they were out of earshot. His anger and language were calculated, though his sentiments were not. "I'll go up and help them."

"Relax, Lieutenant," said Greenstreet. "I fully intend on doing the mission."

"What?"

"I said I would work it out."

"You kinda sounded—"

"Pissed off? Yes. We want two planes to deal with a UAV—what was that about?"

"He's just being careful," said Cowboy.

"You think he would have said that to an Air Force pilot?"

"Turk's pretty straight up."

"And another thing. They're not sharing everything they know. That UAV is the entire reason we're here. What do we know about it? Jack shit."

"They say they're here to get intel."

"They're spoon-feeding us information. That's what I think."

Cowboy didn't think that was fair, but it was really beside the point. They had to fly the mission.

"We had casualties on the ground," he told his commander. "That means we get out there and get some payback."

"We'll get payback." Greenstreet folded his arms. "But we'll do it right."

"That's why I'm here," replied Cowboy. "It's the only way I know how to do things."

6

The Cube

THE APPEARANCE OF THE ADVANCED UAVS IN AN OBscure third world guerrilla battle had set off alarms within the American intelligence community. The immediate consensus among the tech people was that China had leapt several generations in UAV development and was testing the equipment in a place where few would notice. The fact that China had no ties to the rebels who were benefiting—and in fact had every reason not to support them—gave rise to another theory that Russia was actually the country behind the aircraft. This was backed by a smaller group, who had even less evidence on their side. Outlier theories—that Japan or Israel were involved—had occasionally been floated, only to be quickly shot down.

None of the theories tied the aircraft to either Dreamland, which had originally developed combat UAVs, or Rubeo's different firms, which had worked on the AI and some of the avionics and body shaping.

But Rubeo knew they would. And for that

reason alone, he had to figure out exactly what the aircraft were and who was flying them.

Of course, that wasn't the only reason. The combat UAVs had revolutionized air combat. And as dangerous as they were in the hands of China, they could be even more dangerous if controlled by someone else. From what Rubeo had seen so far, they were still being tested. Give whoever was handling them a few more months and they would be even more formidable.

Technically, Rubeo was no longer a government employee, but as the head of the firm that had designed most of the Cube's systems and had an extremely close relationship with the Office of Special Projects, he'd been allotted an office in the deepest basement of the bunker, next to the situation room—convenient, since it allowed him to go back and forth quickly when he wanted. The office was spartan—a wooden desk, a very old, barely padded chair, a single lamp—but that was the way Rubeo liked it.

If he needed to sleep and wanted something more comfortable than the chair, he had a small bedroll tucked next to the desk.

The furniture was spare, but his communications and computing gear was state of the art. The desk sagged under the weight of four different sets of screens and hand-built CPU units, each more powerful than the standard IBM mainframe of only a generation ago.

He'd uploaded data from the UAV to one of his units, where he ran flight and computation simulators, trying to divine what the unidentified UAV was capable of. The parallels to the Flighthawk Gen 4 were striking. But as Rubeo looked at the data they had gathered so far, he went back to the destroyed chip.

He'd called it a processing chip during his briefing, but that wasn't entirely correct. It seemed to actually function as a gateway between other processing chips, or at least that was his engineer's theory. And Rubeo's team had managed to extract a long piece of code from a memory unit embedded in the fuselage remnant.

The code sequence matched sequences used in the early Flighthawks, with an additional "tail" added for the brains used in the Gen 4 version.

There was no way that was a coincidence. While the "tail" solved a number of common problems that *might* be arrived at independently, appending it to the other sequences had been a matter of expediency—why reinvent the wheel?

The sequence had a command syntax: had it been words rather than numerals, it would have had a specific grammar and punctuation indicating that it was a command. But it was encrypted—though it was clearly a command, it was impossible to tell which command it was. To use the sentence metaphor, it was as if all the letters in the sentence had been exchanged for others.

The exchange wasn't random, of course. And since Rubeo had a database of all the Gen 4 commands, breaking the encryption, while not trivial, was not impossible.

The computer back at his New Mexico lab had just done that. The command initiated a "flee" sequence, directing the aircraft to leave the battle ten minutes after the start of the encounter. It had been intended as a fail-safe if the controlled UAV lost its connection to the base; here it was probably being used to get the aircraft home.

But it wasn't the command that interested Rubeo—it was the encryption. The Gen 4 Flighthawks used a software process for the encryption that took advantage of the nano-architecture of hand-built chips off the main circuits. There were advantages to this approach, most notably since it allowed for a more complicated—"robust" was the preferred term—system of encrypting the data in real time, which in turn made the UAV brains harder to hack. The process turned out to be too cumbersome for large-scale production; they could never get the chip count high enough to make it practical. Now, advances in manufacturing made that problem trivial; at the time, though, the process had been a breakthrough. DNA snippets were used as keys.

So here was a fingerprint—the DNA might reveal who had stolen the work, or at least whose work had been stolen.

"Compare vector in cycle Mark 56Z through Mark 987AA7 to typical DNA pattern," Rubeo told the computer.

He waited as the mainframes back in New Mexico churned.

"Pattern would fit on X chromosome," declared the computer.

Rubeo leaned back from the screen. He wasn't sure whether to go on or not.

"Compare the possible encryption key to DNA contained in all personnel files for present and past employees, and in the Dreamland archives."

It took twenty minutes—less time than he had thought.

"Match discovered," said the computer.

"Identify," said Rubeo.

"Gleason, Jennifer. Now deceased."

7

Malaysia

NONE OF THE MALAYSIANS HAD EVER BEEN IN AN Osprey before, and while Turk kept telling them it was no different than riding in a helicopter, they approached the aircraft with expressions similar to those of four-year-olds queuing for a pony ride. The wide-eyed stares continued once aboard the aircraft, whose interior was surely no fancier than the Eurocopters and Sikorskys they were used to. The Marine crew chief winked at Turk as they took off, joking that he could have charged the Malaysians for the ride and made a killing.

Dusk had fallen a few hours before. The sky was clear and there was enough light from the moon and the stars to see a good distance, though the jungle would make that far more difficult. But the darkness favored the Marines, who were not only equipped to fight in it but had practiced extensively to do so.

Sitting between Captain Deris and Private Isnin, Turk checked his gear. The Marines had outfitted him with an M-16 assault rifle and night vision, as well as body armor and a helmet. He had his own smart glasses, which not only tied into Whiplash but also to the Marines.

Though officially the Marines were "assisting" the Malaysians, in actual fact the operation was far more American than Malaysian. The Marines were not only supplying more men, they had redrawn the game plan from start to finish. It was better in any number of ways, and not simply because they had more men at their disposal.

A small group of rebels had been spotted at one of the clearing areas southwest of where they mounted the mortar attack. Apparently exhausted, they had stopped there to rest and restock; the rebels typically cached weapons in different areas for just such an occasion. Located some twenty miles from the base, the area lay along a dirt road that wound up on the side of a ridge. The nearby jungle canopy was too thick for the sensors on the Marine RQ7Z Shadow UAV to penetrate, but the Marines assumed that lookouts had been posted both near the road and at local high points, which would make any force moving on the road itself easily detected.

Their attack plan took advantage of that. Split in two, the assault teams would be dropped at two different landing zones four miles from the rebels, one northeast and one southwest. The group dropped to the southwest would move into a blocking position straddling the road a mile south of the rebels. The other would advance toward the camp from the north along the road. The idea was simple: the rebels would see the advancing unit and move to get away, running into the group at the bottom. They would be "encouraged" to move by an air attack just as the northern force came into sight.

There was a possibility, of course, that the rebels would stand and fight, even though their position was not well chosen for defense. In that case, the hammer and anvil attack would turn into an envelopment, with the southern group pressing most of the attack. This would be a slower operation but it would still allow the Marines to bring overwhelming force against their enemy.

Turk and most of the Malaysians were with the southern group; only Sergeant Intan was with the northern group, providing Malaysian presence more for legal reasons than strategy.

The Osprey taxied for a few seconds then lifted off, flying more as an airplane than a helicopter. Only a few moments seemed to pass before the Marine crew chief walked down the aisle at the center of the aircraft and held up two fingers.

"Two minutes," he said. "Two minutes."

DANNY FREAH DUCKED HIS HEAD INVOLUNTARILY AS HE ran toward the rear of the Osprey. The rotors, just starting to spin, were nowhere near him, but there was something about the windmill sound overhead that triggered the ducking reflex.

"Hi, Colonel, what's up?" asked Corporal Mofitt. The corporal was with Group North, the augmented Marine rifle squad that would attack the rebels first.

"I decided to come along for the ride."

Mofitt gave him a thumbs-up, then turned to the officer next to him. "Sir, do you know Colonel Freah?"

"We met," said the lieutenant, Tom Young. The squad leader got up from the nylon fabric bench to stick out his hand. Danny had met him during the mission brief.

"Hey, Tom," said Danny, sticking out his hand to put the young man at ease. "Don't mind me. I'm just along for the ride. It's your show."

"Yes, sir, thank you," said Young.

Danny knew that the lieutenant would feel a little uncomfortable having a senior officer looking over his shoulder. He wasn't here to criticize or even supervise; he just wanted to be where the action was.

"I'll try to stay out of your way," he told the Marine officer, whose square chin looked a little too wide for the rest of his face. "I couldn't sleep, so I thought I'd make myself useful."

"Yes, sir."

Danny took a seat across the aisle and scanned the rest of the faces in the aircraft. A few were expressionless, eyes locked on some invisible point in the distance. A few looked worried, not fearful exactly but apprehensive. Danny recognized the look, common in men who had never faced combat—concerned that they might let their buddies down.

The majority had nothing to fear in that regard.

There were also a few expressions that spoke only of eagerness. These belonged to men whose adrenaline was already raging, for whom danger and excitement were life itself.

Danny suspected his face looked very much like theirs, even though he did his best to hide his emotions.

Combat was an unforgiving and uncompromising master; it extracted things far more valuable than the momentary adrenaline high. People he loved had died, and worse. That there were many worse things than death was still something that shocked him.

And yet he went to it willingly. More—he sought it out.

There was something about sitting in a metal container hurling toward destiny at a few hundred miles an hour that he could never get enough of.

He studied the lieutenant. He was a good-looking kid, six-two, a little thin but rangy, the way Marines liked their officers. There was something about his intense look that Danny knew his men would respond to. Leadership a lot of times hinged on those subtle signs as much as training and intelligence, even more than courage. The tone of voice, a habit of staring—there were any number of accidental ways that a man might inspire others just by being himself.

"LZ ahead," the crew chief said, walking down the aisle of the Osprey.

"Already?" said Mofitt. "We barely took off."

"Time flies when you're having fun," said Lieutenant Young.

IT TOOK ROUGHLY A HALF HOUR FOR TURK AND FORCE South to reach their positions along the road below the rebel camp. The Marines moved with quiet precision, stretched out in a staggered single file. Their UAV scouting overhead showed that the rebels remained in place. While a handful of men moved in the jungle on either side to ensure there were no surprises, the main force stuck to the road, which allowed them to move quickly.

The Malaysian squad was interspersed with the lead company; though they'd had a long and harrowing day, they had no trouble keeping up. They were spoiling for battle, eager for revenge. Monday Isnin's head bobbed back and forth as he walked, almost like a radar dish scanning for trouble.

The road twisted around the side of a low rise in the terrain. As they reached the area where they had planned to mount their ambush, the Marines discovered it was separated from the road by a thick marsh, which would make it difficult for them to pursue the rebels. Captain Deris had worked them a little closer to the rebels; it was on lower ground, but the surrounding area was better, and they had good fields of fire to the road and beyond. The Marines settled in, sending a pair of scouts ahead to monitor the approach.

The rebels were still far enough away that Force South could relax a bit. The Malaysians took out their cigarettes and began smoking; it was their normal habit.

Marlboros were the preferred brand. They could have done a commercial.

"You know *Mai Thai Warrior*?" Monday asked Turk as he settled against a tree trunk on the jungle floor.

"I don't know him," said Turk, confused. He thought the soldier was talking about another squad member and couldn't place him.

Monday gave him a funny look. "Movie," he said. *"Mai Thai Warrior."*

Turk still didn't understand.

"Hero," prompted Monday. "Movie."

"I know it," said one of the Marines. "Martial-arts movie, right?"

"Great warrior," said Monday. He began mimicking one of the fight scenes. Then he and the Marine traded notes about some of the techniques.

"Great hero," said Monday. His voice was solemn.

"I'll have to check it out," said Turk.

"We watch it together when we get back to city," said Monday.

"It's a deal."

DANNY WENT DOWN TO ONE KNEE NEXT TO LIEUTEN-ant Young as the squad leader stopped to take stock of their position. They were about a quarter mile from the rebel camp, just north of a bend in the road where they would be visible.

"I'm ready to call the planes in," said Young, who was looking at a feed from the Shadow UAV overhead on a hardened tablet computer. About the size of an iPad but several times as thick and encased in rubber, the tablet gave the commander a real-time view of the battlefield. "Looks like they have a lookout on the hill there," added Young. "Just one guy."

"Across the road?"

"Scouts don't see anyone."

"If you can take him, you can get closer to the camp before they see you," suggested Danny.

"That's what I was thinking," said Young. "It's a gamble, though. If he radios back, we won't have surprise."

"True."

Young weighed the chances. There was no right answer.

"I'm going to send my sniper," he said finally. "Take him out. Then we move farther down."

"It's what I would do," said Danny.

FLYING BASHER TWO NORTH OF THE ENGAGEMENT area, Cowboy listened to Greenstreet as he talked to the air combat controller assigned to Group North. The ground unit had just reached its mark north of the rebel site.

"We're going to take out their lookout," said the controller, relaying what Lieutenant Young was telling him. "Once he's out, we can get within a hundred yards before they'll be able to see us."

"How long is that going to take?" asked Greenstreet.

"Ten minutes. We sent a sniper team."

"All right." Greenstreet exhaled heavily. "Let's move it along."

"Problem, Colonel?" Cowboy asked over the squadron frequency after the exchange.

"I feel like shit," admitted Greenstreet. "Rogers gave me his disease."

"I can take it myself, Colonel."

"I'm good."

Cowboy checked his fuel, then ran his eyes over the gauges, making sure the plane's brain agreed with his gut feel that it was operating exactly to spec.

With the exception of a few high clouds to the west, the sky was perfectly clear. The stars twinkled above; the tiny sliver of moon sat between them, a silver comma.

The sensors were clean as well—they were the only aircraft in the skies for a hundred miles or more.

Which meant no UAV. Cowboy wanted another shot at the little bastard. He'd replayed the encounter in his head a few hundred times, seeing how he could have nailed the little sucker.

Next time, he would.

The mysterious little aircraft intrigued the hell out of him. It was fast, and from what Turk had said, very much like a Flighthawk in its approach to air combat. Cowboy had flown against a pair of Flighthawks in a series of training exercises. Of the five encounters, he'd managed to beat the little robot planes exactly once—and been shot down all the rest.

He wasn't particularly proud of that, even if it

came against some of the best Flighthawk pilots in the Air Force. And even if he had the only shoot-down in the squadron.

He wanted a measure of revenge, and waxing the little sucker tonight would give it to him. A robot better than a human? No way—even if that robot was being flown by a team of people in a bunker.

Especially then.

"Basher Two, tighten up," said Greenstreet.

Cowboy acknowledged. The ground commander came on the radio. They would be ready for the first strike in sixty seconds.

IT WAS AN INTRICATE DANCE, BUT IT MOVED EXACTLY AS it had been drawn up by Young and Thomas.

Danny heard a shot on the hill ahead—the sniper took out the rebels' lookout. The Marines began to move in force. The planes swooped down and dropped four bombs on the center of the rebel camp. As they cleared, the Marines attacked the perimeter.

They were within fifty yards of the rebels' makeshift lean-tos before there was any gunfire. And then it was on big-time, tracers and flashes lighting the night.

A few of the Marines, untested in war, were nervous, and it showed: firing on the run, shooting too soon. But it was an almost necessary mistake, and within moments they realized they had to stay within themselves, had to fight the way they'd been trained, the way they'd drilled. The dozens of exercises they'd worked through over the past several months had embedded memory in their muscles. They slowed down, still moving forward but now doing it with more precision. They fired with better purpose, picking targets one by one.

Before the mission they'd been boys, most not old enough to drink legally in the States. In a few minutes this night they became men, and more than that, Marines. They worked together, in pairs, in threes, in fours, as a whole group, never alone.

Used to fighting small, ill-equipped units of the Malaysian army, the rebels buckled. Exhausted from the earlier fight, they had trouble seeing the enemy even in the clearing. As the gunfire intensified, their conviction wavered. The drugs most had used to gather courage earlier in the day had worn off. In chaos, they began to run.

"Hold back! Hold back!" yelled Lieutenant Young. "We're sending the planes in for another run. Sit tight."

COWBOY RELAXED AS THE PIPER IN HIS TARGETING screen settled on the knot of rebel soldiers in the lead. He pressed the trigger on the stick, pickling two bombs, then pulled the plane upward, rising above the target area quickly and preparing to circle back for another run. He glanced right, looking for the infrared image of the cluster bombs he'd dropped exploding, but he was moving too fast and was already beyond the explosions.

"Good hits," said Lieutenant Young over the radio. "Basher, stand off."

"Roger that," said Greenstreet. His voice was weak.

"One, you good?" asked Cowboy.

The flight leader didn't answer. Cowboy saw his F-35 flying above and to his left, about two miles away. He began climbing, aiming to get closer to his commander and make sure he was OK.

"Yeah, I'm all right," said Greenstreet finally. He sounded anything but.

"Sick?"

"Ughhh . . ."

"Why don't you go back, Colonel? We're done here. These guys are just going to mop up. I can handle it."

"Roger."

The answer came so quickly that Cowboy knew Greenstreet must be *really* sick. He altered course slightly, widening his orbit as Basher One angled away.

"Nothing left to do but sing," said Cowboy, humming a song from Drowning Pool as he radioed the ground for a sitrep.

THE FIRST MAN CAME THROUGH THE BRUSH, PUSHING A large clump of brush away as he ducked onto the road. Turk studied him in his scope, waiting until the rebel turned toward him so he had a broad, easy target. Finger against the trigger, Turk squeezed so gently that it seemed to take forever before the mechanism released the hammer and set the charge.

But then everything went quick: three rounds

sped through the barrel, slicing through the man's chest. A misshapen rose bloomed in Turk's viewfinder, and the man folded into the ground.

"Three more, left," said one of the Marines on his right.

The last word was nearly drowned out by gunfire as the others started to fire. The edge of the jungle was suddenly full of rebels. Turk zeroed in on one, only to see him fall before he could squeeze the trigger. He moved his scope right, toward the road; a half-dozen rebels were crouched, trying to return fire. All were down before Turk could aim.

Suddenly there was a loud yell behind him, then a whoop that made Turk think of the battle cries Indians made in old westerns. Captain Deris leapt forward and started to run down the embankment toward the road and the rebel position. In a flash his men rose to follow. The Marines hesitated for a moment, and then they, too, began running.

The battle was over by the time they reached the road. Fourteen rebels lay dead or dying; another two found severely wounded in the high grass on the southern side. Turk used the infrared on his glasses to search the area and found four rebels huddled about 150 yards west in the jungle. They were the only survivors of the rebel force that had attacked the base earlier in the day.

"Are they dead or alive?" asked the Marine captain.

"Alive, but maybe wounded," said Turk. "They're not moving much."

"We'll take the Malaysians up there and see if

we can get them to surrender," said the Marine commander. "Maybe we'll get some intel."

"Yeah, good idea."

THE BOMBS AND CLUSTER BOMBS HAD MADE A MESS OF the rebel camp, and even Danny wasn't prepared for what he saw when he reached it.

Body parts hung from shattered trees; severed torsos littered the ground. The area stank of burnt flesh. One of the bombs had hit an underground spring, and water was seeping everywhere, filling the wide crater made by a five hundred pounder.

Danny's boots squished in the bloody mud. The water made it seem as if the earth itself were bleeding.

Seeing that the area was secure and there were no more rebels in the immediate vicinity, the Marines lit flares for illumination. The light was fickle, as if not even Heaven wanted to look at the destruction.

"We're never going to know how many are dead," said Lieutenant Young, coming over to Danny as he surveyed the scene. "Pretty damn brutal."

"Yeah," agreed Danny.

"Bunch of assholes," said Young bitterly. "Who the hell do they think they're fighting against? Look at them—no armor, shitty Chinese weapons. That kid's what, fifteen?"

Danny glanced at the face. A thick shadow fell across the bottom half, obscuring his cheeks and mouth, but the eyes were clear, large and shiny with reflected light.

"Yeah," admitted Danny. "Sixteen at most."

"What a fucking waste," said the Marine officer bitterly. "What the hell are they even fighting for? Islam? Like God wants them to kill each other. Shit. Idiots."

Young detailed four men to "organize the remains," as he put it. The looks on their faces made it clear they would have welcomed any other order in the world, but it was a necessary job; no support units were going to roll in and sweep up. With Sergeant Intan's help, they chose a dry bomb crater and began moving the dead to it. The burial was intended to be temporary; the Marine command would formally notify the Malaysian government, which would then decide how to repatriate the remains with their families.

In theory, anyway, Danny suspected that the government would not put a high priority on the job.

He checked in with Turk, who told him that South Force had completed the ambush, vanquishing the rebels.

"There are four guys alive in the jungle," Turk added. "They're surrendering. They may have intel on the UAV."

"OK, good." It was unlikely they had real information about the UAV, but they might have details about how the forces coordinated with it and possibly who worked with the rebels. There was scant data on the rebel group to begin with, and any information might be helpful.

"Pretty brutal over here," Danny added as two men passed with a body.

"Yeah," said Turk. "Here, too. That's what they get."

While Danny certainly understood Turk's comment—in a way it was little different than the Marine commander's—he was surprised by it. It was out of character, particularly coldhearted for the pilot.

Fallout from Iran, Danny thought.

With the area now completely secure, the Marines not assigned to provide security pitched in to help move and organize the remains. It was a grim, silent task, performed as much as possible with eyes closed.

Danny watched as one of the Marines picked up a trenching tool and began shoveling dirt into the hole. Two more shovels, the small portable ones carried as gear, were located and the dead began to be covered. Walking away from the grave, Danny saw Mofitt resting on his haunches. He had his head in his hands.

"You OK, Corporal?" he asked.

Mofitt looked up. "I've seen shit, but this is bad."

"Yeah," agreed Danny.

Mofitt shook his head. "They would have done the same to us."

"They tried to. With the mortars."

"True. Mothers."

"You OK?"

"I'm fine," said the corporal, continuing to stare. "Tired, but fine."

8

Suburban Washington, D.C.

Ray Rubeo sat in his office for hours, his mind blank, shaken by the discovery that the DNA key in the UAVs belonged to Jennifer Gleason.

It ought not to have surprised him, he realized. She had been the lead scientist on the project. Whoever had stolen the coding and presumably the plans it was part of had taken her work files and used them with little or no alteration.

Rubeo was an unemotional man, but he felt his stomach queasy and his hands trembling. Jennifer Gleason had been his prize pupil, his best employee, and in many ways his best friend.

Few people could have had access to her work files, which not even Rubeo could see without running a long bureaucratic gamut of checks, balances, and obstructions.

And according to the records office, no one had, since they were sealed shortly after her death.

He saw the expression on her face, her death mask—she'd been beheaded.

Rubeo leaned his head down, shattered by the memory.

Finally, almost unconsciously, he took out his satellite phone and called one of the few people whom he could speak to about her, the one person closer to Jennifer than he was.

Tecumseh Bastian answered on the third ring.

"Hello, Ray," he said. "What's going on that you're calling this late?"

"I . . ." Rubeo stopped speaking. It took a moment for him to regroup. "I think someone stole some of the work we did at Dreamland," he told his former commander. "I need—I just wanted to bounce some names off you."

"Shoot."

"Lloyd Braxton."

"Hmmmph," said Bastian.

"I know you don't like him."

"I have good reason. What has he taken?"

"I don't know if it's him," said Rubeo. He was lying—it had to be Braxton, who was not only a genius but had left Dreamland just before Jennifer's death, and under difficult circumstances. Just saying his name out loud convinced Rubeo he was right.

"So, why are you calling, then?" asked Bastian.

"I need to talk this out with someone I trust."

"Talk."

"I'd . . . I'd like to come up in person."

"I'm too busy, Ray. Talk now."

Rubeo knew Bastian wasn't busy; he hadn't been busy since he left the Air Force following Jennifer's death. He just didn't like interacting with the world, even with Rubeo, who was probably his only friend from the Dreamland days still in touch. Bastian didn't even talk to his daughter, Breanna Stockard.

"I wonder if Braxton could have left with the computer files on the Gen 4 Flighthawk project," said Rubeo.

"I doubt it."

"He might have stolen them before he was cashiered," said Rubeo.

"That's possible," said Bastian. "But I doubt he could have taken much."

"He might not need much," said Rubeo. "A chip, early prototypes. He'd be able to remember much of what he did—he had a phenomenal brain."

"You know he's rich, right? He owns that company."

"I'll have to do a little background work," said Rubeo. "I lost track of him."

"He has a whole foundation," continued Bastian. "He's an anarchist."

"An anarchist?"

"You never were much of a people person, Ray," said Bastian. "That's why I liked you."

Rubeo had nothing to say to that.

"Tell you what—I'm going back to bed. If you want to talk, you know where I am."

"Yes, sir."

"I'm not your commander anymore, Ray." Another man might have chuckled, but Bastian simply hung up.

9

Malaysia

Turk told Basher flight what was going on, then got up and ran to Captain Deris and his Malaysians. The soldiers were advancing warily up the hill as the Marines came down with the captured rebels.

"Pick one of them to question," Turk suggested. "And hold the rest for pickup."

Deris chose the oldest rebel, and led the group down to the road to Captain Thomas and the Senior Marine NCO, "Gunny" Smith. The trio started questioning him, with Deris acting both as inquisitor and interpreter. Turk stood by, listening to the halting dialogue—Deris peppered the man with questions, the rebel answered in monosyllables, Deris translated.

"No more alive, he says. I don't trust him," Deris told the Marines.

"Ask him the size of the force," said Gunny Smith. "We can work the rest out for ourselves."

Deris asked a question. When the rebel answered by shaking his head, Deris began shouting at him.

"Ease up, ease up," said Thomas. "That's not getting us anywhere."

"I have to make him talk."

"He'll just lie to get you off his back," said the captain. "Get someone else. We got three more."

"This one was a squad leader. The others are frightened children. They'll know nothing. Not even their prayers."

Gunny Smith reached into one of the pockets on his tac vest and took out a candy bar. He tossed it to Deris.

"Try making friends and see if that works," suggested the sergeant.

Deris frowned, but started to hand the bar to the rebel. The rebel backed away.

"Tell him it's food," said the Marine.

Another round of shouting ensued.

"He thinks we're trying to poison him," explained Deris finally.

Gunny Smith took the bar back, broke it in two and pulled off the wrapper. Then he began eating half of it.

"Not bad," he said, holding the other half out to the prisoner.

The rebel batted it away. Deris swung his fist, hitting the man in the side of the head.

Turk jumped forward and grabbed the Malaysian captain around the chest. The Malaysian was shorter than him but powerfully built, and Turk had to struggle to hold him off the POW.

"Hey, hey, none of that," said Thomas. "Relax. These fuckers are prisoners of ours. We can't be hitting them."

"He's a criminal," said Deris.

"You're right," said Smith. "But we have to follow the law. *Capisce?*"

"Law? What law? He is criminal and killer." Deris looked up at Turk, who was still holding him. "Why are you protecting him, Turk? He killed my men. He tried to kill you. Why would you protect him?"

Turk stuttered, unable to find an answer—in truth, he agreed with the Malaysian captain emotionally, even though he knew he was not permitted to strike a prisoner. It was Gunny Smith who spoke up.

"Listen, I'd love to slam the son of a bitch myself," he said. "It'd feel pretty damn good. But we need the bastard for interrogation. Intel. This way other people don't get hurt. If that means laying off, not belting him—that's what we got to do. Damn. We're just saving other lives. Maybe people we love, you know?"

"He's right," agreed Turk, wishing he'd been the one to say it.

Deris didn't look impressed. He said something in Malaysian, then put up his hands, signaling to Turk that he wouldn't struggle any more. Turk let him go.

Deris yelled something at the rebel—Turk guessed it was along the lines of, *You're lucky these guys held me back or you'd be dog meat by now*—then turned and stalked back to his men.

"Kind of a hothead, huh?" Gunny Smith smiled at Turk. Then raised his rifle at the prisoner. "Don't try anything or I'll shoot your balls off."

The man may not have understood English, but he certainly understood the threat. He put up his hands. When Gunny Smith gestured for him to sit down, he quickly complied.

"Can you hold on to him while I get some cuffs?" the Marine asked Turk.

"Sure." Turk raised his rifle.

Gunny took a step back, then another, making

sure the prisoner wouldn't try anything. Turk steadied the gun on the prisoner. Dirty and exhausted, the rebel looked even younger than the Malaysians. He stared at Turk with hard eyes, defiant. Turk wondered if he was thinking of trying to run—not to actually escape, but to get shot and die like his friends had.

If he does that, will I be able to shoot him?

Easily.

The answer surprised Turk, yet as soon as it formed in his brain, he knew it was true. He was angry, deeply angry—not at the rebel, not the way the Malaysians were. Their anger was immediate. It made sense—they were mad at the people who had killed their friends.

Turk's rage ran deeper. He was mad at Breanna for ordering him killed. He was mad at the Iranians for cheating on their nuclear agreement and making the attack that had killed so many lives necessary. He was mad at the senselessness of the rebel movement, angry beyond reason at whoever was helping them with cutting-edge technology.

He was mad at mankind in general for being so thoughtless, so careless with life.

And he was mad at himself for not being able to do anything about any of it.

The sergeant came back with the handcuffs. Glancing at Turk to make sure he was watching carefully, he dropped to a knee behind the prisoner and quickly trussed his hands. Then he pulled him to his feet and pushed him in the direction of two of his men.

"Hey, Captain, you all right?" Gunny Smith asked Turk as the prisoner was led away.

"I'm OK. Why?"

"I thought for a minute you were going to shoot me, too," said the Marine. He laughed and reached into one of his pockets for a tin of chew. Wadding the tobacco, he tucked it into the corner of his lip. "Dip?"

"Nah."

"Dirty habit." The Marine smiled. "Best keep away from it." He worked the plug a bit. "You seen a lot of action?"

Turk shrugged.

"I heard you were in Iran," added the Marine. "Top secret shit."

"I was over there," admitted Turk. "How'd you hear that?"

"Word gets around." Gunny Smith worked the plug of tobacco in his mouth. "You don't think we'd work with just any Air Force punk, do you?"

"Well, I wouldn't work with just any Marines," said Turk.

The sergeant laughed, then spit. "You *sure* you don't want some chew?"

"No thanks."

"Let's go try talking to another of these guys, right?"

As Turk started to follow, the radio buzzed. It was Cowboy, in Basher Two.

"Ground, I have more of those UAVs en route," he said. "Six of them, two hundred miles away. And they are moving! Twelve hundred knots, right at my face."

Suburban Virginia

UNABLE TO SLEEP, ZEN LAY FACEUP ON THE BED. BRE-anna wasn't home, and had told him she might not be until sometime the next day. It was worse than when they both worked at Dreamland.

Not really. For all the pressure, things were a lot less stressful now. And safer.

He thought of getting up but knew he needed sleep. He tried diverting his thoughts, but inevitably they came back to his meeting with the President.

She was in campaign mode . . . for him, not her.

"Senator Stockard is here, Madam President."

"Show him in, and bring the coffee, please."

He'd been waiting at the door. He started wheeling in; she met him a few steps inside the Oval Office.

"Jeff, so good to see you. Come on in. Tracey'll bring us some coffee."

"No beer?"

It took Todd a moment to realize he was pulling her leg. She shook her head and took a seat in front of her desk, waiting as he maneuvered his wheelchair. Her aide came in with a tray of coffee and cookies.

"Raspberry filled," said Zen, picking one up. *"My favorite."*

Raspberry cookies. They'd be worth getting out of bed for. But they didn't have any.

No?

No.

"Tracey's very good at remembering things," said Todd, loud enough to make sure her aide heard as she left the office.

"So what vote am I being asked for here?" said Zen.

"Vote?"

"Come on, Madam President. I know you don't engage in cookie diplomacy for no reason."

"Actually, I wanted to say that I appreciated your vote on the NSA bill," said Todd. "Your voice was important in the committee, and it was critical in the Senate. Thank you."

"It was the right thing to do."

Zen picked up his coffee—black—and took a sip. Todd put hers down and plunged ahead.

"I ran into your wife the other day, and I mentioned that I thought you would make an excellent President," she said. "I wanted to follow up on that."

"You're not planning on resigning, are you?"

The remark caught her by surprise. She wasn't, but she wondered if there were rumors.

"No, no," said Todd. "But . . . if I were to decide not to run again, I wonder if you would be the sort of person who would toss their hat in the ring."

Had she said that? It didn't sound like her.

Something along those lines, at least.

"Because I for one would want to be in a position to help that along," she continued. "I think you'd be excellent. And I think you could get the nomination."

"You're not planning on running for reelection?"

"I'm giving it a lot of thought, and will be giving it a lot more thought," she told him. "If I knew someone like you—you specifically—were interested in run-

ning, that would certainly be a factor. And, candidly, I would work to make sure that you were in the best position to do that. If I stayed on for a second term, one way or the other, it would certainly help, I think, not hurt you."

That was as close as any politician would ever come to urging someone else to run. It was an admission—but an admission of what, exactly?

That she was giving up power. And who did that?

Willingly, anyway.

But Todd was different. Todd—well, they'd had disagreements, but at the end of the day she was a strong, moral person, someone with integrity. And a good President.

"Wouldn't Vice President Mantis be the party's likely candidate?" asked Zen.

"Preying Mantis?" She made a face.

They certainly shared that opinion. Her vice president was the most despicable, lying, conniving politician he'd ever met, and that was saying quite a lot.

"I think he can be defeated in a primary," said Todd.

"I wonder if the country's ready for someone in a wheelchair," said Zen.

"We've already had a President in a wheelchair," she said. "Franklin Roosevelt."

"Yes, but the public didn't know."

"I think the public is ready. Certainly in your case." She rose. *"Let's have another discussion in a few weeks. There are people whom I'd like you to speak to."*

"Why exactly aren't you going to run?"

"If I decide not to run," she said, "it won't be because of a scandal, or anything to do with the job."

"No?" He stared at her; she met it.

"I think you know me well enough on that score."

"I do," admitted Zen. "I assume you'd want this absolutely confidential."

"I know I can count on you."

"As much as anyone," said Zen.

He really missed Breanna.

Zen rolled over, closing his eyes and trying to slip back to sleep.

11

Malaysia

COWBOY CONTINUED TO CLIMB, INTENDING TO USE the altitude to help him build speed for an attack. There were six of them, moving tightly in a diamond, with one in the lead, then two, then three. The two aircraft on the ends split off, angling away from the others in what looked like a pincer movement. Cowboy assumed they were going to try and tuck around him if he stayed on his course.

"Ground, the aircraft just split up," he told Turk.

"Yeah, I'm looking at it," answered Turk. The feed from Cowboy's F-35 was being piped through the Whiplash system into Turk's display.

"They're going to come behind me, I think."

"What they're looking for you to do is break one way or the other," said Turk. "Then whichever side you're on, the fighter in the lead and then the one behind will engage you head-on. The idea is to slow you down so the rest can swarm in."

"Yeah?"

"They do it all the time."

"So how do I beat it?"

"Come straight at them. All their attack patterns are optimized for a rear quarter attack because of their weapons," added Turk. "If they're armed, that is."

"You don't think these are armed?"

"We won't know until they attack. No weapons radars."

"Right," said Cowboy. "But they sure look like they're aggressive—they're climbing."

Aggressive or not, neither pilot could fire until they were in imminent danger—fired on or locked by a weapons radar. So they had to wait—or hope for a direct order from Danny Freah, who was empowered to interpret the situation according to his overall mission orders as well as the ROEs, or rules of engagement. So they had to prepare themselves for combat—and yet do nothing.

"If they go hostile, target the middle aircraft," suggested Turk. "Fire your radar missiles."

"Not at the lead?"

"No. They're keying the attack off the plane in the middle. If it diverts, they have to re-form. It's a vulnerability in a large formation—they were originally designed to work in pairs."

"You sure?"

"I'm guessing," admitted Turk.

Basher Three, which was flying top cover over

the base, checked in. He was coming south. Turk told him to stay back over the base—the UAVs might split and make their primary attack here.

"You'll know by their reaction when Cowboy fires," he said.

At the speed they were closing, Cowboy had another thirty seconds before the UAVs were within firing range.

"You think these guys are hostile?" Cowboy asked Turk.

"Hell, yes. Don't you?"

"Yeah, and they're getting close. But the ROEs are pretty specific."

"I'm working on that. Stand by. I'm going to patch Colonel Freah onto the shared frequency."

Danny Freah came on the circuit. His voice was clipped and formal—Cowboy realized he was talking "for the record."

"Basher, state your situation," directed Freah.

"Colonel, I have six unidentified UAVs coming at me in what Captain Mako says is an attack pattern. I want permission to shoot them down."

"Do you feel yourself in imminent danger?" asked Freah.

"I feel I'm about to be fired on, yes sir."

"Permission to engage granted," said Freah.

Wow, that was easy, thought Cowboy. He'd expected an argument, or at least more questions.

The F-35 had two AMRAAM missiles in its larger internal bay, along with a pair of Side-winder heat-seekers on its wings. Cowboy dialed up the radar missiles, designated the two targets, and got good locks on both. Just as he was about to fire, however, he lost his fix—the little UAVs had initiated ECMs.

They also started a countermaneuver. The four planes that had stayed together separated into two groups. One charged upward while the other dove toward the earth.

It took Turk a few moments to figure out what they were doing.

"Dive on the ones that are hitting the deck," he told Cowboy.

It was a counterintuitive move, to say the least. "Why?"

"Trust me."

Cowboy hesitated, but only for a moment. He pushed his stick in, plotting an intercept about five miles to the west, on his left in the airplane. As soon as the nose of his aircraft tucked downward, the two aircraft that had started to climb spun back in his direction.

"Roll on your wing and pull around as close to a 180 as you possibly can," said Turk, telling Cowboy to change direction. "They'll be on your nose in about thirty seconds. You're going to want to fire right away."

"I don't have a lock."

"Do it. They'll get out of there anyway. Then push down and flip over. Look for the two fighters below you."

"Easy for you to say," muttered Cowboy, but he did exactly as Turk had suggested. The Lightning II slid down on its wing, then shuddered as Cowboy fought gravity and his own momentum through the turn. It was more a swerve than a pivot. The tail of the plane stubbornly resisted his input, and for a moment the aviator thought he would actually lose the plane; his airspeed had dropped precipitously, and his altitude dropped so quick he thought he was in a free fall. But the Pratt & Whitney F135-600 kept pumping thrust, the two-shaft power plant exerting some 43,000 pounds of force to shove the aircraft in the direction its pilot wanted. Cowboy grunted, fighting off the g forces smashing against his body as the two bandits moved magically into the sweet spot of his targeting pipers.

The aircraft shook as he fired, the doors to the bays opening and then closing as he pushed down his nose. Gravity seemed to welcome him. His airspeed jumped. He saw the other two planes some 8,000 feet below him, but he was too far off to fire the Sidewinders.

Rather than flipping over as Turk had suggested he pushed steeper into the dive, sure he would be able to close the distance before the planes reacted. But he was wrong; the UAVs seemed to disappear, and before he could react he realized they had managed to pull farther down toward the terrain, temporarily getting lost in the clutter.

Cowboy started a turn, guessing that the UAVs would be ahead on his right. The F-35's radar found them behind him, at very low altitude. He tried to turn toward them but they were already moving away. He started to follow but then saw one of the drones that had split off earlier angling toward him from above. It had worked to within five miles and was closing fast; had he stayed on his course it would have come down right on his tail.

He lit flares and rolled right. Sweat poured from every pore in his body. Cowboy realized he'd made a mistake, leaving himself vulnerable. His RWR lit with a targeting radar—the drone was trying to get him.

It was the signal he'd needed, but it came at the wrong time—now he was the vulnerable one. Cowboy jerked his stick, tightening the turn so hard that he nearly blacked out, the g forces building so quickly that even his suit couldn't quite keep up. But the maneuver broke the UAV's grip. He saw it pass overhead, within range of his missile for a fleeting second.

Cowboy couldn't react quickly enough, and the aircraft flew off. Basher Three, not close enough to take a shot, banked south to continue guarding the base.

It was over. All six of the UAVs were gone, moving back in the direction they had come.

The pilot let out a string of curses. His radar missiles had missed and he felt like a dope, beaten by robots.

"You all right?" Turk asked over the radio.

He replied with a curse.

"It's all right," said Turk. "They wanted to see how you would react. They'll use that for the next encounter."

"Bastards."

"We're tracking them. You did good," Turk added. "You did real good."

"Then why do I feel like an idiot?"

12

The Cube

EVEN AS THE ENCOUNTER ENDED, THE STAFF OF EX-perts in the Cube were analyzing the performance of the UAVs. The evidence was now overwhelming that Rubeo was right—they were using technology developed for the Flighthawks.

They had a traitor on their hands.

"Theft is not the only explanation," said Jonathon Reid, standing with Breanna and Rubeo at a console in the front of the situation room. "They may have salvaged the C^3 automated pilot units from one of the Flighthawk aircraft lost in Africa last year."

"All of the computer units are accounted for," said Rubeo, who had watched the raw video of the encounter with a deeply distressed face. "More to the point—the only transmissions the elint Global Hawk recorded were brief bursts between them. They're using something similar to the system the Gen 4 Flighthawks use. We just don't know what it is yet."

"But it's a good bet it's exactly the same," suggested Breanna.

Rubeo scowled. "It may be better."

"That's quite an indictment of your organization," said Jonathon.

Rubeo looked as if he'd been shot.

"We need to find out who these people are," said Jonathon. "And what else they have."

"Why they're doing it would be good to know as well," said Breanna.

"I believe I know the who, at least," said Rubeo. "Lloyd Braxton. And it may be related to a movement he calls Kallipolis."

"Kalli-what?" asked Reid.

"Kallipolis. It has to do with Plato and a movement of elites toward a perfect world beyond government."

"That's crazy," said Reid.

"That's Braxton," said Breanna.

RUBEO'S PEOPLE HAD PREPARED A SHORT POWERPOINT summarizing Braxton. A poor white kid from the hardscrabble area of Oakland, he'd won a scholarship to Stanford at the tender age of fifteen, graduated at eighteen, and gone across the country to MIT to work in their famous robotics lab. Two years later after winning numerous awards for work combining AI with robotics, he was recruited for a Dreamland project that adapted the physical design of the original Flighthawk to make it more suitable to combat conditions. He stayed to work on projects ranging from the unmanned bomber to nanotechnology. The ability to work across such a broad spectrum of areas was the rule rather than the exception at Dreamland, but Braxton was a standout intellect even there.

What was unusual were his politics, or more precisely his antipolitics. They were as unconventional as his mind. And he wasn't shy about sharing them.

Braxton had flown in the back of several Mega-fortress test beds Breanna piloted, and she had interacted with him in any number of debriefings and planning sessions. They'd chatted numerous times at parties and other social occasions. He constantly intermingled thoughts about Plato and philosopher kings with g forces and artificial intelligence.

But that wasn't why Breanna remembered Lloyd Braxton.

He'd had a huge crush on Jennifer Gleason, who at the time was not only the number two scientist at Dreamland, but was engaged to Breanna's father, Tecumseh "Dog" Bastian, the commander of Dreamland.

Crush didn't begin to describe it. Even obsession didn't quite capture his behavior. Braxton did everything from asking to be assigned to her projects to slyly following her around the base. Things reached a peak when Jennifer came home to her on-base apartment one night and found him inside.

Colonel Bastian—he hadn't been promoted to general yet—had him escorted off the base the next day.

But even though the incident was reported in his employee file, Braxton retained his top level security clearance. Not only that, but he was hired almost immediately by DARPA, the Defense Department's equivalent of Dreamland, and later by the CIA. It wasn't clear what he'd done—most of the CIA projects were so highly classified that even Reid wasn't familiar with what lay behind the nondescript names they were given—but it was obvious that they had to do with artificial intelligence and its application.

Since then, Braxton had left government service five years ago to start a firm in Silicon Valley. Contrary to what his background might have predicted, the company made toys—high-tech racing cars for boys that tied into games on iPads, and a miniature balloon-based UAV that kids could fly in their backyards. The toys didn't sell particularly well—he was underfinanced, having found it impossible get backers—but the technology the toys exploited was considered so valuable that four different global companies bid to buy the entire company. Braxton cashed out with over ten billion dollars—not the biggest payout in Silicon Valley history, but up there. And it didn't hurt that Braxton not only got all the money, as he lacked partners, but paid no taxes on the money, thanks to an extremely clever set of maneuvers that included his renouncing American citizenship and moving his company's headquarters overseas.

In many ways Lloyd Braxton had lived the American Dream. Starting from conditions that could be best described as horrible—his mother was a crack addict—he had become a billionaire. But along the way he'd developed a massive contempt for others who weren't quite as smart as he was. It was an extreme arrogance not just toward other scientists, but toward the human race in general.

After selling his company, he founded a think tank called Kallipolis, a reference to a mythical utopian island ruled by "philosopher kings" in the

ancient Greek philosophy espoused by Plato. Ostensibly designed to advance Plato's teaching that
the world should be run by the best and brightest,
in practice it preached Darwinist anarchy, where
the "rabble" were to be left to fend for themselves
while the "best" were equally free to do whatever
they wanted. Seminars were held on the best way
to leave behind the ties of government authority,
which amounted to everything from taxes and
speeding laws to banking regulations designed to
prevent terrorism.

Kallipolis wasn't simply against intrusive government, something most people could agree
with. The think tank and the circle that developed around it found no legitimacy for any form
of government. Governments were anachronisms
left over from the days before high-speed communication, lightning-fast transportation, and
high-tech computing. Borders were archaic, and
meaningless to the wealthy and intelligent elite.
Which of course Braxton and the people associated with Kallipolis were.

The group claimed governments had no right to
arrest anyone or defend their borders. According
to Kallipolis—or at least the speakers and organizations it gave money to—the best people should
divorce themselves entirely from government and
the rest of the human race. Only when they did that
would humankind evolve to the next level.

What exactly this next level was remained to
be seen. Braxton never said explicitly. But he had
hired a ghost writer to write a science fiction
novel, privately published as an enhanced e-book,

that depicted a unified world ruled by a small, brilliantly intelligent elite.

"Proles"—about ninety-nine percent of the population—lived in peaceful harmony, tending to robots and computers designed by the elite and manufactured by other robots and computers. The peaceful harmony was enhanced by ecstasylike drugs that heightened the pleasure centers of the brain.

In the book, things went off the rails when one of the proles stopped taking his medicine. Unlike standard sci-fi fare, where the rebel prole would have been the good guy rebelling against a jack-booted society, in Braxton's book he was the bad guy, hunted to the end and eventually killed.

Asked by a reporter whether the book encapsulated his philosophy of life, Braxton demurred. "Fiction is fiction," he'd said. "Things happen in fantasy that don't in real life."

But his portfolio of investments—carefully researched by Rubeo when he suspected the connection—suggested otherwise. Braxton bought out a number of small high-tech companies, and was rumored to have purchased land offshore. He had also become very media-adverse; a thorough search of Web news turned up no articles on him in the past eighteen months, and no public statements by him in the past twenty-four.

"THIS IS A NEW SORT OF THREAT," SAID BREANNA, "AN extragovernmental organization stirring up trouble in a foreign country. We've never faced this before."

"There are precedents in the nineteenth century," said Rubeo.

"Is he capable of funding all this without backing from China or Iran?" asked Reid.

"It would appear so."

"The Islam connection," said Reid, referring to the fact that the 30 May Movement in Malaysia was Sunni Muslim. "Maybe Saudi Arabia and some of the Gulf states are helping."

"Braxton doesn't care for religion," said Rubeo. "It's the opiate of the people, to borrow the phrase from Marx. He despises religion nearly as much as governments."

"It's hard to believe private people could put this together," said Reid. "And why?"

Rubeo gestured at his computer. "If you want to read their manifestos, be my guest. In any event, he is certainly capable intellectually of guiding the construction of this technology. He had access to the data. And he has the money to pull it all off."

"I think we have to lay this out for the President," said Breanna.

"Agreed," said Reid.

"YOU TWO ALWAYS PRESENT ME WITH INTERESTING problems," said the President when they reached her via secure video a half hour later. She was in her private office at the White House, due to leave for Air Force One in an hour. She was heading that morning to a NASA facility in Texas to unveil the start of a manned mission to Mars.

"Regardless of what the intentions are here," said Reid, "the technology is impressive, and in the wrong hands will present considerable problems. Used as terror weapons, these aircraft would be difficult to stop."

Reid detailed more of the possible links to Dreamland, which had already been suspected and outlined. The connection to Ray Rubeo and his billion-dollar companies—even if it was indirect—would undoubtedly become a weapon for the administration's political enemies. Rubeo and his company's lucrative contracts had lately become a target for critics. There was absolutely nothing untoward going on, but the secrecy the firms operated in and Rubeo's prickly and hermitlike public personality made for easy speculation.

But that was a matter for the future.

"The Chinese are not directly involved?" asked the President.

"We believe not," said Reid. "But I would have to assume they will grow more and more curious. We can't rule out a situation where they cut some sort of deal with either Braxton or perhaps the Malaysians to capture the technology, as they did with Iran and the stealth drone."

"So, Breanna, Jonathon, what are we proposing?" asked the President.

"We want to pursue them," said Breanna. "Wherever that may take us."

"We're not sure who is protecting them," explained Reid. "And the Chinese carrier task force that was north of the area has moved south. We'll try to avoid a confrontation with them, but we can't make any guarantees."

"Avoid confronting the Chinese, if at all possible," said the President. "I have enough problems with Congress. But get to the bottom of this. And if it's our technology, get it back. I'll deal with the Chinese, and Congress, if it comes to it."

13

Malaysia

DANNY HADN'T SLEPT IN CLOSE TO FORTY HOURS, AND while that was nowhere near his record, he was so tired that his arms ached when he raised them. Rubbing his eyes, he refilled his coffee cup, then walked to a table at the far corner of the mess tent. Pulling his tablet computer from his pants pocket—the machine and its seven-inch screen fit snuggly, but it did fit—he sat down, pressed his thumb on the reader and stared at the camera just long enough for the retina scanner to ID him and show the password screen.

It took two tries and three sips of coffee before he got the password in right; the screen popped to life and he started scanning his secure e-mail.

The first message was from Breanna: the Tigershark and the ground team were en route, due to arrive within twenty-four hours, as was another surveillance aircraft. They would operate out of Sibu airport, about ninety miles north of the Marines in an area considered far less open to guerrilla attack.

The next e-mail was from Breanna and Reid, a formal authorization allowing Danny to call on the Marines for help in an assault on any base believed to be harboring or controlling the UAVs. It included the name of a Pentagon official who had been tasked as a liaison. This was a bit of bureaucracy Danny didn't particularly care for—in effect, a general several thousand miles away had been assigned as a gatekeeper and de facto impediment to the people who were actually on the scene.

Breanna had clearly anticipated that Danny would object to this, and added two sentences to the effect that, once the overall plan was agreed to, General Grasso could be consulted if there were additional roadblocks.

The general is a facilitator only, Breanna wrote. Danny had to smile—he could hear her saying that in his head as he read the words. *But keep him in the loop.*

"Hey, Colonel." Turk sat down across from him, a tray full of fresh bacon, scrambled eggs, and potatoes in his hands.

"Where'd you get the chow?" Danny asked. "I thought the kitchen was closed."

"Cowboy's friends with the cook. Want some?"

"Sure."

"Take mine. I'll be right back."

Turk was up and gone before he could object. Danny spun the tray around but waited until he saw Turk returning from the kitchen area, a big grin on his face and an even heavier tray in his hands.

"These Marines know how to take care of their people," said the pilot, plopping down. "Even found me a cinnamon roll."

"You joining the Corps now?" joked Danny, digging into his eggs.

"I might. If they always eat like this."

Danny thought of bringing up Turk's request for a transfer but decided this wasn't the time. He scanned the rest of his e-mails quickly; they were routine reports on training and procurement, nothing exciting, even if they were critical to the operation of the ground team. Whiplash was in the middle of an expansion program and so many details had to be taken care of that Danny needed another administrative aide. In fact, he'd already been approved for one, but had simply not been able to find the time to begin interviewing.

"So, any word from Washington?" asked Turk after Danny shut the tablet down and put it aside.

"Whiplash Team Two and the Tigershark will be here in twenty-four hours," said Danny. "We have other surveillance assets en route. I want to set up an assault plan that will let us go in as soon as we know where they're flying from."

"Great."

"Which means you should be getting some sleep," added Danny.

"Yes, Dad."

Danny smiled sardonically. He was tempted to give Turk a lecture about the need for him to be in top condition mentally and physically, but held back; he didn't like being a hypocrite.

"What do we do in the meantime?" asked Turk.

"You're going to sleep."

"The Malaysians have another platoon coming up this morning," said Turk. "They have a target to hit tonight."

"Tonight?"

"They managed to get some intel off one of the prisoners. They want to keep up their momentum. They think they have the rebels on the run."

"Where's this target?"

"They say there's a village about twenty miles southwest of where they were that the rebels are using. It's close to the border with Indonesia. It may even be over it."

"If it's over the border, we're not helping them," said Danny. He didn't add that they might not help in any event; the UAVs were now the Marines' top priority as well as his.

"Captain Deris says he knows. They're going to deal with it themselves, if they have to."

"Can they handle coms with the Marines?"

"Captain Deris can talk well enough to get a target nailed down. Thing is, Colonel, the Marines may not be able to support them at all, even if the target is approved," added Turk. "Colonel Greenstreet is out with the flu, and so are Rogers and Haydem."

"I knew about Rogers," said Danny, "but not the others."

"Both of the guys were throwing up like crazy in the air. Only Cowboy's good to go."

"So the Malaysians have to go without air."

"If necessary," said Turk.

Danny suspected that Turk was hinting that he should go, but he didn't rise to the bait; he wasn't sure whether he wanted him to or not. "Can the Marines get other pilots in from the assault ship?"

"They're heavily committed at the eastern part of the island. Big assault under way. I had an idea," Turk added. His voice dropped a few decibels; Danny had to lean closer to hear. "I was thinking I'd volunteer to fly with them."

"I don't know, Turk. The colonel wasn't crazy about you flying earlier. He's kind of proprietary."

"Is that a new word for a jerk?"

"Even so—"

"Cowboy's all for it. And it makes a lot of sense—if the UAVs come back, we'll be able to shoot them down."

"In the Tigershark, not an F-35B."

"I could shoot them down in a Fokker triplane," said Turk.

Danny was no pilot, but he recognized the aircraft as a WWI fighter. He also recognized Turk's statement as typical fighter jock bluster—rare in Turk, though not in the breed.

"I'd prefer to wait until the Tigershark gets here," said Danny. "And I have the rest of the team in place."

"What happens if the UAVs come back?"

"We'll take that as it comes."

Turk rose without saying a word.

"Get some sleep, Captain," said Danny sharply as the pilot sulked away. "That's an order."

TURK STALKED OUT OF THE MESS TENT, ANGRY WITH HIM-self as well as Danny. He'd gone about asking to fly on the mission all wrong, dancing around the subject until the very end, and then blurting rather than calmly laying out all the reasons he should.

The hell with it.

Cowboy met him a few yards from the tent.

"What's he say?" asked the Marine.

"That I should go to bed."

"No shit." Cowboy laughed.

"We have more assets coming so the operation is in a holding pattern," Turk said, trying to calm down. "And the colonel's worried about the border."

"We aren't going over the border. I can guar-antee that."

"Whatever."

"Maybe I should talk to him," said Cowboy. "I'm definitely doing that mission. Greenstreet's OK'd it. And I need a wingman."

"Good luck."

"What are you going to do?"

Turk shrugged and stalked off.

If he'd been in any other place in the world, Turk probably would have hit a bar. He thought of calling Li but decided not to. He'd have to ex-plain why he was mad and would probably end up sounding like a cranky baby. And besides, talking to her would only make him miss her more.

Frustrated and bored, he headed back to his room in the trailer, where he took out his e-reader to read a book on World War II.

He fell asleep within five minutes.

"THE THING IS, COLONEL, I DON'T ONE HUNDRED PERcent know that I'd survive another encounter with the UAVs," Cowboy told Danny. "I do know I wouldn't have made it out of that last one without Turk telling me what to do."

"I agree Turk is a great pilot," said Danny. "It's a question of priorities."

"The priority is getting information on the UAV, right? You're not going to be able to do that if it shoots me down."

"I'm sure that would give us plenty of information," said Danny sarcastically.

"Maybe." Cowboy smiled. "That was a bad example. I'm just saying, we need another pilot, there's another pilot here. It would be great if we could use him."

"What'd Greenstreet say about it?"

"Haven't asked him yet. Figured there be no use dealing with him unless you were good with it."

"I'll take it under advisement," said Danny. "When I know about the Malaysian plans. And when your squadron commander says *he's* good with it."

"Great!" Cowboy jumped up from the table. "Thanks, Colonel."

Why do I think I've just been had? wondered Danny.

14

Offshore the Sembuni Reefs

THE SECURITY ENCRYPTION AND PROCEDURES KALLIPO-
lis employed imposed a significant performance
penalty on real-time communications; it split the
video and audio streams, and so there was always
a slight delay between the video and the sound
during the best of times, and at sea the additional
security and network overhead made it even worse.
It was so bad tonight that Lloyd Braxton had to
look away as Church Michaels spoke; the audio was
nearly a full second ahead of the visual.

"You shouldn't have launched the attack," continued Michaels. "We aren't prepared."

"I have four bases. I have a dozen aircraft. I
have ships, I have submersibles. We're making
more UAVs and weapons. I need the structures
for the distributed intelligence units. When do I
wait for? The next millennium?"

"The involvement of the Dreamland people
makes things much more . . . difficult," said Michaels. "They're not going to back down. It's a
vast escalation."

"On the contrary. The fact that they're involved means there will be no escalation," said
Braxton. "And besides—they are the ones who
have the computing technology. This is the best
way to get it. And we need it. Or else we have to
hire an army and become a government. Which
none of us want."

"I don't see them backing down."

"You're in the Ukraine. I doubt you have much to worry about."

"The bribes are killing me."

Braxton snorted. Michaels had sold his carbon-fiber fabrication business to General Electric for roughly $3 billion worth of GE stock. He had numerous other investments, and had bankrolled at least one black hat hacker operation specializing in credit card theft. He could certainly afford whatever trivial amount the authorities were holding him up for; it was cheaper than legitimate taxes.

"You have all these high-minded ideals," countered Michaels, obviously wounded by Braxton's response, "but how much of this is because you had the hots for Jennifer Gleason and she dissed you?"

"She never dissed me. Ever. Bastian did. Him and Rubeo. Rubeo was the real problem, the sexless prick."

"I'll take your word for it," said Michaels, calling a quick truce. "Rubeo was always decent to me."

"You met him twice."

"Do you really think you can control 30 May? They're Stone Age crazoids. They don't just believe in God, they think He talks to them through the Koran. Give me a break."

"They're useful. For the moment. As I say—we either get the technology that allows the machines to work together or we hire an army. Which do you want?"

The arrangement with the rebels was based solely on mutual convenience, and Braxton put no trust in them. True, when they started, he had hoped to carve out a refuge here in Malaysia, a place Kallipolis could use as its physical base. But after a few months it had become obvious that neither the rebels nor Malaysia would be suitable in the long term. Even if the locals could be dealt with, the Chinese were too active. Apparently aware of some of the technology Braxton was exploiting, they'd tried to infiltrate the rebel network and even reached out through intermediaries to make a deal. Braxton would have nothing to do with them; they were even worse than the Americans.

"What are you going to do if the U.S. sends more than a few Marines?" asked Michaels.

"What we're doing now. We bloody them, and we do it publicly. The President will back off. Her approval rating is sinking. She has all sorts of problems. Don't fret, Christopher. As soon as I have one of the Sabres, I'm gone and on to the next phase. As planned."

"I say, get the ships, get everything the hell out of there. That's the best bet. We don't need this fight. We have all the freedom money can buy. That's what we need."

"What?"

"You heard me. We don't need this. This—it's a pipe dream."

"What happened to your ideals?" asked Braxton, truly shocked. Michaels had been one of his most fervent backers from the beginning.

"I still have them." Michaels's mouth moved for a moment, finishing the sentence. His eyes were intense, but something had changed.

"You're getting married," said Braxton. "You've decided."

"We're not going to a government, or a church," said Michaels. There was the faint hint of a smile on his face. "But we are making a commitment. To each other."

"That's very nice."

"Thank you." Michaels didn't pick up on the sarcasm.

"I'm going ahead as planned. I'll see you in Kazakhstan in six weeks. We can discuss your future involvement then."

Braxton knew there would be none, but it made no sense to declare that now.

"I can't talk you out of this?" asked Michaels.

Braxton frowned, and hit the kill switch, ending the conversation.

Love, he thought bitterly to himself. It was a worse opiate than religion.

15

Malaysia

FINALLY GIVING IN TO THE DEMANDS OF HIS BODY, Danny hit his cot around 1000 hours, planning to sleep for two hours. But he slept until close to 6:00 P.M., when Turk Mako was shaking his shoulder.

"Colonel, you need to check this out," said Turk. "We have hot video—there's a column of rebels coming up from the south. It has to be a couple of hundred guys."

"Wh-What?" stuttered Danny, still half-buried in sleep.

"Come on over to the command post and have a look," said Turk.

Danny folded himself out of bed. His body was stiff, his muscles complaining that the humid air didn't agree with them.

"You OK, Colonel?" asked Turk.

"Yeah." He stretched. "Any coffee over there?"

"Plenty, and it's stronger than the liquid scat the mechanics brew at Dreamland."

"Good."

Danny pulled on his boots and grabbed his tablet on the way out. The Marines were already suiting up for battle, their Ospreys warming on the airstrip.

"Looks like we got their attention," said Captain Thomas. "We're going to hit them when they come through the valley. Both sides."

The Marines would land near the route the rebels were taking. Splitting in half, they would attack from the north and the west, hammering them from two sides. The Malaysians would accompany them.

"We need air support and protection when the UAVs come," said Captain Thomas. "The squadron is down to one pilot, which means one plane. I'm asking for more coverage from the assault ship, but they're way overstretched and it's quite a haul. I don't think they can make it in time."

Danny glanced at Turk. The pilot studiously avoided his gaze.

"Turk may be able to take one of the slots," Danny said. "I'll discuss it with Greenstreet."

"Great. Thanks," added Thomas. "What about you, Colonel? Where do you want to be?"

"I'm going to sit this battle out," added Danny. "I need to coordinate with Washington on our next move."

"Understood."

"With regret," added Danny, resisting an urge to change his mind and go. There was just too much to do before his people got there, and if the UAVs appeared, he would be in a better spot here to monitor them.

CONTRARY TO WHAT HE EXPECTED, GREENSTREET told Danny he had no problem with Turk flying. He didn't necessarily seem pleased, but he was certainly professional.

"If my ground commander wants another plane for more support, he'll have it," said the colonel.

"With Turk flying," added Danny, just to be sure.

"He's a competent pilot."

A lot more than that, thought Danny, but he saw no reason to poke the bear.

"Very good, Colonel. I appreciate your cooperation. He'll get a full update on the UAVs and brief you preflight."

Greenstreet nodded.

"You don't have a problem with Turk, do you?" Danny asked.

"He's a hotshot," said Greenstreet, a tiny bit

of his professional mask slipping. "But we'll live with it."

T
URK TIGHTENED HIS FACE AS BREANNA CAME ON THE screen to brief him on the UAVs. He was going to be professional, and only professional.

Her frown told him he didn't quite succeed.

"Turk, I hope you're feeling well," she said.

"I'm fine," he said.

"We've been able to analyze the encounter and we have a great deal of information for you. The aircraft looked to be modeled after the Gen 4 Flighthawk, though prior to the improvements we made for the New Mexico range."

"Right," said Turk tightly.

"Are you familiar with that project?"

"Somewhat," said Turk. "It was before my time."

"Their onboard maneuver library is exactly the same as Gen 3."

"I recognize that."

"John Rosen will go through it with you if you need him to," she said, referring to one of the analysts on the program who had been brought over to Whiplash to help. Rosen worked for one of Rubeo's companies. "We still have no firm data on the weapons. It's most likely a 25mm cannon based on the tactics and the visual. Fred McCarthy is going to run down the probable capabilities."

McCarthy's face flashed on the screen. A retired Navy intelligence specialist, he had spent several years working for the CIA and was now on loan to Special Projects. McCarthy knew as much about weapons as any engineer—or database, for that matter.

"This is what we think they're firing," he said, holding up what looked like a thick metal needle. "Depleted uranium. High mass, very small volume. Consider it roughly the equivalent of a 25mm round in an M-242—yes, I prefer the Army weapon as an analogue for the following reasons . . ."

While McCarthy certainly knew his stuff, there was a downside to his store of knowledge—he tended to unleash vast amounts of it when explaining even the simplest concept or finding.

The M-242, he said, was used in the Bradley Fighting Vehicle and the Marine Corps LAV-25 personnel carrier; the 25mm gun had itself used depleted uranium rounds, though they were not standard equipment. The material's density gave the DU BBs—as McCarthy called them—an inherent advantage over conventional slugs; a smaller size bullet could carry as much momentum as a larger round, giving it more kinetic energy and thus more penetrating power. But the metal's qualities went beyond that; McCarthy theorized that the rounds were engineered so the rear portion spread as the nose hit, creating a wider "wound" in its target.

The weapon would have an effective range of just over 1,500 meters, about the same as a 20mm cannon. That would account for the tactics the UAVs employed; it had to be relatively close to fire. The weapon would have a fairly good recoil, which in the small aircraft would have a significant impact on its flight energy. It would be fired in very short bursts, perhaps as low as three at a time, and in any event would not carry much ammunition.

The weapon assumptions were being made based on thin data, and so Turk took them with a grain of salt. The Sabres had been fitted with a similar weapon at one point in their trials. But the uranium slugs had proven to be overkill—you didn't need to make big holes in an aircraft to shoot it down—and have a weight penalty as well. The Sabres now used conventional bullets.

McCarthy moved on to tactics, where he and Turk were mostly in agreement. It seemed likely the enemy UAVs were programmed to fly to a certain area, then used a combination of passive sensors to home in on their targets—a simple electronics detector would get them close, where an infrared sensor could take over for the final targeting. The simplicity gave them certain advantages: the aircraft could be small and therefore hard to detect and highly maneuverable. But it also extracted a price. They were surely vulnerable at long range, and they seemed to have to make a rear-quarter attack to guarantee a kill. Cowboy's encounter appeared to prove all of that, and also implied that Turk's suggestion for him to attack at long range had been sound.

As McCarthy continued, the camera pulled back to show the others sitting near him in the situation room. Rubeo was there, and Reid, and a dozen other specialists.

And Breanna, right in the middle, standing, arms folded, lips pressed tightly together, clearly worried.

Is that how you looked when you ordered them to kill me? Turk wondered. Does your conscience bother you now? How would you have gotten this mission done if they'd succeeded?

Hate welled inside him. Then he felt guilty, sad even—he had admired Breanna and her husband Zen greatly. Both were heroes, and at the same time unpretentious, just regular people, at least to the extent possible in Washington, given their jobs.

But Breanna had let him down. She stood revealed as someone who could not be trusted.

Zen was different. Turk still admired the former pilot, who had done so much to make combat UAVs successful and become the first Flighthawk ace. To have come back from a crippling injury, especially at a time when people looked at disabilities as if they were contagious diseases and a mark of bad character, had taken a tremendous amount of courage, courage that Turk himself wasn't sure he possessed. It wasn't just bravery under fire—which Turk certainly did possess—it was the ability to take a long-range view of the battle and to put up with the constant setbacks, large and small, that were inevitable. Perseverance under fire was a different kind of courage, a quality that someone who was impatient, as Turk was, couldn't count on.

"So, bottom line, Captain Mako," said Rubeo, thankfully interrupting the analyst's dissertation. "Target them at long range, and don't let them behind you."

McCarthy turned to him. "I'll defer to Captain Mako on the precise tactics," he said. "But you have it in a nutshell."

"That's pretty much the best way to deal with any enemy," said Turk, even though he knew it was much easier said than done in this case.

"Good luck, Turk," said Breanna.

"Yeah. Thanks." He switched off the feed and went to get suited up.

16

The Cube

JONATHON REID STOPPED BREANNA AS SHE STARTED to leave the situation room.

"A minute alone?" he asked.

"Of course." She glanced around. Except for the two duty officers at the front, everyone else had left to take a break or get something to eat.

"I couldn't help but notice, you looked a little upset," said Reid, his voice barely above a whisper. "Are you worried about the operation?"

"I'd feel better if we had all our assets in place," said Breanna. "And if we had a full force."

"We will in another eighteen hours."

"The UAVs will probably come with this attack," said Breanna. "We really should have our people there. In a perfect world—"

"In a perfect world we'd all be millionaires. But that's not what's bothering you, is it?"

"Things aren't right with Turk. He doesn't trust me."

"Why not?"

"Iran. The order I gave Stoner."

"You did what you had to do," said Reid. "Right?"

"I know, but . . . I can't take back the fact that if he was killed, it would have been on my orders. My fault. My responsibility."

"And what about the several million people your order saved?" asked Reid. "That mission—if we hadn't destroyed the bombs, don't you think Iran would have used them at some point?"

"It's more complicated than that. And maybe they wouldn't have," added Breanna. "We don't know."

"That's true. We can't see the future. What we *do* know is what happened—the bombs were destroyed, and Turk is still alive."

"No thanks to me."

"On the contrary. You sent the one person who had a chance of saving him. You don't give yourself credit for that. Why not?"

"Because Turk doesn't," said Breanna.

17

Malaysia

TURK STEADIED THE F-35B INTO A COMFORTABLE orbit at 20,000 feet. The night was clear, with not even a whisper of wind. The plane felt solid around him, responding precisely to every input. Taking off the other day, he'd been unsure of himself, and the aircraft seemed to have sensed it, reacting with slight jerks and the occasional stutter through the early parts of the flight. Now his muscles moved with smooth assurance, and the plane responded accordingly.

Cowboy flew about a half mile ahead in Basher One. They had the sky to themselves.

"Two, scope's clean. How you lookin'?" asked the Marine, telling Turk he had no radar contacts.

"Copy. Same. Systems are good. Looks like you dialed up an easy one for us."

"The night is still young," answered Cowboy. "Ospreys are off the mat in zero-two."

"Roger that, I copy," said Turk.

As soon as the aircraft carrying the Marine assault units were off the ground, Cowboy swung south, aiming to overfly the area where the rebels were advancing. A Marine UAV was already in the vicinity, providing real-time infrared reconnaissance.

Turk stayed with the Ospreys, tucking down toward 12,000 feet. The transport aircraft were far lower, close to the jungle treetops, hugging the curve of the Earth as they sped south.

Three miles from the landing zone the lead Osprey began to slow. The flaps on its wings deployed as they approached the LZ, and with the airspeed gently dropping, the long engines and their massive rotors began to rotate. The aircraft seemed to swing out as if they were on a trapeze, descending smartly to the ground.

The landing area was a hard-packed dirt road, and there was only room for one of the aircraft at a time. The second Osprey banked a short distance to the north, revolving slowly around a hilltop. Within a minute and a half the Marines on Osprey One were off; it rose and its companion came in. Ninety seconds after touching down, the second aircraft pulled up, having disembarked its platoon.

Still escorting the rotobirds, Turk swung back in the direction of the base. His sensors scanned the air at long range to make sure the enemy UAVs hadn't chosen this moment to appear. The Ospreys had a short run back, but they were extremely vulnerable to enemy aircraft, with no weapons to defend themselves.

Cowboy remained over the LZ. He made radio contact with Captain Thomas and the CCTs—combat controllers—with each platoon.

While the Corps had its own personnel trained to act as ground controllers, they sometimes "borrowed" similarly trained men from different services. In this case they had two of the profession's finest: Air Force special ops pararescuers, both of whom had seen action in Libya just a few months before, working clandestinely with the rebels there.

The Air Force combat controllers were descendants of the World War II pathfinders, paratroopers who'd dropped into Europe ahead of D-day. As the war evolved, the pathfinders had called in air strikes, helping the allies move quickly across Europe. Given jeeps and allowed to ride with the tanks in Patton's spearhead, the small band of sky-dropping daredevils had revolutionized warfare.

In the contemporary military, their Air Force descendants trudged through the mud and gravel alongside troops from every service, from "ordinary" grunts to Tier One SEALs. Able to do anything from locating the landing zone for a parachute drop to creating an airfield in the middle of a jungle, their job today was to direct air strikes if things got hairy. They'd spent a month working with the MEU on the other side of the island. Cowboy had worked with both; they recognized his voice as well as his call sign, and gave him a little bit of ribbing along with their sitrep.

It was a sign that things were going well, Turk thought—they didn't fool around when the situation was tight.

With the Ospreys safely home, Turk returned, taking a high track above and slightly behind the figure eight Cowboy was cutting in the area. He stayed at 18,000 feet—high enough to assist in a ground attack if necessary, while still at an altitude he thought sufficient to deal with the UAVs.

Both F-35s carried two AMRAAM air-to-air missiles in one of their bays, along with a pair of Sidewinder infrared heat-seekers on their wings. Because of the way the aircraft was designed, the wingtips of the F-35B were bare; the Sidewinders were mounted on the last of three hard points on each wing. That left the other four external points and one internal bay for a mix of Redeye cluster bombs and "small" SBD-II bombs. The SBDs were fitted four to a rack, giving the two aircraft considerable versatility if called on for ground support.

Twenty minutes of flying loops and crazy eights left Turk bored, and he found himself half wishing the UAVs would appear. He knew it was wrong—bad karma and all that—but still, he was ready.

Finally, the lead segment of rebels left the jungle and headed for the road north, aiming directly at the ambush point Captain Thomas had plotted. But only a few minutes passed before they left the road again, splitting into two columns along the western side and moving north. The move complicated things for the Marines, but they quickly adjusted, setting up an ambush about a mile deeper in the jungle. That was a good thing for the F-35s—it gave them a little more room to maneuver without going over the border. While Indonesia was powerless to stop them, it had radars in the area able to detect the F-35s when they were carrying weapons under their wings, and any transgression of the border would bring protests at the UN.

On the ground, time was moving quickly; the Marines were hustling through the jungle as quickly as they could, scrambling to make sure they were in place. In the air, time dragged. Turk rehearsed a dozen scenarios in his head, then rerehearsed them.

"They're saying zero-five from contact," Cowboy told Turk after the Marine controller with West Force checked in.

"Roger, I heard."

"I have nothing on long-range scan."

"Copy," said Turk.

"They engage the lead elements, and then we

get called in if they have enough of a target for us," said Cowboy, who was simply repeating the basic briefing. Turk realized he was bored, too. "We may not have a target in the early stages."

"Roger. Got it."

"There's a hill about two miles south of the ambush point, overlooking the road," added Cowboy. "I'm thinking that if the rebels retreat, they may try to take a stand there. We may end up hitting that position."

"Copy."

As Turk began scanning for the position, West Force radioed that they had made contact and taken the rebels under fire. Now came the hardest part of the mission for the pilots: waiting for something to happen, while knowing that the guys on the ground were taking fire.

The battle on the ground—in a jungle, at night, in terrain unfamiliar to both sides—was a confusing mélange of explosions, bullet rounds, and blind cursing. The Malaysians and Americans had the advantage of night vision and superior communications; the rebels had numbers. Surprise was a factor at first, and greatly aided the American force. Their initial volleys of fire drove the rebels back in confusion. But the thick jungle made it difficult to see even with the night gear, and before the allied force could take real advantage, the rebels rallied. The two columns retreated and then consolidated. Better trained or at least better disciplined than the force the day before, the rebels managed to organize a line of defense along a stream that ran down the center of a shallow rift. Lying on the high side of the ground, they used machine guns to stop the Malaysian and Marine squads pursuing them.

But that just gave Cowboy and Turk something to do. With a clear line marking where the enemy was, Basher One and Two went to work.

In the not too distant past, precision ground support meant getting very close and personal to the target—the lower, the better. That subjected the airman to a fair degree of danger from the ground. Most enemy soldiers didn't particularly like being bombed, and could be expected to fire whatever they had at their attackers. Even a rifle could potentially bring down an airplane; there were, in fact, stories of American soldiers in the Pacific taking down Japanese airplanes with their M-1s by striking the pilot.

Getting close to the enemy *still* worked well in certain situations and with certain weapons, but in this case it was unnecessary. The small-diameter smart bombs the F-35s were using allowed the pilots to hit targets beyond sixty nautical miles—making the word "close" in close-air support a misnomer. With a multimode sensor—the bomb could be directed to its target by radar, infrared, and laser as well as GPS and an inertial guidance system—the weapon was as versatile as it was accurate.

Officially, the bombs had a margin of error that allowed them to strike within about a four meter radius of any given target. Unofficially, the margin of error was much less than that, depending on the guidance mode.

Just inside five miles from the target area,

Basher One unleashed four bombs, all guided by GPS locations that he had double-checked with the friendlies on the ground. The bombs hit in a staggered line on the rebel side of the creek, devastating the middle of their position and eliminating both machine guns.

"Woo-hooo," said the controller over the radio as the explosions lit the sky. "Good hits!"

Now it was Turk's turn. He lined up his crosshairs on a cluster of rebels about three hundred yards farther south and closer to the road. Coded with the GPS coordinates from the F-35's weapons system, the two bombs he dished sped toward their destiny. With those off, Turk moved to a second cluster of bad guys in the jungle to the west about a quarter of a mile away. There were about thirty rebels there, gathering for a counterattack; with more area between them and the Marines and a larger count to boot, Turk selected his cluster bombs. The weapons were like dump trucks carrying small packages of destruction; rather than concentrating hundreds of pounds of explosives in a single area, they spread out smaller bomblets, showering the enemy positions.

Turk got another ya-hoo for his efforts.

The air strikes broke the rebels' will. They retreated in confusion and panic, small groups of two and three men bolting through the trees in the general direction of the Indonesian border. The American and Malaysian ground units moved south, capturing stragglers and the wounded. The battle was done. It had lasted less than half an hour.

Back to being bored, Turk blew into his mask. The muscles in his shoulders and his forearms ached, not from exertion but from the almost unconscious tension. His flight suit was damp; he'd been sweating the entire time without even realizing it. It might be a push-button war in a lot of ways, but it was still war; danger waited at the edges, always ready to push its own buttons.

"How's your fuel?" asked Cowboy from Basher One.

"Good," said Turk, checking the gauges. "I have about an hour before bingo."

"Copy. Me, too. You fight well, Air Force. So when are you joining the Corps?"

"When are you joining the Air Force?"

"The hell with the Air Force. I want to be in Whiplash," said Cowboy. The serious note in his voice surprised Turk.

"Really?"

"Hell, man. You bet."

"It's not as glamorous as you think."

"From what I've heard, it's even better."

"I don't know about that . . ."

"I'm serious."

"I can tell," said Turk.

"We'll talk about it when we get down."

Turk started to acknowledge, but Cowboy suddenly sounded an alert.

"Two bogie contacts, bearing 290 degrees, moving like all hell," said the Marine pilot. "Gotta be the UAVs—looks like our night is about to get a lot more interesting."

CLOSING IN

1

Malaysia

DANNY FREAH LISTENED TO THE PROGRESS OF THE battle via radio as he watched the feeds from the Global Hawk and the smaller battlefield UAV. As fractured and contradictory as they were, he felt the radio transmissions gave him a better sense of what was going on. They were more visceral, and he could judge from the excitement in the voices what the men on the ground were feeling about the battle.

They were done; it was over, it had been a good mission, and now things were going to be easy for a day or two or three.

The sudden appearance of the drones changed everything. The two aircraft popped up over the water a few miles from the coast. As they did, the elint-equipped Global Hawk II being commanded from back in the Cube detected a transmission.

The game was on.

"Basher Two, you see those aircraft?" asked Danny.

"Affirmative," said Turk. "We just got them on radar. I was about to radio you."

"Aircraft are considered hostile," said Danny. "You are authorized to shoot them down."

"Copy that. Basher One, you copy?"

"Basher One copies. We're cleared hot. Bandits are hostile and will be engaged. I'm talking to ground now."

Danny got up to reposition his slate computer against the console to his left. Just as he lifted it, the ground shook with two tremendous thuds. He lost his balance and fell to the ground as a third and a fourth round exploded, these much closer.

"Mortars!" yelled someone as Danny struggled to his feet.

"Find those mortars!" yelled Jack Juno, the lieutenant Thomas had left in charge at the base.

Danny got up and looked at the UAV screens to see if he could help. But the Marines were too fast for him.

"Located!" shouted one of the men working the radar that tracked the rounds.

"Well, get some fire on the damn thing!" shouted Juno as the shelling continued.

While the mortar radar had located the source of the rounds, the IR feed from the UAV didn't detect anyone there. Danny punched into the Whiplash com line to ask for help.

He was surprised to hear Ray Rubeo's voice.

"You're under fire," said the scientist.

"Yes."

"Either your enemy is very lucky or they have an extremely thorough understanding of the technology the Marines are using. My vote is the latter, but it's irrelevant," he said. "You notice the thick foliage area where the mortars are firing from?"

"Affirmative."

"They've come down parallel to the ridge and the stream that runs northwest—look at it on the map screen. There is enough water vapor from the stream to degrade the small sensors in the Marine UAV. This is a consequence of the IR-cut filter technology. It's inexpensive, but as you see—"

Danny cut him off. "Doc, no offense, but I'm needing a solution here, not a dissertation on the way the different sensors work."

"We're going to divert the Global Hawk to the area and fly it at five thousand feet," said Rubeo. "We'll supply you parameters to readjust the radar in a moment."

"If I do that, we can't track the UAVs," said Danny.

"What are the F-35Bs for?"

"Yeah, but—"

"Colonel, your aircraft can't be in two places at one time, and at the moment your survival is paramount," said Rubeo, his tone even more withering than usual.

"Right."

The Marines had begun firing back at the mortars, but without noticeable effect. A new source joined in, this one targeting the mortar radar. Before the Marines could return fire, the radar was damaged and put out of commission.

"These bastards are getting some help," said Lieutenant Juno. "Can we get air support back here?"

Turk heard the call from the forward operating base that they were under fire, but without target data for the mortars, there was little they could do at the moment. In the meantime he and Cowboy had their hands full dealing with the two UAVs, which had juiced their engines and were maneuvering to engage the American F-35Bs.

"Trying to climb above us, right?" said Cowboy.

"Yeah," answered Turk. Deciphering what they would do next wasn't that hard; it was figuring out three moves from now that was difficult.

Turk was struck by the fact that the planes were acting differently than they had the day before—rather than trying to remain undetected, they were going out of their way to make their presence known, changing their headings to make their profiles as wide as possible for the F-35 radars to pick up.

Why?

If these had been Sabres or even Flighthawks, it would be because they'd learned something from the earlier encounters. And they were trying to use that to some advantage.

So what had he learned from the earlier encounter? And what would they have expected him to learn, and then do?

Turk guessed they were trying to get the F-35s to use their radar missiles at long range. They must be confident of beating them.

"Let's take a sixty-degree turn east. That'll keep them on our nose as they climb."

"Roger. I'm looking for a lock for the AM-RAAMs," added Cowboy.

"We want to hold on to the radar missiles as long as we can," said Turk.

"Uh, that's not what we briefed."

"Yeah, I know. But hold on to them anyway. It'll keep them from getting too close."

"How's that going to work, kemosabi?"

"I'm thinking. They flew purposely in a way that we could see them; they didn't have to. So I'm figuring they want us to shoot sooner rather than later. It's a guess," he added, as if that were necessary.

A sharp cut by the UAVs as Cowboy got a lock told Turk he was right. At ninety miles away they were in range of the AMRAAM 120D radar missiles the planes were equipped with, but the planes would be able to easily beam the F-35s and temporarily disappear from the radar too far for the missiles' own guidance systems to pick them up.

Turk called another break and brought them back on the scope.

"It's a cat and mouse game," he said. "We have to get closer."

"What are they going to do then?"

"I'm thinking."

The trick was to use their tactics and expectations against them, Turk realized.

"I'll bait them," he told Cowboy. "I'm going to fire the AMRAAMs, then try and get in their faces. They think they sucked me in. You keep your distance until they come after me. When they're both on my tail and you have a lock, fire. The closer you are the better; we don't want them to outrun the missiles."

"How close do you want them to get to you?"

"As close as it takes. I'll tell you when to fire."

THE RADAR ABOARD THE GLOBAL HAWK WAS USED BY the Cube to synthesize a three-dimensional view of the jungle, painting the trees and terrain in gray-greens. There were two clumps of rebels in the shadow of the ridge; Danny gave both locations to the Marines as possible mortar locations. Meanwhile, the Marine's Shadow UAV found a large clump of men north of the camp, less than a mile away.

"They're going to attack once the mortaring stops," Lieutenant Juno predicted, pointing at the screen.

"Can you target them with your mortars?" asked Danny.

"We will if we can. I just lost coms with the mortar team. I'm going to send someone— Mofitt!"

The corporal came over and listened as the spotter gave him the coordinates. Then he took off out of the bunker.

Danny turned his attention back to the displays. Though they were a mile away, the rebels were running toward the perimeter. It was the weakest of the four sides to begin with, and the mortaring had softened it up.

"They'll be at the defenses in five minutes," said

Danny. "There are fifty of them at least. You'll have to shift your mortar attack or we'll be overrun."

"My coms with the mortars are still out," yelled Juno as the bunker shook with another strike. "I've lost two of my mortar men, and a third's injured."

"What about Mofitt?"

"Can't raise him on the radio. I'm going to send someone else."

"I'll go," said Danny. He yelled to Ward, the Whiplash techie monitoring the UAVs, to keep an eye on the targets and feed him their coordinates every thirty seconds.

"Colonel, don't go," warned the lieutenant.

Two rounds landed, one practically on top of the bunker.

"All right," said Juno, giving in. "Get the mortars redirected. I'll organize a counterattack."

TURK CLOSED TO WITHIN FIFTY MILES OF THE TWO UAVs before getting solid locks for the AMRAAMs. He dished them off in quick succession, then buttoned up the fighter, though his stores on the wings still presented a juicy radar picture.

Just as he had thought, the UAVs made sharp turns and switched on their ECMs. Still, the AMRAAMs continued in their direction, and for a moment Turk thought he might have two kills. But the small planes could cut unbelievably tight turns in the air, and now managed to duck under the radar missiles. They were already coming for Turk when the AMRAAMs realized they were hopelessly lost and self-exploded in disgust.

Turk tucked his wing down, pushing his plane lower—and closer to the enemy's flight path. He got a warning that the targeting radar in the closest small aircraft was trying to lock on. He went steeper into the dive, striving for a balance between being an enticing target and a dead one. A warning blared—the small aircraft had locked on him from ten miles away.

Turk waited anxiously for a warning that the small aircraft had fired a radar missile, but none came. The Flighthawk 3s could carry small radar-guided missiles that were effective at twenty miles, but as the UAV closed the distance without firing, Turk knew these aircraft weren't carrying them.

It wasn't much of a possibility, but it was one less thing to have to worry about, he told himself.

Somehow, that hardly cheered him.

"Basher One, do you have a lock?"

"Working on it, Two."

"Keep closing."

"If you stop flitting around, I might have a chance."

Turk rolled into an invert and then let the nose of the plane dive downward, in effect making a large loop in the sky. The maneuver changed the plane's direction 180 degrees; he was now facing toward the two UAVs. He was hoping they would now start turns and come around for a rear quarter attack; instead, the radar receiver warned that they had just locked on to his plane.

Too far for a shot, thought Turk. They were four miles away. He knew he had a few seconds.

A flash of light danced off the front fuselage.

The infrared detector buzzed—the aircraft were firing a laser at him.

Turk pushed straight down into a dive, twisting away from the enemy UAVs. They were on his back, swooping almost parallel to each other so that he couldn't escape by simply going to one side or the other.

"OK," he said over the radio. "This is as close as I want them."

Actually, closer, he thought.

"Fire, Fox One," called Cowboy. "Fire, Fox One."

Turk pushed the F-35B into a tight turn. Gravity punched him in the face and chest, then tried wrestling his hand from the stick. He got a temperature warning in the engine. The gauges began lighting with cautions, and now the aircraft's Bitchin' Betty system chimed in, saying he was going too low.

"Pull up!" said the automated voice, bizarrely calm yet very incessant. "Pull up!"

Turk yanked back on the stick, but he'd miscalculated his momentum; the plane continued to sink.

"Throttle, throttle, throttle," he said, as if he were talking to the plane. He jammed the control to full military power and struggled to keep his nose positioned correctly. He was still losing altitude, unable to overcome the basic laws of physics. His stomach shot into his throat, then fell like a stone to his feet: he was climbing.

He hit his flares and the stores of chaff, desperate to confuse the UAVs any way possible. He could see one of them flying about a mile away, just ahead, banking to come back after overshooting him.

The aircraft was roughly the size of Flighthawk 3s, but with a profile closer to an X-48. Stubby wings extended from a wing-in-body design just like the Gen 4 Flighthawk. But there were a pair of small turbojets at the rear, rather than the single engine of the Gen 4. A twin-boom tail sandwiched the engines, which, judging from the aircrafts' maneuvers, had directional thrust. Adjusting thrust from both engines also probably helped.

Suddenly the aircraft disappeared in a burst of smoke. Cowboy's AMRAAM had caught it.

But where was number two?

DANNY GRABBED THE LIEUTENANT'S M-16 AND RAN out to find Mofitt. He'd gotten about halfway across the compound to the mortar station when he saw a body lying flat on the ground.

Mofitt, he thought. Damn.

He ran to the body and slid down next to him. The man's head raised as he did.

It was Mofitt. He turned his face toward Danny's, his white cheeks covered with dirt.

"Where are you hit?" Danny asked.

"I . . . I don't know."

A mortar round whizzed overhead.

"Come on. Let's get you inside."

"I'm—uh—"

Danny scooped him into a fireman's carry and carried him back to the bunker. About twenty yards from the entrance, Mofitt seemed to lift off his shoulders. Danny became weightless, spinning around on the ground like a top that had just been pulled off the string. A hailstorm descended around him and he slammed into the ground, face-first.

A black and gray kaleidoscope danced around his head as he caught his breath. He knew what had happened—a mortar shell had hit nearby—but somehow he couldn't put that knowledge into any context, much less plan what to do next. His confusion seemed to last an eternity, and when it started to fade it was replaced by a heavy rolling sound, the kind a heavy steamroller would make if it were pushing his skull into the ground.

Danny got to his feet. Mofitt was nearby, on his knees, shaking his head. Danny tried to ask him if he was OK, then realized the blow had left him deaf.

It was a good thing they hadn't reached the bunker. The shell that had knocked him to the ground was a direct hit on a spot weakened by the earlier blasts. It had torn a massive gash in the roof near the entrance, splitting through the metal below the layer of sandbags and dirt.

Danny saw beams of light inside—flashlights. Two men ran up behind him, then began clawing at the dirt and debris that had fallen into the entrance.

Moving in what seemed like slow motion, Danny began to help. The six people who'd been in the bunker were all still alive, but in various degrees of shock. Lieutenant Juno was bleeding from an enormous gash at the top of his head, but his was the lightest injury; his radio man had a compound leg fracture and two broken ribs. Trevor Walsh, the Whiplash technician, was sitting at his bench, dazed and holding his limp right arm against a small but sucking wound at the side of his chest.

"They have lasers," he told Danny. "Turk just called it in."

Danny heard the words from a distance; his hearing was coming back.

"You're wounded," he told Walsh. He repeated it twice, unsure if he was garbling his words.

A corpsman ran in shouting orders, directing that the injured be taken to a second bunker being used as a med station. Danny pointed to him; Walsh got up slowly, trying to help.

The corpsman looked at him and told him to join the rest of the wounded, but Walsh refused, claiming he wasn't so hurt that he couldn't continue to do his job. He went back to his post, adjusted Danny's tablet, then promptly collapsed. The Marine com specialist, his face dotted with gashes and oozing blood, helped lift him onto a stretcher that had just been brought in, then took his spot.

"Colonel, I have Captain Thomas," the Marine told Danny. "He wants to know the situation."

Danny heard the words like faint echoes in the distance. That was a vast improvement from just a few minutes before.

"The radio?" Danny asked.

The Marine handed it to him.

"We're getting a lot of incoming," Danny said into the mike. "We just took a big blow to the command center. The lieutenant is out of action."

"The Ospreys are heading for us," said Captain Thomas. "I'm going to leave a platoon to mop up. The rest of us are coming back."

"We'll hold the fort until then," said Danny. "Wait—"

He leaned over and looked at Walsh's large sitrep screen, which was showing the radar feed from the Global Hawk.

"There's a road about a quarter mile north of the force that's aiming at our northern perimeter," he told the captain. "Big enough for the Ospreys to land. Get them in there, roll them up."

"Affirmative. Can you give me coordinates?"

"I'm going to give you back to your guy who's looking at everything from the UAVs and aircraft. He'll punch this stuff straight to you. Right?"

"Got it, Colonel."

As he put down the radio handset, Danny realized his hearing had returned just in time: he could hear gunfire on the perimeter.

"You stay here," he told the com specialist. "Anyone else who can stand, grab your rifle and come with me."

2

Washington, D.C.

ZEN WOULD HAVE HAD TO HAVE BEEN THE STUPIDEST person in Washington *not* to realize that Todd's overture to him meant she wasn't going to run for President. He would also have to be extremely naive to interpret anything she said as a guarantee that she definitely would support him if he decided to run.

However . . .

At the moment, at least, she was clearly disposed to helping him. And her support would be useful within the party.

Mostly, anyway. And outside the party it was surely a liability. The administration was under virulent attack for what critics and much of the media called its hawkish worldview.

The funny thing was, Zen thought it wasn't hawkish enough.

Be that as it may, his main questions now were: why was Todd not going to run for reelection, and why was she backing him?

He could guess the answer to the latter: she loathed the vice president, who, as he'd told her, would be the most likely candidate, and on foreign policy matters Zen's views were probably the closest to hers in Congress.

So why wasn't she going to run? Did she fear impeachment, which the opposition party was always talking about? Several House members even submitted bills to do just that, but they had never made it out of committee, let alone to the floor of the House. Her allies held a small but firm majority in the House that usually kept the opposition in its place, but there was always the danger that she would do something to anger just enough of them to tip things against her.

So *did* he want to be President?

It was what every little boy wanted, wasn't it?

It had been. Eons ago. These days, only madmen and maniacs wanted to be President.

Zen smiled at himself. He was a little of both. Every fighter pilot was.

There were other things he wanted. Walking again topped the list.

After all these years in a wheelchair, after everything he'd achieved, in the back of his mind that remained a deep desire. Deprived of so much . . .

Had he been, though? One could argue that he'd gotten everything out of life that a man could possibly want: adventure, a great career, a wonderful wife, the most beautiful and brightest daughter in the world—

"Dad?"

He broke from his reverie and saw his daughter Teri standing in front of him. From the looks of things, she'd been there for quite a while.

"Thinking about *senating* again," said the eight-year-old in a voice that dripped of satire. She was never cuter than when she was being impertinent.

"As a matter of fact, I was," said Zen.

"Well, I'm hungry. When are we eating?"

He glanced at his watch—it was closer to bed-time than to dinnertime.

Ouch! That wonderful wife was going to kill him.

"We're eating right now," he told her. "Get your coat."

"My coat?"

"You don't want McDonald's?"

"Yeah!" said his daughter, running from the room as if she'd just won the lottery.

If only every political decision were so easy.

3

Malaysia

BY THE TIME TURK REALIZED WHERE THE OTHER AIR-craft was, it was nearly too late. He threw his wing down hard and hit his flares and chaff, desperate to get his butt out of the pip of the attacking UAV. Fortunately, the laser's relatively small size and its need to pause and recycle between bursts meant that it had only a few milliseconds on target before he was able to dance away. Even so, the high-energy beam put a nasty black streak on the side of the fuselage, momentarily raising the temperature in the engine into the red. Turk jerked the stick and worked his pedals, trying to jink as unpredictably as possible and confuse the always logical computer guiding the UAV. Then, falling way too low to build enough speed to run away, and worried about the engine blowing up, he pulled the fighter into as tight a turn as it could manage and held on, hoping the UAV might make a mistake and turn inside him.

That didn't happen. But when he checked the radar, he realized the enemy aircraft was gone. Somewhere in the middle of his crazy dance he'd shaken free.

"Basher Two, how's your plane?" asked Cowboy.

"I'm OK." Turk glanced at his panel and realized that the alert on the engine was off; whatever harm the laser had done wasn't permanent, or at least wasn't affecting him at the moment.

"You're going in circles," said Cowboy.

"Yeah, I know. I can't locate the UAV."

"It's low."

"Yeah."

Finally, the UAV popped back onto his radar screen. It was below him, barely five feet over the trees, and running northwest toward the water.

Home?

"I'm turning to follow Bandit Two," Turk told Cowboy.

"I have your six."

DANNY FREAH GATHERED SIX MEN AS HE RAN ACROSS the compound. He found another half-dozen spread out along the sandbags and shallow trench at the north side of the camp.

"We need ammo!" said the sergeant who'd taken charge. He was lying on the ground next to the Marine manning a 50-caliber heavy machine gun. "Ammo!"

Danny sent two of the men back to get bullets and waved the others along the trench.

"They're about fifty meters down," said the sergeant, pointing to the trees. "We just beat the first element back. How the hell did they get so close without us seeing them?"

"The water vapor off the stream that runs down

in that direction casts a shadow on the IR sensors," said Danny. "Somebody was pretty damn smart about what our gear can see."

A bullet flew nearby. One of the Marines responded with his M-16.

"Hey! Hold your fire unless you have a definite target," shouted the sergeant. He turned back to Danny. "If they charge, they can overwhelm us. I just polled everyone and we're down to two mags apiece. The machine gun has ten rounds left."

"We can ambush them from the side," said Danny, looking across the terrain. "Get them off balance."

"Good idea if we had more ammo, Colonel."

"It's coming. If they attack before that, we'll have to make them think we do. Just enough to stall them."

"OK."

"I need two volunteers," shouted Danny.

Every one of the men, including the sergeant, put up their hands.

"Just two," said Danny.

All the hands remained.

"Pick two guys. You have to stay here," Danny told the sergeant. "We'll wait until the force starts moving forward, then we cut them from the side. It'll stop them, or at least it should."

"*If* you can get to the flank," said the sergeant as a fresh volley sounded from below. "And if they don't decide to charge you."

4

An island in the Sembuni Reefs

Lloyd Braxton looked up from the screen in disgust. The American fighters had managed to shoot down one of the two Vector UAVs. The autonomous program in the surviving fighter was locked in interceptor mode, and would keep fighting the other aircraft.

That was foolish. But its next logical decision—which it would make if it concluded that the battle was hopeless—would be to return to the base it had taken off from.

That was even worse.

Braxton could override those commands, issuing new ones to direct it to the second pickup point. But if he did, his signal would tell the Americans where he was. He'd be forced to switch bases sooner than he wanted. The rebels were about to overrun the American base, but that would hardly compensate for this setback.

The UAV wasn't ready to challenge the Dreamland technology. But that was why he wanted the Sabres in the first place.

Braxton slammed his hand on the console, then got up and paced around the small cabin. When he calmed down, he went back and gave the UAV the command to fly to another area and, if possible, fight. With that done, he hit the self-destruct sequence on the control gear, then picked up his low-chance-of-intercept radio.

"We have to move," he said, informing the others before gathering his gear to leave.

5

Malaysia

DANNY WAITED UNTIL THE MEN CAME BACK WITH THE ammo before setting out. His two Marines were privates nicknamed Fern and Monk—short for Geraldo Fernandez and Terry Monsuer. Fern was a recruiting poster Marine, six-four, bulging biceps, quick smile. Monk was nearly a foot shorter, and may very well have weighed less than one of Fern's legs.

"We go south, then cut back across the ravine," Danny told them, drawing a map on his palm. "There's a little creek there we'll take up to their flank."

"Right," said Fern.

Monk nodded beside him.

"You guys been in combat before?" Danny asked.

"Ten minutes ago," said Fern.

Monk nodded again.

"That'll do," said Danny, starting out.

The Marines had night gear and Danny had his glasses, but there was enough light around the cleared perimeter for them to use their Mark 1 eyeballs and still see well enough to fight. Danny ran along the defense line, head lowered toward his chest. His mind was clear; adrenaline and the necessary excitement of battle had pushed away all of the little wounds and distractions. He could even hear well enough to discern the sound of brush moving in the distance—the rebels were getting ready to make another charge.

He found the cut and started down the hill, sliding on his butt after about ten feet. The rough stones bruised his hands and legs, but he ignored the light pain, moving across the open ground the Marines had cut to give themselves a clear field of vision and fire. He saw an opening in the trees on his right and headed for it, cutting off Monk as he ran. Four steps into the jungle he stopped—the foliage was so thick overhead that he could no longer see without switching the glasses to infrared.

"Your gear working?" he asked the others.

"Yup!" said Fern.

"Take point," he told Fern.

The Marine grinned and moved ahead, using his night gear to guide them in a winding trail east. Danny and Monk followed. It took ten minutes of trotting and pushing through the brush to reach the point near the creek where Danny had decided they would take their turn. When they stopped, Monk held his finger up and then pointed to his ear.

Men were moving nearby.

A rifle sounded. The rebels were making their attack.

"Can you see them?" Danny asked Fern.

"Negative."

"We need to get closer and get their attention," he said. "Drop when you see them."

THE UAV DIPPED DOWN SO LOW AS IT CAME TO THE shoreline that Turk thought for sure it was diving in. But it continued forward, accelerating to near Mach speed while still managing to fly bare inches over the top of the waves.

Turk could go either as low or as fast as the UAV. But not both. He stayed high, but even so, his passive infrared sensor lost the aircraft.

"Two, you still have him?" asked Cowboy.

"Stand by." The long range scan caught the aircraft as it turned. "He's got four miles on me, angling north. I'm losing ground."

"Fast little devil."

Little was the operable word, as far as the radar was concerned; depending on its angle to the sensors, the aircraft's profile ranged from the size of a swallow to that of a bumblebee. The faceted silhouette had been designed to make it difficult to track from several common angles, rear included.

"I'm going to juice the afterburner and angle north," Turk told Cowboy. "I can come on at a different angle and have a better chance of seeing him."

"You better check your fuel, Air Force. We don't have tankers waiting to gas us up."

"Yeah. I think I can make it," hedged Turk. He made a mental calculation—unless the UAV landed in ten minutes, he'd be into his reserves heading back. "You stay on the heading you're at. I'll do the tracking."

"Roger that. Don't run dry. It's a long swim home."

"Two," said Turk, acknowledging with his call sign.

DANNY SAW FLASHES IN THE BRUSH TO HIS LEFT A second before Fern dropped to his knees. A dozen shadows were moving about twenty yards ahead, focused on the base perimeter.

"There," whispered Monk, coming up behind him.

"Yeah," answered Danny.

Fern had his hand up, watching. Gunfire erupted from the base perimeter, which was roughly two hundred yards away on their left; the rebel vanguard was at the edge of the wood line in front of them, with more rebels behind, just to Danny's right.

"Fire!" yelled Danny, pointing his rifle at the nearest shadows.

The enemy didn't react at first, oblivious in their charge. But Danny's gunfire found its mark, and before a full minute had passed the shadows stopped coming. They were on their bellies in the brush, either cut down or taking cover.

"Grenade!" yelled Fern, tossing one.

"Fire in the hole," answered Monk, throwing one of his own.

Danny saw shapes moving on his right and fired, emptying his magazine. Fern threw another grenade, then a third, as the rebels turned to answer their fire.

Bullets pinged around them, the rebels changing their targets. Danny slid to the ground. Another mag was taped to the one he'd emptied; he loaded it and began returning fire, aiming at the flashes.

The grenades cut down a sizable portion of the rebel force. Confused and no longer confident, they began to fall back. The machine gun at the perimeter began to fire, and suddenly the main body of rebels was retreating. A mortar shell landed in the middle of their path, and the retreat turned into a rout. The assault had been broken.

"Fall back!" yelled Danny, concerned that they might be shot by their own forces if they pursued the fleeing rebels. "Let's go."

They moved back slowly, in proper order—the closest man to the enemy trotted back, tapping his companion as he passed, then taking up a position to lay down covering fire as the others repeated the process. In a few moments they reached the creek where they had started. Danny heard the drone of Ospreys in the distance—the reinforcements had arrived.

"Back to the perimeter," he told his companions. "Good job."

TURK FOUND THE LITTLE UAV ON HIS LEFT, SIX MILES ahead of him. It was well over the water now, heading toward the collection of reefs and tiny islands off the coast.

The UAV had dropped its speed to five hundred knots. Turk lost his radar contact but found that he could make it reappear by tucking his nose down, subtly altering the angle of the radar waves without actually changing course. At 8,000 feet above sea level, he had just enough altitude to play with to keep the target aircraft on his screen.

He tried hailing the Whiplash operator back at the Marine base to see if he was picking up anything else from the Global Hawk, but got no answer.

The reefs and rocks below had long been a collection of hazards for mariners. Most of the rocks dotting the area were either submerged or too small to be inhabited, but there were larger islands in the Ebeling Reefs and the neighboring Sembuni Reefs to the north big enough for the aircraft to land on. Ships passing up from the Java Sea mostly steered through a channel to the west to avoid the hazards. The outer islands and reefs had lately become a haven for pirates, who, though not as accomplished as the pirates off Somalia, practiced the same sort of extortion.

Finally the UAV disappeared from his screen, and Turk couldn't find it. He tucked down, rose, tucked down, moved a bit left then angled east. A brief flicker hit the radar, then nothing.

"I think he's turning east," he told Cowboy.

"My scope is clear."

"Yeah."

"Whiplash Base to Basher Two," said Rubeo, radioing from the Cube over the squadron frequency. "Captain Mako, are you reading me?"

"Two. Go ahead."

"What's your situation?"

"I just lost contact."

"The base has released the Global Hawk and we're flying it back in your direction. It should be in range in five minutes."

Five minutes would be an eternity, but there was nothing to be done about that.

"Some of the people here think it may have doubled back to the island of Brunei," added Rubeo. "Do you have an opinion on that, Captain? Is it feasible?"

"Negative on that," said Turk. "He would have come past us. No way he did that."

"Not even at low altitude?"

"Negative."

"What is your theory?"

"He's got to be heading toward one of those reef islands."

"Thank you," said Rubeo. "Continue your pursuit as you feel fit. Do not endanger yourself further."

"Roger that," said Turk, surprised that the normally coldhearted scientist was actually concerned about his well-being.

Contrast that with Breanna, he thought.

"Where do you think he is?" asked Cowboy, who'd heard the conversation.

"Just like I said, heading for a landing somewhere ahead."

"Might be flying to Vietnam or western Indonesia," said Cowboy.

"He doesn't have the fuel," said Turk. "The airframe is too small. He's gotta land soon. On one of these islands."

"These aren't islands," said Cowboy. "They're spits of dirt."

"He won't need much to land."

Turk started cutting different angles in the sky, altering the direction of his forward and side radars. He got a few blips in the general direction the UAV had been taking but then nothing. It would have at least a ten mile lead on them now; the chase was essentially over.

As good as the sensors aboard the Lightning II were—and they were the best in the "conventional" fighter fleet, and by extension the world—the size and stealth characteristics of the UAV were better, at least at this range. Turk decided that his only option was to hit the gas—he selected his afterburner again, juicing Basher Two over the sound barrier. He held his speed for only a few moments, knowing that every millisecond of acceleration was costing him fuel, and in turn lessening his time in the air.

The UAV popped onto the screen, closer than he thought: five miles away.

It turned to a heading almost exactly between north and east, and for a few moments he had a profile of it from the rear side quarter. Rather than adjusting his course to follow, Turk adjusted his course to parallel it. He got another fleeting glimpse, then another, then lost it.

There's a way to make this work, Turk told himself. *Go farther north and flip around.*

"I'm going to jump ahead," he told Cowboy. "You stay on the present course."

"You want me to follow?"

"No, stay on your heading," said Turk. "You're going in the general direction. I'm going to slide around a bit and try and get a good radar on him. I have an idea."

"Sounds dangerous."

Turk hit his afterburner again, riding it for three seconds before backing off. He started a turn, aiming to push the nose of the plane at the UAV's rear fuselage. He found it only three miles away—the drone had slowed considerably.

"You better check your fuel, Two," said Cowboy.

"Yeah, I know. Listen, Bandit is down to two hundred knots. Gotta be looking to land."

"Where? There's nothing out here."

Cowboy was right. The reef tips were so small even a seagull couldn't call them home.

"He may just be slowing down for fuel conservation," answered Turk.

Or maybe he was running out of fuel. Turk was suddenly closing on the contact at a good rate; its forward speed was down to 150 knots.

"I'm thinking he's going to crash," Turk told Cowboy.

Two seconds later the UAV disappeared from the screen.

6

The Cube

AT SOME POINT RAY RUBEO STOPPED STUDYING THE data flowing across the screen and just stared at the simulation of the UAV in flight. It was impressive, all the more so because it had been developed without the help of a massive government program.

True, vast amounts of it had been stolen or inspired by his own work. Still, to have constructed something so smart and capable—the scientist in Rubeo couldn't help but admire the ingenuity.

But he wasn't here to admire someone else's work—especially when that other person seemed bent on destroying everything he had worked for.

Rubeo tapped his screen, changing the window to see an analysis of real-time performance data. He was surprised to find that the screen was no longer updating.

"What happened?" he asked his team back in New Mexico.

"The UAV appears to have crashed or stopped operating," said Kristen Morgan, one of the operators handling communications with him. "It's off their radars and nothing they do will bring it back. They're close enough to pick it up, or they were."

"Command signals?"

"If there were, the Global Hawk was too far away to pick them up. When you diverted it to protect the base—"

"Yes, I understand. A necessary decision." Rubeo scowled. It was a chess match, and one had to protect his pieces until an advantage could be had. "Compile the data as soon as you can. We need models, everything we discussed."

"Will do."

"And how are we coming with the file on Braxton and his associates?"

"It's thicker than it was. We have a whole range of his shell companies and some contractors."

"Keep working on it," said Rubeo. "Update my files here every hour."

"Not a problem."

"Something he's done will give him away," Rubeo told her. "As brilliant as he clearly is."

7

Malaysia

BY THE TIME DANNY GOT BACK TO THE COMMAND bunker, most of the debris had been cleared and the systems restored. Lieutenant JG Cathy Talaria had taken over and replaced the wounded with fresh staff.

Walsh was back, chest bandaged and arm in a sling.

"Are you OK?" Danny asked.

"Broken arm. The rest is nothing."

"Don't—"

"They lost the UAV," said the techie, changing the subject. He was here for his brain but he shared the tough-as-nails will of the rest of the Whiplash team. "I have the Global Hawk running a search pattern in the area. It has to land soon, at least according to our calcs. It slowed way down before we lost final contact, so it may have crashed."

"Where?"

"Not sure, Colonel. Turk thinks over the water. But it's just a guess."

"Hmmm." Danny leaned down to look at the console. Walsh had a map up on one of the screens showing the approximate search location. There were several small islets in the area, but none were big enough to support a full base. All had been scouted even before Danny first arrived to look for a base; as far as they could tell there were none.

"If it crashes, we need to recover it," said Danny. "Hopefully before it sinks."

"Not going to be easy, Colonel. They're roughly a hundred miles from shore. And that's at a minimum."

"Better to try than give up." Danny went over to Talaria and told her what he wanted to do.

"If Captain Thomas says we can spare the men, I'll lead a squad myself, sir," said the young woman.

"That's your captain's call," said Danny. "Where are the Ospreys?"

"They're both on the ground getting refueled and checked over," said Talaria.

"I'm going to talk to the pilots. Tell Thomas

what I want to do, and ask him to detail a squad to help me, if possible."

TURK FLEW OVER THE AREA WHERE HE'D LOST THE radar contact. There was nothing but dark, empty ocean. He settled into a widening orbit as he searched.

"Basher One, do you have a contact?" he asked his wingman.

"Negative, Two. What are you seeing?"

"Nothing."

"You think he crashed?"

"Possibly," answered Turk. Even in daylight it would have been hard to detect the fragments of the small aircraft on the surface of the ocean. Now, without a fire, there wouldn't be enough for the passive IR sensor to pick up either.

Turk stared out of the cockpit, frustrated. They'd come so far, only to lose the damn thing.

"Basher Two, check your fuel gauges," said Cowboy. "How good are you at treading water, Air Force?"

Turk glanced at his fuel gauge and did some quick math. He had about forty-one minutes of fuel left . . . and it would take about eighteen to get home. They had planned to land with about twenty minutes of reserve, a generally prudent mark.

"I'm a lousy swimmer," Turk told Cowboy. "I'm about three minutes to bingo. I have enough fuel for two more minutes. The Global Hawk is flying this way."

"Basher Two, do you have contact with your bandit?" asked Walsh, back at the Marine base.

"Negative. Lost it. We're trying to get a visual or something, anything, on a wreckage."

"Be advised the Global Hawk just had a fleeting contact about fifteen nautical miles east of where you are. I'm heading the aircraft in that direction. Stand by for a vector."

"Roger that," said Turk, altering his course as Walsh read out the heading. It was almost exactly due east of the point where he'd lost the aircraft.

"Hey, Air Force, you don't have the fuel for this," said Cowboy.

"I got twenty minutes of reserve."

"Turk—"

"Don't worry, I'm not going to break your plane," answered Turk.

"That ain't it, dude," responded Cowboy. "If we have to punch out, I can't swim."

DANNY STRAPPED HIMSELF INTO THE COPILOT'S SEAT OF the Osprey and hung on as the aircraft began its short taxi down the runway. With no way to quickly tie the Osprey pilot directly into the Whiplash communications system, they'd settled for a low-tech solution—he would relay information to the pilot as he spoke through his own gear. It was easier to do that from the second officer's seat.

An unconventional solution, but the Marines liked to brag that they could adapt to any situation, and they seemed determined to prove it tonight.

"What's our ETA to the area?" Danny asked the pilot after they'd swooped into the sky.

"Fifty minutes, give or take, depending on the final location," he told him. "Faster if I could go over Brunei."

"No," said Danny. "Hold off on that. If we get an actual sighting, and if there's a need, then we'll do it. On my responsibility. But I don't want to cause a ruckus without a very good reason."

"You're the boss."

THE UAV HAD SLOWED TO EIGHTY KNOTS BY THE TIME Turk got it on his radar. It had climbed as well; it was now at 8,000 feet.

Why had it climbed?

Eighty knots was slow, possibly close to the slowest speed the aircraft could go and remain flying. It was continuing to decelerate, all the while staying at the same altitude—surely it would have to stall in a matter of moments.

"Basher Two, I'm one mile behind you," said Cowboy. "I have the contact on the radar. It's five miles away."

"Roger. Copy."

"How is it flying?" asked Cowboy. "Airspeed is dropping through seventy knots?"

"Copy."

"What— Damn! Did he just blow up?"

"He just deployed a parachute," said Turk, interpreting the new radar returns. "Come on—we want visuals."

"Remember your fuel."

"Roger." Turk glanced at the gauge. He had ten minutes of his reserve time left . . . and that was with a good tailwind.

But there it was, descending less than two miles from him. He clicked on the radio to tell Walsh.

"Roger that. Global Hawk is three minutes away. Is there a ship there?"

"Negative. Nothing."

"Colonel Freah and a team of Marines are heading there to see if they can recover it. Can you stand by until they arrive? They're about forty minutes off."

"Can't do it," said Cowboy, breaking in. "We don't have the fuel."

"Understood," answered Walsh.

"SORRY FOR INTERRUPTING," COWBOY TOLD TURK. "But I don't want you doing anything rash."

"I wasn't gonna."

"Not a problem, then."

"Roger that."

Cowboy leaned his head to the side until his helmet touched the canopy. The night vision in the helmet made it possible to see, though the range was somewhat limited.

"I see the chute," he told Turk. "It's going down slow. Nothing there, though."

"Yeah."

Earlier, Cowboy had entertained a fantasy of using the F-35B's vertical landing ability to touch down near the UAV's landing spot, grab the thing, and take off. But that wouldn't work here, even as a fantasy.

"Why parachute into the water?" he asked Turk. "Why the hell not just crash and be done with it."

"Probably just following its programming."

"Computers."

The UAV had fallen to 2,000 feet. Cowboy slowed Basher One to just over a hundred knots, watching it go down. The entire experience felt surreal, and for good reason: he was taking a leisurely spin around an aircraft that had tried to shoot him down less than an hour before.

"I wonder if I could snag the chute with my wheel," he told Turk.

"Hey, that's a great idea," answered Turk.

"No, no, I'm kidding."

"I'm going to take a shot at it," said Turk.

"What are you going to do if you catch it?"

"I'll bring it back to the base. Stand by."

TURK LINED UP THE CHUTE IN THE DEAD CENTER OF HIS windscreen. Snagging it was probably a one in a million shot, he thought, but even a slight chance was better than nothing.

The trick was to get close enough to the parachute so he could get it, but not have the engine ingest the cloth. What he needed was a big hook underneath—arresting gear would have been perfect. The tip of a missile might work—except that he didn't have any more.

That left his landing gear, as Cowboy had suggested.

A ridiculous long shot, and a dangerous one, but getting the UAV was high priority, and what the hell—as long as he didn't ingest the chute, there was no downside.

Besides, he'd faced longer odds in Iran, among other places.

The Lightning II shuddered as he deployed the landing gear, and Turk swore it was a reaction to the fact that he was lowering his gear with no land in sight.

The parachute was at 1,200 feet. He had time for one pass, maybe two.

Bitchin' Betty gave him a stall warning as he eased closer to the target. He nudged the throttle slightly, saw the canopy coming on his left side . . .

Too far!

Turk pushed his rudder pedal, sliding in the air.

Come on, baby!

His left wing knifed toward the floating nylon blanket. Turk held steady, not even daring to breathe.

"Missed," said Cowboy. "Damn close. It ducked to the side at the last second."

Turk hadn't counted on the vortex of wind under the aircraft; it had pushed the chute out at the last second, whipping it below and past the wheel.

"Let me try," said Cowboy.

"You're not low enough," said Turk, banking

for a second try. "Get into position to follow me. If I miss, you get it. Be careful not to get it in your engine intakes."

"Yeah, I can see that."

As Turk came out of the turn, he realized that the parachute had fallen faster than he'd thought it would; his wing had given it an extra push. He started to line up, then saw what looked like a whale with a unicorn's horn appear on the surface of the water.

"What the hell is that?" he asked Cowboy.

"Stand by."

Turk's warning system began to blare—a radar had appeared out of nowhere and was tracking him.

"What's going on?" he cursed, hitting his throttle for thrust and cleaning the gear. He came back on the stick, climbing to get higher and give himself room to maneuver.

"It's some sort of submersible," said Cowboy. "It's snagging the UAV."

Turk spun his head but was too far past the sub to see.

"It's in the water—watch out!"

There was a small burst about halfway up the line to the chute—an explosive device cut the connection between the UAV and its parachute. Meanwhile, the submarine dove below the water, the aircraft in tow.

"Damn," said Cowboy. "That's right out of *Star Wars*."

"Or Dreamland," said Turk, banking to try to get a look.

8

Suburban Virginia

Gᴇʀʀʏ "Bɪʀᴅ" Rᴏᴅʀɪɢᴜᴇᴢ ᴡᴀꜱ ɴᴏᴛʜɪɴɢ ʟɪᴋᴇ Zᴇɴ remembered him from Dreamland. There, he had been a quiet if hardworking junior scientist; now he was not only self-assured and expansive, but clearly well off: he had arrived at the restaurant in a Mercedes S, and the watch on his sleeve looked to be a Patek.

He'd also put on quite a bit of weight since the days they played pickup basketball together back at Dreamland, before Zen's accident. At six-eight, Rodriguez was tall enough to be a domineering presence under the basket in any pickup game, but had been so thin that you could miss him if he turned sideways. Now there was no missing him at all. Well-proportioned for his size and ruggedly handsome, he dominated the restaurant like he dominated the paint.

"I'm glad we were finally able to make our schedules mesh," said Rodriguez. "You're so damn busy."

"Not as busy as you," said Zen. They'd been trying to meet for two months.

The waiter came over and cleared their plates. Rodriguez ordered a scotch for dessert. Zen, who'd been drinking water with dinner, asked for a bourbon.

"We have several," said the waiter, who began reeling off a list of boutique brands, none of which Zen had heard of.

"Woodford?" Zen finally asked.

"Coming up," said the man approvingly before sweeping away.

"So what do you think, Zen?" asked Rodriguez. "Do you think you want to try?"

"It's very— It's an interesting idea."

"I know you've been through this a lot," said Rodriguez. "A lot of people have promised that you'll walk again. I can't make a promise. But this process has worked with two other people."

"But there's no guarantees."

"No. Exactly. It's an experiment. That's why we want you, after all."

"The fact that I'm a senator has nothing to do with it."

"No. It raises the bar for us—if we fail, obviously, that's real bad."

"If it succeeds, you have a lot of media attention."

Rodriguez shrugged, and Zen thought of an after-game beer session where Rodriguez had made a similar gesture about his thirty points, giving the credit to his guard—Zen. But even if he was being a bit disingenuous, he was right that they were taking risks themselves, and he'd already agreed to keep everything quiet as it proceeded.

And in any event, so what? If it was a chance to walk again, what was the difference?

"Explain a little more," said Zen. "How much of me are you going to cut up?"

"Just the good parts." Rodriguez took him through the cell grafting techniques—he'd tried something like that in his last year at Dreamland—

but lost Zen when he began talking about the nanolevel microchips that would be placed in his spine and legs.

The drinks came; Zen savored the sweet burn of the bourbon in his mouth.

"It's a long process," continued Rodriguez. "Over the course of a year, like I said. We have to put you into a coma—three times."

"Just three?" joked Zen.

"Yeah. If it works. That bit's only for a few days, but it adds up." Rodriguez laughed nervously. "To you, it'll feel like you're sleeping."

"But I eventually wake up."

"Yeah, that part I can guarantee. Almost guarantee," Rodriguez corrected himself. "That part is basically like a normal medical procedure. It's done every day at hospitals for patients in trauma."

"So this is trauma?"

"Sure. Think about it—it's the reverse of what you went through at Dreamland. You're coming back in the other direction."

That made more sense to Zen than the nanochips.

"The rest of it is the risky stuff," said Rodriguez. "But we've done it on two other people. Whom we didn't have nearly as good medical histories of. So I'm pretty confident, or I wouldn't be here. That, and I still think of myself as your friend, and want to help."

Rodriguez had explained that his well-documented medical history and the length of time he'd been crippled were major assets to the program. When they were done, they would know a tremendous amount about the process and the human body's reaction to it.

"It's a three year commitment," added Rodriguez. "But only the first two are really heavy. After that, it's pretty much just real life."

Zen nodded. They finished their drinks in silence.

"Well, let me think about it," Zen told him.

"There's a lot to think about," said the scientist. "I would . . . I do need an answer relatively soon. A month, tops. There's one other candidate."

"And I have a limited window physically," said Zen, referring to something Rodriguez had said earlier.

"That's right. Your age. We're already pushing the envelope."

"Can't do anything about that," said Zen.

"Not yet." Rodriguez smiled. "Soon."

9

Offshore an island in the Sembuni Reefs

LLOYD BRAXTON BROUGHT THE BEER BOTTLE TO HIS lips and took a small sip. Brewed in Oregon by a small craft brewer, the vanilla porter had a slightly bitter taste; Braxton couldn't work out whether it was intentional or a by-product of its long trip to the South Pacific. He also couldn't decide if he liked it or not—the bitterness seemed to fit his mood, even if it gave the beer more bite than he would normally prefer.

The robot submersible had taken hold of the Vector UAV, so at least they had lost only one craft. The problem were the damn rebels—they were incompetent boobs who couldn't launch a simple attack on a lightly guarded outpost without getting their butts kicked. They'd fired only one of the guided rockets they'd been given, rather than massing them, as instructed. God only knew what other things they'd flubbed.

Hitting the Dreamland people with anything less than a knockout blow was a huge mistake. He'd seen that himself years before.

He still had hope. Whatever else, they'd been bloodied. They'd send a major team now. That would give him his chance.

He looked toward the shore, then glanced at his watch.

Thirty seconds.

Braxton took another sip of his beer, letting the bitterness eat the sides of his mouth. He liked it, he decided; he would order more. Assuming that was ever possible.

A sharp slap echoed over the water. Braxton raised his head and stared at the island, but there wasn't enough light to see what was happening there. He had to settle for the sound of the settling dust and the birds that were fleeing the explosion. The underground compound, his home for the past six months, had just been blown up. Dirt and rocks covered what had once been one of the most advanced private computer setups in the world.

He had others. Braxton turned to the wheel-house.

"Take us below," he told the captain. "We're running behind schedule."

10

Malaysia

BY THE TIME TURK TURNED BACK TOWARD THE SUBMA-rine, it was underwater. His finger practically itched as he ran over the empty surface of the water, the cannon begging to be used, though it would be pointless.

He had a more pressing problem now—he was tighter on fuel than he'd planned.

It got worse as they headed back. At first he thought he'd simply gone dyslexic and got two numbers mixed up. Then he realized that he was leaking. It was a slow dribble, but with his stores so low, it was enough to turn him into a glider well short of the runway.

"I think one of those laser shots got the fuel tank," he told Cowboy. "I'm going to have to think about putting down somewhere."

"Can you make it back to land?"

Turk studied the numbers. Home was out of the question, but he could make it back to the island.

Probably.

"There's a little airport at Kampung," said

Cowboy, naming one of the emergency alternatives the squadron had briefed. "It's near the coast. You might make that."

Turk had to look it up on the map. It was a small airport near the coast. It was reachable—but only if he went straight there. Which presented a problem.

"I can get there if I go over Indonesia," he told Cowboy.

"Better to do that than crash."

"Yeah."

Indonesia snaked around Malaysia on the western coast. Turk picked a spot that would take less than three minutes to cross.

He tuned to the printed radio frequency of the tower at Kampung but couldn't get a response to his hail; neither could Cowboy.

"Place may not be big enough to have a tower," said Cowboy.

"It has a published frequency," said Turk.

"Remember where we are, Air Force. This ain't America."

"Roger that."

The Indonesians had apparently been monitoring the flight, for he got a warning as he approached their territorial waters. He didn't respond to the initial hail, holding his course; by the time the controller radioed again, he was approaching land.

"I have a fuel emergency," he answered, deciding honesty was the best policy.

"Unknown flight, you are ordered to exit Indonesia airspace." The controller had a British accent.

"I intend to. I have a fuel emergency," he repeated. "I am heading for an emergency landing."

Turk wasn't exactly sure what the controller would say; anything from a threat to shoot him down to a gracious offer of assistance was possible. Instead, the controller simply said nothing, which was just fine with him. The Indonesians weren't about to scramble any of their aircraft after him in any event; all of the repercussion would happen after he landed.

Assuming he landed. Then again, if he didn't, he wouldn't care what the Indonesians did at all.

He was over their land long enough to picture himself in an Indonesian jail eating spiders and ants for dinner. It wasn't a pleasant vision, but he soon passed into Malaysian territory, where more mundane worries took over: how far could the F-35B glide without fuel?

The airport was fifteen miles away.

"Walsh, how are we coming with that tower?" Turk asked the Whiplash techie.

"Airport is closed. Has been for months," responded Walsh. "I'm looking at the field— pockmarked pretty bad. Rebels attacked it two or three times before they finally shut it down."

Turk was about to say that it would have to do when Bitchin' Betty interrupted.

"*Warning*," said the automated voice. "*Fuel emergency. Fuel emergency.*"

"No shit, you told me that already," he said.

"Turk, can you make it?" asked Cowboy.

"I can make it," said Turk, tightening his grip on the stick. The runway was five miles away, somewhere in the shadows of the land ahead, unlit and unready for him to land.

DANNY FREAH STARED OUT THE OSPREY'S SIDE window at the ocean. There was still a full hour before dawn, but he could see the ripples on the surface without night vision.

"The submarine is no more than ten miles from us, if that," he told the pilot. "Can we get into a search pattern?"

"Yes, sir."

The Osprey moved into a gentle arc toward the point Turk had given Danny. No matter how advanced it was, the submarine that grabbed the UAV had to be somewhere nearby, but the Osprey lacked gear to track it. The task force with the Marine MEU off the northern shore of Malaysia had antisubmarine assets, but the nearest vessel in the task force was over six hundred miles away.

"You sure it didn't just crash into the water?" asked the pilot. "I mean—submarine picking it up? Pretty far-fetched. For rebels, I mean."

"Not really," said Danny. "Drug smugglers use them off the coast of Florida and the Southeast all the time."

"Drug dealers?"

"These are small subs."

"A lot of money in drug dealing. Can't see it out here."

Danny didn't answer. The pilot didn't entirely understand what they were dealing with, but who could blame him? Small submersibles cost less than a large pleasure boat, but still—why would anyone spend so much money on such high tech to help a band of ragtag rebels?

Ragtag rebels who'd nearly overrun a Marine base, granted.

They'd do it if they were testing their gear. If he didn't know better, he would have sworn he was up against Dreamland itself.

But then that was why he'd been tasked out here to begin with.

"Colonel, I have no contacts anywhere within ten miles," said the pilot. "What do you want me to do, sir?"

"Take another few circuits," said Danny reluctantly. "If we don't see anything, let's go home."

"Yes, sir."

"CAN YOU GO VERTICAL?" COWBOY ASKED. HE'D zipped ahead to check the runway.

"No way," said Turk. "Even if I knew what I was doing. Not enough fuel."

"How much?"

"It's reading zero."

"South end of the field is beaten to shit. I'm thinking you have less than fifteen hundred feet of good cement to land on."

"Yeah."

"Tight but doable."

"I'll take your word for it."

"Come on, Air Force. You're Superman."

"Thanks," said Turk, who was feeling anything but super.

"Come ten degrees north and you'll line up."

Turk made the adjustment. The Bitchin' Betty circuit was having a stroke, warning about fuel, speed, altitude, and the fact that he hadn't brushed his teeth in a week. None of this would be a problem, he told himself, if he could just see the damn runway. It was ahead *somewhere*, but even the vaunted low-light abilities of the F-35's helmet couldn't pick it out.

As he pushed over a cultivated field, Turk thought of using it, but by then it was too late.

"You see the runway?" asked Cowboy.

"Negative, negative."

"Push your rudder, dude. You're off three degrees."

"Which way?" demanded Turk.

"Right."

Turk eased his foot on the pedal.

In daylight, this would have been a breeze. Why the hell couldn't he see it?

His landing lights caught a blank expanse in front of him, then a seam in the ground—the edge of the runway just to the right, as Cowboy had said. Turk started to exhale, then realized he was flying in utter silence: the engine had just run out of fuel.

Bitchin' Betty was not pleased.

"Yeah, yeah," he told the machine. "Watch this."

He held the airplane in a glide just long enough to clear the worst of the holes the rebels had dug with their mortar shells. The F-35B's undercarriage groaned as he bounced across the ripped surface. It jerked to the right as he got the nose wheel down, but held enough concrete to brake just before hitting the turf at the far end of the runway.

Down! And in one piece!

Turk popped the canopy open and climbed up out of the seat. He suddenly felt cold and wet—he'd been sweating so much his suit was soaked through.

Cowboy passed overhead, wagging his wings.

There was a light in the sky a few miles off, coming from the south—it was the Marine Osprey from the base, heading toward him with fuel and a team of mechanics to patch up the plane.

I hope they got beer, thought Turk. And a lot of it.

11

The Cube

RAY RUBEO STARED AT THE LARGE SCREEN AT THE front of the conference room and its map of the area where the UAV and submarine had disappeared. A yellow circle showing the area the submarine could be in slowly expanded.

"Ray?" Breanna leaned across the table toward him. "Are you with us?"

"Yes. You said it's the Vector program," he recounted, still staring. "Submarine launched UAVs. I agree."

"The Vector program was a study for the

Navy that Dreamland participated in," Breanna told Reid. "It used the AI from Gen 4 in a sub-launched variant. The airfoils are different. Jennifer Gleason worked on both."

"And this Braxton fellow?" asked Reid.

"He would have been involved as well."

"The aircraft was recovered by a small submarine, roughly the size of a pleasure boat," said Breanna. "There are a lot of similar craft in Australia and on our coast—rich people's toys. They don't go very deep or very fast, but they're hard to detect by surface ships or planes that aren't looking for them. And the Navy doesn't keep track of something so small."

"Yes," said Rubeo. He got up from his seat and walked toward the wall, staring at the map.

"Wouldn't it have to be pretty substantial to launch a plane?" asked Reid. "Even a small one."

"They didn't launch from the sea," said Rubeo.

"How do you know?" asked Reid.

"You said it yourself, the submarine is too small. The most difficult problem to solve has to do with wings. The wingspan here is too large for the submersible we saw. The submarines are used for recovery only. And it may have been a backup in any event. Remember, it was being pursued, and its mate had been shot down."

"I still see an Iranian or Chinese connection," said Reid. "For me, the submarine clinches it. It could be working with a larger ship."

"Braxton hates governments, all governments." Rubeo pictured the young man: bright red hair, skin so white it seemed almost opaque. Quiet, as a general rule, but when he did talk, passion glared behind his bright green eyes. He was a pure libertarian, a young man who thought Locke was practically a fascist, and had in fact told Rubeo so one late night. Science had to be pure and divorced from the corruption of governments and anything that stole individual freedom.

So governments are a necessary evil? Rubeo had asked.

Governments are evil, period, Braxton answered.

"Politics and war make for strange bedfellows," said Reid. "He may very well have decided that to accomplish his Kallapsis or whatever his nirvana is called, he needs to take temporary steps with temporary alliances."

Reid went back to his spot at the conference table. Waving his hand over the surface, he brought up a virtual keyboard and commanded a small window to appear in the main screen. Typing furiously, he tapped into the joint intelligence network, then over to the Navy tracking site where the latest fleet data was kept. The program showed the last known positions of all fleet vessels, American and foreign. He zeroed in on the South China Sea, then filtered for submarines. The nearest submarines—both American vessels—were several hundred miles away; one was with the Marine task force and another was shadowing a Chinese carrier.

"I would expect that if they were working with the Chinese, we would see a Chinese vessel," said Rubeo. "I realize it's not definitive, but we have checked. I've checked."

"I've requested antisubmarine assets be moved into the area," added Breanna. "The problem is, the Navy doesn't have a lot of them, and they're stretched thin as they are."

A patrol aircraft was being detailed from Japan and would be on station within twenty-four hours. But the Navy was scrambling to find not only a secure base closer to the area that it could use, but a relief plane to extend the search times. Antisubmarine air patrol was not glamorous, and with the demise of the Cold War, had never received the funding it deserved.

"At the moment, our elint drones are the best bet," Breanna said. "We can go back and look at all transmissions in the area, and try correlating that with places that might be used as bases, both offshore and in Indonesia and Brunei."

"It must be offshore," said Reid. "If it were in Brunei or Indonesia we'd have picked it up."

"In a way, it's certainly simpler for us if it's offshore. But the modeling of the possible airport hasn't found any matches."

"The modeling must be wrong," said Reid.

"Obviously. Ray?"

He looked at her.

"If we can get close to one of these, can we take it over?" Breanna asked. "Since it uses our coding?"

"We're looking for vulnerabilities," he said. "There aren't many."

"Isn't there a way to convince it that it belongs to us?" Reid asked.

"Only if Jennifer Gleason told it to," said Rubeo. "And she doesn't appear to have done that."

Malaysia

DANNY FREAH RAN HIS HAND OVER HIS HEAD, MOPPING off the sweat, as he walked down the rear ramp of the Osprey after landing back at the Marine base. He'd never been a big fan of hot weather, and the wet heat of the South China Sea was starting to get to him.

Captain Thomas was waiting on the tarmac.

"Colonel, a word," said the Marine officer, in a tone that suggested he was barely holding his temper. He turned and began stomping toward the bunker.

Danny had heard about Turk's fuel problems, and while he would have preferred it if the pilot had contacted him before crossing Indonesian airspace, it was nonetheless far superior to allowing the aircraft to crash. Washington had already rung with the protests, and Danny was sure the heat was being turned on the administration. But he couldn't figure how the fallout had gotten to Thomas—"stuff" might roll downhill, but the Marine ground commander had no role at all in the decision. At this point, the operation was Danny's, and there shouldn't be any "stuff" falling on any of the Marines, let alone Thomas.

Danny sighed to himself and followed along, prepared not only to defend his pilot but to tell Thomas the facts of life, as gently as possible. He was a good commander; no need for him to get bent out of shape.

Though cleared of major debris, the bunker looked somewhat worse for wear. Several piles of dirt lined the side, and a mangled desktop had been propped against the wall. The Marines had determined that the damage had been done by some sort of rocket rather than a mortar shell. There was no evidence yet about whether or not it was guided, but the direct hit made them strongly suspect that it was.

Thomas had reestablished his "office" in a small corner at the rear. His backup satellite link and other com gear had been set up on a portable table; a laptop was on the floor. It wasn't the most private spot in the world, but the two other men in the bunker were wearing headsets.

"Where did you find Mofitt?" Thomas asked.

"Excuse me?" asked Danny, completely taken by surprise.

"Corporal Mofitt."

"When, during the attack?"

"Yes. I need to know."

It had only been a few hours ago, but so much had happened that Danny had trouble recalling the specifics of the incident. "I was running—he hadn't made it to the perimeter forces," he said. "He—I found him on the ground maybe fifty yards from them. No, I guess it was closer to the bunker, because I brought him back here. Or I started to. That's when we got hit."

"He had made it to the forces?" asked Thomas.

"No," said Danny. "I'm pretty sure he didn't get

there. Because they hadn't heard anything when I went back. What's this all about?"

"Mofitt wasn't hurt."

"Yeah, we were outside of the bunker when the missile or whatever it was hit."

"Before then. Somebody saw him standing in the compound, frozen, a little while before you came by," said the Marine captain. "I think he froze under fire."

"I don't know."

"I'm pretty sure."

"He was fine the other day," said Danny. That encounter was more vivid in his memory. "We had contact, we took fire, he shot back. He seems pretty reliable."

"I'm going to have him shipped out ASAP."

"Don't you think that's a little harsh?"

"No."

Danny mopped the sweat off the side of his head. "What does he say about it?"

"His opinion isn't worth asking."

"He didn't speak up for himself?"

"I haven't talked to him and I'm not going to. I don't need his side."

Shipping the kid out was one thing, but not speaking with him was something else. Danny had met plenty of unreasonably hardass officers in his career, but Thomas didn't come off like that. Maybe it was the fact that his people back at the base had been hit hard; very possibly he felt guilty over it.

Danny came around the desk. He didn't want the captain's men overhearing what he was going to say.

"I might dial it back a bit," he told the Marine. "I'd talk to him first. Sometimes, jumping to conclusions—"

"Maybe you can afford a chickenshit in the Air Force. We're Marines. We can't."

"I think you're forgetting who you're talking to," said Danny, still keeping his voice down.

"I'm not questioning *your* courage, Colonel," said Thomas. "Even if your reputation didn't precede you, I've seen you in action. You got more balls than half my men combined. And I don't have any chickenshits here. At all."

"I'm just saying you might lighten up and give him a chance to speak," said Danny. "And not necessarily for his benefit either. You don't want to come off like someone who just jumps the gun on guys. Talk to him, then decide what to do. Your other guys will notice that."

"What would you do if one of your people froze under fire?"

"First of all, I'm in a slightly different situation."

"How?"

"All of my guys are Tier One volunteers, with a lot of combat behind them," said Danny, using the military term for top-level special operations units. Like the Navy's DEVGRU and the Army's Delta Force, Whiplash had extremely high standards and expectations. "But, regardless, if that happened, before I did anything I'd talk to him. If he was good enough to work for me in the first place, then I owe him the respect of hearing his side of the story."

"*Counsel* him," said Thomas.

"That's the buzz word, yeah," said Danny. "But whatever. I don't know that I'd be trying to give him advice, but I'd talk to him. Maybe something happened that I didn't see. That's all I'm telling you."

Thomas frowned. Danny looked over and saw Walsh walking toward him.

"Colonel, sorry, but I have an urgent message from Ms. Stockard," said the techie. "I think they got a lead on the base the aircraft flew from."

PATCHED AND LOADED WITH A SMALL AMOUNT OF FUEL, Turk took the F-35 from the battered airstrip and headed south to the Marine base. By comparison it looked like a first-class regional airport: the mortar holes had been quickly patched, and there was a controller to welcome him in. The ground dogs waiting at the edge of the tarmac were as eager as any Air Force crew to get the plane back into action; they rushed up as soon as he came to a full stop.

"Thanks for getting my aircraft back in one piece," said the crew captain. "Course if you hadn't, I'm not sure the boys woulda left you in one piece."

"I'll keep that in mind next time," said Turk, pulling off his helmet.

"Ha ha, don't let ol' Gunny spook ya," said Cowboy, coming up and pounding his back. "Good work gettin' in back there. Boys said you came in with no power."

"I like to use every ounce of fuel," said Turk.

Then he turned serious. "Thanks for watchin' over me."

"Any time." Cowboy laughed. "The crew would have cut my legs off if I let anything happen to their plane. Although I think they're warming up to you a bit."

If he was correct, the sentiment didn't seem to extend to Colonel Greenstreet: the squadron leader was waiting for them in the makeshift squadron room/environmental shack/all-around squadron squat. He stared at Turk as the pilot entered.

"What the hell happened out there?" the colonel demanded as Turk began taking off his speed pants.

"We shot down one of the UAVs," said Turk. "Other one disappeared under the water."

"Yeah, but what happened to our plane?"

"Basically, it had a hole burned in the fuel tank," said Cowboy.

"I'm talking to Captain Mako, Lieutenant. Thank you for your input."

"They said something about it loosening a seam," said Turk, careful to keep his tone scientific. "The crew chief's gonna talk to some of our tech experts. They're real interested in the weapon."

"How did you get yourself in that position to begin with?" It was more an accusation than a question.

"He was saving my butt," said Cowboy. "If it weren't for him, I would've swam home."

Greenstreet shook his head, then sighed and walked out.

"Glad you're feeling better," said Cowboy to his back.

"Thanks for standing up for me," Turk told him.

"Hey, what are brothas for?" Cowboy laughed. Changing the subject, he said, "You fly against these kind of things all the time?"

"Enough."

"That's what I want to do," said Cowboy. "I'd love to get that sort of gig."

"As a test pilot?"

"Well, you're more than that, right? That's why you're out here."

"True."

"That's what I want to do," said Cowboy again.

"Really?"

"Damn straight."

"They may be looking for pilots soon," said Turk. He didn't think it necessary to tell Cowboy why.

"You're just saying that."

"No, really. I don't know what sort of qualifications they're going to want. But they probably are going to be interested in anyone who's already been in combat. Of course, you wouldn't only be flying F-35s. You probably wouldn't fly them at all."

"What do you have to do to sign up?"

"You have to talk to my boss, for starters."

"And you can get me in with him?"

"It's a her," said Turk.

"Oh, OK. Sorry."

"I'm just giving you a heads-up."

"Thanks. Do you think she'd want me?"

"I don't know what they'd be looking for, exactly," said Turk. "But I'll try and find out. And I'll put in a good word for you."

"Great. Let's go grab some food."

Another shoulder chuck started Turk out of the trailer and in the direction of the mess tent. But they'd only gotten halfway there when Danny Freah hailed them down—literally waving his arms to get Turk's attention.

"We have a possible ID on the submarine," he told Turk. "It's a civilian craft bought in New Zealand six months ago. We'd like you to take a look and see what you think."

"I didn't see it too well," confessed Turk. "Did you, Cowboy?"

"I think I can remember it."

"Come on, both of you."

"IT DOES LOOK LIKE THAT COULD BE IT," SAID COWBOY five minutes later. He was down on his hands and knees, face practically pushed into the screen of one of the Whiplash displays. A synthetic radar image of what might have been a small pleasure boat was on the screen.

It might have been a small pleasure boat. Or a submarine along the lines of a Seattle 1000, a luxury civilian submarine made by one of the preeminent companies in the business, U.S. Submarines. An engineer with the firm had studied the image and decided that, while the craft wasn't one built by his company, it *possibly* could be a submarine.

Which was roughly Cowboy's judgment as well. *Possibly.*

The submarine had been purchased in New Zealand, supposedly by a Japanese businessman who intended on sailing it to Japan. That was a little unusual, given the length of the journey and the fact that he could have easily had another delivered direct from the States. More unusual was the fact that the submarine did not appear to be registered or docked anywhere in Shikoku province, where the businessman allegedly was from.

But the real reason for Danny's interest was a routine satellite observation photo from a few weeks back that showed the submarine near an island in the area of the Sembuni Reefs offshore of East Malaysia.

The only way to know for certain if the submarine was using the island was to go there. And sooner rather than later. But the Whiplash team was still twelve hours from reaching Malaysia.

That wasn't a problem, as far as Captain Thomas was concerned.

"We have plenty of people for an assault," he told Danny after watching Cowboy and Turk tentatively ID'ing the sub. "Let's get out there."

"How soon can you be ready?" Danny asked.

"We're Marines. We're always ready." He grinned. "We can take off in an hour. Less if you need us to."

Danny turned to Turk and Cowboy. "Can you guys fly cover?"

"If they let me near a plane," said Turk.

"They will," said Cowboy.

"I'll talk to Colonel Greenstreet," said Danny. "Are you guys sure you're not tired?"

Turk shrugged. Cowboy shook his head. "Like the captain said, I'm a Marine. I don't get tired."

"You're going to fly over that island in broad daylight?" asked Colonel Greenstreet. "If they have antiair there, you're going to draw all sorts of fire."

"The satellite images don't show anything like that," said Danny. "Even though they're a couple of days old, I think it's unlikely they moved anything in."

"The photos also don't show your aircraft. Or even that sub," added Greenstreet.

"True."

"It's not the F-35s I'm worried about," said Greenstreet. "It's the Ospreys. They're sitting ducks. You can put an RPG into the side and they'll go down. What you have to do," he added, "is have the F-35s take a couple of runs and try and suck out any defenses. Then you have the Ospreys come from this end, where at least they might have a chance if someone tries shooting at them."

"Agreed," said Danny.

The island was small—maybe ten acres, half of it covered with trees and thick brush. Shaped like an irregular opal, it had a necklace that sprawled from one side—a jagged reef that poked over the waves at several different points and extended for about a half mile.

The working theory was that the sub recovered the aircraft and returned it there for launching. A small rocket engine was attached to the rear of the aircraft, which was then launched from a small gantry like a guided missile. That meant the base could be small and easily hidden in the jungle. Whiplash analysts put the probability of the base being there at only seventy-five percent.

How exactly they came up with the percentage hadn't been revealed.

"So you land here and here," said Greenstreet, pointing at the sides of the island opposite the treed area. "You may need support fire on that tree line."

"That's exactly what we think," said Captain Thomas, the ground commander. "So you have to be ready to bomb the area."

"And there's a possibility they may launch when they see us coming," said Danny. "You have to be ready for that as well."

"Obviously."

"How many aircraft can you give us?" asked Danny.

"I have two pilots, myself and Cowboy. Lieutenant Van Garetn, that is," added Greenstreet, using Cowboy's real name.

"I think we oughta fly Turk out there, too," said Cowboy. "He knows how these things fight."

Danny glanced at Turk, who was standing quietly against the wall on the opposite end of the room. He was staring blankly at the projection of the island. He seemed more like his old self; less angry, a little easier-going. There was always going to be a hard edge to him now, and an even harder core. Danny knew that seeing people who were close to you get killed changed your brain chemistry forever. But maybe Turk was coming out of the worst part of the dark place Iran had left him in.

"We could fly three planes," said Greenstreet. The vaguest note of reluctance mixed into his clipped, professional aviator tone. "We can kit one of them up for air-to-air, and mix the others. If Captain Mako is up for it."

"I'm good," said Turk.

Thomas wrapped up with an impromptu, "Let's get going and kick butt the Marine Corps way."

Danny smiled, but it was Turk who had the last word:

"And if that doesn't work, we'll give them a touch of Whiplash."

13

The Cube

"WE'RE GETTING REALLY GOOD DATA FLOW FROM THE Marine F-35s," said the techie supervising the data collection, Hy Wen. "We're good to go whenever they are."

Breanna nodded. The Cube's situation room—a complex of data stations arranged theater-style in front of a massive wall screen on the very bottom level of the Cube—was packed to overflowing.

Exactly ninety-eight analysts and technicians had been brought in for the project, both to gather and analyze data on the UAVs and to support Danny, Whiplash, and the Marines. It was the most people they'd ever had in the Cube at one time.

The only problem was feeding them. Literally. Greasy Hands Parsons—Breanna's special assistant and majordomo—was currently trying to solve that problem with a cook over at the CIA kitchens. Hopefully, he would solve it soon— Breanna was starving.

She tried to get her mind off food by walking around the workstations. She found Ray Rubeo halfway down, arms folded, hunched over an analyst from the Air Force. The analyst was a cryptographer, tasked with trying to break any encryptions in real time.

"Just like the old days, huh, Ray?"

He frowned.

Breanna sometimes suspected he didn't like people.

Other times she was sure of it.

14

Over Malaysia

TURK HAD GONE MUCH LONGER STRETCHES WITHOUT sleeping, but the stress of combat, and flying an aircraft he wasn't thoroughly used to, was starting to wear him down. The sides of his head felt numb, his eyes were scratchy, and his throat was sore. On top of which, his arms and upper back kept cramping.

Couple more hours, he told himself. *Then we sleep.*

Turk knew from experience that once things got hot—when the Marines went in, or if the UAVs appeared—everything that was bothering him would disappear. The problem was the long intervals of boredom a fighter pilot inevitably had to endure. The briefs, the preflight, the prep, the long flight to target, the ride home—these were all the very thick bread that sandwiched the few minutes of excitement he lived for.

Very thick bread, especially with Greenstreet cutting the slices.

"All right, Basher flight. We're zero five from the target. Basher Two, you are my wing. Basher Three, you are top cover. Acknowledge."

"Basher Two acknowledges," said Cowboy.

"Three," said Turk tersely.

"Sounding a little tired up there, Three," offered Cowboy.

"Negative," said Turk. He was at 22,000 feet, a good 10,000 over the other aircraft. He'd picked that altitude because it was a few thousand feet over the starting point for the Flighthawks' favorite long-range attack routine against ground attack aircraft. Of course, there were literally dozens of different routines the computer guiding the UAV interceptor might use. And in Turk's opinion, the Marine F-35s should worry more about MANPADs—shoulder launched ground-to-air missiles—than UAVs.

"Let's do this," said Greenstreet, hitting the throttle to spurt ahead.

Turk juiced his gas. His heartbeat began picking up. He scanned the sky from left to right and back, checked his readouts, then his radar.

"Nothing," said Greenstreet as his F-35 approached the reef at the side of the island.

The spit of land was so tiny that the aircraft were over it in literally half a heartbeat. Turk stretched himself upright in the ejection seat, alert, on edge—this was the point to watch for a response, for now it was obvious to anyone that they were there.

Nothing.

"Infrared, radar, all systems clear. Nobody home," said Greenstreet. "We take another pass. Stay with me."

They banked wide and came around for another pass in the same direction, this time lower but just as fast. Turk felt himself starting to lose a bit of his edge. He warned himself this was the most dangerous point of the mission, a bit of a lie but a well-intentioned one. He needed to stay alert; he needed to be ready.

"Nothing down there but sand rats," said Cowboy after they cleared the island.

"Low and slow," said Greenstreet.

They took two more passes without drawing a response or seeing anything move on the island.

"I'm going to talk to the Ospreys," said Greenstreet as Basher One rose from the final flyover at 3,000 feet. "They should be here inside ten minutes."

A FEW MINUTES LATER ABOARD MARINE OSPREY ONE, Danny Freah steadied himself at the back of the aircraft's rear ramp, waiting for the Osprey to touch down. He had his gun in his hand, loaded and ready to fire. The F-35s hadn't drawn a response or seen anyone on the island, but that wasn't a guarantee the place was deserted. Danny knew from experience that even the best radar and infrared detection systems could be fooled with patience and creativity. He'd been ambushed too many times in his career to take a landing like this—against a well-equipped and undeniably intelligent opponent—for granted.

"Charlie Platoon! Ready!" shouted an NCO as the rotorcraft settled into its landing squat.

"Ready!" shouted the rest of the company. They were loud enough to briefly drown out the engines.

The ramp fell and the Marines hustled out. They might not be considered a "Tier One" group, but they were as professional, moving quickly across the sand as they stormed the open beach.

The platoon's first objective was to take holding positions along a low rise near the center of the open area of the island. The jets were then called in for another flyover, while the Marines watched for a reaction. That done, two three-man groups got up and ran to the tree line. When they didn't find anything or draw fire, they plunged a few yards deeper. With still no contact, the commander unleashed the unit in a systematic search of the island.

Danny, trailing behind, couldn't have organized them better. But if he'd been hooked up to a lie detector and questioned, he would have had to admit that he was disappointed: if the people with the UAVs weren't here, where were they?

As the ground units scoured the island, Greenstreet had Turk extend his orbit outward, theorizing that the UAVs might be using this as bait and would launch from another base.

A civilian airliner twenty miles to the north provided the briefest of diversions before Turk double-checked its identifier with the Cube. Otherwise, the sky was empty, except for the Marine force.

There were dozens and dozens of little islands and reefs below, but the vast majority weren't big enough for a walrus to sunbathe on. Turk took his circle wider, double-checking his position with the other aircraft as he flew. Trying to stay alert, he ran himself through the possible reactions to a UAV, trying to guess where it would come from. He thought about Cowboy and the pilot's desire to fly with Whiplash.

Then he thought of Li. That was very dangerous—she was distracting even at the best of times. He refocused his thoughts as well as his eyes, examining the islands and waves below.

Turk's attention drifted again. Suddenly he was back in Iran, flying the Phantom that he and Stoner had used to escape in. MiGs were coming after them.

God, am I ever going to get away from them? Flying this old crate, desperate for fuel, a sitting duck . . .

He jumped upright against his restraints. He hadn't fallen asleep, but he'd been slightly dazed, inattentive. He thought of taking one of the emergency "go" pills he had in his leg pocket before something serious happened.

The AN/APG-81 AESA radar system had picked out two contacts at ninety miles, coming fast in his direction from 30,000 feet.

Fast movers. J-15s. Chinese.

J-15s! Chinese carrier planes.

"I have two contacts coming hot from the northwest," said Turk, hitting the mike. "Chinese."

DANNY REACHED THE EDGE OF THE ISLAND AND PUSHED out onto the shallow ledge overlooking the water. If there had been people here in the past ten years, they hadn't left a trace.

The ocean spread out before him, the water shimmering with the afternoon sun. The waves were so gentle that they barely made a sound as they lapped against the rocks skimming the rim of the island.

The place was picturesque, at least. Maybe in a few years some international hotel chain would discover it and set up a massive resort.

"What do you think, Colonel?" asked Captain Thomas.

"Analysts were wrong," said Danny.

"Not wrong—they hedged their bets." Captain

Thomas smiled. "We just happened to be in the twenty-fifth percentile."

He was referring to the estimate that there was a seventy-five percent chance the base would be here.

"How do they come up with those percentages?" asked the Marine. "Dart boards?"

"I think it's dice," said Danny.

"Military intelligence. Oldest oxymoron going."

Danny picked his way across the rocks, skirting the water. The truth was, the estimates the analysts made were usually pretty good; they were able to deal with an incredible amount of data and make guesses based on historical patterns. But in cases where there wasn't a past to speak of, it was all just a guess, wasn't it? Garbage in, garbage out, as they liked to say.

"Hey, Colonel," yelled one of the Marines who'd come out on the shore about twenty yards away. "What do you make of that?"

Danny walked over to the private, who was pointing at the reef. "Make of what?"

"Next to the reef?"

"In the water there. See how it jugs out a bit? Under the water?"

"I don't see anything but the reef," said Danny, staring. The rocks formed a small, shallow cove; the water was lighter, almost a pale green in the sun.

"The rocks and coral and what have you are irregular. There's a straight line there."

Danny stared but he couldn't tell what the private was talking about.

"I'm going to take a look," said the Marine. He began walking out on the sand that had piled up on both sides of the reef.

"Don't fall in," warned Danny.

The private waved his hand. He took a few more steps, then retreated back to shore where he gave his rifle to one of his companions, then pulled off his tactical vest and boots. Stripping to his shorts and undershirt, he hopped into the water, then swam and walked to the part of the reef he'd been pointing to. He glanced around before diving under the water.

"What the hell is that private doing?" growled Captain Thomas, walking out from the brush.

"He thinks he found something," said the man holding his rifle.

"Maybe it'll be his sanity," groused the captain.

The private resurfaced. "It's dug out," he yelled. "Colonel, it's dug out."

"What do you mean?"

"There are metal beams here, and on the other side it's real deep. Watch."

He dove back under the water, bobbed up, then disappeared again. A few moments later he resurfaced farther down the reef. The water there came up to his waist.

"Like it's a little minislip for a boat," said the man. "I think there's a channel that extends out into the ocean."

Danny turned to Captain Thomas. "Do you have any combat divers?"

"No. I may be able to get a diver flown in from the Navy ships with the MEU."

Danny glanced at his watch. "My guys'll be here in a few hours. They'll have gear."

"Maybe we're not in the twenty-fifth percentile after all," said Thomas, a little more cheerful.

"Colonel Freah!" A Marine lance corporal pushed through the trees. "Basher flight needs to talk to you. They have Chinese aircraft heading their way."

TURK'S AIRCRAFT WAS "CLEAN"—THERE WERE NO weapons or other stores on his wings—and therefore almost surely invisible to the approaching Chinese fighters. He had a pair of AMRAAMs in his weapon bay; he could thumb them up and shoot the planes down before they realized he was there.

But of course he couldn't do that. They were all in international airspace. He was not under threat, and without any legal or logical reason to attack.

He *could* do it, though. There was a certain power in the knowledge.

"Basher Three, say situation," radioed Greenstreet.

"Two bogies," he repeated. "Same course and speed as before."

"Stay passive on your sensors. We'll supply the data."

"Roger that," said Turk.

He'd turned off the active radar as soon as the other aircraft were ID'ed. The F-35s could share their sensor data with each other, which made it more difficult for enemies to attack or even know how many planes they were dealing with. At this point it was probable that the two Chinese pilots didn't know he was there.

"We're going to stay north of the island to keep them from getting too curious about what's going on down there."

"May not work," said Turk. "Whatever surveillance aircraft they're using may have picked up the Ospreys earlier."

"True, but it's the best we got," said Greenstreet. "And your colonel suggested it. You keep your eyes on everything."

"Acknowledged."

"And don't shoot."

The two Chinese aircraft were depicted on his radar screen as red diamonds with sticks showing their directional vectors. The bands on the radar circle helped categorize threats as well as organize contacts. As a general rule, the closer the circle they were in, the more serious the threat. The Chinese planes had just crossed from the farthest band into the third circle, sixty miles from the aircraft. They were about ten degrees off his nose to the west, flying an almost parallel course. They were closing on him at a rate of roughly seventeen nautical miles a minute; Turk had somewhere between two and three minutes before they would be able to detect him with their standard radars.

Eons in an air-to-air fight.

Unlike Basher Three, the other two F-35s had bombs under their wings, making them more easily visible on radar. The two Chinese fighters apparently could see them—a few seconds after Turk gave Greenstreet his status, they hailed them.

"Unidentified American planes, you are flying in Chinese territory," said one of the pilots in easily understood but accented English. "Say intentions."

"We are on a routine training mission in international waters," replied Greenstreet. "State your intentions."

"You are in Chinese territory. You must leave."

It was a typical Chinese bluff, and Greenstreet answered it as it deserved to be answered—with quick sarcasm. "Check your maps, boys. This is international airspace and we are not moving."

Turk banked and began to climb in the direction the Chinese fighters were taking. If Greenstreet could be a prig and a pain on the ground, now his attitude was not only appropriate but reassuring. Turk knew he wasn't going to take guff from the Chinese, and there was no doubt about how he would act if fur flew.

The Chinese hadn't switched their weapons radars on, and nothing they were doing could be considered antagonistic.

Obnoxious, maybe, but even there they were low-key by typical Chinese PAF standards. Turk had heard many tales about surveillance planes being buzzed so closely by fighters in the South China Sea that they had lost paint.

Turk had never encountered a real Shenyang J-15, though he knew the aircraft's capabilities and weaknesses from simulations. The

Feisha—or "Flying Shark," as it was called in Chinese pinyin—was a two-engine multirole aircraft capable of hitting Mach 2.4. Either heavily influenced by the Sukhoi Su-33 or directly cloned from the Russian fighter—you could never be completely sure with the Chinese—it featured the latest in home-grown avionics technology. Like the Su-33, it had outstanding flying characteristics, but it was limited in range and reliability by its use of Chinese-manufactured engines, which were not on a par with the Russian originals, to say nothing of Western counterparts. The weight of the aircraft and its need to operate off carriers that lacked catapult systems were further handicaps. The fact that the J-15s were moving quickly meant they would not be able to linger long.

On the plus side, the J-15 had descended from some of the best close-quarters fighters ever built, and would have a distinct advantage against the F-35 at very close range. The American aircraft were meant to destroy enemies at long range, before the enemy even knew they were there. If they weren't allowed to do that, a good portion of their edge over other types would be gone. In a knife fight, superior electronics, ease of maintenance, and long-term dependability meant very little.

The Chinese aircraft repeated their warning, which Greenstreet ignored. Climbing through 25,000 feet, Turk positioned Basher Three so it could swoop down behind the Chinese planes if they kept on their present course. The J-15s, meanwhile, slowed, perhaps fine-tuning their intercept. They seemed to have no idea that Turk was now above them, or even that he was there at all.

Circling north of the operation area, Basher One and Two were between the Chinese fighters and the assault force on the island. As the J-15s closed to within ten miles, they turned so they could pull into a course parallel to them. Turk maneuvered Basher Three toward the point where the intercept would occur. The two Chinese planes throttled back, aligning themselves so they could easily get on the F-35s' tails—a very dangerous position for the Americans.

Turk decided he would return the favor. He pushed his nose down, then gave a judicious tap of the throttle that allowed him to plop down behind them as they hailed Basher flight with yet another warning.

"You are in our airspace," said the Chinese leader. "You will leave or be—"

He didn't finish what he was saying for at that moment he realized where Turk was. He jerked his plane left; his wingman went right. Both dished off flares and chaff even though Turk's targeting radar wasn't active and, except for his positioning, hadn't done anything specifically threatening.

At least nothing that would stand up in a court of law, let alone public opinion.

"We are in international airspace," said Greenstreet calmly. "Conducting routine training missions. You will desist from bothering us."

The Chinese aircraft regrouped to the west. After radioing their controller for instructions, they were apparently told to go home and did so, without comment.

"Tail between their legs and bye-bye," said Cowboy. "That ends that."

"I doubt it," said Greenstreet. Then he added, much to Turk's surprise, "Good timing, Basher Three. We'll make a Marine aviator out of you yet."

15

Offshore an island in the Sembuni Reefs

BRAXTON NEARLY MISSED THE IMPORT OF THE WARN-ing: Chinese agent Wen-lo had been transported in the last few days to the *Mao* carrier task force.

Wen-lo was one of several Chinese agents who'd tried to contact Braxton and reach an "accommodation" with Kallipolis over the past several years. The fact that he had been taken to the Chinese carrier task group operating in the near vicinity meant that he was looking to up his game.

Braxton had never met Wen-lo, but he detested him nonetheless as a pawn of a repressive regime. He hated the Chinese government at least as much as he hated America's, and had vehemently rebuffed all attempts at contact. Other members of Kallipolis would have been far more accommodating; they saw nothing wrong with selling older technology to them. "They'll steal it anyway" was a common excuse.

Braxton did a quick search for additional news on Wen-lo, but the rest of the results were several months old. Wen-lo worked for PLA-N technical intelligence—the Chinese navy. Though still in his thirties, he had the rank of *hai jun da xiao*, equivalent to a rear admiral or OF-6 in the American navy. So presumably he could command decent resources from the task force.

Too many distractions, thought Braxton. He would focus on the Dreamland Whiplash people for now and deal with the Chinese later on.

16

The Cube

IT WAS AS EASY AS CHILD'S PLAY—ASSUMING THE CHILD was very, very bright.

The reef on the target island had helped hide an underwater refueling and stocking area. There was space for two bays; at the bottom below the ever-shifting sand there was an automated mechanism for refueling the submersibles. The equipment was relatively simple—on par with equipment used by robot vacuum cleaners, one of Rubeo's techies quipped—but it was entirely autonomous: there was no need for a human to initiate the process or intervene in any way. It was one more indication of how sophisticated the people behind the UAV system were.

It also gave the intel people numerous leads. Combined with the material recovered from the UAV that had been shot down, they had a large number of leads and were rapidly filling in details about the people behind the drones.

More important in the short term, the underwater structure gave them something to look for. Or rather, it gave their computers a new set of parameters to try to match.

They found a match on an island in the Sembuni Reefs, roughly eight miles away. About a square mile, it was much larger than the island where the submarine station had been found, and also uninhabited. It was just south of the disputed zone with China, along the edge of the main shipping channels.

But they also found a match in a place nearly four hundred miles farther north, on a formation known as Final Reef—and half a dozen other names, depending on who was doing the naming.

The reef was in the contested zone between Malaysia, the Philippines, Vietnam, and China. Malaysia and the Philippines claimed the reef based on its location along the continental shelf; the other two countries claimed the area by ancient fishing rights. In a maneuver designed to boost their claims—not just to that reef, but to the Kalayaan islands—the Philippine government had sent an old American merchant transport, the *Final Pleasure*, to the atoll five years before, using it as a base for a half-dozen Filipino marines who essentially asserted squatter rights there. The Chinese had responded by stationing an ever-changing flotilla of fishing vessels in the area; when one left, another would invariably take its place. Malaysia and Vietnam occasionally sent patrol boats to the vicinity; there had been two shooting incidents over the past eighteen months, with the patrol boats shooting "in the area of" a Chinese fishing vessel and the Filipino ship. There were no injuries in either case, nor had there been a noticeable effect on the conflict.

"The location of this last base is very delicate," said Reid. "Geopolitically—this is potentially a land mine."

"That may very well be why it's there," suggested Rubeo.

"If it's a base at all," said Reid. "There's a single girder at the stern of the ship, underwater."

"The metal is identical to the others," said Rubeo. "We see a rope ladder coiled on the deck. It is certainly worth checking."

"No sub there," said Reid.

"The proximity to the reef makes it difficult to be certain," noted Rubeo. "That entire side of the ship is shadowed by the hull and the reef. But we have no firm evidence of a sub, no."

"They must be working with the Filipinos," said Breanna, "if they have a base there."

"Or they're paying the equivalent of rent," said Reid. "That would be more their style. The images of the merchant ship don't show a large presence, if there's one at all."

Reid pulled up a brief PowerPoint slide show on the island conflict prepared by a CIA analyst. Most of the slides were attempting to put the conflict into the larger context, but three showed the merchant ship and made estimates of its capabilities and the size of the force there. If the conspiracy had a large base on the ship or the surrounding reef, it was *extremely* well-hidden.

"We have to check it out," said Reid. "At a minimum."

"True."

"And even if this is some sort of mistake on our part—even if there is no base on the atoll, the fact that there are two submarines that we can identify, the fact that there are definitely two bases—it's larger than we thought and much more involved."

Breanna waved her hand over the screen, moving back to the slide on Braxton. Even after all these years, she recognized the face—hollow cheeks, bleached white skin, eyes that seemed a size too small for the head. He was still thin, and his hair, once long, was cut to a quarter inch of his scalp. It was prematurely white now, and he had a scar over his right eye, but the stare was familiar.

"If we're serious about finding them," said Breanna, "we have to move quickly. And we can't tell the Filipinos."

"Well . . ."

They looked at each other. Both had worked together long enough to know each other's thoughts.

"If we tell the White House, there's a good possibility things will get very complicated," said Breanna.

"If we tell the President."

"We're authorized to pursue Braxton and Kallipolis already."

"We are."

"I'd say we should just pursue it and not ask for permission," said Breanna.

"I think I have to agree. We already have authorization."

Breanna considered the situation. The Chinese had not registered a protest.

Which was worse? Waiting and possibly missing Braxton, or stumbling into an international incident?

"Better to ask forgiveness than permission," she said finally.

"Agreed. Let's authorize the mission."

TAKEN

——

1

Malaysia

IF THE ENCOUNTER WITH THE CHINESE AIRCRAFT HAD softened Greenstreet's attitude toward Turk, it hardly showed once they landed. All three pilots debriefed the mission together, recording what had happened and filing reports and mission tapes; under other circumstances the squadron leader might have been expected to put in a few words of encouragement if not praise for the pilots he was flying with, but Greenstreet did neither. Not that he said Turk or Cowboy did poorly; he just didn't comment. But that was the way he was—Cowboy seemed surprised when Turk brought it up on the way back to the trailers.

"He's not a rah-rah guy," said Cowboy, shrugging.

"I can see that," said Turk.

"Flies damn well," said Cowboy. "Guy you want on your back in the shit."

"Sure. He could be a little more cheery about it, though."

"I think he's pissed that we weren't allowed to

engage the bastards," added Cowboy. "You could have shot them down."

"Yeah."

"You're just too much, Air Force. I heard your voice—you were *dying* to take those guys out."

"Maybe, I guess."

Cowboy laughed. They'd reached the trailers. "You can admit it. It's our job."

"True."

Cowboy gave him a shoulder chuck that nearly sent him into the wall. "Catch you later," he said, sauntering off to his room.

Twenty minutes later, lying on his cot drifting toward sleep, Turk thought about what Cowboy had said. Was he right? Had he been itching to take the other pilots down?

Maybe he had.

What was wrong with admitting it? Was he worried that it would make him seem too cold-blooded?

He'd been in combat before, killed people, on the ground and in the air. He wasn't jaded about it, or complacent; he didn't take it lightly. It was, as Cowboy said, his job.

And his duty. Just as it was his duty this morning *not* to shoot.

Turk's head floated between sleep and consciousness. He'd never angsted over his job before, and the whole idea of whether he should like shooting down people hadn't really occurred to him. Or if it did, it hadn't been something he spent a lot of time worrying about.

Not that he was worrying now.

I need sleep, he told himself. *Enough of this.*
And just like that, he dozed off.

Six hours later, refreshed by a nap, Danny Freah took one of the Ospreys to Tanjung Manis Airport to meet the incoming Whiplash MC-17. Located near the northeastern coast, the civilian airport was virtually deserted. The MC-17 had just come in, carrying not only the Whiplash troopers but the Tigershark II and eight Dreamland aircraft specialists. After unloading the diminutive Tigershark, they were waiting for a second cargo plane carrying four escort Sabre UAVs.

"There's a sight for sore eyes!" said Chief Master Sergeant Ben "Boston" Rockland, striding toward his boss as he hopped off the Marine Osprey.

"How was the flight?" asked Danny.

"Wouldn't know, Colonel. Slept the whole way."

"How's the team? Will they be able to go out on a mission tonight?"

"Try and hold them back. What do we got?"

As always, Boston's enthusiasm energized Danny. The chief master sergeant was a short, pugnacious, and high-energy veteran. Once one of the few African-Americans trained as a parajumper, Boston had mellowed a bit around the edges over the years—and lost most of the hometown accent that had given him his nickname—but he was still the sort of combat leader Danny found indispensable on an op. He filled Boston in on the latest intel from the Cube: two new bases had been located; each had underwater gridwork similar to the site

Danny had been to earlier. One seemed to have been abandoned recently, the other was much farther north, in territory watched over by the Chinese. There was an old merchant ship there, with six Filipino marines who'd been parked there in a somewhat quixotic attempt by the Philippines to stake a claim to the territory.

"The Filipinos are helping them?" asked Boston.

"Officially, no," said Danny. "But they talk to them once a day. No one seems to be sure what's going on out there. That's why we have to take a look.

"And there's the Chinese," added Danny. "Their carrier task force has moved south, closer to that site. What their interests are, no one seems to know. They sent a pair of planes to check us out earlier, then skedaddled when the Marines got tough."

"Smart move on their part," said Boston.

"What I'm thinking is we use our Marine friends to hit the island I think was abandoned," said Danny. "They go in with their Osprey and support aircraft. Meanwhile, we do a night HALO jump from the MC-17 onto the merchant ship, check it out. We have Turk and the UAVs to back us up, and we run the Ospreys for firepower and to get us out."

"We need permission from the Filipinos?"

"I don't think asking them what's up is a good idea," said Danny.

"How heavily armed are they?"

"We don't know. The only weapons we've seen on the old merchant ship are M-2 machine guns. Ma Deuces," added Danny, using the American nickname, "probably from World War Two. I'd expect they still work, though."

"What about the guys with the UAVs?"

"Not clear."

"But their planes had a laser," said Boston.

"That's right. There may be all sorts of defenses. We have to be prepared for anything."

A roar in the distance announced the pending arrival of the two Whiplash Ospreys. They had rendezvoused north of the island just an hour before. WhipRey One came down from Okinawa, where it had been parked since Danny's first mission here. The second had flown all the way from Hawaii, a trip that involved nine in-air refuels and just under eighteen hours of straight flight time. Though flown entirely by computer, two full crews had accompanied the MV-22/W aircraft from Hawaii; both aircraft would be fully manned for the op.

"So how do the UAVs operate off a reef?" Boston asked.

"We're not sure." Danny shook his head. "They seem to have some sort of launching system that can be easily hidden—one of the theories is that's like a rocket. I'm afraid this is one case where we're going to have to play it by ear and see what happens."

"One case?" Boston rolled his eyes. No Whiplash mission was ever straightforward, by conventional standards.

"I'm not worried about the UAVs," continued Danny. "Turk seems pretty confident that he can handle them."

"I'd bet on that."

"We want the guys who are behind this. And they have to have some large computer operation somewhere."

"One question, Colonel—UAVs, small submarines—sounds almost like a Dreamland setup."

"You don't know how right you are, Boston."

2

Offshore an island in the Sembuni Reefs

SHE WAS THERE IN THE DREAM AS SHE ALWAYS WAS, long hair draped back behind her ears, eyes penetrating, her smile so casual and confident. She was as tall as him, though that didn't say much. Braxton stood only five-six, his height an issue and an impediment when he was young—and surely an issue in his personality, a reason he felt the need to prove himself to every human being he met, except Jennifer Gleason.

In the dream, he saw her get up from the console in the Dreamland operations center, tired after watching the progress of a long night's experiment. She walked toward his station, then leaned over his shoulder. He felt her warmth in the cool room, the light press of her breast against his back.

"Man is meant to evolve," she said. "To become free. The best and the brightest must throw off the shackles that hold them. Governments are oppressive . . ."

A loud buzzer brought Braxton from the dream.

Jennifer Gleason had never spoken like that to him, and never would have; she was the most apolitical person in the world. But the first part of the dream, of her getting up and walking toward him, that had happened. That was real.

Human minds were hopelessly tangled and easily confused.

How much of what he wanted was due to Jennifer, and not the philosophical underpinnings of Kallipolis? Was he just motivated by unobtainable lust?

Braxton had contemplated the question at great length. He was certainly devoted to Jennifer Gleason's memory, far more than anyone. Part of that was due to the beauty of her work— the AI constructs, the melding of hardware and software, the very basis of the brains that flew the Flighthawks and their prodigy: it was beautiful work, so far advanced for its time that it still wasn't completely appreciated, even though the basic architecture was embedded in every combat UAV currently in the fleet.

Braxton had built on her work, and understood it like no one else, with the possible exception of Ray Rubeo. But just as Jennifer had surpassed Rubeo, building on his insights, Braxton had surpassed her.

So it was lust and obsession, but on some higher plane—something worthy of Kallipolis and the future of the elite.

"More work to be done," he said aloud, rising

from the chair where he'd fallen asleep. "Enough self-flagellation. Work. That is the only useful purpose a mind can be put to."

Even though the words were his, in his head they echoed with her voice.

What a strange construct, the brain.

3

The Mall, Washington, D.C.

WALK? OR RUN FOR PRESIDENT?

Zen stopped his wheelchair at the middle of the Vietnam War memorial. He always felt deeply humbled here, as if he were physically as well as symbolically in the presence of so many brave Americans who had sacrificed their lives and futures for their country. In his mind, their sacrifices made his look petty.

He had, it was true, done many heroic things. But he hadn't traded his existence on earth for his country. On the contrary, he had lived a great life—not one without tremendous hardships, but a bountiful one nonetheless.

He hadn't discussed running for the presidency with Rodriguez, but it was clear from what the scientist said that were he to undergo the operation and rehabilitation, he wouldn't have the time to campaign. In fact, he might even have to give up his Senate seat.

He couldn't say he wouldn't do that. Between walking and being a politician—walking was better.

But President?

If he were President, he could get important things done. He could take care of the military, improve veterans' benefits—especially for the wounded and disabled. It wouldn't be easy—being in the Senate had taught him that. But there was still a lot more that he could do. He could have a lasting effect on people, on the country.

On the other hand, he really, really, really wanted to walk again. Just the notion of walking down the aisle with Teri when she got married— how fantastic would that be?

Unbelievable.

In the years after the accident, he'd tried and tried to get his legs back. He'd always thought he would. Gradually, he had come to accept who he was. Accept that he was limited physically.

He'd never been limited mentally.

If the experiment worked, it would help others as well. His medical history made him the perfect candidate from a scientific point of view, but it was even bigger psychologically: if someone who had been crippled for so long regained the use of his legs, how many other lives would that affect? Wouldn't that be even more tangible to them than what he might do as President?

If he even got the nomination. There'd be no guarantee. Mantis would be a very formidable opponent. And then there was Jason Hu, and Cynthia Styron from Wyoming—who would be an excellent President, even if she was probably a long shot for the nomination.

He'd certainly have to do things he didn't want to if he ran. Beg for money. Compromise on his principles. Not big compromises, not at the start. But eventually. That was politics. He hadn't given up his principles in the Senate, and he was well respected by both sides for that. But as President . . .

"Uh, Senator, you wanted to be at that reception," said his driver, who'd come down to the monument with him. "We are, uh, running pretty late."

Zen broke himself from his reverie.

"Let's go, James," he said, wheeling back from the wall. "Time's a-wastin'."

4

Malaysia

GETTING INTO THE TIGERSHARK AFTER FLYING THE F-35 was like trading a well-appointed F-150 pickup for a sleek little Porsche. It wasn't just the size of the cockpit or the fact that the Tigershark's seat slid down to an almost prone position once he was aboard. The aircraft was designed for an entirely different purpose than the F-35. Not needing to be all things to all people, it was optimized as an interceptor—small and quick, highly maneuverable in any imaginable regime, carrying active and passive sensors that could detect an enemy well before it could be detected. The plane was also optimized to work with UAVs—the Sabre drones, combat-optimized aircraft scheduled to replace the Flighthawks in the near future. The Tigershark and the Sabres shared their sensor data in much the same way that the F-35s did, but had the additional advantage of being able to tap into the Whiplash satellite communications network, and from there into a vast array of American military data worldwide.

Turk went through the computer's preflight checklist quickly, making sure the aircraft was at spec after its long trip west. The flight computer happily complied, checking off each box with an audible declaration of *"Green."* The intonation that suggested there was no possible way the condition could be anything other than perfect.

The Tigershark was not a STOL aircraft, but its small size and powerful thrust allowed it to get off the runway at Tanjung Manis in only 2,000 feet. Turk rocketed upward, stretching his muscles— the change in aircraft was as physical as it was mental, his body adapting to the beast's feel.

"Go to twenty thousand feet, on course and at speed as programmed," Turk told the computer. He had loaded a memory chip with the outlines of the mission prior to takeoff. The chip included a backup of his personal preferences—the cockpit temperature, the precise angle of the seat, along with some of his favored preset maneuvers. Some of this was already programmed into the aircraft's memory, somewhat like the driver's setting in a car would be, but the designers had felt it should have a backup that could be easily changed if a new pilot was at the helm.

Turk's path took him west over the ocean, where he would rendezvous with the Marines. Basher One and Two had just taken off from their forward operating base. The Marine squadron was now back to full strength, with its pilots recovered from the stomach flu, and the aircraft that had been damaged by the laser fully repaired. Danny and Greenstreet had opted to keep two of the planes in reserve; the rebels' recent propensity to attack while the planes were gone could not be taken lightly.

Turk's plane flew between the four Sabres in a two-one-two formation—two Sabres about five miles ahead of the Tigershark. The forward aircraft were spread a bit wider than the back, with 5,000 feet separation in altitude. The formation was arranged to provide not only a wide sensor field but also mobility for combat.

"Basher One, this is Shark," said Turk, checking in with the Marines. "I'm about zero-two from rendezvous point alpha. How's your ETA?"

"Five minutes, Shark One. We don't have you on radar."

"Copy that."

If the F-35 was stealthy, the Tigershark was practically invisible to radar. The F-35s could, however, spot it with other sensors, most notably its passive infrared detection system, which would find the aircraft's baffled tailpipe as it drew near. The Sabres, on the other hand, could only be detected at extremely close range while they were at cruising speed.

As the planes rendezvoused, Turk flew close enough to the F-35s to give them a thumbs-up—or would have, had they been able to see into the cockpit of the Tigershark. But unlike every jet fighter since the Me 262, the aircraft did not have a canopy; it was a wing-in-body design so sleek that the pilot could not have sat ninety degrees upright. Instead, its skin was studded with small video cameras that gave Turk a perfect 360-degree view, one that could change instantly from daylight to night at voice command, and was always integrated with the radar and other detection systems.

"Sleek chariot," quipped Cowboy. "Where'd you get that? Mars?"

"You sure it's not a UFO?" said Greenstreet. It was his first attempt at humor since Turk had known him.

"I want one," added Cowboy.

"Don't drool," said Greenstreet. "You'll rust the controls."

Two tries at a joke within thirty seconds? He was on a roll.

"I'll see if I can arrange a demonstration flight," said Turk.

"That'd be awesome," said Cowboy.

The joke was on him—the demonstration flight would actually never leave the ground, as the Tigershark had a rather robust simulation mode.

"All right, let's do this, gentlemen," said Greenstreet, back to all-business. "Shark, you ride over Target One and get us some images. We're with the assault team."

"Roger that."

Turk pulled up the mission map and adjusted his course to fly over the atoll where the submarine dock had been spotted. He could just tell the computer to take him there, but where was the fun in that?

"Throttle max," he said, his hand reaching to duplicate the motion of pushing the throttle to military power.

"*Command accepted,*" said the plane.

For all the world, he could have sworn it added the words: *It's about time.*

DANNY FREAH RAISED HIS HANDS SO THE TEAM JUMP-master could finish checking his rig.

"Good," Melissa Grisif announced finally, turning to give a thumbs-up to the MC-17 crew chief. "We're good to go."

Grisif had joined the Whiplash assault team only two months before; this was her first mission with the unit. But she was far from inexperienced. Grisif had joined the Army Rangers as one of the first female members of the regiment; after two years there, she was selected for Officer's Candidate School, where she graduated at the top of her class. The freshly minted lieutenant went to Special Forces; two promotions later she found herself headed for a desk job. At that point she stepped sideways, getting a slot in an intraservice exchange program that saw SF-trained personnel working with Air Force pararescue jumpers. Six months in she'd seen a notice for volunteers to join Whiplash.

Volunteering to take the team trials represented a serious risk to her career. For one thing, there was no guarantee she would make the cut; if she didn't, she would lose her assignment with Air Force special operations and return to the Pentagon desk job. And if she did make the cut, she would be treated like any other member of the team. While she would still be an officer, many of the privileges that rank usually bestowed would be missing. She wouldn't command a team, at least not at first. As the "new guy" on the squad, she would be given much of the donkey work, just as if she were "only" an NCO. (Whiplash required a rank of E5 or higher, which meant that even the newest recruit had been in the military long enough to advance to sergeant or petty officer. As it happened, no military member—some Whiplashers were CIA—had been accepted below the rank of E6, a technical sergeant in the Air Force. If anything, the people who had come over from the CIA were even more experienced, as most had worked in the military before joining the CIA's paramilitary side.)

Captain Grisif had made the cut. If her ego had been bruised since joining, she never let on. The fact that she had won the position of jumpmaster, an extremely important role in the Whiplash scheme of things, showed that she was already thriving.

The MC-17 was about halfway through its slow climb to 35,000 feet. By the time they reached that altitude, Turk Mako would be starting his pass over the beached merchant vessel. Danny had several plans contingent on what Turk found there, but they all ended the same way: the Whiplash team was getting aboard the vessel and taking it over.

He looked over the rest of the team. With the exception of Boston, everyone was new; the original Whiplash team had been broken up and used to seed new teams, now in training. Chris Bulgaria and Tony "Two Fingers" Dalton had come from Air Force special operations; Eddie Guzman was a former SEAL who had been working for the CIA when he was recruited. Glenn Fulsom, "Baby Joe" Morgan, and Ivan Dillon were all from Army Special Forces. Riyad Achmoody was the eighth member of the team. Achmoody was another CIA recruit, and the oldest member aside from Boston and Danny. A former Army Special Forces officer, he was also the team leader, though with Danny and Boston along, he was the third-ranking member of the unit.

Boston came over and gave Danny a quick thumbs-up. "We're looking good," said the chief. "Cap'lissa's got 'em shipshape," he added, using his new nickname for Grisif.

"Yup."

"I see she even got you squared away," added Boston.

"My rig was perfect," said Danny defensively.

"A woman's touch. That's what you needed." The

chief wagged his finger at his commander. "Something you might think of in your personal life."

"The day I take advice on that front from you," said Danny, "is the day I go into a monastery."

"Just lookin' out for you," said Boston.

"Thanks," said Danny, putting on his smart helmet to check on the rest of the operation.

THERE WAS A MASSIVE DEPRESSION ON THE SIDE OF the atoll the Marines were going to inspect. It looked like a small stadium had been there and then flattened. As Turk circled overhead, he directed Sabre One to descend and fly over the depression low and slow.

The feed from the UAV's low-light and infrared video was piped instantly back to the Cube, where an analyst studied it for a few seconds before declaring it the top of a pancaked bunker.

"That's definitely manmade," said the expert. "Way too symmetrical to be anything but. Be nice to get a ground-penetrating radar and have absolute confirmation," he added. "But I'm thinking that's not in the budget."

"It's not in the timeline," said Colonel Freah, who was linked in via the com unit in his helmet and the MC-17. "Is the place safe or not?"

"Danny, we're not seeing any people on the island," said Breanna from the sit room. "Proceed."

"Understood. Out," said Danny. As the com link to the States turned off, he tapped the back panel of the smart helmet. "The island does not appear to be occupied," he told Captain Thomas aboard the Marine Osprey. "There's a large depression—our experts think it was a bunker that was exploded. You have the image?"

"We're looking at it now." The video had been routed by Whiplash over to the Marine unit via their combat link. "No defenses?"

"None noted. These guys are sneaky and smart," said Danny. "I wouldn't take anything for granted."

"I don't plan on it."

COWBOY COMPLETED HIS PASS OVER THE ISLAND AND banked west. The place looked as deserted as a government office at 4:05.

"I'm going to clear them in," said Colonel Greenstreet.

"Acknowledged."

Leveling his jet out of the turn, Cowboy double-checked the position of the approaching Ospreys, making sure he wasn't going to interfere with their flight path. Then he nudged the stick to climb behind Basher One and gave his readouts a thorough going over. The F-35 was performing like a champion racehorse on a midday warm-up, barely breaking a sweat.

Cowboy's stint out here and his association with the Whiplash people had sparked a conflict in his soul. He loved being a Marine. There was something truly awe-inspiring about the Corps' history. For Cowboy, the link to the very first leathernecks—a name that had come from the collars worn by the recruits during the

Revolution—was a tangible thing, something that didn't simply inspire him, but linked him with a select fraternity of warriors. To be a Marine *and* a pilot made him a member of an even more elite fraternity.

Not that he had necessarily thought naval aviators or Air Force pilots were wimps, but . . . they weren't Marines.

But Whiplash was something else again. It might be primarily Air Force, but it was clearly cutting edge. And at least to judge by Turk and Colonel Freah, the people associated with it were extreme warriors themselves.

Not Marines. But definitely warriors.

Did he have the stuff to join them?

Cowboy certainly felt he did. He *knew* he did. But he'd have to prove it.

The Ospreys came into the beach fast, settling down to let the men off. No matter how calm the situation might look, that was always a tense moment. So many things could go wrong, even without an enemy around.

"Basher flight, this is Shark," said Turk, radioing them from the north. "I'm about to make my run over Whiplash objective. How are you looking?"

"We're good," said Greenstreet. "Everything is clean and quiet. Thanks for your help."

"Roger that. Have fun out there."

"Acknowledged."

Greenstreet sounded ever so slightly annoyed, but as Cowboy had told Turk earlier, that was just his way. Greenstreet was an excellent pilot and a decent leader; he was certainly a good Marine.

Cowboy wouldn't have minded working with someone else, though. Colonel Freah's style—very confident and self-assured, yet easygoing at the same time—was a sharp contrast. It was clear that Freah had been in a *lot* of shit, far more than even the crustiest gunnery sergeants in the MEU. Maybe that was why he was so laid back; whatever happened, it probably didn't compare to the worst of what he'd already seen.

Not that you'd want to cross him: there was a flash in his eyes every so often that let you know he was capable of real anger, and could back it up not only with connections all the way to the White House but physically as well. Then again, why would you want to cross him? He had the air about him that all great commanders had: Everything he said just seemed to make so much sense that you would be a complete idiot to go against his advice.

Cowboy listened as Colonel Greenstreet talked with the Osprey pilots, then checked in with the air combat controllers as the units established themselves on the beach. It was good, it was quiet, they were advancing to the objectives.

Everything was going great. The night was a picnic in the making.

"Basher flight," said Turk from the Tigershark, now nearly four hundred miles to the north. "Are you seeing these contacts?"

"Say again, Whiplash?" asked Greenstreet.

"Two bogies, high speed, coming at you from the west," said Turk. "The combat UAVs are back, and they're running straight for you."

5

The Cube

THEY WERE AGGRESSIVE BASTARDS, WEREN'T THEY?

Rubeo looked at the large screen at the front of the room, which was mapping the location of every unit in the area. The UAVs were coming for blood.

They'd just appeared on the screen, as if from nowhere. That certainly wasn't possible, and it certainly wasn't acceptable. His team had clearly missed something. He picked up the phone that connected to his company's analytic center in New Mexico.

"Check the launch profiles and see where they're likely to have come from," he demanded, without even bothering to give an explanation, let alone greet the techie on the other end of the line. "Coordinate that with everything we know about them—the bases they've used, things Braxton owned, the submarines—we are not doing a good job here. I want more information."

"Right now?"

"I would have preferred yesterday," snapped Rubeo before hanging up.

6

South China Sea, north of Malaysia

EVEN THOUGH THE UAVs WERE APPROACHING, TURK was already committed to supporting the Whiplash operation on the merchant ship and couldn't leave. The best he could do to help the two F-35s was send a pair of Sabres to back them up. Even if they juiced their engines, it would take them close to twenty minutes to get there. The enemy UAVs were less than ten minutes from the Marines.

It was better than nothing. Turk detailed Sabres Three and Four, the ones to his south, to help the Marines, but before dispatching them prioritized protection of the landing force above the F-35s. This way, they'd position themselves to cut off the enemy if they got by Greenstreet and Cowboy.

Once tasked, the Sabres were autonomous, and would not only decide how to carry out their orders but adapt to new situations without needing to be reprogrammed. And they wouldn't quit until there were no threats in the air. Turk told Greenstreet they were en route, then turned his attention to the beached merchant ship and area around it.

Originally beached in the shallows a few yards from the top of the reef, the ship had been driven up the hard rock by the current, waves, and storms. The bow and a good portion of the starboard side of the ship had been lifted high enough to leave the keel exposed. The stern, which seemed to have twisted slightly, sat with the waves lapping just above the screw.

An infrared scan showed that there were two men on the port deck near an ancient .50-caliber machine gun. There were four other men below-decks in a compartment believed to be used for eating and sleeping. Turk assumed these six men were the Filipino marines assigned to occupy the ship against the Chinese, though until the ship was boarded, no one would actually know.

The question was whether there were other people aboard. A modest heat signal indicated the engine room might have more people in it, but it was situated in a way that the analysts couldn't be sure. The Whiplash team would go on the assumption that they were there until proven otherwise.

Six Chinese fishing vessels were arrayed outside the reef south of the vessel. None were armed, but a Chinese Type 010-class minesweeper was about ten miles farther north, on the side of the beached Filipino ship. The minesweeper was the mama bear to the other boats. Here as elsewhere in the South China Sea, the Chinese tended to assert their most aggressive claims with a soft face, posting the seemingly less obnoxious "civilian" vessels close to the enemy, while leaving the muscle just over the horizon.

The Type 010 was similar to the Russian T-43 minesweeper, an older oceangoing craft that was as much a patrol vessel as a minesweeper. Roughly 180 feet long, it had a crew of seventy and carried an array of light weapons, ranging from machine guns to an 85mm cannon. The ship wasn't a threat to the Tigershark, nor would it be an immediate concern to the Whiplash team unless it sailed south. At the moment it was becalmed, facing parallel to the merchant vessel but presumed to be in constant contact with the fishing boats.

As Turk crisscrossed over the area, he piped the feed from his sensors directly to Danny and the MC-17. When the combat cargo craft was about sixty seconds away from the drop point, Turk radioed to make sure they were still "go."

"Roger, Tigershark," said Danny, his voice clear over the dedicated Whiplash com channel.

"The UAVs appear headed for the Marines," added Turk.

"I copied that. We're jumping in thirty seconds. Keep an eye on the boats and that minesweeper."

"Godspeed," said Turk.

DANNY FELT A KNOT GROW IN HIS STOMACH AS THE wind ripped against his body from the open ramp of the MC-17. He'd jumped from airplanes countless times in nearly every condition, but he'd never lost the little nudge of anticipation mixed with anxiety that accompanied the first time he'd given himself over to gravity. No jump was ever truly routine, especially a high altitude–low opening night jump; it was a long way down, with plenty of opportunities for something to go wrong.

"We're ready, Colonel," said Grisif.

He gave the jumpmaster a thumbs-up, and she in turn gave it to the crew chief and then the team. They went out briskly, in single file, walking into the darkness of the night like commuters moving to catch an early morning train.

The rush of the wind untied the knots in Danny's stomach, chasing away the tension. He spread his arms and legs the way he always did, adopting a frog position. When you were a human airplane, freedom and exhilaration far outweighed fear.

The Whiplash team wore suits with special webbing that extended beneath their armpits and between their legs. These acted like wings, enhancing their ability to maneuver toward the target. Dropped some miles west of the ship, each man and woman flew forward as well as fell downward, maneuvering toward the target. Their helmets not only displayed their current altitude, bearing, and rate of fall, but showed their GPS position, a computed course and time to their objective.

It was quite a difference from how things were when Danny had first jumped from an airplane, to say nothing of the WWII Pathfinders who were the godfathers of all American airborne troops. But certain things would never change: the strong brush of the wind, and the hard jerk of the parachute rig when it opened a few thousand feet above the landing zone.

It was a strong tug, and while it didn't catch Danny unaware, it still nearly took his breath away, jerking hard against his vulnerable groin.

"Better than the alternative," the old paratrooper who'd taught him used to say.

Chute deployed, Danny checked his lines with a small wrist flashlight. Assured that he had a good canopy, he tapped the side of his helmet.

"Team, ready?" asked Danny. "Check in."

One by one, they did. Unzipping their leg and arm wings, they sailed to a preset point on the western side of the ship.

"Ten seconds to touchdown," Danny told the team as the deck loomed below him. "Let's do this the way we practiced."

As soon as Turk saw the chutes blossom on his screen, he directed Sabre One and Sabre Two to head toward the minesweeper, just in case the Chinese boat saw them and got curious. The chutes were small and made with an absorbent material that tended to cut down on their radar signature, but only slightly. Anyone aboard the fishing boats with a pair of NODs or even a good set of eyes would be able to see them.

If any of the fishing boats opened fire, he would sink them all. The computer had already stored their locations and computed targeting solutions for an attack; all he had to do was tell the rail gun to fire.

Though still deemed experimental, the aircraft's small-scale energy weapon had been so thoroughly tested that Turk was as confident about using it as he was firing the F-35's cannon. More so, actually, since he had worked extensively with the gun before going to Iran.

Like all rail guns, the weapon used a powerful electromagnetic field to propel a metallic slug at a target. The principle was well-known, and versions had been around for several decades; the real innovation here was the size of the weapon, which fit into the body-long bay of the sleek Tigershark II. The only downside was its need to recycle energy and lower its heat every dozen rounds. Even this, though, was a vast improvement over the earlier incarnations.

Turk looked at the sitrep screen to see how Sabre Three and Four were doing. The Tigershark's helmet provided him with a configurable control and display board; he had arranged several default configurations for the mission. The base configuration, which he was using now, was generally similar to what would be seen in a standard aircraft cockpit—an instrument panel, a 360-view of the outside, and a HUD projection of critical flight data.

Aside from the fact that the HUD display was always in front of him no matter which direction he faced, the major difference between the Tigershark's and conventional cockpits were the virtual video screens, which replaced the glass canopy and could be configured in any form he wanted. Turk had located three "screens" in the bottom-left corner of his forward view. He configured the top screen to give a God's-eye view of his aircraft and what was going on around them—a sitrep, or situational awareness view. The bottom showed the Whiplash link, with messages and other data. He used the middle to select different feeds from the Sabres.

They were still nearly thirteen minutes from the Marines. The F-35s were on radio silence, preparing to deal with the UAVs.

"Five seconds from landing," said Danny over the Dreamland circuit.

Turk returned his full attention to the Whiplash landing. Eleven figures descended on the merchant ship, each aimed at a different point on the deck; once there, they would shed their chutes and head in different directions, aiming to quickly subdue opposition. The two men who were ostensibly on watch were completely oblivious to what was going on; Turk guessed that they were sleeping, as the computer indicated they hadn't moved since the first Sabre passed overhead.

They were about to wake up inside a very bad dream.

The fishing boats seemed oblivious as well. Meanwhile, the Whiplash Ospreys hovered some thirty miles to the south, staying just above the waves so they were completely invisible to the minesweeper's radar. It would take them roughly ten minutes to get to the merchant ship, either to pick up the team or to support it with their chain guns if things got difficult.

Everything in place, thought Turk. Let's get this show going.

DANNY FLARED AS HE HIT THE DECK, THEN PULLED THE toggle to release the parachute. In nearly the same motion he grabbed the SCAR rifle out of its Velcroed scabbard on his chest. The rifle was no different than the weapon issued to other U.S.

special ops troops, with one exception: its sights interfaced with Danny's helmet system.

He was on the starboard side of the deck, the high end of the ship, five feet from a door on the superstructure that led to the compartments below. He ran to the door without waiting for the rest of the team; once through, he began descending the stairlike metal ladder to the corridor that would take him to the engine room.

The ship was completely dark. If there was electricity, it wasn't working here.

"Behind you, Colonel," said Tony "Two-Fingers" Dalton, coming down the ladder.

"Dead ahead," said Danny, running to the second ladder, which would take them to a large, presumably empty area immediately forward of the engine compartment. As he started down, he caught himself—there were no steps.

"Stairs are gone," he told Dalton. Grabbing the side railing, he sidestepped his way down to a crosswalk that ran across the width of the hold. The decking was still there, but so rusted that Danny nearly fell through on his first step. He grabbed hold of the railing there, then decided it would be much easier simply to jump down to the deck below, some eight feet away.

"Catwalk's gone," he said, tacking his gun to his vest before going over the side. He dangled off the rail, then let himself drop. He landed badly, rolling over onto his back.

"Coming down," said Dalton.

Danny scrambled to his feet and stepped out

of the way. As Dalton landed—two feet, perfect balance—he started toward the stern end of the compartment, heading for an opening into the rear compartment.

The trooper tapped Danny's shoulder as he ran. "I'll take point, sir." He passed in front of him before Danny could object.

The waterproof hatchway on the bulkhead was wide open. A dim yellow light shone at the far end, beyond the array of engines. A few inches of water lapped across the deck.

Dalton turned left, out of Danny's view. Another Whiplasher, Baby Joe Morgan, whispered over the radio circuit that he was starting down behind them.

"We're in the engine room," Danny told him. "Searching. Nothing obvious yet."

He had just reached the decrepit boiler when a shout went up nearby. Danny leapt forward, turning the corner, finger on the trigger.

"*Las manos en alto!*" yelled Dalton, struggling with his Spanish. "Put your hands up. All of you!"

The beam from the flashlight on Dalton's wrist played over three men sleeping in blankets on a platform built over the machinery.

"*Rendirse,*" said Dalton, trying to tell them to surrender. "Give up!"

Danny took over. The smart helmet had a language translation program built in, but his Spanish was more than adequate enough to tell them what he wanted them to do.

His rifle didn't hurt either. By the time Morgan joined them, the three men had been trussed with flex cuffs and were sitting against the hull. To say that they looked confused would be an under-statement.

Danny was confused as well. This was the area the analysts thought most likely to be used as the conspirators' control center. Not only were there no computers or other electronic gear of any type, the three men were wearing Filipino uniform tops. While that didn't necessarily mean anything—anyone could put a green shirt on over dirty shorts—they certainly didn't look like tech wizards either.

Disheveled and dispirited soldiers, maybe. They kept asking what was going on, in English as well as Spanish, and one of the men said loudly that the Philippines were allies with America and Danny had better be careful or "our American brothers will *keel* you when they come."

"I'm American," Danny told them. "We'll sort it all out in a minute. Just do what we say for now and everything will be fine. We're not going to hurt you, but we're not taking chances either."

Danny told Dalton and Morgan to take the prisoners topside, where Grisif, Chris Bulgaria, and Ivan Dillon had already secured the two men who'd been on guard. He headed to join the others in what they believed was the Filipinos' bunking area near the bow.

"Boston, what's the situation?"

"Closed door," said Boston. "I'm going to blow it."

"Not too much," warned Danny. "Damned ship's falling apart. One charge may tear it to pieces."

He heard the muffled explosion a few seconds later. The rest of the Filipino contingent—which only consisted of a single man—was in the compartment, sleeping peacefully despite the commotion. In fact, he didn't even react to the boom that took out the door. The reason was obvious as soon as anyone entered the compartment—it smelled like formaldehyde, a result of the burn-off from the homemade still that dominated the center of the compartment.

Roused to semiconsciousness, the man was taken above, to join the other prisoners. Boston and Achmoody began questioning the Filipinos while the rest of the team proceeded to search the ship.

Danny was making his way up into the superstructure when Breanna hailed him from the Cube.

"What's your situation?" she asked.

"I have no command center here, no computers, no nothing," he told her. "We're searching."

"Nothing at all?"

"Negative. Six Filipinos. Every one of them was asleep when we landed. Including the people who were supposed to be on watch."

"Have you questioned them?"

"About to."

"Don't forget, you have a Chinese warship nearby."

"I'm not about to forget that."

"All right. We're watching."

Danny continued into the superstructure. The analysts had guessed it would be in a state of advanced decay, and they were correct. Huge flakes of metal and pieces of broken bulkheads littered Danny's path as he made his way to the bridge.

The space that had been the bridge was now

used only as a lookout area, a fact attested to by a pair of binoculars hanging near the entrance. The navigation and communications gear had been stripped from the ship years before; a handful of wires hung forlornly from the panel, as if longing for their old companions. The ship's wheel was gone, as were most of the metal panels that had once held other controls. Even some of the boards that made up the deck had been lifted out, probably to be used as fuel by the men stationed here.

Danny saw no reason to test the jigsaw puzzle of rotted wood and rusted metal that formed a scrabblelike walkway across the space. He leaned in far enough to scan the compartment immediately behind the bridge—the bulkhead there had rusted into nothingness—and once assured that it was completely empty, backtracked to continue hunting through the rest of the ship's superstructure.

"Colonel, we got one of the fishing boats moving," said Turk from the Tigershark. "It's moving parallel to the reef, not getting any closer, but I think it's trying to get a view of what's going on."

"Thanks, Turk. Keep an eye on it."

"Roger that."

Dalton and Morgan had come up and were working their way through the compartments in the superstructure. Danny decided to go back and see how Boston and Achmoody were getting on with the Filipinos.

WHEN DANNY FREAH HAD DRAWN UP THE PLAN, HE'D predicted that the boarding team would be discovered by the Chinese fishing boats or the mine-sweeper within thirty seconds of landing. Things were going much better than that: they'd been on the ship for more than five minutes before the system told Turk that one of the first fishing boats was starting to move.

"Track surface target one," Turk directed the computer. "Network, scan for communications."

"*Null set*," responded the computer.

It was telling him that the Whiplash network, which was tied into the elint data from the Global Hawk above, was not picking up any transmissions from the fishing boat. There were several possible reasons for this, beginning with the most likely: the fishing boat wasn't using its radio. But it was also possible that the boat was using an extremely sophisticated low-powered radio too weak and too far from the Global Hawk for the signal to be detected.

The fishing boat was clearly curious. It sailed parallel to the merchant ship, passing the stern, then slowed and turned back in the direction it had come. After passing the beached vessel once more, it made another turn and headed in closer.

"Danny, that fishing boat is taking a real interest," Turk told Freah. "What do you want me to do?"

"Just monitor it. Let me know if something changes."

THE FIRST TWO TEAM MEMBERS TO LAND HAD CARRIED down what looked like lightweight machine guns with extra high stilts. These were actually fully automated gunbots, called "mechs" by the team, that could be guided by remote control and used for extra firepower. While some were capable of fully autonomous operation—they could be pre-programmed to guard a base perimeter and fire at anything coming toward them—in this case they were controlled by the troopers who carried them, or Danny himself through an override. He checked on both, making sure they could repel any boarders from the fishing boats, then ran up to Boston and the captured Filipinos.

"What do they know?" Danny asked.

"Nothing," said Boston with disgust. "The guys on duty were drunk and all passed out."

"Drunk?"

"They cook up some moonshine and that's how they spend their days."

"Great."

"Probably can't blame them. Nothing to do on this tub but wait for the rust to make it collapse."

"What about the others?"

"Working on it. They claim to know nothing."

"We have to get them talking. Our friends out there are taking an interest."

Danny picked one of the captive Filipinos nearby and squatted down in front of him, asking in Spanish how many people were aboard.

"I can speak English," said the man. "Why are you here?"

"I'm here because we're looking for people who have stolen computer material and other technology from the U.S.," said Danny, phrasing the situation as diplomatically as possible. "They're also helping rebels in Malaysia, which is against a UN resolution. That resolution authorizes me to use force to stop them."

"And what does that have to do with us?"

"They have a base here," said Danny.

"Who? Where?"

"They're technical experts," said Danny.

"What? We have been here a full month and we are the only ones here."

"No one else?"

The man gave him a confused look. Before Danny could rephrase the question, Melissa Grisif broke in on the team radio.

"Colonel, I found a hatchway off the forward cargo compartment. You're going to want to look at this, sir."

"On my way." Danny looked over at Achmoody and pointed to the Filipino marine. "Talk to this guy."

Clambering down the steps to the hold, Danny kept slipping on the wet rails. There were two inches of water where the ladder met the deck planks; by the time he walked back to where Grisif was waiting, the water came nearly to his knees.

"It looks like the kind of hatchway you'd see on a submarine," she told him, pointing to the round wheel in front of her.

"You try opening it?" Danny asked.

"Yes, but it's locked in place," she said. "At first I thought it was welded or rusted, but there's a little movement when you turn the wheel, and I think it's hitting a bar or something on the other side."

Danny bent down to take a look.

"Get some plastic explosive down here," he told her. "Let's blow it open."

7

Over the South China Sea

COWBOY LOCKED ON BOTH TARGETS, THEN PRESSED the mike button.

"Basher One, request permission to fire."

"Do it!" said Greenstreet.

Four seconds later a pair of AMRAAMs dropped from the F-35's internal bay. The air-to-air semiactive radar missiles launched toward the pair of enemy UAVs, accelerating to a speed of Mach 4.

When they set out, the AMRAAMs used the radar in the F-35 to locate and fly toward their targets. But as they got closer, they switched to their own onboard radars. A few seconds after that happened, the UAVs made sharp turns into the path of the missiles, then disappeared from Cowboy's screen.

His first thought was that the AMRAAMs had hit them. But in fact they were still several miles from their targets. They'd missed, and failing to find the drones as they maneuvered, blew themselves up a few moments later.

"Basher One—Cap, I lost the contacts," radioed Cowboy. "Missiles just self-destructed."

"They must be jamming the radars," said Colonel Greenstreet.

"No indication."

Cowboy turned his aircraft north, heading in the direction the UAVs had been going when they disappeared from his radar.

"Basher Two to Whiplash Tigershark."

"This is Shark. Go ahead, Two."

"I need some quarterbacking. Just locked up and shot two missiles at the UAVs. The aircraft disappeared from the screens before the missiles got close enough to detonate."

"Are they jamming you?"

"If they are, we can't pick it up. I can't find the UAVs," Cowboy added. "Can you see them on your screens?"

"Stand by."

A few moments later Turk came back on line.

"Our tech guys think they're using a selective jammer to mimic your waves," said Turk. "I still have the aircraft on the Sabre long-range scan— they're flying almost perpendicular to your course, forty miles south."

Turk gave him a heading and then GPS readings that could get Cowboy into the area for an intercept.

"How do I deal with them?"

"Close on them. They can only hit certain wavelengths and they need to be picking up your signal steadily. It might help to keep changing the scan. The technique pumps out something like an echo of your signal. Eventually, they won't be able to keep up."

Cowboy wondered when eventually was. He got his answer a few seconds later, as the UAVs popped back onto his screen. They were coming head-on toward him, less than a minute away.

8

The South China Sea, north of Malaysia

TURK STUDIED THE FEED FROM SABRE THREE, TRYING to work out a strategy for Cowboy and Greenstreet.

"See if you can take them north toward the Sabres," Turk told Cowboy. "Get them closer to the Sabres so if they try that radar trick again I'll be able to see what's going on and help. The Sabres need another ten minutes or so to get into the fight."

"Roger that," said Cowboy.

"Think of them as MiGs with only cannons left," added Turk. "They can outturn you, and probably outaccelerate for a small distance. So don't let them get behind you."

"We're trying to climb over them," said Cowboy.

"Might work. Once they get closer I may be able to see what tactics they're following. They're pretty straightforward now."

"Roger that."

Turk glanced back at his main screen, looking

below at the fishing boat that was moving. A light flashed at its bow.

Another light blinked, this one on the third fishing boat. Then a light on the fifth began to blink.

That's weird, thought Turk.

Then he realized what was happening—the little boats were communicating via signal lamps.

And they weren't just talking among themselves. The minesweeper had begun throwing off her slumber. Smoke poured from the stack and the ship began moving toward the island.

"Colonel Freah, the minesweeper's moving," radioed Turk. "The fishing boats are signaling each other with lights."

"Tell me when he's within nine miles," snapped Danny. "That's the range of his biggest gun."

"Not going to take too long, Colonel."

"Noted."

DANNY FREAH TAPPED THE BACK OF HIS HELMET TO end the radio call.

"Out of the compartment," he told the others, fixing the timer on the plastic explosive. "Go!"

He set it for fifteen seconds, then scrambled back to the ladder. He reached the low bulkhead where the others were waiting just as the charge went off.

Though the explosive had been relatively small, the entire ship shook with it. The deck beneath Danny's legs began to wobble; for a moment he thought it would give way.

"Let's go," said Grisif, jumping up. Eddie Guzman, who'd brought the explosives down, followed, leaving Danny temporarily behind.

He caught up to them on the ladder. Water oozed from a fresh crack in the deck ten feet from the landing; it looked as if a giant had tried to fold the ship and given up.

The hatchway had blown open. Wrist lights showing the way, Danny and the others waded over to it. The hatch opened to a space between the compartment bulkhead and the hull; a ladder leading downward sat directly below it.

"I'll check it out," said Guzman.

Danny stepped back to give him room, then reached to turn the radio back on. "Turk, what's with the minesweeper?" he asked.

"Still coming toward you. The fishing boats are moving back," added the pilot.

Not good, thought Danny. They're getting out of the line of fire.

9

The Cube

"I HAVE A TENTATIVE FIX ON WHERE THE UAVs CAME from," said Yanni Turnis, one of Rubeo's top engineers. He was talking to him from New Mexico. "There's an atoll in the Grainger Bank. A cargo container is docked near the lagoon. The satellites reported two flashes on the deck about thirty minutes ago."

"I see." Rubeo zoomed out the map on his display, then focused back on the area of a horseshoe-shaped island with a ship parked to the south. A pair of small boats were tied to a dock at the shore. The image had been taken by a satellite two days before.

"Was the flash analyzed?" Rubeo asked.

"Not considered significant by the Reconnaissance Office algorithms," said the techie. "But look at the data. They have to be UAV launches, don't you think? Check it against the simulation. It matches, perfectly."

Rubeo's technical expert was right. But the distance! It was some five hundred miles from the point where the Marines were operating. To have covered that distance in that short a time was beyond the capability of even the Sabres.

On the other hand, Rubeo hadn't thought Braxton would be able to spoof the radars, even for a limited time, but clearly he had. It wasn't so much the technical problems as the difficulty of manufacturing and packaging it reliably in something as small as the drones. Even the Sabres didn't have that ability.

What other tricks did Braxton have in store?

"The performance specs look almost exactly like the Gen 4s," added Turnis. "They may be a little faster, but turn a little wider. The simulation says they'll bleed off speed pretty fast if you get them to pull over eight g's in a turn—you might get them to go into a flat spin."

The F-35 pilots would black out well before that happened, Rubeo realized. They were best off not engaging the enemy planes—which of course wasn't an option, or probably even a thought.

"Are you talking to the Marine fighters?" he asked Turnis.

"We don't have a direct hookup. They're about to engage the fighters," said Turnis. "I can relay tips to Frost in the Cube if you want."

"Go ahead. I doubt they'll be of much use," added Rubeo bitterly.

10

Over the South China Sea

COWBOY PULLED THE F-35 INTO A TURN, AIMING TO get behind the UAVs as they passed. The two aircraft were doing over eight hundred knots, so fast that there was no way in the world they could slow down enough to maneuver and target him before blowing past.

Except they did.

A laser range finder locked on the tailpipe of the F-35. Cowboy got an IR warning; realizing he was in trouble, he threw the aircraft into a dive a second or two before the UAV's energy weapon fired.

The weapon's beam touched the side of his tail, but the shot was too brief to do serious damage.

The UAVs continued past, moving too fast for him to try his own shot. He tightened his turn and aimed south, hoping to position himself better to ward off their next attack.

"Cowboy, they're not running away," said Turk. "They're going to go south and then sweep around you to hit the Ospreys."

"How do I stop them?"

"They'll prioritize on the biggest threat," said Turk over the radio. "At this point they'll only pay attention to you if they think you're going to attack them."

"Turk, what are you saying?"

"Go right after them. Target them with your radar, open your bay and make them think you're going to attack them. Fire a Sidewinder if you have to—you want them to think you're a real threat. Otherwise, they're going to just keep on after the Marine Ospreys."

"How do you know?"

"Because they didn't just shoot you down. They got you out of the way, then went on. They don't think you're important."

"What do I do once I have their attention?"

"Tangle with them long enough for the Sabres to get there. They'll take care of them. Go! If one of them gets close to the Ospreys, everybody aboard is dead."

"Colonel, you hear that?"

"Copy."

Cowboy slammed his throttle. He didn't mind making himself a target; he just didn't want to be an easy target. What he wanted was a solution to kill the damn things, not to let someone else kill them.

But one thing at a time. Charging after the UAVs, he switched his targeting radar on, even though he had no radar missiles aboard. If it had any effect on the UAVs, he couldn't tell; they were still moving west.

Maybe, thought Cowboy, they're going back to where they came from.

No such luck. The two aircraft began to bank back south, swinging in a wide arc. They were meaning to cut off the Ospreys, aiming at where the rotorcraft would be in a few minutes. Just as Turk had predicted.

"Tell the Ospreys to change course and come north," said Turk, once more breaking in over the radio. "Tell them to go back to the reef."

"They're twelve minutes from the mainland," said Greenstreet.

"They'll never make it. If they turn back, the UAVs will think they have time to shoot you down and then go for them. They're obviously programmed to stop the Ospreys from getting to Malaysia. I can tell by the course."

"Cowboy and I can hold them up long enough for the Ospreys to get away," said Greenstreet.

"Negative," insisted Turk. "Not gonna happen. They'll split and one will go after the Ospreys. I've flown against these things dozens of time, Colonel. Trust me."

"Turk knows what he's talking about, Colonel," said Cowboy over the squadron frequency. "He's been right so far on everything they've done."

Greenstreet ordered the Ospreys to change direction. As they complied, the UAVs turned as well—and kept going, heading straight for Cowboy, whom they now considered an immediate threat.

Cowboy angled his fighter toward the enemy aircraft, heading for their noses. The UAVs had gradually slowed, and were now doing about four hundred knots. He slowed his own speed; the trick now was to get them to come north with him when he turned.

The UAVs held their course, undoubtedly expecting him to fire his missiles before closing. This would be the most logical move, giving his weapons their best chance of hitting the targets while still minimizing his exposure. Instead, Cowboy jammed hard to the right, falling into a twisting turn that left the UAVs on his back, closing from ten miles out.

A human pilot would have strongly suspected a trick—the move had made Cowboy's F-35 infinitely more vulnerable. But if the UAVs were wondering why he had just served himself up on a silver platter, they gave no sign of it, instead held their course.

"Basher Two, Ospreys are two minutes from the reef," said Colonel Greenstreet.

"Roger."

"They're going to put down there. I'll target the UAVs as soon as they land."

"Get closer and wait for me to turn hard north," said Cowboy. "The closer you are, the better the odds of taking them."

"Are you sure you can last that long?"

"Piece of cake."

Cowboy flexed his fingers around the stick, waiting as the two UAVs closed in on him. They'd managed to climb, which would make it even more difficult for him to get away. He'd push left and accelerate. At least one of them would do the same, and extra altitude might take away some of the advantage he hoped to get from surprise.

"Just as they lock, pull back and climb," suggested Turk.

"Are you kidding?" answered Cowboy. "They're above me. That's suicidal."

"No, they won't expect it. They'll have angled down to make their shots and you'll slip right out of their targeting cone. As long as they're five thousand feet above you when you pull back, you're good. You'll have just enough time to break their lock as they pass you."

"What about six thousand?"

"Not gonna work. Keep it as close to five thousand as you can—you can't give them too much time to react. Or too much room. Five thousand's just about the sweet spot."

"Then what do I do?"

"Pick one, get on his tail, and fire your Sidewinders. The Sabres will be about three minutes away."

It sure sounded easy, thought Cowboy. But actually doing it was going to be very difficult. "You sure this is going to work?"

"No. But it's what I would do if I were in your plane."

That was less than the ringing endorsement Cowboy had hoped for.

He nudged down slightly, keeping his plane a little more than 5,000 feet below the closer of the two UAVs. They'd slowed a bit more, which was a temptation—maybe if he hit the afterburner he could shoot away without getting nailed. But even if that worked, he'd leave Greenstreet open to attack.

The UAVs closed to four miles, then three and a half. The RWR was bleeping, pleading with Cowboy: he was about to become dead meat.

"I agree," muttered Cowboy.

And then they were on him, trying to slice him into yesterday's hash. Cowboy yanked back on the stick, then got an inspiration. Why stop now? Rather than simply climbing, he urged the F-35 into a full loop, continuing around until he saw the black speck of one of the UAVs in front of him.

The Sidewinders sniffed the air, trying to find the UAV's heat signature.

"It's right there, right there," said Cowboy, yelling at the missile. He turned left to keep the UAV in his sights, then poured on the throttle to hold onto his target.

The missile finally growled, indicating it had locked on its target. Cowboy fired, then pulled hard right, worried about the other bandit.

He was right to worry. The enemy aircraft had come in behind him. Its weapon caught the top of the cockpit before he managed to turn inside and drop out of the UAV's sights. As he shoved the F-35 back to the north, he heard and felt a loud bang above him: the canopy literally ripped in half, the thick acrylic shattered by the combination of the laser and the high g turn. Cowboy floated for a fraction of a second, as if his brain and body had separated. Then everything roared around him, as though he'd flown into the center of a tornado.

Turk was saying something over the radio, but Cowboy couldn't hear.

Where was the UAV?

Behind him. The gravity and wind nearly overcame him. The plane bucked, the stick jerking from his grip. Cowboy was blind; he pushed into a dive, desperate to get away.

The canopy gave way completely, shattering and flying behind the plane. Cowboy was pushed back in the seat, his hands still on the controls but unable to move because of the force of the wind. The aircraft had slowed and descended precipitously, but it was still a wild beast, some 5,000 feet above sea level, wings tipped.

I'm dead, he thought.

A pair of black shadows passed in front of him. There was a flash in the sky, a jagged red and yellow hand rising behind him.

The Sabres had arrived.

Over the South China Sea

Turk watched the Sabres follow the UAV that had been on Cowboy's tail as it tried to accelerate away. Cowboy's missile had damaged the other aircraft, but it was still flying, heading westward, most likely back toward its base.

They'd take down the one they had first, then go for the other. The enemy had never seen them coming.

With the Marines now in reasonably good shape, Turk turned his full attention back to the minesweeper, which had continued toward the island. He sent Sabre One on a low pass directly over the ship, running from bow to stern, and got a good close-up showing the sailors manning battle stations. The 85mm gun swung in the direction of the beached merchant vessel.

"Colonel Freah, I'm guessing they're getting ready to fire," Turk told Danny. "Like really soon. Minutes, if not seconds. They're nearly in range."

"Radio the warning."

"Yes, sir." They had prepared a brief message in English and Mandarin, declaring that the merchant ship had been boarded by U.S. forces in accordance with a UN resolution against helping the Malaysian rebels and telling the Chinese not to interfere. Turk had the computer broadcast it on all channels used by the Chinese navy.

There was no response. Not that he really expected one.

"Colonel, no response. They're in range."

"Do what you gotta do," replied Freah. "But only if they fire."

In other words—don't shoot until they do. In many if not most situations, U.S. pilots would be allowed to fire on a ship or aircraft that turned its weapons radars on and locked on them. But the recent contentious history of U.S.-Chinese interactions in the South China Sea, where weapons radars were routinely used for provocation by both sides, had led to the more stringent requirement. There was an additional consideration in this case, as the capabilities of the Tigershark's weapon were still secret, and simply using the weapon provided the enemy with information.

The Chinese were also notoriously poor shots. Still . . .

Turk started to object. "Colonel, if I wait until they fire, there's always the possibility—"

"Those are your orders."

"Yes, sir."

"THERE'S A HELL OF A LOT OF GEAR HERE," YELLED Guzman from below. He'd gone through the hull into another opening and a small compartment beyond. "Looks like the frickin' bat cave. And there's another hatchway down at the end."

"I'm coming down," said Danny. "Stand by."

Leaving Grisif near the blown-out hatchway, Danny maneuvered himself down to the ladder and then across the thick screen that ran between the hull and the compartment bulkhead. Water flowed at his feet, trickling down from the compartment above. Danny's wrist light was of little use inside the darkened chamber. He switched the helmet to night vision, which cast everything an eerie gray. He had to turn sideways to get through the opening in the hull, squeezing his body down into a squat.

The compartment was actually a cylinder attached to the outside of the ship via a narrow tunnel. It opened into what looked like a large round hallway lined with computer equipment. Running nearly thirty feet, the cylinder was fourteen feet in diameter, with LED lighting along the top and a metal screen deck at the bottom. There were pumps below, sucking in the water as it leaked down and expelling it somewhere outside in the seabed. They were losing the battle, water slowly inching up toward the deck.

Power came from a device that converted wave energy into electricity, storing it in a large pack of batteries that filled the rest of the area below the decking. Computer servers and other electronic equipment were stacked along the walls; there were two processing stations with multiple screens and keyboards. One of the computers seemed to be on standby, with a small LED lit, but the rest were off and the screens blank.

"Quite a setup, huh?" said Guzman.

"It is. We gotta get this stuff out of here," added Danny.

"It's bolted to the metal frames."

As Danny leaned down to examine it, there was

a loud crack from above. The ship lifted two feet in the air, then settled hard, knocking both of them to the deck.

"Damn," muttered Guzman.

"Yeah," said Danny, hitting the radio Send button. "Team check in."

There was no answer. The short-range communications relied on being near another unit, and with all the metal and water between them, Grisif was now out of range.

"Colonel, look at that." Guzman pointed back toward the entrance to the cylinder connecting them to the rest of the ship. A sheet of water streamed down from a fresh crack at the top. "We gotta get out of here."

But before they could move, the cylinder abruptly jerked downward, pushing them toward the hatchway where they'd come in. The pair fell into the water as it rolled, flopping against the side of the ship as the hatch came loose from its mooring. The tunnel-like connection between the ship and the compartment broke apart. A section rolled under the container and the ship. Crushed and twisted, it blocked their way out.

THE MINESWEEPER'S SHOT ON THE MERCHANT SHIP HIT the reef on the starboard side of the vessel, throwing a geyser of water and coral into the air. It was short, and the Chinese crew didn't get a chance to correct.

"Fire," said Turk. "Disable target."

Current shot through the rail at the center of the

Tigershark, propelling what looked like an aerodynamic railroad spike out of the plane, through the air, and into the center of the shroud covering the 85mm deck gun on the Chinese minesweeper.

Two more shots sped from the Tigershark before Turk told the computer to stop; he was out to disable the gun, not sink the ship. His restraint was not appreciated on the ship, however, especially among the gun crew nor the men in the compartment directly below. Traveling in excess of Mach 6, the rail gun's spikes shattered the Chinese gun and the mechanism that fed it. The spewing shrapnel ignited the explosive in a loaded shell, which not only exploded but started a secondary fire in the gun housing. This quickly spread to the deck immediately below the gun.

Meanwhile, two of the three projectiles continued through the ship after striking the gun. Penetrating the hull, they left relatively small but critical holes, and the ship started listing to its starboard side.

Damage control was complicated by the fire on the deck below the gun and confusion among the crew and the captain; it was not immediately clear where the attack had come from, as neither the Tigershark nor its escorts could be picked up on radar. The minesweeper therefore continued toward the reef—a serious mistake.

The fire showed as a hot glow on Turk's targeting screen, with a damage percentage of one hundred percent in the legend next to it, indicating that the gun was now considered out of action even by the overly cautious computer. But the ship had other guns, and the fact that it was still moving convinced Turk that it remained a danger.

"Target propulsion system on target one," he told the computer.

"*Computed*," replied the computer. It lit three separate target areas that it proposed to strike, two in the engine room and a third a little farther back, on the propeller shaft.

"Eliminate propulsion system," said Turk, choosing to let the computer pull the trigger while he flew the aircraft. The course was computed for him on the screen: dead on his present heading for five seconds, then a slight nudge right; the rail gun was fixed in the Tigershark's fuselage, and could only be aimed as the airplane was aimed.

The gun fired nine times in quick succession, not quite at its full capacity. The shots were true; the minesweeper immediately lost power, its engine and driveshaft obliterated. Its momentum continued to drive it south, but it was off-course, and its list to starboard quickly deepened.

The targeting computer was pleased; it listed the minesweeper's fighting ability at zero percent, and declared that it had only a thirty-three percent chance of surviving.

"Minesweeper is no longer a factor," Turk radioed Danny.

DANNY NEVER GOT THE MESSAGE, AS HE WAS STILL out of range of the other units. He wouldn't have responded in any event, since he had a lot of other things to worry about.

Water, primarily.

A hole in the tunnel allowed air to escape as the seawater rushed in. Danny took one look at the mangled metal and realized they weren't leaving that way anytime soon. He led Guzman to the far side of the compartment, where there was a hatchway that looked like it must connect to the outside. The surface was only a few yards above, at most; all they had to do was open the hatch and get out.

The problem was the hatch: it wouldn't open. At first Danny thought it was because the pressure of the seawater was too great. But Guzman showed him that the hatch swung inward and the wheel itself was locked, just as the one leading there had been.

"Can we blow it off?" Danny asked.

"The explosives are topside."

Danny worked his way back toward the door to the ship, hoping the radio reception would improve. But there was no answer from anyone above.

What a place to die, he thought. How ironic—in the Air Force pretty much all my life, and I'm going to die at sea.

The water gurgled around him. It was just about to his knees.

The pumps were still working, though they weren't able to keep up with the inflow.

Sooner or later the water would rise high enough to cover wherever the air was escaping, and stop the inflow, he thought. If they could get help, they could retreat to the air pocket and wait for someone to blow the door.

"You think there's a radio in these controls?"

he asked Guzman, going over to the panel. "Help me look."

They looked over the controls and started punching buttons. But there was no obvious effect. The water, meanwhile, continued to rise. Air was leaking from somewhere other than the tunnel, Danny realized—more than likely the ventilation system.

There was a crackle and a beep in his helmet.

"Colonel Freah, where are you?" asked Boston, his voice loud and clear in the helmet.

"We're trapped inside a compartment at the base of the ship," said Danny.

"We think it broke off from the ship," said Boston. "I'm above the compartment where the doorway was."

"What about Grisif?" Danny asked, worried about the Whiplasher he'd left behind. "She was watching our backs in there."

"We just pulled her out of the wreck. The hull collapsed. There's a ton of rusted steel between us and you."

The line went dead then. Danny moved back toward the doorway at the ship's end, but got nothing.

"They're working on it," he told Guzman, still trying to find a radio.

"They better work fast," said Guzman.

"Colonel? You there?" Boston came back on the line.

"We're here."

"We're going to try and cut through some of the metal. There's two decks between you."

"The tunnel to the boat's mangled," said Danny.

"That's not going to work. You're going to have to come from the outside. There's a hatch like the one on the inside. You can blow it."

"With you guys inside?"

"There's no other way."

"Shit. All right," said Boston. "We have diving gear on the Ospreys. They're holding ten minutes south. Can you hold out?"

"We don't have much choice," said Danny. He glanced at the water, which was now up above their chests. There was no way they were going to get anyone into a wet suit and into the water quickly enough to get them out. But that was their only hope.

Unless . . .

"Stand by," Danny told Boston. "I need to talk to Turk."

TURK COULDN'T QUITE BELIEVE WHAT DANNY WANTED him to do.

"I see the container on the infrared scan," he said, "but just barely. It's up against the hull."

"Barely's all you need," said Danny.

"Slicing off the end of the canister is going to take at least two passes," said Turk. "And the gun has to cycle through between them. We're looking at five minutes for the whole process, and that's optimistic."

"Then get moving," said Danny.

"There's gotta be another way. Something safer—"

"Believe me, if there was, we'd be doing it."

"Listen, Colonel—"

"That's an order."

"Coming to course," said Turk mechanically. "Stand by."

He needed to climb another 5,000 feet to increase his length of time on target long enough to make the shot. The plan was basically to use the rail gun as a can opener, poking holes in the end of the compartment where they were trapped. Turk would have to drive over sixty rounds through the top of the end cap, destroying it.

It was beyond a long shot. Even explaining to the computer what he wanted to do was difficult; Turk ended up having to forgo the audio AI interface and hand designate a linear target across the top of the cylinder.

Four passes, declared the computer. Ten minutes.

Danny had estimated they had only five minutes of air.

They'd have even less once he started shooting.

"Recompute for two passes," Turk told the computer.

"*Not possible within safety limits,*" it responded.

"Screw safety limits."

"*Unknown command.*"

"Compute two passes."

"*Two passes computed.*"

The computer divided the shooting sequence neatly in half. This meant that the rail gun's temperature would run into the red zone twice.

Turk decided he would change the sequence, taking a few less shots the first time but making sure he had enough left for the second run. It might not be better statistically, but he believed it would let him get more bullets onto the target even if the gun overheated so badly that it failed.

He leveled off as he hit his altitude mark with another minute's flight time, to the point where he had to start his gun run.

What if he missed? He'd be killing Danny and the other trooper in the cabin with him.

The plane is not going to miss. It never does. And I'm going to get them out.

Was that the sort of debate that Breanna had with herself before sending Stoner? *What if he can't get him out? What should he do?*

No. She hadn't debated at all. She thought he should die. It was only a miracle that he'd managed to get out of there alive.

"Colonel, stand clear," said Turk. "Get as far away from the end of that tube thing as you can."

"Come on. Do it."

"Two passes. First set of bullets will—"

"Just go for it, Turk. I don't need a play by play."

Turk took a deep breath, then bit the side of his cheek as the computer prompted him to nose down and start firing.

THE BULLETS FROM THE RAIL GUN CAME SO QUICKLY they seemed to be a saw blade, loud and violent, slapping as well as slicing the end of the compartment. The LED lights at the top and sides remained on, casting the round tube in a strangely yellow and brown glow. Steam flashed from the end of the compartment as the hot metal slugs cooled rapidly as they passed through the water and into the bed of the ocean and reef below. The roar and vibration pitched Danny around, throwing him and Guzman into the deep end of the compartment.

Struggling back to the air pocket, Danny realized they had only a few minutes left. Air gushed out the top holes while water flowed in at the bottom; Turk's shots had made the dire situation even worse.

"When the next wave of bullets hit," he told Guzman. "Take a deep breath and swim for it."

Guzman didn't hear a word. Danny tried to mimic what they should do. Guzman looked at him in a daze, then finally nodded his head.

That would have to do, thought Danny, leaning his head back to get more air.

Turk saw the fishing boats moving in the small screen on the left side of his console, but he had no time to deal with that. The computer counted down the sequence to the shot.

"*Three . . . two . . . one . . .*"

He pressed his finger on the trigger, riding the aircraft along the course laid out by the computer.

"*Warning!*" said the computer as he neared the halfway mark. "*Weapon temperature above optimum.*"

"Yeah," he muttered.

"*Unknown command.*"

Turk held his course, continuing to fire. Shells rammed down the rail one after another, generating momentum as well as heat. The aircraft was pushing right, fighting against the trim adjustments the computer made to compensate.

"Warning, weapon temperature approaching critical."

A caution screen popped in front of Turk's view. A semicircular graph ghosted in front of him, showing the weapon temperature going from green on the left through yellow and into red.

Another graph and warning appeared below, showing fuselage temperature. He was in yellow, edging toward red.

Too hot and the fuel tanks might flash.

"Safety precautions off," said Turk. "AI off. Full pilot control, authorization four-four-two-Mako."

The screen turned red, blinking its most dire warning.

Gotta get Danny out, thought Turk, his finger plastered on the trigger.

AS THE SHELLS BURST THROUGH THE EDGE OF THE compartment, Danny pulled off his helmet and dropped it into the water. With as deep a breath as he could manage, he dove toward the turmoil, hoping to push through as the firing stopped. But the water was so agitated it threw him back before he managed more than a stroke. He slammed against the bulkhead on the ship's end and surfaced, gasping for air.

Guzman bobbed next to him, arms flailing, chin barely above the water. As Danny pointed toward the end of the compartment, urging Guzman to try again, the compartment shifted and began to fall, rolling away from the ship. Danny grabbed Guzman's arm and pushed toward the outer end, hoping the shells from the Tigershark had opened the way.

The water churned as if swirled by a propeller. Danny grabbed hold of the panel on his left and pushed toward the still steaming mass. The shock waves and bubbles of air pushed him toward the top of the compartment and away from the end. He fought back, pushing and groping toward what he hoped was an opening.

Shadows appeared in front of his eyes. There was a round circle—the hatchway handle.

The damn thing is still attached!

They were still trapped. Danny's fingers grabbed the wheel. He pulled himself forward, hoping to somehow find the strength to open it now. As he did, his legs shot upward behind him.

He didn't understand at first. The world swirled and moved violently. His lungs strained. Finally, desperate, he let go of the wheel and allowed the rest of his body to follow his legs upward.

He burst above the surface of the ocean. Wind hit his face—it was a delicious feeling, almost as welcome as the sensation of the air that filled his lungs.

Danny looked for Guzman but couldn't see him.

"Guzman! Guz!"

Realizing he must still be below, Danny ducked under the water. It was too dark to see. He flailed around with his hands, then remembered his wrist light. The light did very little; he saw shadows and shapes.

Something moved to his right. He grabbed at it, felt cloth, then pulled up.

It was Guzman. The Whiplasher surfaced coughing and spitting water.

"My lungs," he gasped.

"Colonel Freah!" shouted a voice nearby. A weak beam of light shone on the water. Danny turned, realizing he was only a few feet from the reef. He paddled for it. Guzman was next to him.

The coral and hard volcanic rock scraped Danny's fingers as he clambered up. The reef was only two feet below the ocean's surface.

"Colonel, you all right?" shouted Achmoody.

"Fine, fine," said Danny, sitting to rest.

Guzman stood next to him.

"Been a while since I did anything like that," said the trooper.

Danny looked at him. "You've been shot out of a submarine chamber?" he asked.

"You wouldn't believe some of the shit they put us through when I was a SEAL," said Guzman.

12

Over the South China Sea

To Cowboy, the battle seemed like an encounter between a hawk and a pair of falcons. The Sabres were slightly smaller than the enemy UAV, and in its damaged state, a bit faster; they worked together, spinning and poking at the other aircraft with their guns as it tried to get away.

While outnumbered, the UAV wasn't completely overmatched; its laser was still operative, and it seemed able to outaccelerate the Sabres for a few seconds before they could catch up.

Cowboy was both fascinated and frustrated watching the three planes—fascinated because he'd never seen a dogfight between UAVs, even in an exercise, and frustrated because he was simply a spectator. He tried maneuvering into a position to catch the enemy UAV as it dodged the Sabres, but the little planes were simply too maneuverable for him to get a firing solution with his Sidewinder or cannon.

"Basher Two, you're getting pretty far north," said Greenstreet.

"I'm trying to nail that other drone," explained Cowboy.

"Negative. Your mission is to support and protect our people."

"Roger that. Understood."

It felt odd to leave the Sabres, as if he were leaving comrades in the middle of a fight. They were only drones—and yet they were comrades, weren't they?

"Whiplash, your Sabres are going north with the other UAV, trying to get it down," he radioed Turk. "I have to stay with my Marines."

"Yeah, roger that, they're good, they're good. They know what they're doing."

"Uh—"

"Have my hands full right now. Trust the machines."

"Roger that," said Cowboy. Though that wasn't exactly what he was thinking.

It's a brave new world. I want to be part of it.

Don't I?

"Basher Two, the Ospreys are going to take off and go home. We're escorting them. Check your fuel."

"Roger, acknowledged. I'm coming," said Cowboy, turning back south.

13

Over the South China Sea

TURK ZOOMED HIS LOW-LIGHT CAMERA FEED ON DANNY and Guzman as they clambered back aboard the wrecked merchant ship. The shell from the minesweeper had collapsed a good portion of the forward deck and enough of the hull. The ship had not only moved a dozen yards but bent inward at the middle; if it had been a rusting hulk before, it was now more like a pile of junked metal. The girder that had been used to dock submarines at the stern was fully exposed, pushed up on the reef by the shifting of the ship.

All but one of the Chinese fishing boats were moving to assist the minesweeper. The lone exception was sailing across the area below the reef at about four knots, apparently trying to keep watch while not getting close enough to be fired on.

Turk turned his attention back to Sabres Three and Four and their continuing tangle with the enemy UAV. The other aircraft had managed to hold them at bay so far; it couldn't escape but it wasn't being shot down either. It was a tribute to the original combat programming, which was now nearly a decade old.

Turk ached to respond himself—he was sure he could take the enemy plane down—but he knew his place was here.

"Tigershark, what's the situation with the minesweeper?" asked Danny, back aboard the decrepit merchant vessel.

"Dead in the water. The fishing boats are going to its rescue."

"The Ospreys will be here in zero-five," said Danny. "We're going to see if we can recover the compartment with the gear."

"How, Colonel?"

"I'll let you know when I figure it out."

"WE HAVE LINES WE MIGHT BE ABLE TO USE TO LIFT it," the Osprey pilot told Danny over the radio. "What's the weight?"

"I have no idea."

"A cubic foot of water weighs sixty-two pounds," said Rubeo, who was listening on the circuit back in D.C. "Based on the rough dimensions, the volume would be roughly 4,616 cubic feet. That's—"

"Way the hell too heavy for us to get it in the air," said the pilot. An Osprey could lift some 60,000 pounds, but that included its own weight.

"What if we dump the water out first," suggested Danny.

"It's not going to work, Colonel," said the Osprey pilot. "It's going to be too big."

Danny didn't want to leave the cylinder there for the Chinese to inspect after they left, but blowing it up seemed like a waste.

"How long will it take you to get the equipment off?" Rubeo asked.

"Hours," said Danny. "We only have two diving suits. Everything was bolted to benches."

"If you can show me the gear, I can tell you what to take," said Rubeo. "Assuming time is a constraint."

"It is," said Danny. "I don't know how long before the Chinese carrier task force responds."

"Do your best, Danny," said Breanna.

"Always."

Danny took off the borrowed helmet and looked over at Boston. "Who are our best divers?"

"Guzman's number one. After that, take your pick. Probably Dalton."

"They're going to need torches. And a video up to the deck so we can send it back to Rubeo."

"We have one torch, Colonel."

"It'll have to do."

Danny went to the bow where the Filipinos had been confined. Still cuffed, the men were somewhere between stunned and resigned. He suspected that most if not all were happy to see the black smoke curling from the minesweeper. At the same time, they knew there would be hell to pay, and they were undoubtedly concerned about the consequences.

To a man, they claimed not to know anything about the secret compartment at the bottom of the ship. They had rotated in it for a six-month stint only a few weeks before; the Filipino in charge—a short noncommissioned officer who gave his name as Bautisa and only came forward after being outed by the others—theorized that the last group had installed it.

Danny didn't believe them, but at this point that was irrelevant. His main problem was getting the gear out and everyone back to land.

"Guzman, Dalton, get up on the Osprey and get into gear. Everybody else, get the prisoners ready to go back to Malaysia aboard Osprey Two." Danny noted a few smiles among the Filipinos as they realized they were getting off the ship. "Boston, you take them back. I'll stay here with the divers and Bulgaria and Grisif to load the equipment. Everyone else goes."

"What are you going to do if the Chinese attack?" asked Boston.

"Turk sinks 'em and we get the hell out. Same as we would if you were here."

"But in that case, I'll miss all the fun."

"Get going."

TURK WIDENED THE ORBIT HE WAS TAKING AROUND THE reef, made another check of the Chinese vessels, then refocused on the UAV dogfight.

He wondered if the Sabres would have done better with a lightweight laser. Probably not—it required a longer hold on target to do damage than the cannons they held. Sometimes advances in tech seemed awesome, but in the real world they didn't fare as well.

In theory, the dogfight should have been over in ninety seconds or less. Two against one was a pilot's dream, as long as you were in the two part of the equation. But the enemy UAV seemed to know every move they would make in advance.

Which of course it did, since they were all playing by the same playbook. Turk was a little too far away to override their programming, and wouldn't have tried anyway—once he did so, he'd have had to pay full attention to the battle or risk losing it. And his main focus had to be with Danny and the team below.

Turk checked the UAVs' fuel. Without the prospect of a refuel, he'd have to call them back in a few minutes.

Suddenly, his long-range scan lit on alert— two Chinese J-15 fighters were coming from the northwest. He clicked the mike button.

"Colonel Freah, we have another wrinkle," he told Danny.

Washington, D.C.

WHILE NOT ENTIRELY UNANTICIPATED, THE CHINESE decision to interfere complicated the situation immensely, and Breanna and Reid had no choice but to alert the President.

She wasn't thrilled.

Her first question was: Are our people OK?

Assured they were, and that the operation was continuing, her second was more pointed: How the hell did you let that happen?

"It wasn't up to us, Madam President," said Reid, who with Breanna had retreated to Breanna's private office to make the call to the White House. They sat across from each other, Breanna's desk in the middle; the President was on the speakerphone, talking from her car as she traveled in the Midwest.

"The Chinese decided to shell the reef and put our people in danger," continued Reid. "They were warned that it was an investigation."

"And the Filipinos?" demanded the President.

"All safe and accounted for," said Breanna.

"You realize they are our allies!"

"Yes, ma'am."

"Did it occur to you that you should check with me to see if they should be attacked?"

"They weren't attacked," said Reid.

"Jonathon, I'm surprised at you," said Mrs. Todd. "The political implications here—"

"I think they would have been even more extreme had you been apprised of the operation ahead of time," said Reid.

The President didn't say anything, but Breanna swore she heard the sound of teeth gnashing together.

"I assigned this to Whiplash precisely to avoid complications like this," Todd finally said.

Breanna watched Reid's face as he struggled to come up with an appropriate response. Given his long personal relationship with the President, he was always the one to talk to her in situations like this, but it clearly took a little something out of his soul every time he did. Just for a moment, he stopped speaking as a public servant and talked as a friend, and that friend felt as if he'd let another friend down.

"The Chinese unfortunately became far more aggressive than we had hoped," said Reid. "I believe their presence was noted in the briefing and—"

"Don't go all CYA with me," snapped the President. Though extremely measured in her choice of words for the media, she was more than capable of the occasional salty expression, and the abbreviation for *Cover your ass* was hardly her worst. "What's the situation now?"

Reid's pained expression made Breanna jump in. "The Chinese minesweeper is dead in the water," she told the President.

"They have casualties?"

"We believe so," said Reid. "We expect the Chinese aircraft carrier task force to respond."

"The raid was a success," said Breanna, repeating what they said earlier and trying to elaborate. "We have discovered a technical center used by the conspirators. It's a submerged cylinder about thirty feet long and filled with high-tech gear."

"Can it be recovered?" asked the President.

"Not with the forces we have presently employed," said Reid. "We would need a salvage vessel. But the Chinese are very close. They would undoubtedly get to it first."

"We can't give it to them," said the President. That was one thing about Todd—she could shift gears quickly. "On the other hand, I don't want to start a war over this—assuming you haven't already."

"Yes, Madam President," said Reid.

"Can this cylinder be destroyed?"

"We believe so," said Breanna. "We're trying to salvage some of the gear first."

"Do so," said the President. "But avoid further confrontation with the Chinese. And be nice to the Filipinos. Be very nice."

"Always our intention," said Reid.

There was a slight pop on the line; the President had hung up.

"Not happy," said Breanna.

"I didn't expect her to be," confessed Reid.

15

The South China Sea

DANNY HAD COME TO THE SAME CONCLUSION BEFORE Breanna gave him the orders: the container would have to be blown up in place ASAP.

In the meantime, though, they needed to keep the Chinese fighters from making things more complicated.

"Turk, is there a way to delay the Chinese fighters without shooting them down?" he asked the pilot.

"I'm not sure."

"Be creative. Try and delay the Chinese without engaging them, if at all possible," he told Turk. "I need twelve minutes."

"Easier said than done, Colonel. What if they fire at me?"

"If you are in imminent danger, then take them out. But otherwise—"

"I'll come up with something."

Danny switched over to the local circuit. "Guzman, you ready up there?" he asked the Whiplasher, who was dressing in the diving gear on the Osprey.

"Two minutes."

"We have ten minutes to get what we can and blow the damn thing up," Danny said. "Let's move!"

The Osprey with the Filipinos finished loading and pushed up from the boat, circling away from the reef. The breeze on Danny's wet clothes got his teeth chattering.

With the other Osprey gone, the one with his divers moved closer, descending to a few feet above the water and playing its searchlights across the side of the stricken ship. The rear ramp opened and two figures jumped down into the water.

Danny checked his watch. The Chinese fighters were nine minutes away.

Turk left Sabre Two to orbit over the reef, keeping watch in case one of the fishing boats got frisky. Then he and Sabre One went to play with the Chinese.

After ordering Sabre One to lock down its weapon, he put the plane in a climb to the north. Then he turned the Tigershark onto a direct intercept for the course the Chinese fighters were taking.

It would be much simpler to shoot them down, but then again, as Whiplash's chief pilot, he was supposed to be creative. And Danny's orders were an open invitation to have some fun with them.

"Plot an intercept with Bandits One and Two for Sabre One," he told the computer.

A dotted line appeared in the sitrep screen on the right. Turk turned the virtual screen into a three-dimensional display by curling his fingers and figuratively pulling the screen out into his hand. The gesture allowed the holographic image to show depth and different angles. Turk turned the map on its base so he could see how close the aircraft would get at the intercept.

The computer, following its normal protocols, kept them at a relatively safe thousand yards—much, much too far away for his purposes.

"Reduce distance at closest intercept to enemy aircraft to ten meters," Turk told the computer. "Plot intercept for both aircraft."

The computer complied, its only protest a flashing yellow line on the plot to show it was ill-advised.

Turk agreed.

"Reduce distance to enemy aircraft to five meters," he told the computer. "Add event—fire flares—at closest intercept point."

A little more diddling—he altered the course so flares would be launched right in front of the Chinese planes—and all was ready.

Still invisible to the Chinese fighters, the Tigershark was moving at just under Mach 1. The J-15s were flying at 20,000 feet, side by side and relatively close together—less than a hundred yards, very tight for a Chinese flight.

Turk, about 5,000 feet above them and aimed at a point between them, juiced his throttle. He felt a twinge of perverse pleasure as the Sabre began its dive toward the unsuspecting Chinese pilots.

He was close enough to see the flash of the first flare. The J-15 pilot took a moment to react, then threw his plane into a frantic twist to get away. The other pilot followed a few seconds later.

The radio exploded with Chinese expletives and

questions about what was going on. Fortunately, both planes had been high enough that they had plenty of air to use to recover from their maneuvers; they could easily have spun themselves into the ocean if they'd been at low altitude.

Recovering from their panic, they began to climb out to the west. By now Turk's plane was close enough for their radars to pick him up.

They weren't sure what he was—one of the pilots thought improbably that he was a cruise missile, the other a UAV. They circled and radioed back to their carrier for instructions.

"I bought you some time," Turk told Danny. "But I can't guarantee they'll stay away."

"Give me two more minutes," Danny told him. "We're setting the charges to blow the container now."

DANNY NEEDED MORE THAN TWO MINUTES, A LOT more, but he knew there was only so much Turk could do. As Dalton handed one of the computing units up to Grisif on the reef, Danny yelled at him to set the charges.

"That's all we're taking," he shouted. "We gotta go!"

Dalton held up his hand, flashing five fingers. Did he mean they had five more things to retrieve, or they needed five more minutes?

Danny rolled his hand, signaling that they had better hurry up. Dalton gave him a thumbs-up, then disappeared below the waves.

"I'm seeing those Chinese planes on the radar,"

said the Osprey pilot, who was holding the aircraft in a hover nearby.

"We're working on it, Two Fingers," said Danny.

"Understood."

THE LANGUAGE SECTION IN THE TIGERSHARK'S FLIGHT computer was not its strong suit, and the translation of the Chinese fighter pilots' conversation left something to be desired. It wasn't clear from the text on Turk's screen whether the carrier told the aircraft they could fire or not.

The activation of their weapons radars a moment later settled the issue: cleared hot to nail the American pirate.

Turk, now ahead of the enemy and not in a position to launch his own attack, hit his ECMs and turned east, protecting the reef. The lead Chinese plane fired a missile, then abruptly started its own turn in the opposite direction. His wing mate followed. The missile was a PL-12 radar-guided weapon. Occasionally compared to the American AMRAAM, the missile used a radar touted in the press as being "antistealth," presumably meaning that its long-wave characteristics were able to detect and defeat stealthy aircraft other missiles couldn't. That might have been the case for planes using the stealth techniques employed by China's air force, but the Tigershark was a far different animal. The Chinese missile lost the Tigershark within seconds, then fell victim to the electronic countermeasures, which tricked it into believing it was near enough to its target to explode.

The turn by the Chinese pilots momentarily convinced Turk they had given up, and he slid around to pursue them. But they flipped back almost instantly, and within seconds he got a fresh launch warning.

The Chinese had fired more missiles—not just PL-12s this time, but PL-9 heat-seekers: seven missiles in all.

Obviously they thought there was strength in numbers.

DANNY FREAH HELPED GUZMAN GRAB THE HORSE collar from the Osprey, then hung on as a winch began pulling the line back up to the side door of the MV-22. The rotor-tilt aircraft seemed to strain with their combined weight, though in fact the pilot was simply maneuvering against the wind.

The crew chief grabbed Danny and pulled him into the aircraft with a jerk that sent him tumbling to the floor. By the time he recovered, Dalton was holding the radio-controlled detonator for the explosives in his hand.

"I thought they were on timers," said Danny.

"They are," said Guzman, his wet suit still dripping. "But they didn't go off."

"What?"

Guzman pointed at his watch. "Should have gone thirty seconds ago."

"Hit it," Danny told Dalton.

The trooper did. Nothing happened.

"Damn it," cursed Guzman. He turned toward the door of the Osprey.

"No, no," said Danny.

"Somebody's gotta check that charge, Colonel. I set it, I'm the guy."

"There's not going to be enough time," said Danny. "And besides—"

A muffled explosion outside cut him off. They looked out of the cabin in time to see a small geyser rising where the container had been.

"Better late than never," said Dalton. "Timer must have been mis-set. What was with the radio?"

"Don't worry about it," said Danny. He glanced toward the crew chief, back by the cockpit. "Get us the hell out of here."

16

The Cube

RUBEO FOLDED HIS ARMS ACROSS HIS CHEST.

"Braxton bought controlling shares of that shipping company a year ago," he told Reid and Breanna. "Right around the time he bought the manufacturer of the submarines. That cargo container ship ought to be our first target."

"I agree it has to be checked out," said Breanna.

"The Agency has made a pretty thorough examination of shipping through the area," said

Reid. "And no ties to Braxton or the companies he owns were found."

"That's because the agency is not looking in the right places," said Rubeo. "This is the name of the company: Aries 13."

"Yes, I know. But what's the connection to Braxton?"

"Aries 13," said Breanna. "May thirteenth—the day Jennifer Gleason died."

"Yes," said Rubeo. "Precisely."

"How do you have this information on Braxton?" asked Reid.

"My people have been doing research that the Agency should have," said Rubeo, barely holding back his contempt.

"Are you implying that we're not doing our job?"

"I'm implying that I'm being put in a bad position here," said Rubeo, "with implications that my companies have an intelligence leak."

"We've never said that," countered Reid.

"It's implied."

"I don't think this is the time or place for this discussion," said Breanna. "We have work to do."

"I've turned over the intelligence my people have obtained—"

"Legally, I hope," said Reid.

"If you have a problem with me or my companies, our contracts can be revisited," said Rubeo.

Breanna put her hand on the scientist's shoulder. She had never seen him quite this agitated before; in fact, she might not have believed it possible for him to show *any* emotion. But apparently even the hint that he was less than patriotic—

which she gathered was his real objection to some of Reid's remarks—was enough to set him off.

Good for him. Maybe.

"I believe Ms. Stockard is right," said Reid. "Let's work through this."

"Agreed," said Rubeo, though his tone made clear he was anything but satisfied.

17

In the air over the South China Sea

TURK HIT HIS ECMS AND DISHED OFF ENOUGH PYROtechnics to mark the Fourth of July. The Chinese missiles exploded in a series of plumes that covered the northwestern sky.

Though south of the explosions, Turk was close enough to be buffeted by the air shocks, but shrugged it off.

The Chinese pilots had turned back north and hit their afterburners. They also decided that they had shot down Turk's plane with the barrage. You couldn't blame them, really—after all, it was no longer visible on their radar.

They radioed their "victory" back to their carrier and were promptly ordered to return. Additional planes were on the way to escort the minesweeper and chase the Americans off the reef.

As tempted as Turk was to pursue them and burst their bubble, he had other priorities.

Unfortunately.

"Whiplash Shark, how do you read?" asked Danny over the Whiplash circuit.

"Read you good, Colonel."

"We're returning to base."

"Roger that. Chinese aircraft heading back. There's another flight on its way to the reef. The Chinese think they shot me down," Turk added.

"Let them think that. What about the UAV that tangled with the Marines?"

"I'm just about to go check," said Turk. "I was planning on sending both Sabres to escort you back while I do that."

"Acknowledged. Good. Listen, Turk, that UAV that attacked the Marines—it's not a priority right now. We pulled some gear out of the container that the geeks want to look at, and I'm sure they'll get a lot more information from that. I don't want you risking yourself, or the planes for that matter."

"Roger that, Colonel."

"All right. Let me know if the situation changes."

Turk gave the instructions to Sabre One, did a quick check on Two, which was already with the Osprey, then pulled up the map to show where the other two Sabres were.

West of him, about to lose their connection to his plane.

What?

"No way," Turk told the computer.

"*Unknown command.*"

"Range, Sabre Three and Sabre Four, from Tigershark."

"*Two hundred miles.*"

"How are they connected to my command?"

"*Connection via Whiplash satellite system, satellite 34G. Connection about to terminate.*"

"Maintain connection," Turk told the computer.

"*Connection is automaintained,*" replied the computer, meaning that it had no control over it. In theory, at least, it should be very strong; the planes themselves were doing something to cut it.

"Plot course for intercept," Turk told his flight computer as he put the Tigershark in the general direction of the wayward Sabres. He jammed the throttle, increasing his speed. He couldn't keep the afterburner on very long, though, as he was already close to bingo.

He put his radar on long scan but found nothing. Turk did a quick calculation; at their present course and speed, he'd catch up in ten minutes.

It was going to be a long ten minutes. The sky in front of him seemed completely empty; not even the enemy UAV was around.

"*Connection to Sabres lost,*" declared the computer.

"Reset."

"*Command unavailable.*"

"Locate Sabre Three and Sabre Four."

"*Aircraft are not responding.*"

"Detect them."

"*Aircraft cannot be found.*"

"Why the hell not?"

"*Unknown command.*"

"Someone ought to program you to understand curse words," said Turk.

ACES

—

1

Over the South China Sea

SEARCHING THE AREA WHERE HE SHOULD HAVE MET the Sabres left Turk with a strange sense of déjà vu, as if he'd woken up back in Iran. Nothing made sense.

He had the enemy UAV they were following on his infrared scan. It had been flying low, barely inches from the ocean where it was lost in the reflective clutter of the waves, but now he could see it clearly, running two miles ahead at a speed of just under a hundred knots. Turk closed the distance, sure the Sabres would appear in the infrared screen. But they didn't.

He was about to call Breanna for instructions on what to do with the UAV—he assumed he was to shoot it down—but before he could it abruptly dove into the water.

Marking the spot on his GPS, he resumed his search for the Sabres, using every sensor he had, including his own eyes. But the sky was empty for a hundred miles in every direction.

"Colonel Freah—Whiplash Shark to Leader,"

said Turk, clicking the radio. "Colonel Freah, I have a problem that doesn't make any sense."

"Go ahead, Shark."

"I can't find the Sabres. They're gone."

"Say again?"

"The enemy UAV just crashed into the water. I have the location. But the Sabres aren't here."

"Did they crash?"

"Negative, as far as I know." It was certainly a possibility, of course—maybe even a probability. But something was very wrong. Why had they broken the connection? It had happened while they were still flying. Had they been damaged? It didn't really make sense.

"They just went off the radar screen," Turk told him. "I thought maybe there was an ECM or something. But then when I got close—there's just nothing here."

"Have you talked to the Cube about it?"

"Not yet."

"Do it." Before Turk could switch back, Danny added, "What's your fuel situation?"

"It's tight," acknowledged Turk. "Do we have a tanker available?"

"Negative. Negative. Be careful of your reserves."

"Yeah, roger that."

The Tigershark's sensor data as well as its location and vital signs were being pumped back to Whiplash, and Breanna had seen the UAVs disappear from the screen.

She, too, was baffled, as was everyone in the situation room.

"We're guessing they must have sustained damage somewhere," she told him. "But we don't have a theory yet."

"I can search the route they took," volunteered Turk; he'd already turned back in that direction. "There were a few atolls, and maybe—"

"Negative, Turk. Your fuel is low. Return to base."

"I have a few more minutes to play with."

"You are into your reserves already," insisted Breanna. "Turn that aircraft around and get back to land. I don't want to lose you, too."

That's a change, thought Turk as he complied. Probably she's just worried about losing the plane.

2

The Cube

RAY RUBEO LEFT THE SITUATION ROOM AND WALKED down the hall to his office.

Even if he didn't suspect Reid was trying to pin some of the blame of Kallipolis and Braxton on loose security at Dreamland when he was there—Rubeo had been the head scientist—losing the Sabres without any explanation was a major disaster. While the techies all thought they'd simply been damaged and dipped into the water, Rubeo had far greater fears.

While he trusted the Whiplash computer system and its security protocols—his firm, after all, had designed them—he suddenly couldn't trust all of the people who might eventually be given access to them. And so as he sat down he took a small iPod-like device from his pocket along with a cord; unplugging the keyboard, he inserted the device in its place, then reconnected the keyboard. The device added another layer of encryption and would destroy all traces of his keystrokes in the system once the session was over; there would be no record of what he typed when he was done.

Rubeo typed a series of commands to connect him to his own computer network. Once he was authenticated—ID'ing the physical device he was using was just a start—he began typing commands.

Retrieve the file on Braxton, he typed into the computer. *Retrieve all files related to radar. Highlight Project Ghost and any related projects. List any associates on projects . . .*

Rubeo typed for a solid five minutes, commanding the computer to search not just his files, but any file anywhere on the Internet. That meant government files as well, not all of which he was authorized to see.

This was too important a problem to worry about formalities.

Five minutes later he was looking at the paper Braxton had written on neutralizing telemetry data via sympathetic waves.

Obviously, Braxton had done more work since then.

Rubeo sifted through the other retrievals until he found the files on encryptions.

"Ray?"

Rubeo looked up to find Breanna at the door.

"What's going on?" she asked. "Are you all right?"

"Braxton was able to override the command broadcast protocol. The only possible motive was to steal the Sabres. And the only reason for that was to get their distributed intelligence architecture. That's what he wants."

"You don't think the aircraft crashed?"

"Not at all. They've been captured," said Rubeo. "We'll have to study the data, but my guess is, the same techniques he's using to hide the radar signatures were used to disguise the telemetry he sent to the Sabres. The only possible reason he would want them, though, is the distributed autonomous computing. That's the real difference between them and the Gen 4 Flighthawks. If he was simply tweaking our nose, he could have done it earlier, rather than taking them on such a long flight west."

"You're saying that his plan was to steal these aircraft all along?" asked Breanna.

"I don't know. I would say he and his people anticipated the opportunity. The way the aircraft think and communicate is unique. And obviously they are very valuable, even with the computing units."

That was quite an understatement. The AI system was envisioned as the centerpiece of a small army of units working together and on their own with minimal human guidance. It was the stuff of science fiction, but it was well within their grasp.

"If they have our control system, we've got to change it," Breanna said.

"Not until we get the Sabres back," said Rubeo.

"If we change it now, they'll realize we know what they're doing and how."

"You have a plan for that?"

"I will. As soon as I figure out a way to get past the encryption in real time."

Breanna nodded.

Clearly, Rubeo thought, she didn't realize how difficult that task actually was.

DEVELOPMENT OF THE ARTIFICIAL INTELLIGENCE MODules that piloted the combat UAVs was a long and tortuous process. Thousands of people had eventually worked on the project, and over a hundred were still working on it, making improvements every day. But despite the many variations and evolutionary changes, the core of the AI systems came from a common seed, a set of chips and programming protocols that Jennifer Gleason had originally developed at Dreamland. In the wake of the accident that robbed Zen of the use of his legs, the scientist had revamped the original designs and added what she called "piping" into the chip structure that functioned as a kind of emergency override. When a numerical pass code "flowed" down the pipeline, it could control the brain.

The pass code was a little more complicated than a standard password, as it changed on the fly. It got its basis from DNA sequencing. At the time, this was thought to be an almost foolproof identifier—the researchers could literally lick a finger, put it in a reader, and thus establish their identity with both ease and physical security.

Since that time, various work-arounds had been discovered, and easier methods used, but the pipeline was an integral part of the chip construction. It was similar to a reptilian brain deeply implanted beneath the human cortex.

Rubeo wasn't sure exactly how the pass code was being exploited. Overcoming it was theoretically possible, but difficult. A much quicker solution was to use the pass code themselves—which he had done by deciphering the part of Jennifer's DNA used in the communications.

The problem was that a different and much longer strand was being used for the command sections, most likely on a rolling basis where the keys changed according to a formula he would have to crack. He needed the rest of Jennifer's genotype, and even then would face a difficult task of sheer force computing to break the encryption into a "simple" code.

Braxton had obviously gotten his hands on Jennifer's full genotype somehow, not just the small section of the X chromosome, as Rubeo had originally thought. But there was no record of the rest.

A lock of hair? That was probably how Braxton had done it.

The only thing the scientist could think of was exhuming her body.

"God, this is grisly." Breanna shivered as he told her.

"We'd need a court order," said Rubeo. "Or approval from next of kin. Your father."

Breanna's body turned ice cold, as if she'd plummeted into an icy lake.

Jennifer's DNA? How had Braxton even gotten hold of that?

What would her father say?

"Time is certainly critical," Rubeo told her. "We have to locate the UAVs before Braxton has a chance to study them carefully. And before the Chinese get there."

Breanna's mind drifted back to the last time she'd seen her father, Tecumseh Bastian. It was at Jennifer Gleason's funeral. He'd asked for a special waiver to allow her to be buried at Arlington Cemetery. It was only right, he'd argued; she'd served the country for years as a scientist, and then died on a Dreamland operation. But the request was denied.

Bastian had blamed internal politics and a vendetta against him by some in the military hierarchy and new presidential administration. There was certainly some truth to that. The general had been pilloried by Congress and the Joint Chiefs of Staff following the operation that resulted in his wife's capture and beheading. But Jennifer also hadn't met the criteria for waivers, and the new President could hardly be expected to make an exception.

Breanna heard Rubeo's voice from a distance, as if he were summoning her out of a dream. "Will you?"

"I'm sorry," she said.

"Will you ask him?"

"I haven't spoken to my father in several years, nor seen him in ages," she said. "I'm ashamed to say I don't even know how to get in touch with him."

"I do," said Rubeo. "But I can't promise that he will take your call, let alone agree to our request."

"What's the number?" Breanna asked.

3

Rural Pennsylvania

TECUMSEH "DOG" BASTIAN SHOULDERED THE RIFLE, then watched through the scope as the buck made its way through the trees on the hill opposite him. It was eight hundred yards away, surveying the edge of the open field below the slope.

Eight hundred yards was a very long shot, even with the customized Remington 700 rig in his hands. Dog had shot elk at that range and come away with a trophy, but that was a different gun and many years ago now. His hands remained rock steady, but his eyes were no longer what they once were. Even as he peered through the scope, his right eye began to water and the left to quiver.

Still, he had the big animal in his crosshairs as it started down the slope.

Ten years ago he would have taken the shot.

Ten years ago he wouldn't have been here.

Bastian followed the deer through the scope. It was moving west, toward an old abandoned farm. He could swing around, cross the stream that divided the two hills, and come out in a small copse where it was likely to be browsing.

"Going to make me work a little, are you?" he said to the buck as if he were a few feet away.

The air was crisp, without a discernible wind. This piece of Pennsylvania—his piece of Pennsylvania—was deserted and empty, the one place on earth where he felt entirely alone and secure.

Dog reached a trail that had been cut some eighty years before by the previous owners—a Boy Scout council—and turned to follow it. The old blazes were faded and in many cases gone with the trees they'd been painted on. The trail itself was so overgrown in spots that only someone who had been over it many times could pick it out.

Dog could do it with his eyes closed. He'd been over it a hundred times in the past three months alone. Two blue, he called it, after the original markers. He legged down to the stream, where a rope and tree plank bridge was still the best way over the water for a considerable distance.

The wind began to pick up as he started down the trail. It shook the bare tops of the trees, gently at first, but by the time he reached the bridge, dead twigs were raining from some of the taller, crowded limbs. Worse, the wind was at his back, which would send his scent toward the deer.

He'd have to give up the hunt. Temporarily.

"You win today," said Dog, turning around for home. He could use some tea.

There was a time when just thinking of the word "tea" sent him into the blackness, even as he insisted on keeping up the ritual. He was beyond that now, and while he couldn't say that about many things that reminded him of Jennifer, that one thing, the one habit she had left him with, was something he was grateful for.

She would have liked the crispness in the air. Not the hunting, though. She loved to run and hike and climb rocks and mountains, but she didn't like to hunt. She always said it was because she didn't have the patience for it. And she didn't have great eyesight—she wore glasses or contacts from the time she was a child. But she could handle a rifle with aplomb.

He thought it was more an aversion to killing for sport. So much of her work involved killing, indirectly, that doing it outside the job was something to avoid.

Dog unslung his rifle as he reached his cabin. There was nothing in the house worth stealing, and he could tell just by looking that he had no human visitor, but twice now he'd surprised bears near the back. A woman two towns over had come home one night to find a small black bear sitting in her living room. That hadn't ended well for the bear or the house, though the woman at least escaped without injury.

He eyed the side yard carefully, glanced around his parked Impala, then went up the stairs to the porch. He stooped down to look through the front window.

All clear.

Dog opened the front door, which he habitually left unlocked. He put his rifle away, then went to the kitchen to start the kettle. He was just pouring the water when the phone began to ring.

Dog rarely used the phone and wasn't about to answer it now. He concentrated on filling his kettle.·

The answering machine picked up on the fifth ring.

"Daddy?"

Breanna's voice, halting, timid, crossed the tiny space of the old-fashioned kitchen like a ghost peeking out from the closet.

"Daddy, I—we need your help." Breanna was stuttering, stumbling over her words, the same way she had when she was little and had to tell him about poor grades in school or some other disappointment that seemed monumental to her. "It has to do with the Sabre combat UAVs, and their AI. I know you may not want to talk to me, but if you could talk to Ray, or even Jonathon Reid, we would appreciate it. You have Ray's number, I know. Here's Jonathon's . . ."

Dog listened as she gave Reid's CIA phone number and then repeated Rubeo's number.

He took a step toward the phone, wanting in his heart to answer. But the distance was too great, the pain too much. He shouldn't and didn't blame her, and yet it was too hard to get the phone, and too hard to talk to her.

Dog stood in the empty kitchen, the walls closing around him. Water spit fitfully from the faucet as his pot overflowed.

Finally he shut the water off and found the lid for the kettle. The igniter on the burner had long since stopped working. Taking a match from the box he kept nearby, the sturdy hands he had counted on earlier when hunting shook so badly he nearly missed the striker patch on the side of the box.

4

South China Sea

THE MOMENT OF VICTORY WAS ALSO A MOMENT OF high vulnerability, for it was a moment not only of imbalance but also hubris. Vanity was a great weakness, seductive and difficult to overcome.

And yet, Braxton couldn't help but feel a swell of satisfaction as he steadied the two Sabre UAVs for a landing in the lagoon of the atoll two miles from the tug. It was a moment of triumph years in the making, and not simply because he had found a way to defeat Rubeo and the scientist's military masters. He had defeated the brightest brain trust of the most powerful nation in the world. His triumph was one of historical proportions. He stood on the precipice of a new age, a time when nations no longer mattered. From this day forward, individuals were their own sovereigns; democracy had evolved to a higher level.

At the moment it applied only to a select few, but eventually the shackles of world government would be thrown off by all. Braxton had no illusions. Governments, from the biggest to the smallest, would fight the new age. History was not on their side, but there would be many casualties. He aimed not to be one.

The computer flying the two aircraft indicated they were nearly at stall speed. Braxton watched as the computer settled them into a gentle landing on the calm water of the lagoon. Unlike his craft, these weren't optimized to survive a water landing, but he'd programmed the flight computer to compensate as much as possible. The Sabres skipped along the surface like stones, slowing gradually as they came toward the beach. He'd planned on them landing on the sand together, but an unanticipated change in the wind caused the first Sabre to slip into the water about twenty yards before the sand. The second aircraft continued on its own, hitting the sand and continuing about thirty yards up the gentle slope before spinning right and flipping over. The cameras he had posted on the island showed that it remained intact despite the crash.

Braxton logged out of the computer and got up from the workstation. Opening the hatchway to the deck, he was surprised by how muggy the night air was—the computer room was kept at a constant sixty-seven degrees.

"We'll rendezvous at Point North as planned," he told Fortine, who'd come over from the cargo vessel to wait for the next step.

"Do you need help?"

Braxton shook his head. "No, we're more secure by keeping a low profile. Talbot and I can handle it," he said, nodding at the sturdy seaman who was standing near the rope to the launch below. "We'll meet you as planned. It shouldn't take very long."

5

Malaysia

THE WHIPLASH MOBILE COMMAND CENTER HAD ARrived and been set up by the time Danny Freah returned to Tanjung Manis Airport. The self-contained trailer, delivered via MC-17, had an array of high-tech gear, but perhaps the most critical piece of equipment was a fully automated coffee machine that ground whole beans and brewed a cup of coffee at the touch of a button. Danny had two cups as soon as he got back from the reef.

The coffee wasn't much of a luxury, but it was the only one he permitted himself as he reviewed the mission with Turk, who landed shortly after he did.

Ray Rubeo's assessment that the Sabres had been the aim of the plot all along did little to assuage Turk's guilt over losing the aircraft. The fact that the scientist believed there was little Turk could have done to prevent their theft had no effect either. He watched the videos glumly, and gave monosyllabic answers to Danny's complicated questions on tactics and the aircraft flight characteristics. Rubeo wasn't sure when the aircraft were taken over and was hoping that Turk could help narrow the area. But instead of analyzing the situation, Turk seemed only capable of berating himself.

"Look, you had nothing to do with it," Danny

told him finally. "But the more you blame yourself, the more it keeps you from doing your job now. We have to figure out where to look for the aircraft. And then we have to get them back. And that's what we're going to do."

"Yeah."

Danny watched Turk examine the flight map. He was still young, still a kid, and yet he'd been through so much—even before Iran.

"Come on, lighten up, Turk," Danny told him. "Believe me, if Ray Rubeo says you had nothing to do with it, you didn't."

"Yeah . . ."

"He's not exactly Mr. Personality, but there's nothing about those systems he doesn't know. If he says you're not responsible, you're not. Breanna doesn't think you were, Reid doesn't, and I sure as hell don't. Get your head back in the game."

"Yes, sir."

TURK REWOUND THE MAP OF THE INCIDENT, struggling to accept what Danny had said. He was right about Rubeo—the scientist didn't mince words for anyone, or make excuses, even for himself.

So, back in the game.

What the hell happened out there?

He played the tape over, watching the positioning of the different aircraft and guessing what they were doing. He compared it to what he would have done, and to the literally hundreds of exercises he had with the Sabres.

"I think I know where it happened," he told

Danny. "They should have nailed the target on this maneuver here. See how they crisscross? That's not programmed, and it doesn't make sense. So it's right where they closed for the attack."

Turk reached for the keyboard and brought up a sitrep screen showing the positions of all three aircraft about sixty seconds before the moment he was focused on.

"See this maneuver here?" he told Danny. "That's purely spur of the moment—they're not preprogrammed to do that. They're talking to each other, and the move makes a lot of sense. The enemy UAV dives. That is preprogrammed. He pretends to be getting speed, hoping they fly by him. But they're working together, and they won't do that."

"And they're not under the enemy's control yet?"

"No, because look—here they make their move and get two bursts off and then stop firing. Because they lose the target. Except they shouldn't," added Turk, reexamining the encounter. He brought up the gun camera view from Sabre Three. "He should still be firing there . . . I wonder if it has to do with the weapons radar being on."

"How?" asked Danny.

Turk shrugged.

"Let's see what Rubeo thinks," said Danny.

As usual, Turk was baffled by his interaction with Rubeo. The scientist stared straight into the camera above his video screen as Turk told him what he'd realized. Rubeo didn't even blink.

Breanna was sitting to his right. Turk could see her shoulder in the corner of the frame. Part of him wanted to talk to her directly, to say something like, *See? I'm more valuable than you thought. What would you have done if they killed me like you wanted?*

Another part of him thought that would be pathetically juvenile. Besides, he was winning just by being here.

He caught her face as she rose. It looked white, drawn—Turk, surprised by how old and pained she appeared, stopped speaking.

She glanced at the camera, then quickly turned away. What was she thinking?

Remorse, maybe?

If she apologized to him now, in front of all these people, would he accept it?

"The attack radar mode was switched on only at that point?" asked Rubeo.

"Yeah," he said. "They don't use it until they're close because the other aircraft can home in on it more easily."

"It may have masked the command transmission," said Rubeo. "Or initiated it."

"Yeah," agreed Turk, struggling to get his mind back on the subject. "It may have had something to do with the weapons radar going into targeting mode."

"So you theorize that the returns from the radar are actually instructions," said Rubeo.

"Um, I don't theorize anything."

"Possible." The scientist began talking about

wavelengths and transmissions and data feeds. Quickly lost in the technical discussion, Turk glanced over at Danny Freah, who shrugged. It was hard to stop Rubeo once he started explaining something.

"I'll spare you the actual technicalities," said Rubeo finally. "Your insight does track with some of our thinking. The question of more immediate import is where they went next."

"They had enough fuel for five hundred miles," said Turk. "They could reach Vietnam, or eastern Malaysia."

"Or any of a dozen places in between," said Danny.

"The best theory is this archipelago," said Rubeo. He brought up an island group three hundred miles north, near Vietnam. "The Navy will be starting the search of the area at daybreak."

"I think that's too far," said Turk.

"You just said they had fuel for five hundred miles," said Rubeo. "And your estimate is a little short. Besides, this is the only place with airfields that we're not monitoring."

"They were landing the other UAVs in the water," said Turk. "I just think that they'd want to be closer. Near the intercept. Because, what if something goes wrong—what if the Sabres get shot down? You want to recover them. Easily. Five hundred miles away? Anything could happen."

Rubeo played with the lobe of his ear, considering.

"We have several search plans under way," said Reid, speaking for the first time since the session started. "And we do believe that the UAVs must have been operated from someplace closer. We have a possible location for that station."

"They had that many bases?" Danny asked.

"It would make sense to have several," said Reid. "They need to move around, and be sure of having a safe haven."

"We have circumstantial evidence on this one," added Breanna. "A link to Braxton's business holdings."

"So where is this?" asked Danny.

"A container ship and tug that have been sailing in the vicinity for several weeks," said Breanna. "It's currently anchored about fifty miles north of where the aircraft were last seen."

"We should check it out immediately," said Danny.

"I'm glad you agree," said Reid. "How soon can you put together a mission to do so?"

6

The Cube

BREANNA GOT UP FROM THE CONSOLE AS SOON AS the call with Danny was finished. She needed to take a long walk, but there wasn't time for that. There wasn't time for anything.

She settled for the kitchenette suite across from the lower conference room. It was a poor substitute.

"You must be floating in that stuff," said Jonathon Reid, entering the room as she poured herself a fresh cup of coffee.

"Almost." She took a sip; it was hot, but a little bitter.

"Our call to the President is in five minutes," said Reid.

"I know."

"Do you want me to take it myself?"

Breanna shook her head. "No."

"This wouldn't have happened if she had agreed to our original plan," said Reid. "If it had been a full Whiplash mission from the very start."

"I don't know about that."

If the conspiracy had been out to get the UAVs from the very beginning, the results would have been the same, Breanna realized.

Except for the Chinese, maybe. Though even there, there was no way to tell.

"You're blaming yourself," said Reid. "That's foolish. You're not to blame."

"No, but I'm responsible," said Breanna. "The buck stops here."

"And here," said Reid. "Should we take the call in the conference room or your office?"

"Conference room. Change of pace." She smiled weakly.

A tone announced that a communication from Air Force One was incoming. Reid took his seat and directed the computer to open the line. Breanna closed her eyes while the encryption synchronized, readying herself.

"Breanna, Jonathon, I understand the Chinese ship is no longer on fire," said the President as soon as the line was established. Her face loomed in the large holographic screen at the front of the room. "We measure that as progress, I assume."

Reid started to answer, but the President cut him off.

"I also hear that we've lost two Sabres," said Todd, clearly in a bad mood. "What's the explanation?"

"The conspiracy appears to have taken over the controls via a transmission that mimicked one of the original command overrides," said Breanna. She spoke quickly, not because she was nervous or wanted to get it over with, but because she felt it would be better if she was the one who told the President rather than Reid. The military aspects of the operation were hers, not his. And of course there was the Dreamland connection. "It was a vulnerability we hadn't anticipated. It affects all of the combat UAVs, not just the Sabres. I've asked the Pentagon to ground all versions of the Flighthawk until we have a solution."

"For how long?"

"We're not sure," admitted Breanna.

"And we're working on getting the aircraft back?" asked the President.

"We are," said Breanna.

"What are the prospects?"

"I can't honestly say."

"We believe we have located another of the conspiracy's bases," said Reid, cutting in. "They're on two ships, a cargo container carrier and an oceangoing tug. We think they may have used the cargo containers to hide some of their equipment, perhaps even the minisubs they use."

"How many bases do these people have?" asked the President, clearly exasperated.

"They have a lot of money."

"If they were spending it on feeding the poor, we wouldn't be talking about it," said Todd bitterly. "What are they going to do next?"

Reid shook his head. "We'll know more if we take those ships."

"Take them."

The President seemed to be staring directly at Breanna. She knew this wasn't true—Todd was merely looking at the camera above her screen on the plane. Still, Breanna felt as if she was on the spot.

And she deserved to be. The "leak" had turned out to be far greater than she or Reid had feared. Nothing in this operation had gone entirely as planned. Breanna knew it wasn't her fault, or Reid's—but someone had to take responsibility.

"What else?" asked the President.

"I think that's it," said Breanna.

"It's quite enough," snapped Todd. "Update me. Try to avoid doing any more damage to our relations with the Chinese. And stay away from the Philippines."

"If the Chinese attack—" started Reid.

"Defend yourself, of course," said Todd. "But try to keep them out of it, if at all possible."

There was a pop on the line as it shut.

"I understand the Secretary of State has been talking to Beijing for the past hour," Reid told Breanna, breaking the silence. "I would have liked to have heard the conversation. The secretary doesn't like to be woken up in the middle of the night."

He smiled, clearly meaning the comment to somehow cheer her up. But Breanna couldn't find anything humorous in the situation whatsoever.

"I have to go over to the big house for a breakfast meeting," said Reid, using his new favorite expression for his office in the headquarters building across the campus. "I'll try to get back for the operation. If there are any delays or other complications—"

"I'll let you know."

"We'll get through this," added Reid. "Always darkest before the dawn."

"I'm sure you're right," she managed.

ALONE IN THE ELEVATOR TO THE SURFACE, REID thought about Breanna and the conversation they had just had. She was taking the matter far too hard, blaming herself, and Whiplash, for things that neither had any control over. The seeds of the conspiracy had clearly been planted years before. The vulnerability in the UAVs was extremely serious, but surely a solution would be found.

Breanna was working herself too hard. He couldn't remember when she'd had a vacation. While the same could be said about him, he didn't have a child or a spouse to take care of.

When the crisis passed, he decided, he would urge her to take some time off. It was only right.

7

Malaysia

Neeeding to move quickly, Danny decided to fly down with Turk to the Marine base and talk about a possible strike using Captain Thomas's men. Despite the fact that they'd only returned a few hours before, the Marine commander told Danny they'd be ready to launch as soon as their Ospreys were ready to go. That would be in another two hours, shortly after dawn.

That was sooner than Danny had dared hope. While he would have preferred operating at night—and with more rest—the proximity of the Chinese took away those luxuries.

"The technical people are working on a way to counteract the Sabres and the other UAVs," said Danny. "But we're concerned about the proximity of the Chinese carrier task force. The cargo container vessel is about two hundred miles from the carrier group. If the carrier group gets any closer, we're going to go in right away."

The Marines had practiced taking down a cargo container vessel before the present deployment, and Danny agreed that it made sense to give them that assignment while his team took the ocean-going tugboat nearby.

With the Ospreys operating so far from land, one of the aircraft would be used to refuel the others. While that would give the teams on the ships more support, it would also limit the size of the boarding teams by a quarter. It was a necessary trade-off.

"I'll work out the logistics and talk to you in an hour," Danny told the captain. "If anything changes, I'll let you know immediately."

"Good."

"One more thing—I'm a little concerned about security at the airport now that we have our trailer there. I'm going to need all my men for the mission. There's no threat at the base, but—"

"How many people do you want?" asked the captain.

"A squad?" asked Danny. "We can augment them with our perimeter gear."

"Absolutely. They can go back with you on your Osprey."

"That would be ideal," said Danny.

TURK LISTENED AS COWBOY WENT OVER THE UAV encounter. The more he talked about the other planes, the more Turk wished he'd been there. Even if it had been a plot to steal the Sabres, he still felt he could have figured out a way to get the better of them.

The combat UAVs were the key. Turk knew from analyzing the Sabre video that they were roughly the equivalent of the latest Flighthawks, with the exception of the laser weapon. That was truly an advance, but even that had its limitations. It had to fire for several seconds to be effective; more importantly, it could only be used at short range. There were a small number of vulnerable places on a target as well.

"Think of it as a cannon that's effective from three miles out," suggested Turk. "Don't let it get on your tail, and don't give it a clean shot at your fuel areas, even for a second."

"It needs three, though," said Cowboy.

"That's what the techs say. Anything less just gives you a hot foot."

"Best thing is to take it down as soon as you see it," said Colonel Greenstreet.

"Can't argue with that," said Turk.

Turk diagrammed a few of the basic maneuvers he expected the planes would favor, and the best way to deal with them. None of the tactics were revolutionary, though they did take advantage of the UAVs' proclivities as well as the flight characteristics.

"Never try and outturn them," Turk warned. "But they don't accelerate as quickly as you'd think. And they have a lot of trouble in a two-on-one situation. The first thing they'll do is dive."

"Why?" asked Cowboy.

"That's the way they're programmed. I think it's because they were flying with Megafortresses originally, and their role was to keep interceptors away from the mother ship. So if they were overwhelmed and couldn't come up with a strategy, the default was to move away from the Megafortress. Because the EB-52s were typically flying at a high altitude, that meant going down."

There were other tactical reasons, but the relevant point was simply knowing what they would do. Turk talked for a while more about tactics ranging from when to hit chaff to the need to use radar missiles at relatively close range so the UAVs had less time to duck them. By the time Danny Freah appeared at the door to summon Turk, he was talked out.

"Looks like I gotta get moving," he told the Marines. "We'll hook up when we have the op details. Basic plan, let me deal with the biggest UAV threats, you guys watch the teams on the boats."

"And anybody that gets past you," said Cowboy.

"I don't think anybody's gonna get past him," said Greenstreet.

Turk glanced at the Marine officer. It was a vote of confidence—the first one he'd gotten from him.

"Thanks," said Turk. "But if something does, I know you guys'll nail it."

Danny NOTICED A FAMILIAR FACE AMONG THE DETAIL sent to help protect the Whiplash trailer: Corporal Mofitt.

The corporal steadfastly ignored him.

Just as well, thought Danny. Not my business.

The plan for the takedown of the two ships was as simple as it was dangerous—the Ospreys would broadcast warnings to the ships that they were to be inspected for contraband, then deposit teams via fast-rope onto their decks. If there was any resistance at all, the bridges on both ships would be raked with gunfire from the Whiplash Osprey. Continued resistance would net an attack from the Tigershark. They'd stop short of sinking the vessels—but only just.

The next few hours were a whirl of preparations. Danny studied the latest intelligence and conferred via satellite phone with Captain Thomas, who had refined the takedown plan on the cargo ship. Thomas also suggested Danny take a squad of Marines with the Whiplash team to act as reinforcements, in case something went wrong on either ship.

Takeoff was set for 0800, with H hour at 0910. They were good to go.

As Danny signed off with Thomas, there was a knock at the door to the Whiplash trailer. Boston poked his head in.

"Marine wants to see you, Colonel," said Boston. "Says it's personal, but important."

Danny guessed it was Mofitt. He was right: Mofitt, head down, shambled into the trailer as soon as Danny said he could come in. His manner reminded Danny of a puppy who'd peed on a rug.

"Corporal? What can I do for you?" Danny asked as Boston disappeared.

"I need another chance, sir."

"How's that?"

"Captain Thomas thinks I'm a coward, and that's not true. I know I froze, and you saw me, and I'm not going to lie about that. But—"

Mofitt stopped abruptly, as if he'd suddenly lost the ability to talk.

"Listen, I know you went stiff," said Danny gently. "I also know that you didn't freeze the day before when you and I went out and we came under fire. It's just one of those things. It happens. You move through it."

Mofitt looked up, surprised. "Captain Thomas doesn't seem to think so. He said I'm an embarrassment."

"I can't speak for your captain, son. I can tell you what I would do if I were in *your* position—I'd deal with it, and move on. I'm sure you've dealt with adversity before."

"Yes, sir, I have."

"See."

"Maybe you, uh, could say something to the captain? All I want is another chance."

"I don't think he'll listen to me."

"Sir, he has a lot of respect for you. A lot."

Danny nodded. He saw no point in telling the corporal that he already had talked to Thomas. "I'll give it a shot. But I can't tell him what to do."

"Thank you, sir. Thank you." Mofitt's head bobbed up and down. "All my life, I just wanted to be a Marine. I just wanted to prove myself. But— that day. I don't know. That day, that moment even. It just got to me for that one time."

"I'm sure."

They stood facing each other for a long, awkward moment. Finally Danny told him that he had many things to do.

"Of course," said Mofitt. "Listen, I'm sorry. I—I really appreciate it. Thank you. Thank you. All I need is another chance."

DANNY REMEMBERED MOFITT'S WORDS AN HOUR later when the Whiplash team boarded the Osprey to start their operation. The Marine backup unit that was supposed to ride with Whiplash had yet to arrive in their Hummers.

He went to Sergeant Hurst, the head of the security detail, and told him that he was taking him and his men as backups; the Marines en route would take their place as the security force.

Hurst didn't even try to suppress the smile on his face.

"Leave two men here to watch everything," Danny told him. "Boston—Chief Rockland—will take care of them. I'll tell your commander I made the switch. And make sure Corporal Mofitt is aboard the Osprey."

"Mofitt, sir?"

"Yes," said Danny. "I think he deserves another chance."

The sergeant narrowed his eyes, but then nodded. "Yes, sir. As you say."

8

Aboard Air Force One

"I HARDLY THINK CHINA WILL GO TO WAR OVER A MINE-sweeper," President Todd told the Secretary of State, Alistar Newhaven, over the secure video connection. "Especially since they took the first shot."

Newhaven frowned. The lighting in the State Department "tank" made him look ten years older than he was, and he was no spring chicken to begin with, as the saying went.

"I'm just reporting their stance," he told her. "They're calling it a provocation."

"Theirs or ours?"

"They are one-sided, obviously."

"We have tape and plenty of evidence, and frankly they ought to be glad that we didn't sink their damn ship and destroy their aircraft."

"Madam President, we have come so close to a rapprochement, and now it's going to go up in smoke."

"I'm not going to knuckle under to bullying tactics. Reiterate our earlier statement. We are chasing international outlaws in accordance with the UN resolution," said Todd, trying to speak in as diplomatic a tone as she could muster, "and in the interests of justice and safety, they would do well to stay the hell out of our way. Fix my verbiage, obviously. But make it clear that we're not backing down. That's my position."

"I wasn't suggesting we back down—"

"Good."

Newhaven started to say something she thought was an objection. Todd cut him off. "If you can't do that, then submit your resignation."

He looked stricken. "I was about to say that I had no problem with it."

"Good. I'm glad we agree." Todd flicked off the call and hit the next one in the queue—Charles Lovel, the Secretary of Defense.

"Mr. Lovel, you're up to date, I assume?" she

said, knowing that he was. "The Flighthawks are grounded until further notice?"

"They are. We're in the process of providing a fix." He switched the topic quickly, subtly attacking Whiplash and its unique command arrangement. "I have to say, Madam President, that this would have been better from the start if the CIA was not involved. The operation should have been launched by the Navy."

"In a month, when the rebels they were supporting were in full control of eastern Malaysia."

"I don't think that would have happened. And here we have basically your private army—"

"You're starting to sound like certain members of Congress," answered the President. "Whiplash is under joint control, Mr. Lovel. Your department is responsible for the people."

"They answer to the Joint Chiefs, not me."

"I'm not in the mood for a turf battle," warned the President.

"I'm not starting one. The Joint Chiefs are recommending that our submarine move between the Chinese and the Whiplash operation," added Lovel. "Frankly, I'd recommend a greater show of force."

Now it was Todd's turn to argue for restraint. "We don't want this to escalate too far if we can help it," she told the secretary. "Nor do I want to call attention to the fact that we've lost two of our most advanced UAVs. Responding too strongly will only make them more curious, not less. How capable is the submarine?"

"Very. But it doesn't have a land force. Or an air arm."

The submarine Lovel was referring to was the *Connecticut*, a Seawolf-class sub that had been assigned to shadow the Chinese carrier. It was currently running a pair of unmanned submersibles known as ROUVs—remote-operated underwater vehicles—within a few hundred yards of the carrier. The ROUVs were not capable of attacking the Chinese carrier or its escorts, but were recording data and could be used to divert attention if the submarine did attack. The sub itself was roughly a mile outside the defensive screen.

The U.S. Navy had two aircraft carriers and their escorts near the Philippines, but Todd hesitated sending them south.

"Let's see what Whiplash comes up with before we make any further decisions," she said.

"Very well. But I've asked SOCCOM to move a SEAL team into position aboard the *Reagan*. They're as capable of Whiplash in a situation like this— This isn't a case where high-tech alone can get the job done. If anything, it's been just the opposite."

The remark, to Todd, was one more indication that the Secretary of Defense wanted to shut Whiplash and the Office of Special Projects down. He'd never particularly liked either the group or the arrangement with the CIA, arguing that all special operations should be handled by SOCCOM, or the Special Operations Command, which was in charge of the SEALs, Special Forces, Rangers, and other spec op units.

While occasionally accused of being cowboys, SOCCOM was a highly disciplined operation with a clear chain of command—and not coincidentally enjoyed a very tight relationship with the secretary, who had made sure several of his friends had high places in the command structure.

"Thank you for your assessment, Charles," said Todd, filing her observation away. "We'll reconvene when we have news."

9

South China Sea

BRAXTON HAD TO HAND IT TO THE DREAMLAND PEOPLE: not only had the Sabre UAVs landed intact, but their self-diagnosis modules declared they were in fit shape and ready for action pending refueling. It was far better than he had hoped: even the second generation Flighthawks would have experienced some damage to their wing structure.

While it was their "brains" he wanted, the Sabres' airfoils would be of great interest to several countries, and could undoubtedly fetch a considerable sum if sold. The question was to whom. The two most likely candidates were China and Iran, but neither was suitable. Braxton hated the Chinese, and knew the Iranians could never be trusted, as an earlier attempt at a deal with them had proven.

Russia was a possibility, though that would also

carry risks. The country's prime minister was mercurial, which meant those under him were mercurial as well; they were as likely to try to steal aircraft as they were to actually pay for them, and Russia's annoying tendency to insist on using Russian banks to initiate payment might even help the U.S.: for some reason, Russian officials refused to believe that the NSA routinely watched all large transactions, and would undoubtedly use that lead to break into Braxton's financial network.

But the other countries that could afford to pay the amount of money the UAVs were worth were allies of the U.S., at least nominally, which would make dealing with them even more difficult. The only one he really would trust would be Israel, but they had a strong relationship with President Todd, who had backed them most recently on the Syrian partition.

All of that was to be worried about later. Right now Braxton had to get the aircraft aboard the launch and meet up with the cargo container.

Given their abilities, the Sabres were not only small but surprisingly light. Much of the UAV's operational weight came from the fuel it carried; three-quarters empty meant it was light enough to be easily handled by two men. In fact, Talbot could probably have handled it by himself; holding the left wing, Braxton mostly steered as they carried the aircraft off the beach and onto the bow area of the long launch. With a wingspan barely as big as the average desk, both aircraft fit nicely in the front of the boat. Lashed down to the deck, they looked a little like stingrays with short tails.

As soon as the aircraft were secured, Talbot backed the launch off the shoal, turning carefully toward the open sea. Satisfied that they were in good shape, Braxton eased himself forward to examine the Sabres. It was hard to believe that aircraft so small and sleek could be so deadly.

If his own UAVs were advanced—as aircraft, he reckoned they were close to the second generation Flighthawks, though not quite as fast—these were a step or two beyond. Even smaller than the Flighthawks, they were built around a lightweight but powerful jet engine and a 25mm cannon. The main electronics, consisting of custom-made chips and IC circuits, were distributed along the aircraft, rather than concentrated in one place; they couldn't be accessed without disassembling the spine of the aircraft.

The bulge of the rear part of the engine on the underside of the aircraft was similar to that on his airplanes—not a surprise, given that his engine was an earlier version of the Sabres'. The nozzle and variable thrust mechanisms at the back of the planes was both strikingly simple—two perforated pieces of metal, one over the other, made up the body—and yet effective, acting as both a thermal dissipater and directional thruster at the same time. Unable to access the interior of the molded unit, Braxton surmised it was controlled by a coglike mechanism that aligned the perforations as well as changed the length and shape of the tailpipe, adding a vector effect to the thrust.

It would be a shame to sell the technology, he thought. They should keep it for themselves.

"We're being hailed," said Talbot from the wheelhouse.

"By who?"

"A Chinese patrol craft."

"Screw them," said Braxton.

"I'm not answering."

"Do they have aircraft up?"

"Not clear," said Talbot. "Nothing on the passive radar."

Braxton took the binoculars from the shelf next to the wheel and scanned the horizon. There was a dot in the distance to the north, directly in their path. It was too close to be the cargo container ship.

"Let's go to Daela instead of the rendezvous," he told Talbot.

"Got it."

Daela was the last of their reef hideouts. Larger than the others, with good vegetation covering a third of the land, Braxton had used it for the early tests of the UAVs. It was claimed by Vietnam as well as China and Malaysia, and nearly equidistant to Vietnam and Brunei.

Talbot immediately changed course, consulting the GPS to come to the right heading. Within minutes the blip on the horizon disappeared.

Braxton wondered if he'd been too cautious. He was about to tell Talbot to turn back to the north when they were hailed again, and this time told to stop dead in the water or face an attack.

"They can't possibly be talking to us," said Braxton.

"They're using the Malaysian registration number of the launch," said Talbot.

"How would they have gotten that?" Braxton asked. It was a rhetorical question—surely the Chinese had plenty of spies in Malaysia who could have supplied it. "It has to be a bluff."

"Should I answer?"

"Absolutely not."

Braxton went back to scanning the horizon. The way in front of them was clear, but there was another shadow now to the north.

"It may be a trick from the Dreamland people," said Braxton, thinking out loud.

He had defeated the locator circuitry in the Sabres as part of the process of taking them over. It had to have worked, he thought; otherwise they would have been all over him when he recovered the planes, if they even let him get that far.

Were the Chinese really following?

"Talbot, when was the last time you used the launch?" he asked.

"Couple of days ago, after we left Brunei."

"Was it scanned?"

"For bugs? Of course."

But they were tracking them, weren't they? How?

Braxton went to the GPS unit.

"Has this been tampered with?" he asked, examining the holder plate. "These screws have been replaced."

Talbot bent to look at it. "I think you're getting paranoid."

"No. It's either been monkeyed with or replaced. It may even be the same unit; they just have to know which signal is pinging the satellites. Damn."

He yanked it out and threw it in the water,

though if it had been bugged, the damage was already done.

The speck to the north was growing exponentially. Braxton noticed that it was above the water—a helicopter.

He took out the H&K 417 from its case beneath the seats.

"I can handle the gun if you take the wheel," said Talbot.

"Just steer."

In a few minutes the helicopter revealed itself as a drone—an unmanned reconnaissance aircraft used by the Chinese navy and generally flown off small patrol vessels. It was rare that they were this far from land.

Braxton hesitated as it approached on the port side of the launch, unsure whether shooting at it would make things worse. It came within thirty meters, passing without slowing or seeming to notice. As it circled back, Braxton raised the gun. He waited until the black bulb of the aircraft's nose filled his scope, then fired on full automatic, sending two long bursts at the middle of the aircraft. Seemingly unfazed, the aircraft continued past on the starboard side, flying for about a half mile before turning back toward him.

"I can't believe I missed," said Braxton, aiming again.

This time the bullets burst the forward portion of the fuselage. The hardened plastic and metal splattered into the air. Part of the shrapnel damaged the rotors, and the aircraft's tail began to spin slowly. Braxton poured the rest of the magazine into it; flames began spewing from the gas tank as it quickly rotated itself down into the water. It crashed with a satisfying hiss.

Braxton had barely any time to savor his victory—two more drone helicopters appeared from the same area as the other. Meanwhile, the dot on the horizon that had been following them had grown considerably larger and separated into two small fast patrol boats. They looked like speedboats, barely bigger than Braxton's launch—but considerably faster and undoubtedly armed.

"How far are we from Daela?" he asked Talbot.

"Ten miles."

"We have to get there ahead of them," said Braxton, slamming a new magazine box into the gun. "Or we're through."

10

South China Sea

TURK TRIED TO RELAX AS THE TIGERSHARK RACED toward the cargo container vessel and the ocean-going tug, its array of sensors and optical cameras working overtime to record everything below. He was at 25,000 feet, not quite invisible to the naked eye but certainly far enough away that he'd look like little more than a blur in the distance. Neither of the two ships seemed to have a radar system capable of tracking him, let alone direct a weapons system to shoot him down. And yet he somehow felt vulnerable, as if he were being shadowed by an enemy he couldn't identify, let alone defeat.

It wasn't the fact that he didn't have the Sabres escorting him, although it felt strange to fly without them. Nor was he really worried about the Chinese fleet sailing a few hundred miles away—he knew he could fly the pants off a dozen J-15s.

But the fact that someone had managed to take over the Sabres—had proven they were more advanced and smarter than OSP, Dreamland, Rubeo, and everyone else—that was a little unnerving.

And that, he decided as he checked his course, had to be the problem.

The Sabres were grounded until the brain trust figured out what was going on, but Turk had to now wonder if they could take over the Tigershark as well. It used a completely different intelligence system to help him fly, but its interface connected with that of the Sabres. Maybe these bastards could worm their way in through the UAVs' interface.

Rubeo had insisted it was impossible—but wouldn't he have said that about the Sabres as well?

"Whiplash Shark, we need you to take another pass at high altitude," said Danny Freah over the radio. Freah was in one of the Osprey assault aircraft, heading toward the ships.

"Roger that, Colonel. Stand by."

Turk brought the Tigershark through a bank and came back over the two ships a lot slower this time. He zoomed the infrared image on the left side of his screen, using the computer's filter to identify where the people were. There were about twenty on the deck of the cargo carrier, and only eight topside on the tug. The infrared could get no images of anyone belowdecks.

"The cargo containers are shielded from the penetrating radar," noted Danny. He was looking at his own set of images. The tops of the containers were lined with multiple layers of material arranged to confuse the penetrating waves of lower-powered units such as those carried by the Tigershark. "We need you to keep an eye on them."

"Roger that."

Turk selected the array of cargo containers on the forward deck, then instructed the computer to alert him to any physical change in that section. He took some more slow circuits of the area, extending his orbit to a five mile radius around the cargo ship. She was moving at about twelve knots, a decent pace for the vessel, though as far as Turk was concerned she could have been standing still. Satisfied the area was clear and the sensors hadn't missed anything obvious, he pushed down to 15,000 feet and started a run directly over the two vessels. Nothing had changed; the same number of people were on the decks of each ship.

"All right," said Danny, watching the feeds. "We're ten minutes from go. Make your last pass at H minus 02 minutes."

"Roger that," said Turk, checking his time.

DANNY FREAH FORWARDED THE IMAGE OF THE TUG-boat to the helmets of the rest of the Whiplash assault team.

"We have eight people on the deck of our ship," he told the troopers. "No weapons are visible. We go in exactly as we planned. Secure the bridge and work down. Everyone good?"

One by one the Whiplashers chimed in. Achmoody, now the team leader with Boston back at the base, pointed out that six of the crewmen were on the stern deck. He suggested they land some of the Marines with the two Whiplashers assigned there, assuming the crewmen on deck remained roughly where they were.

"That way it will be easier to hold them without having to shoot anyone," he explained. "If they see a bunch of people, they're more likely just to stay put and not make a fuss. Safer for them, easier for us."

Danny agreed. He went over to the Marines and showed them the setup using his tablet, then asked if they'd have a problem fast-roping down.

"Fast-roping is our middle name," said Sergeant Hurst, the Marine NCO in charge.

Danny rolled his eyes, then called over Baby Joe and Glenn Fulsom to work with the Marines.

"Four Marines go in on the stern," he told the sergeant. "The rest remain aboard as reserve; we use them on whichever ship needs support. These guys will lead you down."

COWBOY TOOK HIS POSITION ON GREENSTREET'S WING, then checked his systems one last time. The plan was to buzz the cargo container ship fast and low, a show of force ahead of the assault. They'd ride bow to stern, with about twenty feet clearance directly over the deck—assuming, of course, that Turk didn't see something happening before then.

If he did, they'd deal with it. Besides the small-diameter bombs, two of the four F-35s in the squadron formation were carrying "Slammers"—ARM-84 SLAM-ER Block 1Fs, long-range anti-ship missiles capable of sinking the large cargo ship with a single hit. While not quite as capable as the newer ALAM-ATA Block 1G—a Slammer with the ability to change targets and "reattack" following other missile hits or misses—the weapon was more than capable of dealing with a lumbering cargo vessel.

Cowboy was not carrying a Slammer; tasked to be on the lookout against the drones, he had a pair of AMRAAMs and Sidewinders to go with his small-diameter bombs.

Satisfied that his aircraft was ready for the fight, Cowboy pushed his head back against the top of his ejection seat and tried to slow-breathe away the growing tension and adrenaline. He needed to stay loose and relaxed—nearly impossible tasks this close to showtime. He was like a football player waiting for the Super Bowl to begin; it was just too damn important, too damn exciting, to calm down for.

He loved it.

Working for Whiplash would be like this all the time. Whatever it took, he was going to find a way to get there.

First, this, Cowboy reminded himself. *Let's get this show on the road.*

Turk watched the numbers marking his altitude drain on the screen. He'd taken the Tigershark down to 5,000 feet above sea level—low enough to get 4k images of every bolt head on deck.

It was also low enough to get him blown out of the sky if he wasn't careful. So even though this looked like a cake walk, he knew he couldn't take it for granted.

"Two minutes," he told Danny over the Whiplash circuit. "Moving in."

The Flighthawk bucked a bit as he started out of his turn toward the stern of the cargo carrier, shaking off a burst of turbulence. The sun glinted off the waves, round and bright and big. The back end of the cargo container looked like the squashed bulbous rear of a hippopotamus. The ship sat high in the water, fat and awkward. It was large enough to fit three stacks of containers top to bottom on the stern deck behind the superstructure, eight across. But there were only two there now, brown rectangles whose sides and tops were dotted with patches of rust.

The superstructure, which included the stack for the engine exhaust and all the important crew compartments from the chart room to the bridge, rose high above the stern deck, some eight stories—or container equivalents—high. There was a man on the rail at the starboard side, looking out toward the stern.

There were two large crane structures on the long forward deck. They looked like massive beams or pieces from a suspension bridge; they made it possible for the ship to load and unload containers and other items in ports unequipped to handle large-scale container operations. Turk went straight over the middle of the structures, drawing a line that split the ship in half.

Three dozen containers sat on the forward deck area, arranged in an irregular pattern from one to four high, which left plenty of room not only on the deck itself but on each successive layer, except for the highest, where a single container sat near the centerline of the vessel.

Turk's flight over the ship lasted no more than a second or two. Rising as he cleared the vessel, he slid left, riding his wing into a tight twist that got him headed back toward the two ships. This time he put his nose on the tugboat's bow and let his altitude bleed down to 3,500 feet, exactly. His airspeed had slowed as well, though at 250 knots the Tigershark wasn't exactly standing still.

Unlike its cousins that worked in harbors, the oceangoing tug was a good-sized vessel, nearly three hundred feet long, with a boom behind the wheelhouse big enough to haul the cargo carrier behind her. The flat stern deck was long and low in comparison to the rest of the ship, but it still towered over the waves; the tug was small only in comparison to its companion.

These guys have got serious amounts of money, Turk realized as he pulled the Tigershark away from the two ships.

It was of course an obvious fact—they would never have been able to build the UAVs otherwise, let alone grab the Sabres—but he hadn't considered the seriousness of the threat they posed until now. It wasn't just that they could take American secrets and use them against her interests: the conspiracy could, in effect, change the entire order of world politics.

Turk might have considered this further, or at least scolded himself for coming so late to such an obvious conclusion, but for a blaring warning that nearly pierced his eardrums—someone aboard the cargo ship had just launched a missile at his tailpipe.

11

South China Sea

Braxton was less than four miles from the island, but he wasn't going to make it before the Chinese reached him.

He'd gone through nearly all of his ammunition trying to push the helicopters away. At least ninety percent of his bullets had missed—the robots were quick and small, and he was shooting from a moving boat. They ducked and weaved and moved off, and when one finally went down, a fourth took its place.

He had a single box of ammunition and an RPG launcher with a single grenade. But that wasn't going to do it. Sensing that he was running low on ammo, the helicopters moved across their bow, egging him to fire.

Braxton picked up the rifle, then decided against firing it. He guessed that they wouldn't actually allow a collision and told Talbot to keep the throttle wide-open. The aircraft zoomed close, the lead helicopter coming within inches of striking the forward prow of the launch before edging upward.

Maybe he could shoot it down on the next pass, but what was the point? The two motor torpedo boats chasing them were now practically even with them, flanking their sides. Small craft with a machine gun dominating the forward deck and a pair of stubby torpedoes on either side of their gunwales, the boats looked like souped-up versions of World War II American PT boats, with long platforms at the rear for the robot helicopters. The Chinese boats had sleek, speedboat-style hulls and open cockpit-style wheelhouses—and, more ominously, three or four sailors aboard each, pointing Chinese ZH-05 assault rifles at them. They flew Chinese flags from their masts.

"You will stop or be sunk," said the Chinese commander over a loudspeaker.

"You gonna use the grenade launcher?" Talbot asked him. His face had grown increasingly pale as they'd fled; Braxton thought it might turn transparent soon.

"If I do that, they'll rake us with their guns. I can't sink them both."

"Right. But what do we do?"

"Keep steady. Once we're on the island they can't touch us."

Another two miles and they would be there,

and then he could do just about anything. But it might just as well be 2,000 miles. Braxton grabbed the radio and called Fortine back on the cargo vessel.

"We are about to come under attack from the Americans," said Fortine, before Braxton could say anything. "They've warned us they're going to board."

Braxton was taken by surprise, and momentarily forgot about his own predicament. "Are you sure it's the Americans?"

"Yes. They've said as much. We're fighting back," Fortine added. "I'm not going to be taken prisoner."

"The Chinese have caught up to us," said Braxton. "Do what you think is best."

He was talking more to himself than to Fortine. He might have tried to talk someone else into surrendering, but he'd known from the start that the fatalist captain would never give in to any government.

"We will win in the end," said Fortine.

The line was covered with static—one of the Chinese boats was blocking the transmission.

"You will surrender!" said the Chinese commander over his loudspeaker. "There will be no other warnings!"

Just in case they didn't get the message, the machine gunner in the boat on the starboard side fired a dozen shots into the launch's bow. They weren't simply warning shots—the bullets splintered the side of the craft.

"All right," Braxton told Talbot. "We'll let them

take us. We'll have to think of something on the fly."

Talbot frowned, but he, too, had reached that conclusion. He put his hand on the throttle and slowly killed the engine.

12

South China Sea

TURK HAD BEEN FIRED ON DOZENS OF TIMES BEFORE. But that didn't lessen the amount of sweat rolling from the back of his head down his neck, or keep a knot from forming in his stomach. A cloud of small decoy flares automatically exploded behind his aircraft as a laser-detonating system hunted for the enemy warhead, but even so, he and his aircraft were perilously close to twenty-some pounds of high explosive.

It might not sound like a lot, but up close and personal with an airplane, it was more than enough to ruin a day. The Tigershark's small engine red-lined as Turk pushed the aircraft away from the missile; he held steady until he saw the missile explode harmlessly behind him, far enough away that the shock blast was lost in the wake of the aircraft's escape.

Now it was his turn. Turk banked out of his climb, lining up on the rear deck of the cargo container ship. There were three men there, one with a bino, and two others working over a case.

The computer ID'ed the kit as a 9K38 Igla, a Russian-made antiaircraft missile known to the U.S. and NATO as the SA-18 Grouse.

"I have two targets preparing a MANPAD," said Turk, recording what he was seeing as well as broadcasting it to Danny. "Preparing to take them out."

"Cleared hot," said Danny. "They've ignored our warning."

Actually, thought Turk, they'd answered it, pretty emphatically.

The rail gun shook the aircraft as he fired, its slugs accelerating to several times the speed of sound as they left the plane. The first one struck the missile's solid propellant. The explosion obscured the rest of the target area, and Turk couldn't see that the next two slugs killed the men.

He was already aiming at the radar above the superstructure. He took it out, then wiped out the radio mast and the compartment directly below it. The big ship ceased transmitting any radio signals at all.

But it was far from dead.

"Container G7—roof opening," said the computer.

It took Turk a few seconds to understand what the Tigershark was telling him—one of the containers was hiding a weapon.

"Radar active," warned the computer.

Turk was ready. Accelerating toward the ship, he aimed his nose at the container highlighted on the screen. He got off three rounds before he passed; the last slug ignited an explosion and small fire.

Three more containers popped their tops in the

time it took for the Tigershark to climb and then turn back.

"*Aircraft launching*," warned the Tigershark computer.

"Whiplash assault team, hold back," radioed Turk. "We have resistance—they're launching three UAVs, combat UAVs similar to the ones encountered last night by Basher flight."

"Roger that," replied Danny. "Standing by."

COWBOY COULD SEE THE AIRCRAFT SHOOTING UPWARD from the cargo vessel like arrows suddenly appearing from small puffs of black-fringed white smoke. The three aircraft attacked the sky at seventy-degree angles, propelled by rocket motors that quickly lifted them several thousand feet.

"Request permission to engage enemy aircraft," he asked Greenstreet.

"Do it!" said Greenstreet. "I have One and Three. You're on Two."

Cowboy designated the second target. But before either he or Greenstreet could fire, the first UAV exploded in the air—Turk had taken it out with his rail gun.

"The UAVs are mine," radioed the Dreamland pilot. "You guys wipe out those containers on the foredeck."

"Acknowledged," said Greenstreet.

FOR ALL THEIR SOPHISTICATION, THE ENEMY UAVs were using a simple and relatively primitive launching system. Fitted with a booster section, they were lifted on a vertical gantry about forty-five degrees, then fired into the air. The rocket at their rear propelled them for a little more than sixty seconds before their own engines took over. Only then could they maneuver.

Taking the first two aircraft down was like hitting ducks on a carnival firing range. Turk brought the Tigershark onto a line just above the first UAV, put two shots into the body of the aircraft and a third into its booster, then turned hard to his right to get on the tail of the second UAV.

The enemy aircraft slipped out of his targeting cone before he could line up. He held on, following as it continued to climb. The Tigershark couldn't match its speed, and after a few seconds Turk realized he'd have a better chance at getting it after the booster separated. Leaving it for last, he slid down on his wing toward the fourth and final aircraft to launch, just now climbing below him to the south. The computer had already dotted out an intercept; all Turk had to do was follow it.

Danny Freah was asking him something over the radio, but Turk couldn't spare the attention. Greenstreet radioed something else about staying clear, but Turk lost it in the background noise.

Now, he told himself as the aircraft came up into the middle of his targeting cue.

The Tigershark rumbled with the shock of three slugs firing in quick succession. Only the first one hit: the other two passed through the debris field where the aircraft had been.

As Turk turned his head to look for the UAV he'd given up on earlier, the Tigershark shrieked at him—the enemy was diving from above, training its laser weapon on his fuselage.

DANNY FREAH FROZE THE IMAGE OF THE CARGO SHIP and the tug. A machine gun had been brought up to the forward deck of the tug. More ominously, there was a man running along the starboard side with what looked like a grenade launcher in his hands.

"Basher One, we have individuals running along the starboard side of the cargo ship," he said, radioing the Marine aircraft. "They appear armed. We'd like to take them out before the Ospreys come in."

"Affirmative, Whiplash," replied Greenstreet. "We're going to unzip some of those cargo containers and then we'll clear the rest of the vermin off the decks."

Danny thought of ordering them not to bomb the containers; he would have greatly preferred getting whatever was in them intact. But they weren't worth risking the lives of the Marines.

"Understood, Basher. We're holding position until all clear."

"Won't be long, Colonel. Hang tight."

COWBOY TILTED HIS NOSE TOWARD THE CARGO AIR-craft and pickled his bombs, dropping a dozen of the backpack-sized weapons in quick succession.

Each pair of the bombs had been programmed to hit a different cargo container. He was so close and the ship moving so slowly that he probably didn't even have to use any guidance at all. But why take chances? The weapons system in the Lightning II had locked on to each container via its radar and optical guidance system, and subtly steered each bomb directly to the programmed sweet spot. In quick succession six large containers blew up on the forward deck of the ship. One began to burn, sending a large plume of smoke into the air.

Greenstreet had already made his run and was circling back.

"Freah said there's a guy on the starboard side with an RPG," said Greenstreet. "You see him?"

"No."

"Let's take a closer look. Follow me in."

WITH ONLY A FRACTION OF A SECOND TO REACT, TURK started to dive away from the pursuing aircraft, pushing the Tigershark's nose down steeply and ramming the throttle. But the UAV had anticipated this, and while it lost its aim point for a moment, it was quickly back on Turk's tail.

It's flying a pattern and I can beat it, Turk reminded himself.

I'm flying against a Flighthawk. What do I do?

Up and roll back.

He jerked his stick back, abruptly putting the Tigershark into a climb. At the same time, he hit his chaff, blowing out a cloud of tiny strips and pieces of metal foil intended to confuse radar missiles homing in on the fighter. It also confused the Dreamland-designed UAVs at close range because of a peculiarity in how they flew in close pursuit: since the target's maneuvers were bound to be extremely rapid, the original C^3 computer programming took over the flight at close range, following the locked target and enabling the remote pilot to concentrate on firing.

Dishing out chaff when pursued at close range by a normal fighter wouldn't do much; the pilot would simply use his eyes to guide the plane. But here the computer had to switch from its radar guidance to infrared or video mode. Either way, there was a delay—only a few seconds in this case but long enough for Turk to put his Sabre on its back and roll behind the enemy UAV. As he did, he noticed an entirely unexpected result—the UAV was now trailing smoke from its right wing.

How had that happened?

The only explanation—or at least the only thing he could think of—was that its laser weapon had heated the chaff, which damaged the aircraft as it flew into the cloud.

There was only one way to test his theory—try it again.

That meant not only giving up his position now, which with a flick of the wrist would put him in the perfect spot to shoot down the enemy drone, but letting the UAV get back on his tail and zero in on him.

That was exactly the sort of trade-off Turk had been taught *not* to make as a combat pilot. Take the sure kill, leave the experimenting to someone else. But if he didn't do it, he wouldn't be sure it worked.

He held tight to the UAV's tail. The UAV started a tight turn left. Turk suspected this was a deke—generally, when surprised by the up and rollback sequence, the Flighthawks would fake left and then break right, trying to accelerate away to reprocess the threat's abilities. He waited a moment before reacting; sure enough, the UAV tucked back toward him. But instead of rolling to keep it in his gunsights, Turk stayed straight.

It took the UAV a second to realize it was not being followed. It took another half moment to evaluate what that meant—was it a trick, or was it flying against someone who was dumb? Because all it had to do was come back left and it would find itself in a perfect position to eviscerate its foe.

Turk waited. He was no more than a mile ahead of the aircraft, a fat target for the laser.

It began to fire. Turk hit the chaff. This time he held his course but accelerated, wanting to make sure the UAV flew directly into the chaff, or at least had reason to.

There was an explosion behind him strong enough to send a shock wave against his wings.

"*Bogie Two destroyed*," declared the computer.

Turk banked back in time to see the UAV disappearing in a fireball.

"All UAVs destroyed," he radioed Danny.

COWBOY SAW A FIGURE RUNNING NEAR THE RAIL ON THE starboard side of the cargo ship as he approached. Just as Greenstreet cleared the ship's stern, the man stopped. Something flared from the rail—the man had fired an RPG at Basher One.

It was an act of complete futility, as the F-35 was well beyond the reach of the rocket-propelled grenade. But it also sealed the man's fate. Cowboy, his gun selected on the armament panel, pressed the trigger and danced a few dozen bullets into the side of the ship and the enemy standing there.

He was past the spot before he could see what happened. Greenstreet radioed, asking what was going on.

"You had somebody firing on your tailpipe," replied Cowboy. "Little grenade launcher."

"Did you get him?"

"Oh, yeah."

"We need to run in again before we clear the Ospreys."

"Roger."

Cowboy followed his flight leader into a wide arc that took them back around to the bow of the cargo container. Smoke was rising from several areas on the ship, and there was now a gaping hole and mangled metal where the man with the RPG had been.

"No threats obvious," said Greenstreet as they cleared.

"Roger."

Rising back in the sky after the pass, Cowboy tried to sort out what he'd seen. He didn't feel bad about having killed the man—he was an enemy, and had obviously been trying to kill him. He did, however, feel a certain touch of sadness or maybe regret that he had to do that.

"Whiplash, Marine Force, container ship is on fire," radioed Greenstreet. "You have people on deck on both ships. No missiles seen. Machine guns and launchers down."

"Acknowledged," said Danny.

13

South China Sea

THE CAPTAIN OF THE CHINESE PT BOAT WAS A SHORT, thin man in his early fifties with a wispy moustache. Nearly bald, his forehead bulged forward, and with his head at least a size too big for his otherwise diminutive body, he looked almost like a bobble-head doll. He spoke excellent English, much better than the man who'd handled the bullhorn, and it was clear from his manner that he was not a man to be taken lightly.

"You are a prisoner of the Chinese People's Liberation Army Navy," he told Braxton after two sailors lifted him aboard his PT boat. "You will comply with my orders."

"*Nǐ hǎo,*" said Braxton, saying hello and adding that he and his companion were in international waters.

The Chinese commander ignored Braxton's attempts at Mandarin. "You are in territory claimed by the Chinese government," he said in an accent that made him sound like a world-weary American. "You are carrying weapons of war. You are now my prisoner."

A man in civilian clothes stepped out from the cockpit area. Dressed in jeans and a hooded sweatshirt, he was in his mid-twenties. But though he was the only man aboard the small boat who wasn't in uniform, he had the swagger of a commander, and even the boat's captain gave him a deferential glance as he came forward.

"You are Braxton," said the man, whose English pronunciation was as polished as the captain's but several times more energetic. He was tall, and towered over not only Braxton and the boat captain, but everyone else on board, including Talbot. "We have been seeking you out for a long time. My name is Wen-lo." He smiled and extended his hand.

Braxton eyed it warily, then shook it. The man's grip was strong, firm though not oppressive. Wen-lo stood about six feet tall; the loose sweatshirt couldn't quite hide the fact that he was on the plump side. His skin was very pale, several shades lighter than the captain's.

"I've read your manifestos and admired your work for a long time," said Wen-lo. "I studied your first papers at Stanford and have followed you ever since."

If the remark was calculated to make Braxton like Wen-lo, it backfired badly—he hated Stanford and everyone associated with it. He also realized not only that he was being flattered, but that the flattery was a thin veneer intended to ease Wen's conscience about whatever violence would ultimately follow. Because that was what government goons always did: lied and then forced you to do their master's will.

Nonetheless, Wen's phony eagerness told Braxton there was hope of escape yet.

"It's good that we met," he told the young man. "We might cooperate in many ways."

"Yes," said Wen-lo brightly.

"Right now the Americans are attacking my ships," said Braxton. "I need them to stop."

"It's unfortunate that's happening," said Wen. "But it's none of my business, nor of my country's."

"You could intervene," said Braxton.

"That is impossible," interrupted the captain. "We are under orders not to engage the American force. We can take no action against them."

Wen-lo responded sharply in Chinese, and the two men began to argue. They spoke too fast for Braxton to understand more than the bare gist of what they were saying. The captain had been ordered directly by Beijing—that part was repeated several times—not to engage the Americans unless fired upon or given orders from the carrier task force. Wen-lo, meanwhile, emphasized that the captain was not in charge of the operation, that he, too, had orders from Beijing, and that he would be the one who decided what was done— even by the carrier group.

"My forces can fight for themselves," said Braxton finally. "I can use these aircraft."

"How?" asked Wen-lo.

"I have launchers on the island. I'll turn everything over to you after the attack. As long as my people are saved. Without your intervention," he added, speaking directly to the captain.

The captain wasn't impressed. He and Wen-lo began arguing again. Wen-lo finally took out a satellite phone.

"You speak Mandarin?" the Chinese boat captain asked Braxton, glancing at Wen-lo.

"Not very well," said Braxton.

"I hope well enough to realize that I will not be fooled by you," said the captain. "I know this is a trick."

"You wouldn't try to get your people freed? If they were attacked, you wouldn't help them?"

"My men will shoot you if you try to escape. We are not friends."

"I don't want to be friends. Temporary allies is more than enough."

The captain gave him a sour look.

Wen-lo held the phone out to the captain triumphantly. The older man waved his hand at it, in essence surrendering.

"Proceed to the island," Wen-lo told the captain, ending his call. "The fleet is going to respond to your distress call and intervene, Mr. Braxton. In exchange, you will cooperate with us to the fullest extent."

"Do I have any other choice?" asked Braxton.

14

South China Sea

"WE GO IN FAST AND HARD," DANNY TOLD HIS TEAM of Marines and Whiplash troopers. "They're armed and hostile. If they surrender, good. Otherwise, we do what we have to do."

There were a few thumbs-up; the rest nodded cautiously. It was a professional response, but Danny missed Boston and his enthusiastic, *Let's do it!*

The Whiplash Ospreys, both heavily armed, rode in first, one skimming near the tug and the other toward the bow of the cargo vessel. Orders were broadcast over the standard marine channels and the loudspeakers, telling the captains they were going to be boarded and warning them that force would be met with force.

Danny moved to the side door where the fast-rope apparatus waited.

The team had practiced exiting from the aircraft so many times it was almost like a rote exercise. Muscle memory took over. As he moved to the door, Danny glanced at the machine gunner covering the ship and noted that he wasn't firing; the tugboat at least had surrendered.

He grabbed on and swung down, sliding quickly but under control. The deck pitched as he hit, but he adjusted and landed squarely. He let go of the rope, regained his balance and trotted forward.

Bullets flying or not, it was still a precarious

moment. Taking over a ship was never an easy task. Even in an exercise, things could go wrong. Just a few months ago a promising young Whiplash trooper had broken both legs when he slipped during a fast-rope exercise, and that had been on land.

The teams fanned out quickly, securing the bridge and the forward deck. Making his way up the ladder, Danny heard Achmoody giving terse instructions over the radio. They had prisoners— the men at the stern were being instructed to keep their hands high in the air.

The tugboat captain was standing near the ship's wheel, hands at his side. He was Asian— Japanese, Danny guessed. His spotless white shirt was freshly stained with perspiration under both arms. The lone mate with him—a woman in her forties, Hispanic—stood near the wheel, hands in the air. Guzman was looking over the equipment while Bulgaria and Dalton covered them.

"I am in international waters," said the tugboat captain. "You are committing an act of piracy."

"You're under arrest for the theft of U.S. property," said Danny. "And for assisting the shipping of contraband to a UN member nation. I'm asserting my right to search your ship."

"You are breaking the law," repeated the man.

"Hey, dude, you shot at us," said Guzman. "You're fucked."

"There were no shots from our ship," said the captain, addressing Danny. "You had no resistance."

"We're going to search your boat," Danny told him.

"You have no authority."

Not in the mood to argue, Danny told Dalton to search the captain and his mate for weapons, then cuff them. Guzman, meanwhile, had figured out the controls. He stopped the tug in the water, applying just enough of the screw to keep her position steady.

"How many people do you have aboard?" Danny asked the captain.

"I have eight hands, not counting myself. You will find my papers already laid out there, with the log."

"Small crew for this big a vessel," said Danny.

The captain shrugged. The bridge was fully automated, and it was certainly possible that the ship could be run with only a handful of people. But Danny didn't quite believe him.

"Dalton, you're with me," he said as soon as the captain and the mate had been handcuffed. "Guzman, secure those papers and get us closer to the cargo vessel."

"You got it, Colonel."

TURK MADE A SLOW CIRCUIT ABOVE THE TWO SHIPS AS the Ospreys rose. The boardings had gone off without a hitch, with no resistance on either ship. He was surprised—given the initial reaction from the cargo container vessel, he had expected a serious gunfight. But apparently the bombs from the F-35s had dampened the crew's appetite for a fight.

They had also killed and injured at least a dozen

people, and started several small fires. Black smoke drifted upward in bunches, angry fists pounding the air.

Turk stretched his shoulders and then his legs. It was far too early to relax—the mission had several hours to run, at least—but it appeared the heavy lifting was over, at least for him. A destroyer that had been with the Marine expeditionary force on the eastern side of the island had just checked in. Tasked overnight to sail west, it headed toward them at flank speed and was roughly three hours away.

Turk checked in with Basher flight. The Marines were flying their own patrol orbit at 5,000 feet, making a large figure eight over the two ships.

"Whiplash Shark, we're all getting close to bingo," said Greenstreet. "If you've got things under control, we're going back to the base to refuel."

"Roger that, Basher One," Turk told him. "Clear skies ahead. Looks like things are settling down."

"Affirmative. Nice flying," Greenstreet added.

"Thanks."

"He's slipping," said Cowboy. "Took him all of five minutes to get them all."

"It wasn't more than three, I think," said Greenstreet.

"You should have let me have one of those bogies," added Cowboy.

"I was feeling greedy," quipped Turk. "See you guys later."

Wɪᴛʜ ᴛʜᴇ ᴛᴜɢ ꜱᴇᴄᴜʀᴇᴅ, Dᴀɴɴʏ ʟᴇꜰᴛ Aᴄʜᴍᴏᴏᴅʏ ɪɴ charge of the search and called the Osprey to take him over to the container vessel. While the Marines had secured the ship with surprising speed and ease, the search of the massive vessel was proceeding slowly. Not only did the containers have to be opened and inspected one at a time, but a bomb had knocked out power through most of the ship. Worse, fire had spread to a compartment below the container deck.

The Marines had captured a dozen crewmen. Four more were killed in the air attack and another six wounded. The wounded were being triaged on the forward deck, a few yards from the prisoners, who sat with their hands on their heads, nervously whispering to one another as Danny's Osprey lowered itself to a clear space nearby.

"Most of the crew are Filipinos," said Captain Thomas, leading Danny to the superstructure a few moments later. "They don't seem to know much."

"Somebody had to be operating the aircraft," said Danny. "They can't launch on their own."

"Maybe, but we haven't found them yet. Ship's intact," added the Marine captain. "But I'm not sure we're going to be able to put the fire out."

"I'm going to send one of the Ospreys over to the *McCain* to pick up a skeleton crew," said Danny. The *McCain* was the destroyer detailed to sail west and help them. "They'll help."

"Good. This way," added Thomas, pointing to a set of metal steps that went up the side of the superstructure. "The captain is a Frenchman, or at least he has a French accent. Won't give his name. Ship's papers say it's Fortine."

"Fourteen?"

"Spelled F-o-r-t-i-n-e."

"Hold on."

Danny stopped and tapped the radio button at the back of his glasses to transmit back to Whiplash headquarters. He gave the name to the desk tech, who told him that Rubeo wanted to have a word.

"Colonel, there were radio transmissions detected from the vicinity of the two ships as the aircraft launched," said the scientist.

"Yeah, roger that. We're looking now."

"The signals do not appear to have come from the cargo container vessel," continued Rubeo. "Looking at the mast antenna of the tug, we believe that it is configured to allow it to control the aircraft."

"The tug? Really?"

"I would suggest you search both," said Rubeo.

No shit, thought Danny.

"You gave Betrand the name of Fortine," added Rubeo. "Be careful with him. He was a French naval captain."

"Right."

Rubeo turned him over to another analyst, Jeremy Von Schmidt.

"We've updated the schematic of the cargo carrier," said Von Schmidt, one of a dozen naval officers helping interpret the intel at the Cube. "We can lead your teams around the fire."

"Punch that right through to Thomas," said Danny.

Achmoody checked with an update from the tug: The team had discovered that several of the compartments below the main deck were locked and booby-trapped. They were assessing whether they could be disarmed or blown in place without endangering the ship.

"All right," Danny told him. "In the meantime, get somebody up to the radio room and send video back to the Cube. We're looking for something capable of controlling the UAVs."

"Probably in one of those locked-down areas," suggested Achmoody.

"Agreed—but let's eliminate the other possibilities."

Danny checked the communications space on the cargo vessel himself. Outfitted with the latest satellite communications and a 4K high-definition television screen that had to be at least seven feet in diagonal, it was big enough to host a sports bar. But the room was almost entirely empty except for a few office chairs and the radio equipment. There were no joysticks or the dedicated consoles that typically were used to control UAVs, let alone the array of servers and other computer gear ground stations generally needed.

Danny sent video back to the Cube, then went up to the bridge to talk to the ship's captain. Fortine was sitting on a chair at the side of the bridge, face pale but with his arms crossed, and even before he answered Danny's questions it was clear he wasn't going to be very cooperative.

"So you're French?" asked Danny. "You served in the French navy?"

"I'm sure you know my entire background," said Fortine.

"Why did you join Kallipolis?" Danny asked.

"I didn't join—I started it."

"I thought Lloyd Braxton started it."

"There were several of us—hundreds," added Fortine, continuing in an accent that sounded more British than French. The movement was one of historical proportions, he claimed; from the small seed he and the others planted, a massive movement would grow.

"You're a military person," said Danny. "Usually anarchy doesn't sit well."

"We don't believe in anarchy," said Fortine.

"What do you believe in?"

"Freedom."

"From everything?"

Fortine gave him a sarcastic grin. "If you are willing to open your mind, I will be happy to debate the matter with you. But not at the point of a gun."

"I'm not pointing a gun at you."

"But you are armed, and you clearly intend me harm. You attacked my ship—"

"Your ship attacked my aircraft," answered Danny. "You were warned not to resist. You are in violation of several international laws. Smuggling weapons and providing assistance to rebels and terrorists," Danny added quickly, seeing that Fortine was about to object. "Your own country voted for the UN resolution forbidding that, and in fact has its own laws—"

"I have no country," said Fortine. "I have re-nounced my citizenship. And I am in violation of no laws."

"Firing on aircraft is certainly against interna-tional law," said Danny.

"Defending my vessel and my crew against pi-rates is my right, and my duty."

"What other arms are you carrying?" Danny asked. "Where is your cargo manifest?"

"I showed that to the first officer who entered the bridge."

"Where's the real manifest?"

Fortine smirked. "Always the government goons play their games and word tricks."

"You can help us save your vessel from sinking," suggested Danny, "by telling us what else we have to worry about."

"I will not assist you in any way," said Fortine. "You can't hold me. You have no authority."

"I have plenty of authority," said Danny.

"Guns, yes."

"And those, too."

Danny decided not to bother wasting any more time. Thomas met him on the external ladder as he was going off the bridge.

"We've searched the engine room," said the captain. "No contraband so far. Nothing that looks out of place."

Several of the crewmen were eager to talk, but to a man they insisted they were merely hired hands, paid nearly four times the going rate and treated far better than they would have fared ordinarily. They knew nothing of Kallipolis, and while they thought it was "beyond odd" that they had spent the last several weeks sailing in the same waters, none had seen any UAVs or heard of any plans to attack anyone, let alone Americans. All were shocked when the containers were opened to reveal the launchers.

"What about the guys who tried to shoot down our planes from the stern?" Danny asked.

"They say they were the mates in charge," explained the Marine who'd taken charge of the interrogation. It happened that his mother was Filipino, and he spoke Spanish with an accent similar to theirs. "I don't know how much to believe them, but none of the dead guys look Filipino. They're all dressed differently, with button-down shirts. For what that's worth."

"A shirt makes them an officer?" Danny glanced at Thomas, who shrugged. "Any of the wounded talking?" he asked.

"Not about anything important," answered the interpreter. "Most of them are pretty messed up."

"See if you can get any information about the tug, about people coming and going, where they've been, that sort of thing."

"Questioning them that extensively is going to take time, Colonel," said Thomas. "Much better off bringing them back ashore."

"As soon as we do that, we have to alert their embassy," said Danny. "Besides, we're going to be out here for a while longer. How many EOD guys you got with you?"

The unit had four men with explosives or EOD training and experience, though none were technically considered specialists. Danny decided to leave two aboard the cargo ship in case the search there turned up anything; the other two came back to the tug with him.

He was just hopping off the Osprey when Turk's voice, high-pitched with excitement, came over the Whiplash circuit, breaking through the chatter of the search team.

"Whiplash leader, we have company," warned Turk. "I have eight Chinese fighters on long-range radar. And they are trying to set a new world's speed record getting here."

15

South China Sea

Braxton led Wen-lo down the concrete steps to the bunker where the Kallipolis tech room was hidden. While not as expansive as the one at Gried that he had blown up, it was nonetheless well equipped—and perfectly positioned for what he needed to do.

Wen-lo's greed and hubris would help.

The lights automatically turned on as he approached the door to the bunker. Laser beams scanned his face; once his identity was verified, the door would be unlocked unless he said anything—a precaution against his being forced at gunpoint to let anyone in.

He remained silent until they were inside.

"We have launch facilities on the south side of the island," he told Wen-lo, steering him down the corridor from the small foyer. "I can activate them from here. And then your men must carry the UAVs into position."

"Of course."

The quickness of the answer told Braxton that Wen-lo didn't intend that he would get that far. He adjusted his plan accordingly.

Most of the crew of both boats had come ashore with them. All heavily armed, they followed quietly but quickly, stepping in unison at times so that they reminded him of the storm troopers in the Star Wars series. It made for quite a crowd in the narrow hall.

"I have to ask your men to step back," Braxton told Wen-lo. "If the computer sees weapons, it won't open."

"I don't believe you."

"Computer, open," said Braxton.

The door stayed shut.

Wen-lo reached beneath his shirt and took out a 9mm pistol. It was a Chinese knockoff of a Glock, one Braxton had never seen before.

"Open the door," said Wen-lo, raising the barrel of the gun so it pointed toward Braxton's head.

"It won't as long as your gun is out. There's nothing I can do."

"Do it."

Braxton took a deep breath. "Open door," he told the computer.

It stayed shut. Wen-lo pushed the pistol against his temple.

"Don't you think there'd be precautions?" asked Braxton, trying to keep his voice calm. "You've seen the technology we have. You know that we are enemies of the Americans. You think that we are fools?"

Wen-lo pushed the muzzle back and forth.

"The computer is reading my heart rate right now," said Braxton. "If it doesn't get back down below sixty-eight beats a minute, we're not getting in at any point, whether you have a gun or not."

That was a bluff, but one Braxton felt he could get away with—as was the caution about the weapons. He had actually thought of instituting such a precaution when he built the system, but decided it might prevent him from bringing a gun into the room when he needed one.

Wen-lo lowered his pistol, then told the others to step back.

"Give your gun to someone before you come inside," said Braxton.

"No."

"Then walk to the end of the hall, out of range of the camera, and put it under your shirt. There can only be two of us in the control room at a time. The computer will count the heartbeats."

"We'll all go in."

"You don't really think we're going to fit, do you? It's a little closet." Braxton pointed to the wall. "That panel will open and reveal a glass window. Your men can watch everything. There's a room with a monitor farther down the hall; I'll send a feed there. But you'll see—the room is too small for more than two people. Even two can be a squeeze. It wasn't planned as a conference room," he added. "It's just for a pilot. And the aircraft only needs one pilot."

"To fly two airplanes?"

"To fly a dozen. Two dozen," Braxton added with a veiled contempt. "What do you think this is all about? That's why you want it, right? You don't give a crap about the UAVs. Drones are nothing. It's the AI, and the distributed intelligence. What these things can do. That's the value. The brains."

He'd touched a nerve. Wen-lo told his men curtly that he was going in by himself, and they were to watch from the doorway and through the window. After they had moved back and Wen-lo holstered his pistol and pulled his shirt over it, Braxton nodded and pretended to be calming himself.

"OK," he said, giving the key word as he looked at the floor. "Open door. Please."

The lock buzzed. Wen-lo pushed ahead of him, entering the control room. Braxton followed.

He hadn't been lying when he said it was small; the main console was exactly six feet long and ran the entire length of the room. Six video screens were arrayed at its head in two rows, with keyboards and two joystick-style controllers. Computing units were stacked around the rest of the room. There was just barely enough room to pull the chair out.

He sat down, then started to reach for the switch that would open the panel on the window. Wen-lo grabbed his arm.

"You want your men to see us or not?" Braxton asked.

Wen-lo let him hit the switch. The panel moved up, revealing the thick window separating the room from the hall.

"It will take a few minutes for the computers to boot up and everything," he told Wen-lo. "It will get hot in here, too. Listen, we need to get the Sabre UAVs off the boat and onto the launchers. Can you have some of your men do that?"

"Where are the launchers?"

"The south side of the island—the path to the left of the bunker will take you there."

"How are they launched?"

"I'll show you," said Braxton, pulling over the keyboard. "First, we need to launch the aircraft that are mounted, so we have room. What are you worried about? You have my man Talbot as hostage. I'm not going to trick you."

Wen-lo went to the door and spoke to his men, sending four of them away. Braxton moved his hand to the switch that would close and lock the door, hoping Wen-lo would go outside into the hall. But his Chinese antagonist kept it open, his body against the jamb.

All right, Braxton thought to himself as he called up the launching panel on the computer, on to Plan D.

16

Over the South China Sea

Turk continued to climb. As the Tigershark passed through 25,000 feet, he noted that the Chinese fighters had separated into two groups, both with four planes apiece. The first, flying on a direct course for the tug and the cargo ship, had just reached 30,000 feet. They were two hundred miles away but moving well over Mach 1; they would reach the area in roughly twelve minutes. The other group, flying to the west, were lower and slower. If they kept on their present course, they would reach a point about fifty miles west of the ships a few minutes after the first group.

Turk could engage the first group, but without the Sabres it would have to be at close range. That would make it difficult to shoot them all down before the other planes were in a position to threaten his guys below.

Of course, he wasn't authorized to shoot anyone. Just the opposite. He radioed Danny for instructions.

"You can intercept the Chinese aircraft," Danny told him. "But don't fire on them."

"With respect, Colonel—"

"Those are your orders. If they change, I'll let you know."

Bullshit, thought Turk.

"Computer, prepare intercept for Bandit Group

One," he said. "Plot an engagement for all four aircraft."

"*Computing.*"

ABOARD THE TUG, THE TEAM HAD DISARMED TWO EX-plosives and was working on the last, which would allow them to enter the lowest deck level of the ship. Achmoody estimated it would take ten minutes to get the device disarmed; they would need another five to check the passage for other booby traps by sending a small robot equipped with an explosives "sniffer" down the corridor.

"Don't rush it," Danny told Achmoody. Then he went back up on the deck to talk to Breanna on the Whiplash circuit.

"The Chinese are coming," he said as soon as she acknowledged.

"Yes, we see."

"Can we shoot them down?"

"Only if they are an active threat," she said. "We're informing the White House now."

"If we wait until they come, they may be difficult to deal with."

"I realize that, Danny. If you feel you have to protect yourself," she added, "do what you have to do. I'll back you up. It'll be on my orders."

"Thanks," he said.

AS SOON AS COWBOY HEARD DANNY HAILING GREEN-street, he knew what was up, and exactly what

Greenstreet would say as soon as the brief transmission ended.

"Basher flight, we're going back," said Greenstreet a few seconds later. "Three and Four—dump your bombs. We're dealing with Chinese fighters."

TURK LIKED THE FIGHTING BALLET THE COMPUTER HAD projected, but he also knew it would never work out that pretty.

It had him going head-on against the lead aircraft, nailing it and then taking down the jet on its right wing. From there he was to flip around and take the farthest plane in the group before accelerating to nail the last. Maybe he could get the first three if they didn't react quickly, but there was no way he was going to catch the last plane. Once he saw what was going on, the Chinese pilot would dive and accelerate. Granted that would take him out of the immediate fight—an achievement the computer would find acceptable when diagramming an engagement—but it would leave the American units vulnerable to a later attack.

It was academic, though. Turk had orders *not* to fire.

What to do? It was highly unlikely that they would fall for his flare trick a second time, and besides, they were moving too fast for him to try it.

The only thing to do, he concluded, was climb and wait.

He thought of putting out his landing gear and tossing tinsel out to increase his radar signature so they could pick him up. It might scare them off, or it might provoke them into turning on their targeting radars. But there was no guarantee they would do either. And it would cost him the element of tactical surprise, which might be of use if he was ever allowed to attack.

The idea of disobeying his orders kept occurring to him. He was trying to get out of Whiplash, wasn't he?

But some part of him just wouldn't let go. Even though he *thought* he knew better, his training insisted that he follow the command of his superior, assuming he still had faith in his judgment.

And bottom line, he *did* trust Danny.

"Recompute intercept at this point," Turk told the computer, pointing near the ships.

17

The White House

PRESIDENT TODD WAS WELCOMING A GROUP OF schoolchildren to the Oval Office when David Greenwich, her chief of staff, appeared at the door.

It never seemed to fail—just when she was doing something she truly enjoyed, there was an important interruption.

"Now children, I have a question for you," she told the dozen fourth-graders, all of whom had come to Washington following a national history competition. "How many would like to be President someday?"

One hand went up, albeit very slowly. Then another, still tentative, and finally the rest.

Thank goodness, thought Todd. Many days no one wanted her job.

"Well, I can't make you President," she told the class. "But you can see what it is like to sit in my chair. Would you like that?"

The chorus of "Yes!" nearly rattled the walls.

"Teachers, please arrange that. Mr. Devons will help you." She smiled at the assistant education secretary, who was escorting the group. "Make sure everyone gets their picture taken."

As the children lined up, the President discreetly walked to the door.

"The Chinese have sent aircraft against Whiplash," whispered her chief of staff.

Todd led him out into the hall, out of the others' earshot.

"Have the Chinese been warned off?" she asked.

"They're in the process of trying that. They wanted you to know that they may ultimately shoot them down."

"If that's what it takes," said Todd.

"You want to call in Senator Peterson and the Speaker," suggested Greenwich.

"Round up the usual suspects, eh?" Todd smirked.

"The Chinese ambassador has called you twice this morning. I'm sure he won't be silent."

"Congress will complain one way or another," said Todd. "We need our technology back. Prepare the situation room. I'll go down for an update as soon as I finish with the children. We don't have to worry about the Chinese—they won't go to war over this."

"It's Congress I'm worried about. They'll use anything to say you're going beyond your powers. They'll accuse you of trying to start a war."

"I'll deal with Congress. I know there'll be fallout, David. But better to deal with it over the incident than to lose the technology as well."

"Yes, ma'am," said the chief of staff.

"If I dealt with China the way the leaders of Congress wanted," added Todd, "I'd be letting them take control of the world and kill my people in the process. And that will *never* happen on my watch."

18

The Cube

RAY RUBEO SAW THE ALERT FROM THE NAVY'S STEALTH UAV and immediately went to the information screen. Four aircraft had just launched from an islet about fifty miles east of the two ships.

They had to be Braxton's.

Rubeo called up a map of the area, zooming in on the little ellipse of sand and overgrown jungle.

It looked very much like the tiny island close to Malaysia where the bunker had been blown up. It hadn't shown up on the geographical match search because it was thought to be outside the range of the UAVs.

Assumptions.

Rubeo picked up the phone that connected him to his New Mexico lab.

"Have we cracked the command coding yet?" he asked.

"Sorry, Ray. We're working on it. It's pretty damn complicated."

"They're launching more combat UAVs," said Rubeo. "Can we observe their transmissions and back-engineer the encryption?"

"We're on that but it looks hopeless. We need either the back door or just brute force, which is already what we're doing."

"Keep at it."

Rubeo put the phone back down. Breanna was standing next to him.

"They've launched more aircraft," she said.

"Yes," said Rubeo.

"Do you think they'll do anything with the Sabres?"

"It's a possibility," admitted Rubeo. "But if their main intention was stealing, more likely they're using this to cover their retreat."

"If they were interested in retreating, why launch the aircraft at all?" said Breanna. "We didn't know about this base—they could have hidden there."

"Yes." Rubeo nodded. They were missing something.

"Can you take over the planes?" Breanna asked.

"We know how we can transmit, but we can't get around the encryptions they're using. Not yet."

Pena Gavin, the head of Cube security, entered the room and walked down to the station where they were standing.

"Breanna? Do you have a moment?" she asked. "I need to talk to you about something."

"It's not a great time—"

"I know, but . . . there's—someone at the gate needs to see you."

"Not now," said Breanna, annoyed at what seemed a trivial interruption. The security officer shifted uncomfortably, seemingly struggling to find the right words. "Tell him to go to the Pentagon office," added Breanna. "I don't have time—"

"It's your father."

19

Daela Reef

THE LIMITED INSTRUCTION SET IN THE COMBAT UAVs meant that Braxton had to continue guiding them for two minutes after the booster separation; only then could he direct them to the two ships and let them go.

Monitoring the aircraft as they climbed out from the launch area, he saw from the passive radar sensors that the Chinese had sent fighters in the direction of the ships—and another set toward him.

There were American aircraft over the ships as well: three Ospreys. While he couldn't see it, Braxton guessed that the Tigershark would be there too, with or without its Sabres.

Which gave him a better opportunity than he had hoped for.

He set his four UAVs on course for the area over the ships, and instructed them to defend the ships against all unfriendly aircraft—a default preset that allowed the planes to use all of their programmed maneuvers to fight until there were no more contacts in the air.

"Your planes are in the air," said Wen-lo. "Now, take us to the launcher."

"I have to program them all first," said Braxton. "Or they'll just fly around over the island and bring the Americans here. We don't want that, right?"

The wide-area plot showed Braxton that the UAVs would reach the area of the ships at roughly the same time as the Chinese did. That was perfect. He started to get up, then sat back down as Wen-lo walked to the door.

"I'll be right there," he said, deciding not to leave anything to chance. He designated the lead Chinese aircraft as the primary target for the first UAV, then cleared the screen quickly so Wen-lo couldn't see what he had done.

"All right, let's go," he said, jumping to his feet. "We have to get the Sabres loaded ASAP. The

Americans are bound to send more aircraft and other reinforcements."

20

South China Sea

EVEN THOUGH HE WAS CURRENTLY FLYING WITH PASSIVE sensors only, so he couldn't be easily detected, Turk could see the approaching combat UAVs thanks to the input from the Cube. There were four of them, exactly like the ones he'd dealt with earlier. They were heading straight for the Chinese J-15s.

If the Chinese saw them, they didn't react. The UAVs were also apparently using passive sensors, no doubt more sophisticated than anything the Chinese had.

Turk clicked into the Whiplash circuit to talk to Danny. "Colonel, Kallipolis has launched UAVs."

"Four of them, right? I just heard."

"Just a guess here, but they look like they're going to attack the Chinese."

"Warn the Chinese that we're conducting an operation," said Danny. "Tell them to stand off. And tell them about the UAVs. Make it clear that they are not ours."

"No way they'll believe that," said Turk. "But yes, sir."

Turk broadcast the warning. He got no response.

"Listen guys, I know you can hear me," he said, dropping the formal tone he'd used at first. "No shit, there are four combat UAVs running right at you hot and heavy. And they will shoot you down. Believe me; we've dealt with them."

"Stop your tricks, American," responded one of the Chinese pilots.

"I'm not playing tricks. I'm above you to the south, about twenty-five thousand feet. I know you can't see me. The four UAVs are low, they're coming from the east, and they can take you down in a heartbeat."

"We see you south."

"That's another flight. I'm over the ships. Those UAVs are just about on you," added Turk, seeing the plot. "They're going to attack. They're climbing—"

"You are playing a trick."

"I'm not."

"Order them away."

"Those aren't our planes," answered Turk. "They're being run by high-tech pirates who've stolen technology and are helping terrorists. That's what this operation is all about."

The Chinese pilot didn't answer—verbally. Instead, he turned on his weapons radar, targeting the Ospreys.

The Ospreys immediately began evasive maneuvers. Their electronic countermeasures could adequately fend off the Chinese medium-range radar missiles; heat-seekers and cannons would be a different story.

"Don't threaten our planes or I'll be forced to shoot you down," said Turk.

"Stand down, American," said the Chinese pilot.

A second later there was an electronic shriek over the circuit—the UAVs had fired their lasers in unison, destroying the lead plane.

THE EXPLOSION SHOOK THE SHIP SO BADLY THAT DANNY fell against the railing on the catwalk around the bridge.

"What the hell is going on?" he asked Achmoody over the radio.

"Robot set off one of the bombs," replied the trooper. His voice sounded shaky. "There must have been a motion detector at the far end of the corridor that we didn't see. It blew out the entire passage."

"Anybody hurt?"

"Just egos," said Achmoody. "The explosion put a pretty big hole in the bulkhead. We're starting through now."

Danny had barely turned around when he saw a black cloud appear in the sky to the north.

"Turk, what's going on?" he asked.

"The UAVs are engaging the Chinese aircraft. The Chinese think they're ours," he added.

"Tell them they're not," said Danny. Then he had another thought. "Can you help them? Keep them from being shot down?"

"You want me to help the Chinese?"

"Yes."

"Colonel—"

"Do it, Turk."

"Roger that," snapped Turk.

21

The Cube

BREANNA'S THROAT FELT AS IF IT HAD TURNED TO stone. She could barely breathe, let alone swallow. She stood just inside the inner door at the top of the Cube entrance, in front of the elevator to the lower levels. Two security aides, submachine guns in their hands, were at her side.

"Daddy, why are you here?" she asked.

"Ray said you needed help. If you don't want me—"

"Did he tell you what we need?"

"There was a text that said something about DNA coding."

"We need Jennifer's body exhumed," said Breanna. She hadn't seen her father in nearly five years. He looked thinner, scruffier, yet somehow younger than she remembered. Emotions were flooding through her; it was a struggle not to scream at him.

"No, you need her DNA profile," he said. "It was analyzed. I have it here."

He held up a small USB flash drive.

"It's part of her password," added Tecumseh Bastian. "I know what you need it for—it'll let you in the back door of the AI programs she worked on. All of them. Braxton stole it, didn't he?"

"You know?"

"We suspected. That's why he was fired."

"I thought . . . he was harassing Jennifer."

"He was. But that's not why he was fired. She's all on this disc, her DNA. Not her." Bastian smiled, but it was a sad, wistful smile. "Over seven hundred fifty megabytes. She designed it herself."

Breanna hesitated, then reached out her hand.

"It's password protected, the drive," he told her. "I'm not sure which password she used. She had a couple."

The elevator opened behind her. Ray Rubeo stepped out. For a moment Breanna felt as if she were watching them on a video screen.

"Ray," said Bastian.

"General."

"I brought the drive with the sequence."

"You should come downstairs," Rubeo told him. "I may need you."

"It's not up to me."

Breanna looked at her father. He still had his clearance, though after everything that had happened, Breanna didn't know whether she should let him down or not.

There could be anything on the drive.

And did she want to trust him?

What she wanted was to yell at him, to ask why he had run away, walled himself off from her and Zen and their daughter. Leaving the military she could understand, mourning Jennifer Gleason she could definitely understand, but deserting her?

Blaming her. Along with the others. That was the reason.

"We need to move quickly," said Rubeo. "I suspect that the launch of the UAVs is aimed at providing cover as they make off with the Sabres. It's the only logical explanation."

"Sabres?" asked Bastian.

"A lot has changed since you've been gone, Tecumseh," said Rubeo. "We can discuss it later. I need the sequence now. Breanna?"

"I'll take the flash drive," she said.

"It might be more useful to have your father with us," said Rubeo. "To get past the passwords quickly."

"All right, yes, let's go, come on," said Breanna, turning swiftly. "He's with me," she told the guards, and then in a louder voice, repeated it for the security system monitoring their movements.

22

South China Sea

THERE WAS NOTHING TURK COULD DO TO HELP THE first Chinese fighter; his plane was already fried so badly, the pilot barely ejected before it blew to bits.

But in the seeds of that victory lay the enemy UAVs' demise. They flew over the destroyed J-15's path, banking south as a group while computing which target to hit next and how. Their course took them nearly perpendicular to Turk, and far below. He tipped his nose forward, turned slightly, and even before the rail gun was ready to fire he had locked up the lead UAV.

The Sabre rocked as three slugs sped from its nose. The UAV was a small target, but that just meant there wasn't much left for the third bullet to hit. The first shattered the main section of the aircraft, destroying the "brain" as well as blowing a hole through the main fuel tank; the second slug blew through the engine. All the third could find was a large piece of shattered wing engulfed in flames.

Gently pressuring the stick at the right side of his seat, Turk put the Tigershark on the tail of the UAV at the end of the pack. The aircraft was starting a turn to the north; Turk rode with it, staying just to the outside as he waited for the small plane to swing back in reaction to his presence. It did so, then twisted sharply, spinning its wings and heading toward the waves.

It looked for all the world as if the plane had malfunctioned into a weird spin and was out of the game. But it was just a trick—one Turk had seen on the range many times. He followed, waiting for the UAV's wings to flatten out. As soon as they stopped rotating, he fired a burst that caught it back to front, splitting it in two.

While Turk was busy following the UAV through its phony spin, the Chinese J-15s made the mistake of trying to tangle with the other two. As Turk looked skyward, he realized that the

Chinese had managed to catch one of the UAVs in a sandwich between them.

"Break off, break off," Turk warned. "Let me get them."

There was no response from the Chinese fighters, and no indication that they had even heard him. The lead Chinese fighter accelerated upward, trying to swing the trailing UAV into a scissors maneuver where his wingman could fire heat seekers from behind. He was doing a reasonable job of jinking out of the UAV's sights, but he hadn't accounted for the other UAV, which suddenly attacked him from the side.

The J-15's wingman fired a pair of heat-seeking missiles, but they went off course, apparently fooled by decoy flares the lead Chinese plane launched as he tried to escape. He turned hard west, only to have his right wing fly off—sheered clean by the UAV's laser weapon.

The second flight of Chinese aircraft to the west turned in their direction, riding to the aid of their comrades. Inexplicably, two of the aircraft fired medium-range missiles—crazily, Turk thought, since they couldn't possibly have locked on the targets.

If the missiles were intended to get the UAVs' attention and break their attack, it didn't work. The pair climbed east, preparing to circle back. By now it was clear the UAVs were following an order to attack the Chinese planes; they were closer to Turk's Tigershark but ignored it, even though his active radar was now telling them where he was.

"All Chinese aircraft, break east," radioed Turk, trying to get them to move toward him and make it easier to get the UAVs. When they didn't respond, he gave them a heading and told them he would cut between them and the two surviving UAVs. But both J-15s near him continued south, toward the ships, as if they were intending to attack.

"The UAVs are your enemy," he told them. "Not the people on the ships."

They either didn't hear or didn't care, instead activating their attack radars to try to launch missiles on the large cargo carrier.

COWBOY SAW THE TWO CHINESE J-15S LINING UP FOR shots on the big ship.

"I have Bandit Two," he told Greenstreet.

"Roger that, Basher Two. Firing Fox Three."

The F-35s launched their AMRAAMs toward the Chinese planes. At roughly the same moment, the air-to-surface missiles the J-20s were carrying dropped from their wings, heading for the cargo vessel. It was a sitting duck.

Suddenly, something exploded a mile and a half from the ship, directly in the path of the missiles. One of the missiles, which had started to arc for a final attack, abruptly dove and exploded. The other veered sharply, then wobbled back toward its course.

Turk had managed to get his aircraft between the missiles and the ship, and deked one of them into exploding with a shower of chaff. But the other was still moving toward the vessel.

TURK SAW THE SECOND MISSILE MOVE INTO HIS PIPPER and squeezed the trigger without a solid lock. He got off three shots, but only the first was on target, and even that barely hit, blowing a hole through the rear propulsion area of the missile. The warhead had enough momentum to continue into the cargo ship, striking it near the bow.

Time moved in slow motion. His maneuvers had taken him below 5,000 feet; his forward airspeed had dropped below 250 knots. Both the UAVs and the Chinese fighters were somewhere above and behind him.

In other words, he was dead meat.

"Come on," he told the Tigershark, leaning on the throttle and ignoring the warnings that he was being targeted. "Go! Go! Go!"

COWBOY'S THUMB WAS JUST ABOUT TO PRESS THE cannon trigger to nail the J-15 on Turk's tail when he realized that one of the UAVs was going to beat him to it. The Chinese pilot had been so intent on getting Turk that he'd ignored the slippery UAV behind him.

A nudge left, and Cowboy had the UAV in his crosshairs.

He fired a half second after the UAV's laser burned a hole in the J-15's tail.

The resulting cartwheel of explosions warmed Cowboy's heart.

"Yee-haw!" he shouted over the radio. "Scratch one UAV!"

"Let's stay focused," scolded Greenstreet. "There's a lot of work to do."

23

Daela Reef

BRAXTON LED WEN-LO OUT OF THE COMMAND ROOM and back into the bunker's hallway.

"We have only a few minutes," he said. "Once the UAVs reach the ships, we need to be back to control them."

Wen-lo said nothing. The two guards who'd been standing in the hall stepped into line behind them, their automatic weapons clutched against their chests.

Braxton felt his heartbeat rising. Adrenaline was surging through his body so badly that his eardrums felt as if they were going to explode.

Was that possible? He certainly felt something. It was almost a high.

He'd felt this way when the deal to purchase his company was about to go through.

And years before that, working late with Jennifer Gleason. He'd tried to tell her that night how he felt about her, but he was too tongue-tied, too shy, and the moment and opportunity passed.

He'd always thought there'd be another chance. But things had changed too rapidly after that.

A lesson.

He walked to the end of the corridor, but instead of going to the main entrance, turned and opened a door at the side. There was another door just inside the tiny corridor.

"Where are you taking us?" demanded Wen-lo, grabbing his shoulder to stop him before he could open the second.

"To the launching area. Your men should be waiting."

"No, I've changed my mind," said Wen-lo. "You're coming back to the boat."

"You're reneging on our deal?" Braxton felt his face flush.

"What deal?" asked Wen-lo, drawing his pistol.

"Just relax," said Braxton. He raised his hands slowly, then glanced at Wen-lo's goons, who'd raised the barrels of their guns. "You need my help. I'm very valuable."

"I've seen your interface. It's no more advanced than the general Flighthawk controls. I mastered those long ago."

Braxton took a step back so that his foot was against the door. He needed to open it, but at the moment that didn't look possible.

"You're going to need help with the Sabres," he said as calmly as he could manage. "Someone who can take them apart and examine them. Someone who's worked on the systems already."

"I have my pick of engineers. You'll work for us, or you'll die," said Wen-lo.

"Quite an offer."

"Take it or leave it."

"Let me shut down the launch area, then."

Braxton turned and put his hand on the interior door. Wen-lo grabbed him and pulled him back.

"What is in there that you want?" he demanded. Without waiting for an answer, he told one of his men in Chinese to open the door.

Braxton dove to the ground as the hallway seemed to explode. A bright light flashed—the door and nearby hall were rigged as a giant flash bomb. The first door had been engineered to protect against the blast, but with it open, the concussion shocked the small space; it quickly filled with smoke.

He couldn't see, he couldn't hear, but he knew what he had to do—he leapt to his feet and ran to his left, back into the hall and the foyer, heading for the main door a few yards away. One of the guards scrambled after him, firing as he ran.

"Close door!" Braxton yelled as he reached the threshold. A thick metal panel slammed down behind him. It caught the guard in the arm, severing it as it closed.

Braxton fell against the steps.

"Gas them," he told the security system. "Suffocate the bastards. Gas them and kill them all."

24

South China Sea

THOUGH HE KNEW THE PLANES WERE POISED TO attack, Danny was so intent on the hidden compartments they'd discovered that he stayed below, moving forward with the team as they checked the tugboat's corridor. In short order they found two control rooms, both with gear that looked exactly like the ground stations for Flighthawks.

There was another compartment that looked like an arms locker. It had a full array of weapons, from rifles to grenade launchers. All looked brand new.

"Colonel, there's something behind this panel in the corridor," said Achmoody.

Danny went out to take a look. Achmoody and Glenn Fulsom were standing along the bulkhead, looking at the wall's surface.

"Are you sure there's a panel there?" asked Danny.

Achmoody held up a handheld sensor unit that detected magnetic fields and used them to find cavities and openings. There was a gap in the wall behind the panel that matched the dimensions of a hatchway.

"It's behind the metal, so the smart helmet radar can't detect it from the hall," added Achmoody, referring to the low-power detection unit built into his Whiplash helmet. The device was intended for urban warfare situations, and could easily scan through conventional plaster and plasterboard walls. Metal was more problematic, though it took relatively sophisticated techniques to fool the system.

Kallipolis had proven they had those in spades.

"Can you get us in?" Danny asked.

"We have to blow a hole through. It's thick."

"Let's do it."

Danny went back topside as the demolitions were set. As soon as he reached the deck, he saw a fresh plume of smoke rising from the cargo ship's bow.

"Captain Thomas, what's going on over there?" he called over the radio.

"Bow of the ship was hit by a missile, an Exocet or something like that. No injuries here, but we're taking on water."

The missile was actually a Chinese YJ-82 (also known as a C-802), but the comparison to the French-made Exocet was apt. Even though its body had been splintered by Turk's slug, the armor-piercing warhead of the missile had enough kinetic energy left to pierce the hull and deck area before exploding, ripping a gaping hole at the front of the ship. The container carrier was taking on water at an alarming rate, and even an experienced crew would have their hands full keeping her afloat.

"Abandon the ship," Danny told Captain Thomas. "We found the control rooms over here. I'll have the Ospreys pick you up."

"Roger that."

The Osprey pilots had moved south, trying to stay clear of the air battle raging above. They were still easy targets, but the pilots didn't hesitate when Danny told them the Marines needed to be taken off the ship. It was Turk who told them to wait.

"Colonel, let me mop this up first," he said, breaking into the transmission over the Whiplash common channel. "Then they can come in with no danger . . . and they won't be in the way."

"We're fighting time."

"I just need a few minutes. It's simpler if they stay where they are."

"Understood," replied Danny. "You clear them in. Don't let those Marines get wet."

"Not gonna happen."

A hatch work of contrails crisscrossed the sky. Two columns of black smoke rose in the north and puffs of black and gray were scattered along the horizon. But the scene was too pretty to suggest the ferocity of the raging air battle.

"Colonel, we found something on the stern deck you might be interested in," said Corporal Mofitt, trotting over to Danny. "Looks like a hidden passage below."

Danny followed him to a spot beneath a life raft, which the Marines had pulled away. The prisoners were standing nearby; two seemed angry, the others simply resigned.

"Locked shut from the inside, sir," added Mofitt.

"I think we can blow it," said the team's sergeant, coming over.

"My explosives guy is below," said Danny. "I'll get him up here."

"I can do it," said Mofitt. He held up a small block of C-4.

"Go ahead," said Danny. "Don't use too much."

He stepped back and then called down to Achmoody. They'd gone through the panel and found what the trooper called a rat's nest of small, interconnecting rooms.

"We can hear sounds," said Achmoody. "We think there are people."

As he finished speaking, Danny heard the sound of automatic weapon fire in the background.

"Correction," said Achmoody. "We found some people. And they're armed."

TURK BANKED IN THE DIRECTION OF THE LAST UAV. IT was five miles west, trying to follow the lone surviving Chinese fighters. If the J-15 lit its afterburner, it would escape; the UAV could not stay with the larger aircraft. But for some reason the Chinese pilot turned back toward the ships.

And Turk.

The UAV cut down the distance between them, driving toward the J-15's rear quarter as the Chinese fighter pilot flew a nearly straight line toward the plane he thought was his enemy. Turk endeavored to save him, even though he suspected the pilot wouldn't return the favor.

Starting a good 10,000 feet below the other two aircraft, Turk managed to close the gap to about 5,000 as he pushed into a firing slot to hit the UAV. Before he could fire, the drone realized it was being targeted from behind and gave up on the J-15, veering left.

Turk decided he would take advantage of his discovery of the aircraft's laser weakness. He turned to follow the slippery UAV through the turn, letting the Tigershark get thrown out ahead of the slippery drone as it cut a tighter radius. That put the UAV behind him—right where he wanted it.

The RWR shrieked; the drone was trying to lock him up. But the turn had been so tight that the aircraft had lost considerable speed, and the gap between its nose and Turk's tail was too wide for it to fire.

Ordinarily, that would have been a good thing—but Turk *wanted* his enemy to shoot. He corrected slightly in its direction, then waited for the UAV to catch up. It was just about in range to fire when Cowboy radioed a direction to him.

"Break left, break left!" rasped the Marine.

"No, no!" yelled Turk over the radio, but it was too late—a pair of heat seekers flashed from the F-35's wings. Turk made his cut in the sky, diving away from what was now a one-on-one furball between Cowboy and the UAV.

TINY FLARES POURED FROM THE BACK OF THE DRONE like little matches thrown by a pyromaniac. As Cowboy's missiles sniffed for the heat source, the plane managed a cut so sharp that it looked like it was flying sideways. Knowing his missiles would miss, Cowboy started a turn to line up another shot. But the F-35 couldn't match the smaller robot's maneuverability, and within seconds he lost sight of the UAV.

It didn't take a sixth sense or advanced radar to know it would now angle behind him. Cowboy started weaving desperately in the sky, drawing a convoluted ribbon that made it difficult for the UAV to get a bead on him. He saw Greenstreet passing in Basher One below him, and then the

Tigershark—very disappointing, since it meant they weren't in position to blow his pursuer out of the air.

"Let him target you and start to fire," said Turk over the radio. "Then hit your chaff."

"What?"

"Do it," said Turk.

"Where are you?"

"Trust me."

"Let this bastard lock on my tailpipe?"

"The chaff will blow him up. Make sure you hit it when I say."

I don't see how, thought Cowboy to himself.

TURK TIGHTENED HIS TURN AND THEN ACCELERATED, trying to get on the UAV's tail. But he was just too far away to get a lock.

The drone was tight on Cowboy's six. What Turk was telling him to do surely went against every instinct the Marine aviator had, not to mention years of training. But it was the only way to get out of the situation if Turk couldn't get a bead on the UAV.

The enemy robot tightened its noose around the F-35's tailpipe. Even if Cowboy didn't make a mistake, he was going to get creamed in a few seconds.

The laser fired.

"Do it!" yelled Turk. "Chaff! Chaff! Chaff! Keep your course straight!"

The rear of the plane seemed to explode. Turk felt a hole open in his stomach—he'd gotten his friend shot down.

In the next moment there was another explosion, this one with fire. Cowboy's plane hadn't blown up at all—Turk had seen the canisters of chaff exploding. The reflected laser beams had destroyed the UAV.

"You're clear, Basher Two," Turk told Cowboy.

"What the hell just happened?"

"You overloaded his flashlight," said Turk, easing off the throttle and running his eyes quickly over the indicators.

THE HATCHWAY ON THE STERN LIFEBOAT DECK BLEW with a discreet *car-ufff* and a small puff of smoke. Mofitt ran over and kicked it with his foot, shoving it out of the way. He fell to his knees, peered down, then disappeared into the hole before anyone could stop him.

Two Marines hustled forward to join him.

"Careful!" yelled Danny. He stepped back to ask Achmoody what was going on.

"Two guys down here, both with assault rifles," reported the trooper. "We're gonna hit them with gas."

"Hold off. We found a passage down," said Danny.

There was a shout from the hatchway and then a run of gunfire.

"Our guys are behind them!" Danny told Achmoody. "Our guys are there."

There were more shouts, then silence.

Damn, thought Danny. Why did I let them go down?

Mofitt had surely acted on impulse, undoubtedly wanting to redeem himself. But there was a difference between acting bravely and being a fool—he should have been more careful.

I should have been more careful, thought Danny. I should have stopped him.

A head popped up from the manhole. "We got 'em," said the Marine who emerged. The second grunt came up behind him, then Mofitt.

The corporal was drenched in sweat, but he was smiling.

"They were loaded for bear," he said. "The Whiplash guys are getting them."

Right on cue, Achmoody came over the radio and told Danny they had gotten the two men who'd fired at them. Both were dead. Achmoody said they looked like technical people—Europeans and Asian, dressed in shorts and T-shirts, with flip-flops.

"Their footwear clashed with their AR-15s," added Achmoody, delivering the gallows humor with a straight, even tone. "These guys had a box of magazines between them. Would have taken us all day to get them out if you hadn't sent the Marines down."

"They went on their own," said Danny. He was proud of Mofitt, even as he realized the Marine had been a little reckless. But sometimes you had to go overboard to show others who you really were.

"There's a hatchway out the side of the ship," said Achmoody. "Might be one of those submarine ports we found on the beached boat. Looks just like it."

Danny glanced over at the prisoners. Two of the men were barefooted and wearing shorts; the others were in jeans with sneakers or work boots. He hadn't even noticed.

"Sergeant, get those two guys in shorts and bring them over here," he said.

The sergeant whistled to one of the guards, then started shouting instructions. Mofitt started over with one of the other Marines.

Danny turned and put his hand over his ear, listening as Turk reported in on the situation in the air. Someone shouted behind him. He whirled around in time to see Mofitt race across the deck and throw himself into one of the men wearing shorts, who'd grabbed something from near the life raft.

As they tumbled over the side of the ship, there was an explosion.

The man had grabbed a bomb disguised as a fire extinguisher in the raft and tried to detonate it. Mofitt had saved at least a half-dozen lives, including Danny's, at the cost of his own.

25

Daela Reef

WHILE THE SABRES WERE LIGHT FOR AIRCRAFT, BRAXton couldn't bring them all the way to the launch pad on his own. But there was no need—all he had to do was bluff the four Chinese sailors guarding them into helping him.

"We need to get the UAVs loaded," he told them, speaking in English first and then Mandarin.

"Commander Wen-lo said to leave them here," said one of the men in English that was better accented than Braxton's Chinese.

"If you want to go argue with him, go ahead," said Braxton, holding out his hands. "He's talking to someone in Beijing, and he's pretty pissed. The guy has quite a temper."

The sailor hesitated, then ordered the others to help. They had the aircraft on small trolleys; pushing and pulling, they took them to the launching area.

The launchers rode rails out from the trees, rising to launch the planes. After launching, they were programmed to prostrate themselves—to Braxton, they looked as if they were begging for more.

He went over and helped the men slide the Sabres onto the launch slots. He would have preferred refueling them—the underground tank had a hose assembly hidden in the foliage a short distance away—but there wasn't time, and he calculated that it wouldn't be absolutely necessary.

"Come on, come on," he said, directing the men to push the second UAV into position. Only two of the four were working. "You and you, go help!" he barked.

They frowned but went over. As they did, Braxton walked to the edge of the clearing. An oblong green box sat in the dirt half covered by castor oil plants. He reached in, fumbling until he found the thumb reader.

"What are you doing?" asked the Chinese sailor he'd been talking to.

As Braxton straightened, he raised an AR-15 from the chest. Sweeping the spray, he emptied the thirty-round box into all four men.

One of the sailors, though wounded, didn't fall. Braxton whirled around and grabbed another gun; when he turned back, the man had disappeared.

Cursing, Braxton ran after him. If the man made it to the beach, there would be trouble; already it seemed likely that the wily captain of the PT boat would send someone to check out the gunfire. Braxton was just about to give up when he saw something moving through the brush to his right; he stepped over and put a three-round burst into the man's head.

Blood was gurgling from the back of the sailor's skull when Braxton got there. It was an odd thing to see, unnatural and yet pleasing somehow.

"Back to work," Braxton told himself, whispering as if someone might overhear. "Clear the air and launch the Sabres, and get in the plane to go. *Go!* The revolution has begun."

26

The Cube

Tᴇᴄᴜᴍsᴇʜ Bᴀsᴛɪᴀɴ ѕᴀᴛ ᴅᴏᴡɴ ɪɴ ᴛʜᴇ ѕᴇᴀᴛ ᴀᴛ ᴛʜᴇ rear of the Cube's situation room. It was almost déjà vu—he'd been in rooms like this count- less times, most especially as the commander of Dreamland.

But it wasn't déjà vu. The room was different, smaller, with less people but even better tech. And his daughter was in charge: confident, mature, moving around with a grace and assurance that shocked him.

It shouldn't. She'd been a well-accomplished pilot even back at Dreamland, and that was years ago now, nearly a decade.

God, he felt so old. He *was* old.

"Are you all right?" asked Ray Rubeo, putting his hand on Dog's shoulder. That was another change—the scientist *almost* seemed human.

He was human, of course, even if he chose not to admit it. He was the last friend Bastian had. Certainly the only one who'd stood by him.

"I'm OK, thanks," said Bastian.

"It's going to work," Rubeo told him. "Ten more minutes and we'll be in. It's a rolling key that uses parts of the strand. Thank you. We'd never have gotten it without you."

Bastian nodded.

"We'll get our aircraft back," said Rubeo.

"Good."

"More planes are launching from the island!" said one of the techies down in front. "The signature is different from the earlier ones—could be the Sabres."

Rubeo hurried over to see. Bastian watched with some satisfaction as his daughter moved slowly toward the workstation. Only a pilot could be that calm when things were going to hell.

27

South China Sea

THE MARINES RECOVERED THE BODIES FROM THE water in a matter of minutes. The man who had grabbed and detonated the bomb lost his hands in the explosion; Mofitt was intact, though it was obvious the concussion and internal injuries had killed him instantly.

They carried him to the forward part of the ship, then arranged for the Osprey to pick him up.

"He was a brave man," said the sergeant. "He got a bad rap."

"I heard," said Danny.

"You can't tell what you're gonna do under fire," added the Marine. "Every time's different. But his impulse here—he saved us. Deserves a medal."

"Damn straight," said Danny. "Damn straight."

Turk tried hailing the Chinese pilot whose neck he and Cowboy had just saved, but he refused to respond. At least he wasn't continuing the attack: the J-15 was flying in a wide orbit above the ships.

The four J-15s that had been west were about two minutes away. They, too, were refusing to answer Turk's queries.

A voice with a strong Boston accent came over the radio. "This is USS *McCain* contacting Whiplash Tigershark," it said. "Can you update us?"

"*McCain*, roger that," said Turk, responding to the destroyer's query. "Here's what we got . . ."

The *McCain* was the fourth ship in the Zumwalt class, a sleek, tumble-home wave piercer equipped with an array of high-tech gear. Unlike her earlier sisters in the class, the *McCain* was equipped with SPY-3 and SPY-4 radars, exactly as her designers had intended. The powerful dual band radar was "painting" all of the aircraft in the region—except for the ultrastealthy Tigershark, which was too far from the destroyer to be seen by it.

The ship was a little less than fifty miles away, cruising at top speed. The Chinese aircraft were within range of its SM-2 Standard ship-to-air missiles, so when Turk finished the conversation and saw that the Chinese planes had begun to turn back west, he assumed that was the reason. But a few seconds later the Cube told him what was really going on.

"There's been a launch from the island where

the UAVs came from," said Greenstreet. "These are larger—it's a good possibility it's the Sabres."

"No shit," he said, turning the Tigershark in that direction.

WITH THE MARINES EVACUATED FROM THE CARGO vessel, Danny had Guzman take the tug a safe distance away. Though he was a SEAL, Guzman had never served aboard ship, and now joked that he was doing more "Navy stuff" with Whiplash than he'd ever done as a sailor.

Danny was just about to compliment him on his seamanship when Breanna contacted him on the Whiplash circuit.

"More UAVs have been launched from the island to the west," she said. "The same place where the others launched from. We think they're the Sabres."

"All right. We'll get over there ASAP."

"Hold on, Danny. There are two Chinese PT boats on the island's shore, and the four J-15s are headed that way as well."

"We can deal with them."

"We're working on a way to get the Sabres back," she said. "I don't want you to launch until we're ready. There's no sense putting you in danger."

"The Chinese are weak right now," answered Danny. "I can deal with a couple of PT boats. And Turk can drive off the fighters."

"He's low on fuel," said Breanna. "I want you to hold him back."

"Understood," he said, though he wasn't sure he could.

28

Situation room, the White House

THE PRESIDENT PUSHED THE BUTTON TO ALLOW THE call to go through. The Chinese premier's face popped up onto the video screen. The bright lights of the Beijing conference room turned his face almost purple. Todd had been in that very room four years before; it was clearly modeled after the CIA situation room shown—incorrectly—on many televisions shows.

It was empty then. Now it was packed with aides.

"Mr. Premier, we have a problem in the South China Sea and there is no reason for it," she said. "Your forces have interfered with our operations against pirates, who as you now know attacked you as well as us and the Malaysians. We have tried to use restraint dealing with your forces, even after they fired on us. I have to tell you frankly, that restraint will certainly cause me political problems here."

Actually, anything she did would give her political problems, but she didn't feel the need to detail that. Nor did she give the premier a chance to respond, continuing quickly.

"Pirates have stolen some of our aircraft, and

we are in the process of getting them back. This is a deep and far-reaching conspiracy. They have been helping arm rebels in Malaysia. Several of their robot aircraft attacked your aircraft. Our people tried to shoot them down before they attacked you, but your pilots did not follow our instructions to help."

"Your drones attacked my country's planes," said the premier. His English was very good; he didn't need a translator.

"No. Those are not our drones. They attacked us as well. We will provide evidence. We have a common enemy here," added the President. "If you allow us to continue our work without interference, we will eradicate them."

One of the aides stepped forward and whispered something to the premier. Todd noticed that the defense minister was sitting with a very glum face on the premier's right.

"Minister Zao, I'm sure you've gotten a report from your fleet by now," she told him. "You see how capable this enemy is. We can defeat him, but only if you don't interfere."

The minister pressed his lips together but said nothing.

Todd knew that the Chinese were in a difficult position. While they had a carrier task force within a few hours' sailing time, the UAVs had just proven more than they could handle. With the U.S. destroyer on the way, not to mention the ships escorting the MEU to the east, they were clearly outgunned. And that was without even factoring in the submarine trailing the carrier.

But a conflict, even a lopsided one, would greatly complicate the already thorny relations between the two countries. Todd wanted to avoid that if she could. She also wanted to increase the odds of getting the Sabres and their technology back.

"We will not interfere with your forces if you combat the pirates," said the Chinese premier finally, reaching forward to end the call. "But this matter is not over."

"I didn't expect it would be," she told the blank screen.

29

Over the South China Sea

FROM THE MOMENT TURK KNEW THAT THE SABRES HAD been launched, he was sure he was going to get them back. It didn't matter what he had to do, he *was* going to get them.

"Basher One, I need to go west," he told Greenstreet. "There are more UAVs in the air. Can you hold here and deal with the Chinese if they get nasty?"

"Affirmative," replied Greenstreet. "We have the ships."

"You need a wingman," said Cowboy. "I volunteer."

"I'm good on my own," answered Turk.

"No, take Basher Two," said Greenstreet. "We'll cover the ships."

"I don't need a wingman," Turk told Cowboy.

"I'm not going to argue," answered the Marine. "I'm just going to watch your back."

"All right. Stay close."

The Tigershark was only a little faster than the Sabres, and while fifty miles didn't seem like a lot, they had enough of a lead that—properly exploited—it would be impossible to catch up before his fuel situation got critical.

Turk knew that if he seemed like a threat, they'd come back for him. But the Tigershark wasn't a threat from long-range; it didn't carry any missiles.

The F-35 did, however.

He pressed the mike button to tell Cowboy to fire a missile at the Sabres. Then he hesitated—he was going to tell Cowboy to make himself a target.

Cowboy was a good pilot, but the Sabres were flown by a command system that was the culmination of years of combat experience and flight science. Flying against them was like flying against all of the air aces ever, from von Richthofen to Zen Stockard. And he'd be doing it in an aircraft that wasn't just inferior to them, but wasn't designed to be an air superiority fighter in the first place. Even Turk would have trouble defeating two Sabres at once.

"Whiplash Tigershark—Captain Mako, this is Breanna Stockard," said his boss over the radio. "What's your fuel state?"

"Uh . . ." Turk knew exactly what she was getting at, even without looking at the calc screen. "I got plenty of reserves."

"Turk, I don't want you putting yourself in jeopardy."

Kind of late for you to think about that.

"We don't think you have enough fuel," she continued. "Don't be foolish. It's one thing to take risks. It's another to be . . . to be stupid about it."

Her voice seemed to crack.

A legend appeared on his main screen: VIDEO ACCESS REQUESTED.

Turk enabled it. Breanna's face filled the top left-hand screen.

"Turk, I'm serious," she said. "You are more valuable than the planes."

Her face was worn, tired. She was in the main situation room at the Cube, leaning toward the camera at the top of her workstation. If there were people behind her, they weren't visible to the camera.

"I don't want you to sacrifice yourself," she said when he didn't answer. Her eyes welled up; her voice was soft. "We're working on a set of instructions you can transmit to take over the Sabres, but it may not be ready in time."

"I'll shoot them down if I have to."

"I don't think that's possible."

"Sure it is."

Breanna's lower lip quivered. She wanted to say something else, but the words were choking her up. "Turk—"

"I got this," he said. "Sorry, I gotta go. If you get that coding, tell me right away."

He killed the video.

FLYING THE F-35 WAS PRETTY MUCH A PILOT'S dream—it was the newest aircraft in the fleet, arguably one of the best ever made. Getting a chance to sit in the pilot's seat was without a doubt one of the highlights not just of Cowboy's Marine Corps career, but of his life.

So why was he feeling huge pangs of jealousy just staring at the back end of the sleek aircraft Turk was piloting a few hundred yards ahead?

The Sabres weren't visible on his radar yet, but he assumed Turk could see them. He certainly acted like he knew precisely where they were.

Were they going to shoot them down? Or was Turk going to simply "capture" them once they got close?

Cowboy assumed the latter, but he was ready to do combat with them. He assumed it would be even more intense than the furball with the combat UAVs he'd just finished.

Bring it on, he thought. Bring it on!

"Basher Two, do you have the Sabres on your radar?" asked Turk.

"Negative."

"Do you have AMRAAMs?"

"One," answered Cowboy. "I have two Side-winders and my cannon. I'm good to go."

"We're not going to catch them this way," said Turk. "I need to get the Sabres to turn back and come for us."

"Let's do it."

"I want you to fire your AMRAAM," said Turk. "It may lure them back."

"I don't have them on my radar," said Cowboy.

"If I give you a general heading, can you fire them in bore-sight mode?"

He was asking Cowboy to fire the missile without a lock. While not often done, the missile did have the capability to fly into the general direction of any enemy aircraft and then use its own radar to lock on to the target.

"If that's going to work," said Cowboy.

"I don't know," admitted Turk. "Assuming the Sabres react, they're going to come after you. They're going to make you their primary target."

"Yeah, that's not a problem."

"They're tough little fighters to deal with," said Turk. "I'll issue commands to take them over, but we may end up shooting them down. We can't let them fall into enemy hands."

"Roger that."

"They haven't responded to the general control signal already, which is . . . bad."

"Then we'll shoot the bastards down if we have to, right? Isn't that why we're here?"

"That's why we're here. But you're going to be the target once you fire."

"Yeah, well, you'll nail them if I don't."

"Stand by for a bearing."

30

The Cube

RUBEO PROPPED UP HIS HEAD ON HIS FISTS, STARING at the computer screen as the DNA coding was read into the encryption formula, trying to unlock it. They had plenty of transmission to work with—the two Sabres were "talking" to each other, using their distributive computing power to decide what to do about the planes pursuing them. But Rubeo's team hadn't been able to get past the changed encryption, let alone get deep enough into the systems to figure out how to take them back over.

With all the computing power at his disposal, it was still taking minutes to grind through the damn thing.

Had Braxton done this? There were so many damn possibilities.

The screen blinked, then flashed with a new message: WORKING.

They'd found the encryption key. Now all they had to do was get into the Sabre programming, examine it, then rewrite it.

Like climbing Mount Everest in shorts and sneakers in the middle of the winter, and setting a world's record for the hundred yard dash along the way.

Rubeo thought back to the earliest days of the Flighthawk program. There was always a fear that the planes would take off on their own.

It seemed silly now, as if they'd all watched *I, Robot* or *2001* a few too many times.

But they'd put in a knockoff code that reset everything. Jennifer had come up with it, joking it was an S&M "safe phrase."

He'd been so sheltered he'd had to ask what the hell that was.

What the hell was it?

"Ray, we have some sequences ready," said Kristen Morgan, back in New Mexico.

"Stand by," he told her. "Captain Mako, I will have a transmission for you to try," he said, punching in the connection. "We will start with the basics, a simple recall. I don't expect that to work," added Rubeo. "We will then have it initiate a response and a data dump. You will receive a great deal of telemetry. You'll be best off flying by hand as it transmits, to avoid any error induced by processing delays."

"That's how I always fly," responded Turk.

"Good for you," responded Rubeo dryly, though for once he wasn't being sarcastic.

B REANNA GOT UP FROM HER STATION, OSTENSIBLY TO refill her coffee cup, but actually just to walk off some of her excess energy. At times like this she really missed flying. The effect of all the übertechnology in the room ultimately reminded her how far from the action she was.

She wanted to be the one in the danger seat, not Turk. She hoped she was not sending him to his grave.

She'd done that already. It wasn't really fair to him that he had to go through it again.

And there was her father, standing like a statue near Rubeo at the back, arms folded, looking not awed, not even old, but exactly as he'd once looked in the Dreamland situation room, waiting and watching as his people were on a mission. He'd sent them into danger countless times—often, he was right there with them.

At the time, she'd questioned whether he should be out there. Even a colonel—his rank when he first arrived and for a considerable time afterward, though he was surely doing the work of a general, and one with more than one star—was expected to command from a distance, not duck fire at the front. Leading from the front didn't mean making yourself the spearhead, which her father often was.

But now she understood why he'd done it. Ordering someone to risk their life was a hell of a lot harder if you were sitting in a bunker yourself.

Her father glanced over and saw her.

"Nice place you got here," he said.

Then he smiled. She hadn't seen that smile in a long, long time. It felt enormously good.

"Thanks," she told him. "We had a good model."

31

Over the South China Sea

THE SABRES IGNORED THE AMRAAM UNTIL THE MIS-
siles began searching for them.

Then they got pissed off.

"We got their attention," Turk told Cowboy.
"They're coming back for us and they're getting
the lead out."

"I'm seeing them up on radar now," said
Cowboy.

"Do a one eighty. Head back from where you
came. Don't be slow. I'll pick them up."

"You don't really think a Marine's gonna run
away from battle, do you?"

"It's what I need you to do. I have to fly with
them long enough to give commands. Or shoot
them down."

"Roger," said Cowboy, clearly reluctant.

The Sabres had a standard maneuver to change
direction quickly, climbing and flipping their
wings as they topped into a loop. The variable
control surfaces and wing-in-body design—not
to mention the lack of a pilot—allowed them to
withstand g forces that would shatter a normal
aircraft, and so they could change direction in
far less space. They couldn't defy physical laws,
however—it was impossible to transfer all their
energy and momentum to the new direction.
That gave Turk a little bit of a breather. He flew at
them, transmitting his "takeover" code, the com-

mand which would normally retrieve Sabres into escort mode.

The planes ignored it.

He tried a verbal command and then decided he would have to treat them like hostiles: he told his weapons radar to target them.

The Sabres didn't react.

"I need your attention," he said, pressing the trigger of the gun.

Three rounds shot out in the Sabres' direction. He was way too far to get a hit, but the Sabres' control computer realized he was trying to kill them. They talked it over between themselves and decided there was only one reason that could be—surely this enemy had found a way to spoof their mother plane's silhouette. That decision overrode the safety protocol that kept them from targeting him, and they promptly began tracking him as an enemy.

In a traditional dogfight, a two-on-one advantage is not insurmountable, especially if the single aircraft is flown by a superior pilot who understands the limitations and advantages not just of his plane, but of his opponents'. Still, a numerical advantage in the air is just as potent as one on the ground. The enemy must be approached with skill and savvy. All things being equal, a head-on attack is usually not advised.

Which was one of the reasons Turk undertook it. The other was that he needed to play for time to let Cowboy get away.

The Sabres were flying a so-called "loose deuce," a time-honored side-by-side formation that allowed either (or both) planes to go on the attack as well as support each other. The distance between them was roughly the same as their average turning radius; whichever plane Turk focused on, the other aircraft could get on his tail with an easy maneuver.

Rather than aiming for one or the other, he beelined toward the area between them. This forced the Sabres to decide on a strategy; Sabre One turned to meet him, while Sabre Two tucked into a dive but stayed on course.

Besides calculating counters to his move, the artificial intelligence that flew the planes was also evaluating his tactics and, in an effort to predict what he would do—his intelligence or stupidity— though it didn't use these terms. The fact that he had gone after *two* planes head-on didn't win him points in the IQ department, but the AI had to consider whether this might not be a trick—to put it crassly, was the move so dumb that something was going on that the computer didn't know?

In the next few moments Turk gave the Sabres every reason to think that was true. Rather than continuing the course to take on Sabre One, or tucking his wing left and going after Sabre Two— or, more prudently, getting the hell out of there while he still could make a clean break—he pulled his nose up and aimed for the sun. This necessarily slowed him down, and made him a dandy target for Sabre One.

Just as the aircraft locked him up in its weapons radar, Turk dropped the Tigershark toward the earth as hard as he could. Sabre One was temporarily without a shot, but it strove quickly to make up for that, dropping into a dive. Meanwhile, Sabre Two banked south, trying to head toward Turk.

"How's that sequence coming?" Turk asked Whiplash. "I got the transmission gateway open. You can transmit directly."

"Yes," said Rubeo, in a tone that suggested Turk's IQ was perhaps ten points below moron level. "We are doing that now."

If anyone thought he was a moron, it was the Sabres; he now had both aircraft behind him, not a very good place to have an enemy in a dogfight. But the aircraft were worried that it was a trick: the Tigershark's airfoil demonstrated it had high capabilities, and it had already convinced them that it was their mother ship. So rather than attacking with the all-out abandon a human pilot might have used, the planes remained cautious. Sabre Two closed on Turk slowly, while Sabre One stayed above and behind, just in case.

Turk took his pursuers downward, weaving and bobbing in a ribbonlike pattern that teased Sabre Two but didn't allow it to get close enough to take more than a single shot. Since its autonomous programming prevented the aircraft from shooting anything less than a ten-shot burst with a ninety-five percent degree of probable accuracy—the programming was there to preserve the limited ammo store, and could be overridden remotely— Turk knew he was in relatively little danger as long as he had sky to maneuver in.

But then as he turned hard right, he saw that Sabre Two had broken off and was climbing up behind him. The planes had given up targeting him.

Why did they do that?

The answer was provided by the flash of a Sidewinder exploding a half mile away: Cowboy had come back to protect him.

At the worst possible moment, thought Turk, cursing.

COWBOY KNEW THE MISSILE WAS GOING TO MISS before he fired it—all-aspect or not, the Sidewinder was too far from its target to guarantee a hit. But what he wanted was to break the Sabres' lock on his wingman. It looked like Turk was about to get nailed, and he needed to do something to get the UAV off his back.

It worked. The Sabres left Turk. The only problem was, they were coming for him.

Cowboy jerked the plane into the sharpest turn he could manage without blacking out. As gravity threatened to cave in his chest, he got a warning that the other Sabre was targeting him. This was followed by a run of black BBs across his wing.

Possibly I bit off more than I could chew here, he thought.

SEEING THE F-35 AND THE SABRE LOCKED IN A TIGHT turn, Turk scrambled to get close enough to get the plane off the Marine's back.

"Take him lower!" he told Cowboy. "Go as low as you can, break out of your turn when I tell you."

Turk's idea was to kick off the Sabre's safety protocols. Like most moves born of desperation, it didn't really work—the Sabre slowed to compensate for its better dive qualities, but it remained virtually locked on Cowboy's tail as he veered lower and lower, passing through 5,000 feet. The F-35's ECMs were going full blast, which did help, since it meant that the Sabre had to stay close to get a lock. But that was going to be immaterial as soon as Sabre Two got in the mix—which it was aiming to do now, starting downward from above.

"Come toward me, now!" ordered Turk. "Just flat out toward me!"

"It'll lock."

"Not long enough to fire. Do it!"

The F-35 and the Sabre accelerated in Turk's direction. Turk lit the rail gun. The first slug flew right at the Sabre, missing only because the aircraft dove at the last second.

Sabre Two changed its target, coming for Turk instead of Cowboy. Turk had used nearly all of his available energy to get into position and fire; he was flat-footed.

He managed to evade, turning and diving, dropping close to the water—close enough to get his safety protocols annoyed. As the Sabre closed, he hit his last bit of chaff and took a turn, practically losing his wingtip in the water.

The Sabre sailed past, climbing to get away from the waves.

"I need you to stay close to the Sabres," said Rubeo over the Whiplash circuit, "and to turn off your ECMs. I need sixty-five seconds to transmit. You have to be within a mile. Closer is even better."

"Turn off the ECMs?"

"In the F-35 as well," said Rubeo.

"If he does that, he'll get shot down."

"If he doesn't, he'll get shot down anyway."

Rubeo's logic was undoubtedly correct. But Turk still hesitated—it was one thing to make himself a target, and quite another to tell someone else to sacrifice himself.

But it was the logical thing to do. And it was the only thing that would get the Sabres back and accomplish his mission.

"Cowboy," said Turk, "they're going to try transmitting a command to retake the Sabres. But they need us to turn off our ECMs."

"Roger that."

"I don't think you understand—that Sabre is right on you. It'll nail you."

"We gotta do what we gotta do."

"Hit every store you have—everything," said Turk. "Then punch your gas, turn off the ECMs. And run."

"Is that all?"

"Hold on. Let me get closer to your tail—we'll do it on my count. Twenty seconds."

32

South China Sea

DANNY FREAH WATCHED THE OSPREY PICK UP THE last of the downed Chinese pilots. He wasn't the only one watching—the J-15s were circling overhead, with the F-35s above them.

It wasn't going to go down as one of the great moments of international cooperation, but at least no one was firing at one another. The Osprey had been invited to bring the downed Chinese pilots back to the Chinese aircraft carrier; Danny decided to grant permission. It was the sort of bold move that would undoubtedly get him cashiered if the Chinese decided to renege on their cease-fire, but he felt it was the right one.

The Whiplash team, meanwhile, had assembled to board another Osprey and go west to the island where the UAVs had launched from. Danny was leaving the small Marine contingent aboard the tug; the *McCain* should be there within an hour.

The bow of the container carrier had slipped just about to its gunwale in the water, but the rest of the craft showed a surprising reluctance to sink any farther. It was likely that there was just enough buoyancy in the ship to keep it afloat. In any event, it would shortly be someone else's problem: once the *McCain* arrived, the Navy would take physical custody of both ships. The destroyer captain was optimistic that his people could put out the fires and salvage the rest of the ship. Two other Navy vessels, both salvage craft, were on their way to help.

So for now, Danny decided he could devote himself to more pressing matters: the island where the UAVs had launched from.

"Saddle up, Whiplash!" he shouted as the Osprey lowered itself toward the tugboat. "Last man aboard buys the beer tonight. Last man besides me," he added, realizing he was bound by duty and custom to be the last man in the aircraft.

33

South China Sea

TURK WAS SWEATING SO BADLY HE PRACTICALLY SWAM in his flight suit as he raced to catch the Sabre on Cowboy's tail. The other UAV was somewhere behind him, but he couldn't worry about it now—he had to do what he could to save his friend.

"Now!" he yelled. "ECMs off!"

The computer complied, as did Cowboy.

The Sabre didn't react. Turk was hopeful that meant it was now under his control, but a half second later he saw something puff on Cowboy's wing. The Sabre was firing.

"Break right, break right," Turk told him.

Cowboy managed to do so, temporarily breaking the lock. Turk fired several shots, even though he wasn't lined up properly.

The Sabre ignored it.

"Left, left," he told Cowboy.

This time the F-35's maneuver brought the Sabre close enough to Turk's line of sight for him to put a few slugs in its path. They didn't hit, but the aircraft did break off.

Turk took that as a cue and veered right—barely ducking Sabre Two as it came up behind him.

Keep it up, keep it up, he told himself.

Rubeo's voice came over the radio. "Turk, I need you to broadcast a command to the Sabres. It's a code. It's going to sound . . . ridiculous. But do it."

"Go!"

"Give it as the command sequence."

"All right. What?"

" 'Jennifer is your mother.' "

There was no time to argue. Turk keyed the mike, switching to the Sabre's command channel.

"All Sabres, Command sequence: *Jennifer is your mother.*"

A legend flashed onto his screen.

SABRES REQUEST: RECONNECT AND SAFETY?

"Computer reconnect!" he said, his voice even louder than before. "Reconnect. Safety! Safety! Sabres knock it off. Sabres knock it off. Free flight pattern two! On my back."

The UAVs abruptly began to climb. They were back under his control.

"They're ours," Turk told Cowboy. "*They are ours!* Let's go home before they change their minds."

34

Daela Reef

FROM THE MOMENT THE TWO SABRES TURNED WEST rather than following the course he had programmed, Braxton knew he had lost them.

It was bitter. Years of work, and now failure.

Nonetheless, he had to think of the long term. He had to complete his getaway.

The Dreamland people were certainly watching the island by now. But that was just fine with him. Talbot was still with the Chinese, but he was of little value—muscle mostly, he couldn't tell them anything important, certainly not about the long-term plans.

Braxton had lost today. Tomorrow he and the movement would be victorious. They had the force of history on their side.

He pushed the button to set the timer, then left for the west side of the island.

35

Daela Reef

WHEN DANNY SAW THE BLACK COLUMN OF SMOKE IN the distance as the Osprey approached the island, he leaned forward into the cockpit and asked if the pilots could get the Chinese PT boat commander back on the radio. A few seconds later he was greeted by the captain's strained but polite English.

"What was the explosion?" Danny asked.

"We have lost several men," said the commander. "The enemy appears to have blown himself and his installation up."

That sounds pretty convenient, thought Danny.

"I have received orders to cooperate with you," said the captain.

"As have I," said Danny. "We have a common enemy."

"Yes."

"We'll search the place as soon as we get there," Danny told the captain. "We'll be there in five minutes."

"A little closer to ten, Colonel," said the pilot.

"They'll wait, I'm sure."

TURK HAD NEVER REFUELED THE TIGERSHARK OFF AN Osprey's "buddy pack" system, but the basic procedure was the same as refueling from a regular tanker, assuming you adjusted for the speed, the lack of director lights, the turbulence, the strange looking gear, and most of all, the corny Marine jokes.

"Come on, Air Force, you can do it," laughed Greenstreet. Depending on your point of view, he was either directing the refuel or harassing Turk from a short distance away.

"If a Marine can do it, I can do it," answered Turk.

"Hell, if Cowboy can do it, anybody can do it," answered Greenstreet.

"He just puts it on automatic and lets the computer do the flying," said Cowboy.

"I wish."

In fact, Turk *could* do that, and would have on a standard refuel. But he didn't feel like taking any chances with computers at the moment, not even the Tigershark's.

Sabre One and Two had just enough fuel to make it back to the airport; he would fly them there, and then land himself, if Danny's search of the island didn't turn up anything.

He thought about Cowboy as he unhooked from the Osprey. The mission had turned the tables on Turk—while he hadn't ordered anyone to actually kill Cowboy, he'd certainly put him into very grave danger to accomplish the mission. It *was* different, he told himself, very different.

And yet in a sense it wasn't. Because he knew that if getting the Sabres back meant killing Cowboy, he would have at least considered it.

Rejected it, probably. *Definitely*. But thought of it.

Breanna had sent him to near-certain death in Iran because he was the only person in the world who could have accomplished the mission. And it was her job to send him.

Actually, no: he'd volunteered. Just as Cowboy had. They had told him about the risks. He just hadn't completely believed them.

When things went bad, Breanna did the only thing she could do: send someone after him.

Maybe saving him had been more of an option than Stoner had said. Maybe that was the real reason she'd sent Stoner: without a doubt, Stoner was the only person who could have pulled off that mission and gotten him back alive.

Or maybe not, Turk thought. The bottom line was the mission. It was Breanna's job to think about it, to put it above her own wishes—and above his own life.

He still felt . . . not quite the same as he had felt about Breanna before. But he understood. In his heart, he understood.

"Hey, leave some for the rest of us," said Greenstreet. "I'm into my reserves myself."

"Roger that," said Turk.

He dropped down from the Osprey.

"See you guys in town tonight," he told the Marines. "We'll settle up on who owes what beers."

"Fine with me," said Greenstreet. "As long as I have the first round."

36

The White House

THE PRESIDENT CHECKED HER WATCH, THEN GOT UP from her desk.

"I'm going to go take a nap," she told her scheduling secretary. "We have a bit of a lull."

Her secretary looked shocked, as did the handful of aides standing nearby. Mary Christine Todd never took a nap in the middle of the day.

"It's a new thing I'm trying," she told them cheerfully. "I've been reading this book by Dr. Wayne Muransky on power naps. We'll see if it works. Hold my calls."

A succession of *Yes, ma'ams* followed her as she made her way to the residence. Her husband was waiting, as were her guests.

"There you all are," she told the doctors and their two nurses. "I'm sorry I'm late. We had a bit of a . . . situation."

"Of course," said Dr. Chambers. "Are you ready to talk about the procedure?"

"Let's have a little coffee first," said Todd's husband. She noticed that he looked worried. It was the first time in years—probably since the night she told him she was going to go ahead and run.

There was a good reason why—she'd already decided against the treatment, which had a minuscule chance of saving her life. The only reason she was taking the meeting was because he'd insisted.

Begged, really.

"Who wants coffee and who wants tea?" he asked. They'd dismissed the staff for the meeting.

"I'd love something stronger," joked the President. "But I do have to get back to work."

The others laughed. "Humor is a great weapon against cancer," said Chambers.

Not really, thought Todd, going into the dining room, but it's probably all I have.

37

The Cube

Breanna nodded as Danny finished reporting on the situation at the island. The bunker had been imploded, exactly like the one they had discovered earlier. The Chinese had lost several men, including a high-level intelligence agent who had been working for well over a year trying to track Braxton.

"The PT captain doesn't appear all that broken up about it," added Danny. "But he's not going out of his way to cooperate."

"And Braxton?" asked Breanna.

"No trace of him. Presumably he's in the bunker somewhere. But . . ."

"But?"

"There are some bodies aboveground," said Danny. "Possibly he escaped. I just don't know."

"All right. The Navy is sending a SEAL team to secure the island. As soon as they arrive, you can come home."

"All the way home?" asked Danny.

"We have the Sabres back. We have the technology from the tugboat and the other base. Our mission is accomplished."

"Yeah, I guess it is."

Breanna smiled at him. Danny was tired—as tired as she'd ever seen him. But she suspected it was a *good* tired, the sort that came at the end of a job well done.

She signed off, momentarily basking in her own

sense of accomplishment—they had gotten the Sabres back and closed down a powerful if quixotic conspiracy.

And her organization had been exonerated.

There was much work to be done—on business and personal matters.

She turned and walked back up the steps, looking for her father.

He wasn't there. Ray Rubeo met her instead.

"Where—" she started to ask.

"He's gone," said Rubeo gently. "He's not ready."

"But . . ."

Rubeo grimaced.

Somehow, Breanna managed to keep her tears to herself until she was alone in her office.